# Rebels and Rules

## Wishes and Chances Series: Book Three

by

Suzie Peters

First Published in 2018
by GWL Publishing
an imprint of Great War Literature Publishing LLP

Produced in United Kingdom

ISBN 978-1-910603-56-7  Paperback Edition

GWL Publishing
Forum House
Sterling Road
Chichester PO19 7DN

www.gwlpublishing.co.uk

# Dedication

For S.

# Chapter One

*Nine Years Earlier*

*Becky*

"I suppose you ought to get dressed," Nick said. She heard the reluctance in his voice. It mirrored her own, but it gave her a warm glow to know that he wanted her to stay naked and curled up in his arms just as much as she did.

"Do I have to?" She looked up at him. God, he was gorgeous, even with his clothes on. He was wearing jeans, a white shirt, and a pale gray waistcoat. This was what he wore all the time – it was like Nick's trademark, as was his dark disheveled hair, which he wore at collar length.

"We're already late," he murmured, leaning down and kissing her. She felt his stubble brush against her skin and shivered at the contact. "I told Eliot we'd be there." She sighed and went to move away from him, but he pulled her back. "Doesn't mean I wanna go," he said, smiling, and she couldn't help but smile back.

He'd arrived about thirty minutes beforehand, just as Becky had stepped out of the shower and wrapped herself in a bathrobe. Kelly, whose flat she shared, had opened the door to him, only wearing a towel herself, which she'd wrapped around and tied just above her ample breasts. She was gushing and simpering to the point where it was embarrassing and, to escape her, Becky had suggested that Nick join her in her bedroom. He'd agreed, removing the robe almost as soon as they'd closed the door, and they'd been lying on her bed ever since. She'd suggested that he could get undressed too, and he'd told her, in between kisses, that he wanted to, but if he did, they'd never get to the Eliot's party. As far as Becky was concerned, that would have been absolutely fine. She didn't want to go anyway. And not just because she wanted to be in bed with Nick. Kelly was going too, and Becky knew she'd be wearing something revealing and sexy; something bound to grab Nick's attention, which made her feel even more insecure than usual, especially as she also knew Nick had asked Kelly out before her – he'd been honest enough to tell her that.

"Hey…" He waved his hand in front of her face. "You're daydreaming."

"Hmm." She nestled into him again, not wanting to tell him about her jealous fears.

"C'mon," he said. "Time to get up."

She pulled away from him unwillingly and shifted to the edge of the bed, clambering off and walking round to the dresser, where she stood with her back to Nick, combing out her long, straight, dark hair. Then she opened the top drawer and grabbed a pair of white lace panties, bending over and pulling them on. She heard the soft groan from behind her and turned to face him. He was watching her intently, his steel gray eyes on fire.

"Keep doing that, and we won't be going anywhere," he murmured, his voice deep and sexy.

She smirked, then turned and bent over again, this time to pick up her shoes from the floor. She didn't need them yet, but wanted to tempt him all the same.

"Jeez, Bex," he said and she heard him move, then felt him come up behind her, his body pressed against hers, his arousal obvious through his jeans. She stood upright and leant back into him, his hands coming around her, cupping her breasts. "What are you trying to do to me?" he asked.

"I'm not trying to do anything," she whispered.

"You're a tease," he murmured into her hair, before planting gentle kisses on her shoulder and moving up to her neck.

"No, I'm not. I deliver on my promises, Nick."

"Yeah… don't I know it." She felt his right hand move down, across her flat stomach and inside her panties, his fingers finding her sensitized clitoris. He rubbed gently and she rocked her head back against his shoulder, sucking in a deep breath. "You're really wet," he whispered into her ear.

"Because I want you." She ground her hips back into him, feeling him hard against her.

He groaned again, more loudly. "I want you too."

He increased the pressure on her clitoris, moving his fingers faster and harder over her swollen nub.

"I—I'm gonna come," she stuttered.

"Not yet, you're not." He pulled his hand away and spun her in his arms so she was facing him, panting hard.

"Nick…" she breathed.

"I want you like this all night," he murmured, his eyes dark with desire. "And later, I'm gonna take you back to my place and make you come so fucking hard."

"Oh God… yes." She felt her legs giving way and he held her up.

He waited until her breathing had calmed a little. "You okay?" he asked.

"Apart from feeling frustrated, yes," she said, looking up at him.

"I can handle frustrated," he replied, grinning at her.

"We're going back to your place after the party?" she said, her brain finally unscrambling a little.

"Yeah. Didn't I tell you?"

"No." She leant back in his arms. "No. You didn't."

"Ah, well… Tony's already gone home for the summer. He left this afternoon. So we've got the place to ourselves for once." Nick shared a flat with another law student, Tony, who didn't like him having women to stay over. Nick thought it was a little weird, but it was Tony's place and he respected the guy's rules, so they hadn't yet spent a whole night together, being as Becky didn't like the idea of Nick sleeping at her place either, not with the too tempting Kelly in the very next room.

"We do?"

"Yeah. I guess you could pack an overnight bag…" He left the sentence hanging, and looked down at her, expectantly.

"My dad's coming to pick me up tomorrow morning, to take me home, but…"

"But?" he queried.

"But I can stay at your place tonight, if you want me to?"

"Oh, I want you to." He leant down and kissed her, his tongue finding hers and letting her feel his need.

"I guess I'd better pack then," she said, when he finally broke the kiss.

"And maybe get dressed too?" he suggested. "You can't go to the party like that."

"Do we have to go to the party at all?" she asked, picking at one of the buttons on his shirt. "Can't we just go straight to your place?"

He chuckled. "We'll just go for an hour or so, then we'll make our excuses and leave."

"Okay," she said reluctantly. She knew that if Nick had promised Eliot he'd be there, he wouldn't let him down. She put her arms around his neck and leant into him. "I can't wait to sleep with you," she whispered.

He pulled her close, crushing her against him. "We won't be sleeping, baby," he said softly. "This is gonna be our first night together, and our last for a while too. I've got no intention of letting you sleep at all."

Becky didn't get around to packing. They spent the next ten minutes kissing, before she finally got dressed. They agreed they'd come back to her apartment and she'd pick up her things then – they had to drive past her place to get back to Nick's anyway. It wouldn't be a problem.

Nick held her hand as they went out into the living room, where Kelly was waiting for them. Becky sucked in a breath and knew that her mouth had dropped open. What on earth was Kelly wearing? Whatever it was, it left nothing – absolutely nothing – to the imagination. There was a trend on the catwalks for sheer fabrics, and Kelly had gone to town with it, whilst evidently deciding to abandon underwear at the same time. Her dress was cream in color, with a silver embroidered pattern, which strategically covered her nipples, but left the outline of her breasts showing. Becky allowed her eyes to drop, and let out a gasp. It was so obvious Kelly wasn't wearing any panties, even though the embroidery just about hid the essential area, but as she turned to pick up her purse, her ass was completely visible.

"Jesus," Nick muttered under his breath, but Becky wasn't sure if that meant he liked what he saw, or not, and she didn't want to look at him, fearful of what she might see in his eyes. All of a sudden her red sundress, that Nick had told her looked sexy a few minutes earlier, seemed wholly inadequate.

"Do you like it?" Kelly asked. "It cost a fortune." Becky wasn't in the least surprised. The Youngs – Kelly's family – had money, lots of it, and affording the dress would have been no problem for her. Whether her parents would have approved of her wearing it without anything underneath was another matter, but they were back home in Fall River, where the two girls had grown up. Although they hadn't technically grown up 'together', because Becky's parents weren't from exactly the same part of town, when they'd arrived at Boston University and discovered they were both from the same place, it had made sense for them to room together… Well, it had felt like it at the time. Becky had started to regret that decision almost as soon as it was made; like the first night, when Kelly had come home the worse for alcohol, with an athletic-looking guy, who she'd dragged into her bedroom, and entertained loudly until the early hours of the morning.

Luckily, both she and Nick were both saved from having to make up an answer by the ringing of the doorbell.

"That'll be Tyler," Kelly said, moving to answer it.

"What's he doing here?" Nick whispered to Becky.

"He's taking Kelly to the party," she replied.

"Really?" Becky glanced up at Nick's face. He was clearly surprised. "I didn't know he was interested in her."

Becky wondered if Nick was envious of Tyler, but didn't get the opportunity to dwell, before the man himself entered the room. He was the antithesis of Nick; blond, tidy, perfectly groomed in smart pants and button-down shirt. He seemed to be the light to Nick's dark. But she preferred Nick's dark.

"Good evening," he said, formally, looking Becky up and down. "You look lovely."

"Thank you," she muttered, feeling embarrassed.

"Shall we go?" Nick suggested.

"We could all go together, couldn't we?" Kelly suggested.

"No." Nick and Tyler spoke at the same time.

"It's not practical," Tyler continued.

"No, it isn't," Nick confirmed, giving Becky's hand a squeeze. Then he gave her a tug and they headed for the door, followed by Tyler and Kelly.

As they began their drive to Eliot's house, Becky looked over at Nick, wondering what he was thinking, whether his mind was full of images of Kelly and her obvious attributes, and whether her own were now diminishing in his eyes.

She blinked back her tears and looked out the window.

It was exactly a week since Nick had taken her virginity, but she'd already lost count of the number of times he'd made love to her… and it was always glorious. He always seemed to know exactly what she wanted, and he delivered – every time. She smiled, just for a moment, before recalling yet again how Nick had wanted to go out with Kelly for months and months before he'd given up on her and asked Becky on a date instead… just five weeks ago. And in that one spectacular evening, had put an end to her years of pining for him.

Nick had filled her head, her heart – her life, really – since she'd first seen him three years ago, at the beginning of their Freshman year. Now, as their third year was drawing to a close, he was finally hers… well, she hoped he was. He was certainly dating her, taking her to the movies, for walks, and out to romantic dinners. He kissed her a lot. She liked his kisses; they were warm, passionate, exciting. He held her in his arms all the time, and she really enjoyed the feeling of his strong muscles binding them together. A couple of weeks ago, he'd used his tongue, and his fingers to bring her to orgasm and, for the first time in her life, she'd experienced the other-worldly joy of letting herself go completely; letting the man she loved take her to that place beyond pleasure. And as of last Friday night, he'd become her lover. He'd called himself that, smiling down at her as he'd entered her for the first time, so tenderly. He hadn't said 'I love you', so she didn't really know how he felt about her, but then she hadn't said those magical words to him either; even though she knew he was everything to her… and more.

She brought her hand up to her neck, fingering the silver locket Nick had bought her last Friday – a really sweet gesture for their one month anniversary. He'd given her that just before taking her to bed…

"What the hell is Kelly playing at?" Anne-Marie murmured in Becky's ear.

Becky shrugged. She couldn't reply. She couldn't talk, because she knew if she did, she'd cry.

She was confused, hurt, embarrassed… and deeply humiliated.

When they'd arrived, nearly an hour ago, Nick had told her he'd go and get them some drinks, leaving her standing near the living room window, while he'd headed into the kitchen. But he'd only gotten halfway across the room when he'd been accosted by Kelly, who'd managed to keep his attention ever since. Becky had stood there watching them, and on three separate occasions – just three – he'd looked over at her and either winked or smiled, but he'd made no attempt to get away from Kelly… none whatsoever.

"Are you okay?" Anne-Marie asked.

Becky nodded.

"Can I get you a drink, or anything?"

"No, thanks," Becky managed to say, although she knew her voice wasn't normal. Anne-Marie drifted away into the crowd and Becky looked over to where Nick and Kelly were talking. Why was he doing this? He'd implied that he couldn't wait to take her home to his bed, that he wanted to make love to her – all night. When they'd pulled up outside Eliot's house, he'd leant over and kissed her, and told her they'd spend some of the night, in between making love, talking about how they could try and get together over the summer break. She knew already that he was planning on working at his dad's boat yard and she had a job lined up at a hotel in Fall River, but he'd said nothing was insurmountable... not if they wanted to be together. So, why was he doing this?

"You don't look very happy." The voice was too close and she flipped her head around, to be faced by Tyler. She stepped back instinctively, although the window was right behind her, leaving her nowhere to go.

"I'm fine," she murmured.

"You don't look fine." He moved closer still. He smelt of strong liquor and an aftershave she didn't like. It was sweet, cloying. "You look very uncomfortable."

*Maybe because you're in my space*, she thought, but she didn't say anything. She was far too polite.

"They get on real well, don't they?" She looked up at Tyler, his blue eyes gazing down at her, and he nodded toward Nick and Kelly, still deep in conversation on the other side of the room. "You should see them in class," he added. "They're as thick as thieves."

Becky felt her heart lurch in her chest. She had no idea what Nick got up to during his classes. He, Tyler and Kelly were all at the Law School, while she was studying Hospitality Administration.

"To be honest, I don't know why I bothered inviting Kelly tonight," Tyler continued. "It's so obvious she's only really interested in Nick." He looked at Becky. "And he's always had a soft spot for her, hasn't he?" He hesitated for a moment. "I mean... I know he's seeing you, but that's just a casual thing, right?"

Becky wanted to scream at him that it was anything but casual... it was *everything*. Well, it was to her, anyway.

"I'm sure Nick would have asked Kelly out again, if she hadn't been seeing Dale..." Tyler's voice droned on in her ear.

Dale and Kelly had shared precisely two dates – and Kelly's bed – over the weekend that she and Nick had got together. Becky couldn't really see how that would have stopped Nick from trying again with

Kelly, if he'd really wanted to. He'd only have needed to wait a day or so…

"And he never stops talking about her," Tyler continued, leaning back on the wall beside her and folding his arms.

They stood in silence for a moment and Becky watched Nick and Kelly. They talked animatedly; he waved his hands around, and listened attentively, like he was interested in what she had to say. She moved closer to him and said something that made him laugh, throwing his head back a little. Had this been what he'd wanted all along? Had the rest of it – the dates, the walks, the dinners, the words, the necklace, taking her virginity – had it all just been a series of lies… lies he'd told her to get closer to Kelly?

She sucked in a breath and tried to stop the tears from falling, just as Nick glanced over, then turned back to Kelly again, before the two of them headed across the room straight toward her and Tyler, who pushed himself off the wall as they approached.

Becky stared down at the floor, unable to make eye contact with anyone.

"Hey," Nick said as he came to stand in front of her.

She didn't reply.

"I'm sorry," he said eventually, "I never got you that drink, did I?" She looked up now. He was smiling down at her. "I'll go and get you one."

She wanted to tell him not to bother. She wanted to tell him to take her home, but he'd already turned and was walking away.

"Nick!" Kelly called after him. "Hold on. I'll come with you."

He slowed and let Kelly catch up with him, and Becky gazed after them as they left the room. Just as they turned to disappear into the kitchen, she noticed Kelly lean up and plant a kiss on Nick's cheek. She heard herself gasp and bit back the tears.

"Oh, Becky," Tyler said, moving closer again. "Don't let it get to you. Some guys just can't help themselves."

She turned to him and noticed the concerned look on his face, his eyes piercing hers.

"Dance with me," he said, nodding to the other end of the room, where the furniture had been moved to one side and a few couples were moving vaguely in time to the music. "It'll take your mind off things."

Becky hesitated for a moment, then realized that, whatever she'd thought she had with Nick, she'd clearly been wrong. It might have been love for her, but it was obviously just a game to him; he wasn't serious about her at all… and now that Kelly was interested in him, Becky knew she didn't stand a chance. Kelly was the one he'd always wanted, and she was making herself more than available. Hell, she was positively trumpeting her availability.

"Okay," she said to Tyler and offered him her hand.

He smiled down at her and led her through the crowd of drinking, laughing, talking people. Then, as if on cue, the music changed and a track started playing that was much slower. Becky thought she recognized it. She thought it was by The Fray… maybe? She wasn't sure, and at that moment, she really didn't care.

"Just forget about him, he's not worth it," Tyler whispered, pulling her into his arms. She let him, going limp, like a rag doll. Someone turned up the music, and she felt it wash over her, just as Tyler placed his mouth next to her ear and echoed the lyrics now filling the room, murmuring, "I'll look after you," as she started to sob into his chest.

## Nick

He laughed at Kelly's observation of the way the class had handled the juvenile delinquency seminars they'd been attending for the last few weeks of the semester. Nick had to agree with her that some of their classmates had been fairly juvenile and delinquent themselves. He glanced over at Becky again. Tyler was standing beside her, although she was staring at the floor now, rather than looking at the weasel. Thank God. 'Weasel' was a good description of Tyler. He had a kind of pointy face and beady eyes. Well, Nick thought he did, anyway. He also took way too much interest in Becky, or at least he had done for the last few weeks, ever since Nick had been seeing her. What the hell he was doing here with Kelly was a mystery to Nick, not that he seemed to be paying much attention to his date. He seemed far more keen on talking to Becky…

"We'd better be getting back to our dates, don't you think?" he said to Kelly.

"Oh… I guess." She sounded disappointed. "Thanks for helping me out, Nick. I knew you'd know the answers."

"It's no problem." He turned to walk away, but she pulled him back again.

"You're sure you didn't mind helping me?" She looked up at him through her thick eyelashes.

"No, Kelly. It's fine." She was pushing her breasts forward, her hard nipples poking into the sheer fabric of her dress and Nick was finding it hard to know where to look. He thought her dress was cheap… although he knew it was probably anything but, knowing Kelly and her ability to spend money. He wondered how she could show herself off like this, and marveled at how he'd ever been interested in her. Well, he guessed that was obvious really. She was flaunting the reasons for everyone to see. And, for Nick, that was the biggest turn off of all.

He glanced back at Becky again, wishing Tyler would just leave her alone.

"Come on," he urged Kelly and this time, she let him lead her over to where Becky and Tyler were standing by the window.

"Hey," he said, standing in front of his girl. She looked beautiful, but kind of doubtful, and he wanted more than anything to take her away from this place, back to his apartment and to his bed, to spend the night with her for the first time ever, and maybe – just maybe – tell her how he felt about her.

She wasn't responding, but maybe she was a little mad with him. He'd promised her a drink, probably about an hour ago? And he had let Kelly kind of monopolize him.

"I'm sorry," he said, "I never got you that drink, did I?" Now she looked up at him and he thought he saw something in her eyes. He wasn't sure what it was… Hurt? Uncertainty? Either way, he didn't like it. He smiled down at her. "I'll go and get you one." Then he could come back, they'd find a quiet spot and talk, and then he'd get her away from here.

He turned and had just moved away when he heard his name being called. It was Kelly – again.

*For Christ's sake.* "Hold on…" she yelled. "I'll come with you."

*Really?* Couldn't she just give him a moment's peace?

He slowed his pace just slightly and let her catch up as they headed toward the kitchen, and then, just as they turned the corner to exit the room, she leant up and kissed him on the cheek.

He stopped. "What the hell did you do that for?" He glared down at her.

"Because I wanted to," she purred.

"Well don't." He didn't dare look back into the living room, but he hoped they'd gone far enough into the kitchen that Becky wouldn't have seen that little display.

"Oh, come on, Nick…" Kelly simpered.

"Leave it, Kelly." He moved away from her, and went through the kitchen, down the short corridor, to the bathroom beyond, which was – fortunately – vacant. He locked the door behind him and sat down on the closed toilet seat, leaning forward and putting his head in his hands.

What had he ever seen in Kelly? He was willing to admit he'd been interested in her for… well, years. They'd met in their first class together in that first week, and he'd been utterly smitten – as had every other guy in their class – by her long blonde hair, pale green eyes, and pouty lips, and her hour-glass figure didn't hurt either. He'd followed her around like a lapdog for a few months, and then he'd seen some guy leaving her apartment block – enjoying a passionate farewell kiss on the doorstep – early one morning, while he was out for a run. It was then that Nick had realized she was maybe a little faster and looser than the girls he was used to, back home in Somers Cove.

Still, the attraction hadn't waned, although he'd stopped following her so much… well, there were only so many times he wanted to watch her with other guys. And Nick wasn't idle, or lonely. He'd taken the chance to sleep around a little himself. He'd even admitted to himself that he was doing it in the hope Kelly would be jealous. She hadn't been, of course – she hadn't even noticed – but he'd had some fun, so what did it matter?

And then, one evening just before last Christmas, he'd finally had the opportunity to ask her on a date. He'd been quite cool about it, despite his nerves, and she'd looked him up and down, as though appraising him before giving him her decision, and then she'd laughed, real loud, and told him that she wouldn't be seen dead with a guy who dressed like him, who didn't even know how to comb his own hair… and she'd flounced off.

He sat back and stared at the ceiling, shaking his head. Considering her reaction, he might be inclined to wonder why she was behaving the way she was tonight – except he'd already worked that out. He knew exactly what Kelly was doing and it made him dislike her even more. She hadn't been interested in him when he was single, but now he was dating Becky – her friend – he'd suddenly become a whole lot more tempting. *What a bitch…*

He let out a long breath and tried to calm down. He thought about Becky and smiled. She looked real sexy tonight in that red sun dress… much more so than Kelly in her see-through effort. Becky exuded sensuality and an innocent charm that had him hooked from the first time she'd served him in the coffee shop, where she worked on Tuesday and Friday afternoons, and all day on Saturdays. Of course, he hadn't known she was Kelly's friend at the time… After her rejection, he'd kept himself to himself for a couple of months. Then, as winter was just starting to fade, he'd discovered the coffee shop and started using it as a quiet place to study. He liked it there, it reminded him of the coffee shop back home, where his sister Emma had a part-time job. He missed Emma – a lot. And one Friday, when he had the place pretty much to himself, Becky had come over to clear his table and see if he wanted anything else. Her voice was all shy and tentative, and he'd looked up into those golden brown eyes and, when she'd smiled down at him, he'd just fallen for her. It was that simple. All thoughts of Kelly, and every other girl he'd ever known just evaporated.

He'd waited a couple of weeks, spending as much time there as possible, and discovering that while her name tag said 'Rebecca', everyone called her Becky, and that she was studying Hospitality Administration in a completely different part of the campus, which was why he'd never met her before, and then one Friday evening, five weeks ago, he'd plucked up the courage and nervously asked her to the movies. She'd smiled, that slow, beautiful smile of hers and said yes, and he thought he'd died and gone to heaven. Finding out that she shared an apartment with Kelly was tricky, but there wasn't anything he could do about it.

Becky seemed shy and self-conscious and, after they'd been seeing each other for a couple of weeks, she finally told him that she'd liked him for a long time. He'd wondered how she'd even known he existed, and she'd explained that she'd seen him around, looking at Kelly, watching her. He'd felt embarrassed then, and had clarified that Kelly meant nothing to him – not now. He explained his dumb infatuation and she'd seemed to understand. He'd been tempted that night to tell Becky how he really felt about her – that he was in love with her – but he'd wondered if that might seem a little crass in the circumstances. Instead, he'd kissed her tenderly, and held her in his arms… and things had become quite heated. In between breathless moans and sighs, she'd made it clear she wanted more, so he'd given her what she needed, bringing her to orgasm, firstly with his fingers, and then his tongue. He'd asked for nothing in return, making that whole evening about her… And just watching her come apart had given him more satisfaction than any sexual experience of his life.

He shifted on the seat. Just thinking about that night made him hard.

A smile settled on his lips as he recalled the nights that had followed… Her orgasms – and there were a lot of them – and his. Her innocence was beguiling, but she'd learned fast, and the end results had been spectacular.

And then, a week ago, he'd happened to be passing the antique jewelry store between his apartment and one of his lecture halls, and he'd seen the necklace in the window. It was perfect; a silver chain, with a heart shaped locket, featuring a geometric pattern. It was an art-deco piece and it was beautiful, like Becky. He'd bought it there and then. He hadn't put anything in it; he'd left that for her to do, and after he'd given it to her that evening, he'd taken her to bed and they'd made love for the first time… and it was her very first time. Even as he was taking her virginity, he knew the memory of that night would stay with him forever.

As she'd lain in his arms afterwards, all satisfied and sleepy, he'd reached a decision… Becky may not have been the first woman he'd ever made love to, but she was going to be the last. That's one of the ways he knew he was in love with her. He'd always taken his chances when they presented themselves, and he'd never really waited for any woman. He'd slept with quite a few different girls over the years, while he decided what to do about Kelly – because, as much as he'd thought he wanted Kelly, he wasn't willing to sit around and wait for her to be available – but with Becky, it was different. He knew that, from then on, he'd be faithful to her. There would be no-one else for him, ever again.

"Hey… can you hurry up in there?" The male voice from the other side of the door woke him from his daydream.

"Sorry," he called and got to his feet.

He opened the door and passed through, letting a tall, skinny-looking guy go in after him.

Nick made his way back to the kitchen. He hoped by now that Kelly would have given up waiting for him, but he was out of luck. When he went back in, she was standing by the door and her eyes lit up like a firework display when she saw him. He grabbed a couple of sodas from the countertop and made his way over, hoping to bypass her.

"Nick," she said softly. "What's wrong?"

"Nothing. I'm just neglecting Becky. I should get back to her."

"Why?" Kelly asked. That was a dumb question if ever he'd heard one.

"Because she's my girlfriend?" He said it like a question, to try and show her how dense she was being.

She laughed, but not in the vicious way she'd done when she'd turned him down. This was more of a tinkling giggle, with a softer tone. "Oh dear," she said mildly. "You don't get it at all, do you?"

"Get what?" he asked, trying to duck past her again.

"College isn't the place to do serious relationships, Nick."

It obviously wasn't for Kelly, and he knew a lot of other people who slept around. Hell, he'd done that himself for the last couple of years, but he and Becky were different.

She moved a little closer. "Why don't you come upstairs with me?" she whispered, taking the sodas from him and putting them down on the countertop beside her. "I'll show you a much better time than Becky ever could."

"Kelly, I'm not interested—"

"How do you know?" she interrupted. "Look, it doesn't have to be upstairs. We can go out to your truck, or even back to your place, if you want. I don't mind where we go…" She moved right next to him, her body touching his. He could feel her breasts against him, and he tensed. She wasn't turning him on – not in the least – but he knew he had to be real careful about what he did next. He couldn't afford for her to misunderstand or misinterpret his actions. "I guarantee you won't be disappointed," she murmured softly, running her hand down his chest.

He took a step back. "No, Kelly. I've told you, I'm not interested. I'm with Becky, and you're with Tyler."

Now she did laugh… loudly. "I'm not with Tyler," she said, "not in the way you think. And if you honestly believe you're with Becky, you're a lot more naive than you look."

He felt his skin crawl. "What do you mean?" he replied.

"I mean," she said slowly, moving closer again, "that Becky gets it, even if you don't. Do you honestly think she's sitting around the apartment when she's not with you?" She looked up at him, but her face had become a blur as his blood pumped loudly through his ears, disorienting him. "She's playing the field, just like everyone else, Nick. You need to wake up."

He was frozen to the spot, unable to believe the words spewing from her mouth.

"Come with me," she said, taking his hand, "I'll prove it to you."

Nick let her lead him back into the living room, and stood with her to one side of the door. Becky and Tyler weren't by the window anymore and he scanned the room, looking for them. It didn't take long to find them, and when he did, he felt his blood turn to ice, watching as his life disintegrated in front of him.

At the other end of the room, a space had been cleared, and a few couples were dancing to a piece of music he didn't recognize. It was a slow number, and Tyler was holding Becky close in his arms, swaying her gently from side to side, his hands resting just above her backside. Her head was lying on his chest. They were lost in the music, and the moment, it seemed.

"See?" Kelly whispered in his ear. "She's not the person you thought she was, is she?"

Nick shook his head slowly, unable to take his eyes from the woman he loved, even though she was in the arms of another man.

The track ended and he watched as Tyler leant back a little. Even from this distance, he could see him looking down into Becky's eyes. She had her back to Nick, so he had no idea what she was doing, but he knew the expression that would be written on her face. He'd seen it for himself often enough in the last five weeks.

Then Tyler placed a finger under her chin, raising her face a little, and he leant down and kissed her, his mouth on hers. It was then that Nick felt the pain. It started in his chest, cutting him in two, cleaving its way through his body and wrenching his very soul apart.

How could she? How could his Becky do this?

Except she wasn't *his* Becky, was she? That much was obvious.

"I'm sorry," Kelly said and he dragged his eyes away from the car crash in front of him and looked down at her. "I wish you hadn't had to see that." He studied her face for a moment. Her eyes were twinkling and she wore the pout so well…

"Come here," he said, and took her hand, just as the music started up again. He pulled her onto the dance floor and held her body close to his, feeling her breasts crushed against his chest. Over her shoulder, he watched as Tyler pulled back from the kiss, keeping a firm hold on Becky and moving her in time to the music again, a soft satisfied smile on his face. Tyler started to turn them, and Nick knew that in just a few seconds, Becky would be facing him. He'd have to see that same contented expression on her face too, and he couldn't bear it.

"Hey," Kelly said, leaning back a little in his arms. "Remember me?"

He looked down at her. "Yeah… I do."

Without thinking, he leant down and captured her lips. They were warm and soft. He felt her tongue enter his mouth, delving for his. He responded, a little half-heartedly, letting his tongue caress hers, as her hands moved down between them. *No way!* He wasn't in the mood for that, certainly not with Kelly. He grabbed her hands and, holding them in his, kept the kiss going a little longer…

# Chapter Two

## *Becky*

Becky wished, more than anything, that Nick would come back from the kitchen, even if he was still with Kelly. She needed him. She just hoped he needed her too. The thought that he might not brought back the tears to her eyes and she buried her head in Tyler's chest again, and almost immediately wished she hadn't, as he tightened his hold on her, seemingly taking her action as a sign that she welcomed his attentions.

This dance may only have been one track, but it seemed to go on forever, and he occasionally sang the lyric into her ear, which was weird, given that it was a love song.

The music finally stopped and he pulled back a little. Becky knew she must look a mess, having spent the last five minutes crying, and she stared at his chest until she felt his finger beneath her chin, raising her face. That felt uncomfortably intimate and she stiffened. Then she saw the look in his eyes and tensed even more. Oh God… he was going to kiss her…

His lips were harsh, not soft and gentle, like Nick's. And she felt his tongue brush across her lips, making her gasp. He took the opportunity to dart his tongue inside her mouth, deep and hard, almost choking her. His hands roamed over her and he pulled her closer. She felt trapped. She could feel his erection pressing into her hip and she tried to back away, but he held on tighter still. Becky felt tears welling in her eyes. Where was Nick?

The music started up again and Tyler broke the kiss, staring down at her. He wore a self-satisfied smile on his face and started to move her again, turning her to face the other end of the room.

She heard her own sob as she saw Nick just a few feet away, kissing Kelly, their lips locked. She could see Kelly's hands move down between them and closed her eyes. She couldn't bear to watch her friend touching the man she loved, not like that, not so intimately. Again, she buried her face in Tyler's chest and wept. He held her close, moving his mouth next to her ear.

"I did try to warn you," he said.

Even so... even though Tyler had warned her, she still couldn't believe Nick would do this to her. He'd seemed so genuine, so kind and loving. If she hadn't believed in him, she'd never have let him... *Oh, God.* She sobbed again. She'd let him touch her, taste her, make love to her... take her virginity. And this was what he was really like? The worst kind of man there was... A cheat.

The music changed twice more and the tears just wouldn't stop, no matter how hard she tried.

"Let me take you home," Tyler whispered.

She nodded, grateful for the chance to escape. She didn't want to see how far Nick would let Kelly go, now he'd finally got his wish; now he'd finally got the woman he'd evidently wanted all along.

"Thank you," she said quietly. "That's very kind."

"My car's outside," he told her and, taking her hand, he led her through the crowd, passing Nick and Kelly, who were still kissing.

Becky couldn't bring herself to look at them, and turned away as she passed.

The journey home was quiet, apart from Becky's occasional sobs. Tyler didn't say anything, although occasionally he reached over and either took her hand, or gave her leg a slight squeeze, trying to comfort her, she supposed. As if he could. As if anyone could.

He parked up outside the apartment block and came around to her side, opening the door and helping her out. Then he walked her up to the fourth floor and stood beside her as she fished inside her purse, looking for her key. Eventually she gave up.

"I can't find it," she wept. "I know it's in there…"

"Let me try." He took her bag and delved inside, finding the key first time, putting it in the lock and opening the door for her.

"Thank you," she said, feeling useless.

"Can I come in?" he asked as she pulled the key from the lock again.

She turned and shook her head. "I don't think so." She wanted to be by herself for a while. She went in through the door.

"Rebecca," he said, using her full name, which hardly anyone ever did, not even her parents. "You're upset. I think I should stay with you."

"That's very kind of you, Tyler, but I'd really rather be by myself."

"I'm not sure that's a very good idea." He moved closer, his foot across the threshold.

"I'm fine. I just need some time to think."

"Thinking's overrated, especially at a time like this."

She wasn't in the mood for humor, although she thought he meant well.

"Really, Tyler." She put her hand on the door and started to push it closed.

"I'll call you," he said.

"You don't have my number…"

"Yes, I do. I got it from Kelly."

"You did?"

"Yes." He moved forward. "I'll call you to make sure you're okay."

"I'm going home tomorrow," she said.

"I'll still call."

He didn't wait for her to answer. Instead, he smiled, then turned and left.

Becky closed the door softly, and leant back against it, before sliding to the floor. She rested her head in her hands, and let the tears fall freely.

Becky had no idea how long she sat there, with her back to the door, and the tears flowing down her cheeks, but after a while she realized that Kelly might come home, and she had no intention of letting her supposed friend see her like this.

She clambered to her feet and made her way into her room, closing the door behind her. She contemplated sinking down to the floor again, but decided she'd had enough of sitting. So instead she started packing up her belongings. Her dad was driving up in the morning to collect her and take her home for the summer vacation. She'd intended to leave most of her things in the apartment, ready for the next semester, being as Kelly's parents owned this place, and were leaving it vacant through the summer, but she'd already decided she wouldn't be living here next semester. She'd find somewhere else to live, and she didn't really care where it was.

It took about an hour to pack her things. She didn't have much; just her clothes, some books and a few ornaments. Once it was all done, she stacked the boxes and bags by the closet ready for the morning and got undressed, ready for bed. The last thing she removed was Nick's locket. She was tempted to leave it behind… but she couldn't, and she popped it open, looking down at the picture of him, the one she'd taken on their second date – when they'd walked in the park, in the late afternoon after their lectures had finished. The light had been perfect and he'd looked so handsome, and so happy, smiling at the camera.

She snapped the locket closed again and, getting to her feet, she tucked it away in the top of one of the boxes, with her books.

Maybe one day, she'd be able to wear it again… maybe.

She climbed into bed, naked as usual, and pulled up the comforter, then stared at the ceiling, wondering how it had all gone so wrong. She'd thought everything was perfect. Well, pretty damn perfect, anyway. She was in love with Nick, and he'd seemed to like her, even if he didn't love her. He spent a lot of time with her, and was affectionate and caring, kind and considerate. She felt the tears behind her eyes again and blinked hard.

The front door opened, banging up against the wall behind it.

"Shhh. Be quiet…" she heard Kelly whisper, loud enough to wake anyone.

A male voice laughed and Becky chilled. It had to be Nick.

"Come on," Kelly said, and Becky heard footsteps, then a door open and close. It was the door to Kelly's bedroom, right next to her own.

There was a pause, of maybe a few minutes, then she heard the creak of the bed, and a giggle. And then a more steady, rhythmic squeaking of the bedsprings, accompanied by soft moaning. The male voice groaned occasionally, but said nothing distinct. After several minutes, the creaking became more pronounced, slightly faster.

"Please… yes. Oh, fuck. Fill me… now!" Kelly's voice carried through the apartment, and Becky heard a loud guttural male grunt, followed by several moans and groans from both of them as they calmed.

She curled herself up into a ball, sobbing quietly into her pillow, listening to the silence, until about half an hour later, Kelly's bedroom door opened again and she heard the man leave.

She got up early the next morning, showered, and dressed, then sat in the kitchen and wrote Kelly a note, explaining that she wouldn't be back the next semester. Kelly would have to find someone else to share the apartment. She thought it would be for the best… for everyone.

## Nick

With just three weeks to go before the end of the summer break, Nick had to admit, it had been horrendous so far. He'd been unable to focus on anything properly, and had spent most of the time being berated by his father for not concentrating on any of the tasks he'd been given.

His lack of concentration was hardly surprising, when all he could think about, even now, so many weeks later, was that night at the party. He was still haunted by the sight of Becky kissing Tyler, and seeing her leave with him, knowing that she'd probably end up in bed with him and maybe even spending the night at his place. That was one thing he and Becky had never done. They'd touched, tasted, licked, kissed, held, caressed… and made love. Man, had they made love. Within the space of a couple of days, she had turned from an innocent virgin into an insatiable lover. She could come, over and over, and still beg for more. Being with her was like a drug. He needed more each time he was with her. But through all of that, they'd never slept together for a whole night. Of course, he'd intended for her to stay with him on the night of the party. But she'd gone home with Tyler instead.

As he spent the hot summer days and sweltering nights at his parents' home, in the seaside town of Somers Cove, Maine, where he'd grown up, he tortured himself, remembering that night in infinite detail. He recalled Tyler's hands on Becky, her lips against his, their bodies pressed together…

He recalled his own kiss with Kelly – the detachment of it, the wretched feeling of disappointment that accompanied it. Not that it was surprising he should feel disappointed. Kelly wasn't Becky, and Becky was the only woman he wanted.

Watching Becky leave that night had broken him and he'd told Kelly he wanted to go home almost straight away. She'd looked up at him, a smirk forming on her full lips, and told him that was just fine by her. He could do whatever he wanted. She was going to stay, but as far as she was concerned, he could go. He'd looked down at her and, for the first time in his life, had been sorely tempted to hit a woman. He hadn't. He'd left, the realization that he and Becky had both been played, dawning on him, even before he'd reached his truck.

Of course, if he'd been thinking straight, he'd have seen it sooner. He'd have worked out that Kelly was bullshitting him, the moment she'd said Becky was playing the field. Becky wasn't playing anything. She'd been a virgin until a week before. He knew that better than anyone, being as he'd been the one to take her virginity. Unfortunately, Nick hadn't been thinking straight, and it had only dawned on him after he'd left the party; after Becky had already gone home with Tyler.

He'd contemplated going straight round to Becky's, telling her what had happened, how Tyler and Kelly had set them up. He'd even started in the direction of her place, but half way there, he'd stopped and pulled over, parking up at the roadside. What was the point? If Becky really cared about him, she'd never have let Tyler do what he did. If she was interested in Nick, Tyler wouldn't have stood a chance. She'd let it happen too… and she'd broken his heart in the process.

So, he'd gone home, settled into the boredom of helping out his dad at the boatyard… well, doing all the work, while his dad sat back and took it easy, would be a better way of putting that. And he'd tried to mend his broken heart.

Emma had helped – not that he'd told her there was anything wrong, but Emma always helped. She was four years younger than Nick, and she meant the world to him. Although he'd been away at college for a lot of the last three years, they'd stayed in touch. They'd always been there for each other. She kept him grounded, made him appreciate everything he had – even when he sometimes thought he had nothing. He tried to keep her cheerful when things got too much, which they sometimes did for Emma. He loved her, and knew he'd protect her if anyone ever tried to hurt her. He also knew that feeling was entirely mutual.

Emma was thinking about going to college herself. With one more year of high school, the decision was fairly imminent, and she was thinking of trying to get a place at catering college, being as that was what she really wanted to do.

"Mom and dad want me to study something more academic," she said to him early one evening, as he sat with her in the coffee shop. During school time she usually only worked on Saturdays, but over the summer, she'd taken on some extra shifts.

At the beginning of his vacation, being in there had been a kind of torture, as it reminded him of Becky, but as the days passed, he found the memories slightly easier to bear, and the coffee shop – and Emma's company – gave him some solace; more than he got from being on his own, anyway.

"You've gotta do what's right for you, Em," he told her. He knew how much pressure their parents would be putting on her and he knew she'd need his support. "Do you want me to talk to them?" he offered.

"Thanks." She smiled up at him across the counter. "I'd love to say yes to that and let you deal with it for me, but I have to learn to fight my own battles."

"Not while I'm here," he said.

"I've got time to work on them." She shrugged. "I know I'm not cut out for anything academic. I'm not even sure I'm cut out for college, but I know I can cook."

She certainly could. Emma had always been able to cook… even if their parents would have preferred her to follow a more scholarly path.

"Why don't you think you're cut out for college?" he asked.

She hesitated, looking down at her fingers. "I'm just scared about leaving here, and being on my own. Everyone else will be going with their friends. I know Jake and Cassie will be going to the same college," she mused.

"And?" he urged.

"And I'll be the only person from here who's going to catering school. I'm not sure about being on my own."

"You'll be fine, Em." He tried to sound reassuring, and after a few moments, she smiled at him. She had an amazing smile. One day, some poor guy was gonna fall hard for her, there was no getting away from that.

"Is everything alright?" she asked him, taking him by surprise.

"Yeah," he lied. "Why?"

She stared at him. "Oh, I don't know… You've been different since you've been back this time. Quieter, more thoughtful."

"I've just got a lot going on," he said. "I'm going into my final year. It's a lot of work."

She nodded, but he got the feeling she didn't believe a word he was saying. She could always see right through him.

The summer came to a close. By the end of it, he'd finally persuaded his dad that he was never going to take over the boat yard, not even if hell froze over. He was studying law because he wanted to be a lawyer, so there was no point in his parents expecting him to take over their business. His dad hadn't hidden his disappointment, and had made noises about selling up, because Nick had let him down – even though Nick had always told him he wasn't interested in boats. Nick didn't let the guilt-trip get to him, and returned to Boston in the fall with a clear conscience, at least as far as his parents were concerned.

On the drive back, he reasoned to himself that he'd managed to get through most of the first three years of his time at college without meeting Becky. All he had to do was survive another few months, then he'd graduate. He could do that…

He knew where she worked, where she went to study, and where she lived – with Kelly – so all he had to do was avoid those places, and he'd be fine. He'd be just fine, except for the aching wound in his chest. The one Becky had put there.

In his first seminar, he took his seat, got out his laptop and decided to try and put Becky out of his head for the next couple of hours, and focus hard on studying. Then he looked up and found Tyler sitting right in front of him. *Fucking marvelous.*

Part of him wanted to move, to change seats, or even classes, but he didn't. After a few minutes, while the other students were still filing in, Tyler turned and smiled at him.

"I wondered if I'd see you," he said casually. "I hope you're not gonna hold a grudge over what happened," he added.

"Why would I?" Nick tried to sound nonchalant.

"Well, I know you and Becky were together for a while," Tyler gloated… at least, he seemed to be gloating, anyway. "But she's with me now."

"I know." Nick couldn't see the point in playing ignorant, or rising to the jibe.

"She's staying at my place," Tyler added, twisting the knife. "She moved out of Kelly's apartment, and she's still looking for somewhere else." He grinned. "But I'm hoping to persuade her to stay on with me permanently."

"I'll bet you are." Nick gave Tyler a fake grin, then turned toward the lecturer as he started to speak, trying desperately to ignore the gnawing pain in his chest.

Later, in his own apartment, Nick sat in the dark, staring out the window, knowing Becky was out there with Tyler, maybe lying in his arms, probably naked. He imagined Tyler might have just made love to her, and Nick shuddered, thinking about Tyler's body invading Becky's. He'd never forget the way she looked when she climaxed, the way her skin flushed, her eyes fluttered closed, and her breasts heaved. Or the noises she made, her building sighs and moans, her screams and cries, the way his name sounded on her lips, and her whole body seemed to clamp around him...

Thoughts of his beautiful girl filled his head.

Except she wasn't his girl anymore. Tyler had wanted Becky, and he'd used Kelly to get to Nick, distracting him so he could take advantage of Becky... and as much as Nick had tried to blame Becky, he knew he was just as guilty. If he hadn't let Kelly divert him; if he'd been more attentive to what was going on, and not left Becky's side, none of this would have happened.

No matter how much this hurt, he knew Becky was still the only woman he'd ever love; the only woman he'd ever want to be with. They were meant to be together. Tyler wasn't right for Becky, not in the least... and one day, she'd work that out.

And when she did, he'd be waiting.

# Chapter Three

Present Day

*Becky*

"Which one?" Becky mused to herself, holding the two dresses out in front of her. They were both floor-length, but there the similarities ended. One was navy blue, strapless and fitted, with beading on the bodice and a ludicrously tight skirt; the other was bright red, more stylish, off the shoulder, with a fuller skirt. She shook her head. She'd saved up and bought the red one herself; Tyler had chosen the blue one for his company's Christmas dinner the previous year… There was no contest, really. She re-hung the blue one in the closet and put the red dress into the purpose-made cover, hanging it on the back of the door – the door that was locked. It was always locked, even though Tyler was rarely home in the evenings. She just felt safer knowing he couldn't get in.

She checked her watch. It was nearly ten o'clock, and she zipped up her suitcase before sitting beside it on the bed, and wondering – not for the first time – whether she should just leave now. If she did, she'd get to the hotel in Maine sometime between twelve-thirty and one in the morning. But then they weren't expecting her until tomorrow lunchtime – two days before the grand opening on Saturday evening. She knew they'd be busy, and the last thing they needed was her arriving ahead of time. She was there to check up on them and make sure things ran smoothly; they wouldn't thank her for getting there early. She doubted they'd thank her at all, especially if she found too many faults, but it was a job that had to be done.

She'd spoken to her boss, Mark Gardner, the owner of the new hotel – along with dozens more in New England – about ten days ago, and he'd asked her to travel up to Maine to help get the new staff settled in and iron out any teething problems. She'd told Mark about her worries over being close to Somers Cove – because she'd known a guy from there when she was at college. She hadn't mentioned Nick's name though, and Mark had reassured her that she needn't go anywhere near the town itself. In any case, she knew Nick had probably moved on long ago. Of course, he'd also told her Emma was from Somers Cove and that she'd grown up there, so there was every chance she'd know Nick – or at least know of him – but that would only matter if they actually talked about him. As long as she avoided the subject, it'd be fine. Besides, she'd only be seeing Emma at the opening and she'd be busy all evening. She thought it unlikely they'd socialize. She didn't usually see Mark outside of work, unless they were away on business, when they might have dinner together. No, it would definitely be fine, she reassured herself. She'd told Mark she'd be there – and she'd stay on for as long as necessary. What she hadn't told him was how relieved she felt at the prospect of being away from home for a prolonged period. He'd probably guessed though. Mark knew about Tyler. Well, he knew some of it. He knew the parts she'd chosen to tell him, when it had all gotten too much and she'd been unable to hide her distress from him. All she had to do was get out of the house without Tyler realizing how long she was going to be away for. He wouldn't like a prolonged absence, but once she was gone, what could he do about it? She tried not to think about that too hard and focused on deciding whether to leave now, or wait until after he'd gone to work in the morning…

The sound of the front door slamming brought her back to her senses with a bump, and she found herself gripping on to the edge of the bed, her knuckles whitening.

What was he doing here? She checked the time again, glancing at the clock beside the bed. It was a few minutes after ten. He never came home this early… *Why tonight?*

She listened as he banged around downstairs – in the kitchen, she thought – then tensed even more as she heard his footsteps on the stairs, passing her room and going into his own at the end of the corridor. Again, she heard a few crashes as he bumped into the furniture, and she wondered just how drunk he was.

Silence descended and she hoped he'd fallen into bed. She waited. Ten minutes went by without a sound and she felt herself relax, just a little.

"I know you're in there…"

His voice close against the door made her skin prickle, and she stared at the wooden panels, picturing him standing right outside. She sat, silent, shaking.

"Rebecca. Don't ignore me." His voice was more menacing this time, slightly deeper.

"W—what do you want?" she managed to say.

"Let me in," he replied.

"No." The locked door gave her a feeling of bravado, even though she was still shaking.

"Open the fucking door, Rebecca." He was angry.

"No. Go and sober up first." *By the time you've done that, I'll have gone*, she thought to herself.

"I'm gonna count to five," he said slowly. "Either open the door before I get there, or I'll break the fucking thing down." There was an ominous pause, and then she heard him shout, "One!"

She hesitated. She had her phone… it was in her purse on the chair by her dresser. She could call the cops… but they'd never get there in time.

"Two!" he yelled.

She got up, her legs unsteady, and went over to the dresser, fumbling desperately in her bag and finding her phone.

"I'll call the cops," she called out.

"Go right ahead," he replied through the door. "We both know who they'll believe, don't we?"

He was right. She knew he was. He could lie his way out of anything.

"Three!" He continued the countdown.

Could she call Mark? She knew it would be like a red rag to a bull as far as Tyler was concerned. And, in any case, Mark was living up in Maine now. What could he do?

"Four! Don't make me break this door down," he threatened. "You know you'll regret it, if you do… Rebecca." There was a warning note to his voice that terrified her, and she dropped the phone onto the thickly carpeted floor. "I mean it."

"Okay. I'll open the door." She knew only too well what he was capable of, and that there was no-one close enough to help her. Her bravado had abandoned her.

She moved quickly across the room and turned the key, stepping to one side as he entered the room, and watching as he looked around, his eyes settling on her suitcase.

"What the fuck is going on?" He rounded on her.

"I'm packing…" she mumbled.

"I can see that. Why are you packing?" He came and stood in front of her.

"Because I have to go away on business."

"You're always away on business," he sneered. "But you never take that amount of stuff with you." He pointed to the large case, lying on the bed. "What's happening here, Rebecca?"

"I'm gonna have to stay away a little longer this time," she told him. "It's to do with the new hotel."

"Oh, really?" She heard the doubt in his voice. "And it's got nothing to do with you banging Mark Gardner behind my back?"

She sighed. *Not this again…*

"There's nothing going on between me and Mark," she said as patiently as she could. "He's my boss. He's engaged—"

"So? You think no-one ever fucked their boss? You think engaged guys don't fool around?"

No, she didn't think that at all. She knew better than to think that.

"His fiancée's pregnant," she added, hoping that would shut him up. The smirk on his face told her she was wrong.

"That's even more reason for him to come after you…" He moved closer. "He's probably not getting much at home now."

She didn't reply. It was clear – as ever – that nothing she said was going to change Tyler's view of her relationship with Mark, no matter how many times she told him she wasn't interested in her boss, and that everything between them was purely professional.

"Nothing to say?" he sneered.

"What's the point? You don't believe me."

"Why would I?" he yelled. "You've done nothing but lie to me since you started working for him."

"I've never lied to you." She raised her own voice now. "And I've never cheated on you either… that's your field of expertise." She wanted to bite back the words. They might have been true, but she knew she'd regret them. He'd make sure of that.

"Is it any surprise? Who'd wanna fuck you?"

"Mark – according to you," she snapped.

That had stumped him, and he glared at her for a moment.

"When are you leaving?" he asked, seeming to calm a little.

"First thing in the morning."

A mean smile spread slowly across his lips and he took the final step needed to stand right in front of her. "Well," he said quietly, "if you're gonna be away for as long as this suitcase suggests, I guess I should probably remind myself what you feel like."

An icy chill spread through her.

"W—what I feel like?" she murmured.

"Yeah." He reached out and grabbed her, pulling her into his arms.

"Let me go!" she shouted.

He didn't reply, but kept a firm grip, placing one hand behind her head, moving his own closer to kiss her. She twisted, trying to break free, but she wasn't strong enough and his lips locked with hers. She tensed against him as his tongue pressed into her closed mouth.

He pulled back, staring at her. "Let me in," he growled.

She shook her head, unwilling to even open her mouth to speak.

"Fucking let me in, Rebecca." He glared at her. "You've shut me out for too damn long."

She glared at him, using anger to hide her fear, the memories of the last time he'd touched her still fresh in her mind, despite the intervening months.

"Nothing to say?" he goaded, his eyes darkening as he pulled her toward the bed. "Well, I guess I'll just have to give you something to remember me by…"

"No!"

"I wasn't *asking* you, Rebecca."

She ducked away from him, but he grabbed her again and dragged her to the bed, pulling her suitcase onto the floor, and pushing her down onto the mattress in its place. He stood above her but she sat up, shifting backwards, desperate to escape.

"Where the fuck do you think you're going?" He leant over, caught hold of her ankles and pulled her back, pushing her down again, and keeping his hands firmly on her shoulders this time. "It'll hurt so much more if you fight me," he warned. "You're my wife. I'm entitled to this."

"You're what?"

"I'm not gonna say it again." He knelt on the bed, his legs between hers, pushing them apart. He rested one arm across her neck, while he placed the other between her breasts, letting it rest there. He stared at her for a moment, then clutched her blouse between his fingers, tearing through the fabric and ripping it open, exposing her. She gasped and moved her arms across to cover herself. "Don't fucking move," he ordered, leaning more heavily on her neck. She struggled for breath and let her arms fall back down by her sides again, closing her eyes. "Open up," he said. "I want you to watch me fucking you."

She did as she was told and he grinned. "Well done." Sarcasm dripped through his words.

He moved down and lifted her skirt, pushing it up higher to reveal her flesh colored lace panties.

"He likes these, does he?"

She looked at him. "Who?"

"Gardner. Why? Who else are you fucking?"

She sighed again. "No-one."

He didn't reply. Instead, he pulled her panties to one side and inserted two fingers inside her, roughly. "Hell, Rebecca. You're not even thirty yet… you can't be drying up already, surely."

She blinked back her tears. Did he honestly think she'd be aroused by what he was doing?

"Or have you forgotten what a real man feels like?" he added, leaning back and releasing her. She felt the panic rise inside her as he undid the button on his pants, lowering the zipper and pulling them down around his thighs, his boxers joining them.

She had to stop him. She might not have such a lucky escape this time as she had before… "Do you think you're a real man?" she mocked, hoping she wouldn't regret her words.

"I'm more of a man than Gardner, that's for sure." He leant forward, ripped her panties from her and let the tip of his erection rest against her entrance. "Remember the last time you went away?" he asked, threateningly. She nodded her head. "Remember me saying I was gonna mention you to Jed and Si, and see if they'd like to try you out for size?" She swallowed hard and nodded again. "Well, I wasn't fucking kidding. I've spoken to them both already, to see how they feel about it, and they're both real keen. So fuck nicely now, or I'll give them a call." He smirked. "They could be here in less than ten minutes. What a sight that'd be… Miss Goody Two Shoes taking two cocks." He shuddered. "Fuck, that makes me wanna come already."

"You disgust me."

He laughed. "You think I give a fuck? Now, take my dick and fuck me like you mean it."

"No." She brought her thighs as close together as she could.

"You want me to hurt you?" he threatened.

"Nothing you can do to me can hurt me," she lied, her voice a mere whisper. He stared at her like he didn't understand. "I'm not yours to hurt." He stopped, leaning back a little. "The only man who can hurt me is the man I love, and that's not you. My heart's never been yours. It was always Nick's. Always. So whatever you do to my body, *you* can't hurt me…"

She wasn't quick enough. She didn't see him swing his arm back, or his fist as it approached her face. She felt it strike though, just below her left eye. She felt the explosive pain, like the whole side of her face was broken, cracked by the blow of his clenched fist.

He stood, and she felt the release from his oppression, despite the pain radiating through her head.

"You fucking bitch!" he shouted, pulling up his shorts and pants, breathing heavily, his shoulders heaving as he paced. "You think Nick Woods ever wanted *you?* He tried you, and when he realized what a useless fuck you are, he banged Kelly instead. And who can blame him? He wanted someone who'd actually do something, other than lie there like a plank of wood." He laughed. "Ha! He couldn't get away from you fast enough, could he? You might have loved him, and maybe you still do but, believe me, he *never* loved you." He glared down at her, then turned and, without another word, left the room. She heard his footsteps on the stairs and then the front door slamming.

She waited a few minutes, to be sure he'd actually gone, before letting out a sigh of relief.

She raised her head off the mattress, ignoring the thumping pain, and looked down at her disheveled clothes. He'd ripped her blouse and panties beyond repair, although her bra was intact, not that she really cared. She felt the first tear land on her cheek, but wiped it away gently, aware of the bruising.

Slowly, gingerly, she clambered to her feet, walking into the adjoining bathroom, where she ran a face cloth under the cold water, before holding it against her bruised cheekbone. She stood for a moment, but then fear overcame her. What if he came back?

She dropped the face cloth into the basin, and moved back into the bedroom, undressing and leaving her clothes on the floor where they fell. She grabbed fresh underwear and put it on, then a pair of jeans and a blouse, and sat on the edge of the bed, quickly dressing. She put on a pair of flat shoes, picked up her phone from the floor, where she'd dropped it, and put it in her purse, which she threw over her shoulder. Then, taking her suitcase, and the dress from the back of the door, she fled the bedroom… and the house.

For the first hour of the drive, she didn't even really think, she just put the car in gear, put her foot on the gas and hoped for the best.

It was only when tiredness started to overwhelm her that she realized she'd better stop, and pulled up at a roadside motel. She could complete her journey in the morning. For now, she just wanted to rest somewhere safe, and this was the safest place she could think of; because Tyler had no idea where she was. She wasn't altogether sure where she was herself.

As she set her head down on the stiff pillow, she curled her body up, hugging her arms around herself. She'd taken one hell of a gamble bringing up Nick's name like that. Tyler had told her on their wedding night that she needed to forget Nick Woods had ever existed. He didn't want to hear Nick's name on her lips ever again – not even in her sleep. She was married to Tyler Howell, and she'd better not forget it. She sobbed, recalling that night… the insulting words he'd used; the brutal way he'd taken her. Considering it was their first time, and that they'd waited until they were married, she'd hoped for love, kindness, consideration, maybe even a little romance. What she got was pain and abuse – the story of her marriage, as it turned out.

She shifted, trying to get comfortable, and wondered how different her life might have been if she hadn't listened to Tyler all those years ago at that damned party. She'd got it wrong that night. Very wrong. She'd hurt Nick; she'd trusted the wrong man, and she'd behaved appallingly. But she'd paid a high price for her mistakes… a really high price…

## *Nick*

"I don't understand why you can't go…"

Nick sat opposite his business partner, Tom Allen, a frown settled firmly on his face.

"I've already explained." Tom pursed his already thin lips and glared at Nick. This wasn't that unusual. Tom was forty-five, with dark hair, graying at the temples, and was maybe a little overweight. In Nick's view, Tom was straight-laced, always suited and booted, tidy, well-groomed, the picture of a small-town lawyer. In return, Tom found it hard to handle Nick's attitude to convention; the fact that he wore jeans, a shirt, a waistcoat, and a tie – but only if absolutely necessary – whether in the office, meeting a client, or in court. His hair was untidy – or it seemed that way to Tom – his chin was stubbled, and he gave the impression of being so laid back, it was hard to believe he was paying attention at all. That attitude rankled Tom. What rankled more though was the fact that Nick was by far the better lawyer. "I've got to go out of town... well, out of state, actually."

"Yeah, you've told me that. The question is, why? You accepted this damn invitation from Mark Gardner. I'm not interested in his new hotel."

"I can't see what your problem is. He's practically family now." Tom was referring to Mark Gardner's recent engagement to Nick's sister, Emma.

"Which means I don't mind having a beer with him, or watching the Patriots, or going for dinner with him and Emma. That doesn't mean I wanna go to the opening of his damn hotel. You're the one who said we should put in an appearance. So, you should be the one to attend."

"Except I can't, because—"

"Because you've gotta go out of town." Nick leant forward. "If you want me to get trussed up in a tux, and tolerate a night of small talk and boredom, the very least you can do is explain why."

Tom huffed out a sigh, seeming to admit defeat at last. "I've made arrangements to spend the weekend with an old buddy of mine from college. I haven't seen him since Ethan was born." Ethan was Tom and Cathy's oldest boy. He'd just had his fifteenth birthday.

"Okay, so you haven't seen the guy in fifteen years. What I don't understand is why you have to meet him this weekend. You had a prior engagement."

"Garrett's a busy man," Tom explained, twisting his pen between his fingers. "If we don't meet this weekend, it's gonna be something like three months before he's free again."

"So?"

"It's business, Nick."

"Business?" Nick was surprised Tom hadn't mentioned this before. It would have made more sense to lead with this side of the excuse, especially considering they were partners. "What kind of business?"

"He owns a huge construction company. GHC Engineering?"

Nick nodded. He'd heard the name. In fact, he'd heard it quite recently. He just couldn't remember where…

"They've been awarded a big state contract to build a new highway." Ah. That was it. Nick recalled seeing something online about this; an article and photograph of the Massachusetts State Senator, shaking hands with some overweight, pompous-looking guy… presumably Tom's friend, Garrett. "The contract's worth millions," Tom continued.

"So?" Nick didn't see the significance.

"Garrett wants Allen and Woods to be his legal representatives on this new project," Tom explained.

"And we need this, do we?" Nick asked.

"It's worth a fortune."

Nick stood, placed his hands on the edge of Tom's desk and leant over. "I didn't know we were worried about money, but if we are, why did you turn down Mark Gardner's work? He offered that to me just a couple of weeks ago, and you turned it down flat, because you said we couldn't handle it. And now you're going after something that sounds so much bigger? It doesn't make sense."

"It makes perfect sense." Tom shifted back in his chair, refusing to let Nick's bulky six-foot-four frame intimidate him.

"Why?" Tom didn't answer immediately, so Nick pressed on: "What kind of work are we talking about here?"

"Nothing for you to worry about…" Tom glanced out the window.

Nick felt a familiar prickling in his spine, the one that always alerted him when something didn't add up. "This is corporate work, Tom," he said.

"Yeah. So?"

"So, you can't handle it. Corporate law isn't your thing. We both know that. And that means it's gonna fall on me, which means I'm entitled to know what you're getting us into."

Tom stood now. He was a couple of inches under six feet tall, but he still had a presence. "I'm not an idiot, Nick. And whatever you think, I'm more than capable of handling this. Besides, Garrett's insisting I deal with it personally."

"Until he sees what a fuck-up you make of it," Nick muttered.

Tom rounded on him. "Stop being so damned patronizing. This guy's gonna pay us a fortune. We're both gonna be very rich indeed." He smirked. "You can finally get out of that shitty trailer you've been living in, and build the house you've been talking about for the last four years."

"Screw the house," Nick retaliated. "There are more important things than money – or houses."

"Such as?"

"Such as principles. Such as doing the right thing."

"Principles don't pay the damn bills. We need something like this."

"I offered you something like this. Mark was happy to give us as much work as we could handle, without over-stretching us, and pay us well for doing it."

"This is worth a lot more than Mark Gardner was gonna pay." Tom let out a long sigh and rested his hands on the edge of his desk, looking up at Nick. "You're gonna have to trust me on this," he said. "And you're gonna have to attend the hotel opening on behalf of the company."

Nick felt his shoulders drop. "Okay… I'll go," he murmured.

"Do you even own a tux?" Tom asked, smiling lightly.

"Of course I own a fucking tux. I just don't wear it much." He ran both hands through his long hair, pulling it back behind his head. "You owe me," he said, glaring at Tom.

"I don't know what you're making all this fuss about. Emma's gonna be there."

"That's the only reason I've agreed." Nick's voice was getting gruffer by the minute.

"Then stop sulking."

"No."

Nick rummaged through the closet in his trailer, pushing countless white shirts to one side until he came across his tux, still wrapped in the dry cleaner's cover – thank God. He couldn't even remember the last time he'd worn it, but at least he'd got it cleaned.

Pulling it out, he closed the closet door, and lay the black suit on his bed. He stared down at it, his mind filled with images of a modern, sterile hotel foyer, crowded with the great and the good from the local area, all boring each other rigid.

He shuddered at the thought and left the room, switching off the light as he went through into the living area. Grabbing a beer from the refrigerator, he sat down at one end of the black leather couch, turning and putting his feet up. As he took the first gulp straight from the bottle, and swallowed it down, he started to wonder why a large Massachusetts-based corporation would choose to send their legal work to a small-town outfit in Maine, and when it was that Tom had become so obsessed with money… and why.

# Chapter Four

## *Becky*

She had to admit, she was impressed. Even with her sunglasses on – a necessary addition, not just because it was sunny, but to hide the black eye that now disfigured her face – the hotel was spectacular.

Becky had been working for Mark Gardner for three years, and he wasn't short of impressive hotels, but this was something else. Elegant and serene in its clifftop surroundings, the Gardner Oceanic was the perfect flagship for the company.

Becky parked her BMW Z4 in one of the staff spaces and climbed out. She loved driving the little gray sports car, but there was no denying, it had caused her some trouble. Mark had bought it for her roughly a year ago, and Tyler had completely overreacted, assuming this was payment in kind for services rendered. No amount of begging had stopped his fists that night. But she was grateful he'd only used his fists.

She left her case in the car, grabbing her purse from the passenger seat, and walked into the lobby of the hotel, through the revolving glass doors, where the illusion of serenity came to an abrupt halt. It was chaos. People were running around, some carrying boxes, or bags... others just running, fraught expressions on their faces. The noise level was high too, mainly caused by the number of people who seemed to be shouting at each other. This didn't look good at all.

A tall man, probably in his mid-twenties, with dark brown hair, wearing jeans and a t-shirt walked up to her. He seemed calmer than all the others, his expression resigned, rather than panicked.

"Are you Becky Howell?" he asked. Now he was standing beside her, she noticed his eyes were a really unusual shade of green, or maybe they just seemed that way because of the sunglasses she didn't dare take off.

"Yes," she replied.

He offered her his hand, and she shook it. "I'm Jake Hunter," he explained. "Mark told me to look out for you."

"Ahh. You designed this place?"

"Yeah." He turned and looked around, then started walking toward the reception desk, letting her fall into step beside him. "Sorry about the madhouse," he added.

"I was expecting it to be a little crazy, but nothing like this," she replied, smiling.

"Neither was I, to be honest."

"Is Mark here?" Becky asked, putting her purse down on top of the glass reception counter.

Jake shook his head. "No. He's avoiding the place until Saturday." He shrugged. "Can't say I blame him."

"And where's Austin?" Becky was referring to the manager of the hotel, Austin Lewis, who she'd met twice; firstly when she'd interviewed him, and again, when she'd introduced him to Mark after he'd been hired.

"Upstairs somewhere."

Becky looked up at Jake. "Can I just say, this isn't looking good."

"You can say it," Jake replied. "Doesn't mean anyone's gonna listen to you."

"Meaning?"

"Meaning I've been trying to get Austin to listen to me for the last hour and a half. I'm getting nowhere…"

Becky took a deep breath. "What are you trying to talk to him about?" she asked.

"We've got some snagging issues," Jake explained.

"Such as?"

He pulled a sheet of paper from his back pocket, unfolded it and handed it to her. She read it through.

"This is nothing major."

"I know. But I need to turn off the mains power for about an hour."

"Then turn it off."

"Austin told me I couldn't."

"Screw Austin."

Jake smiled. "I'd rather not."

Becky let out a laugh. "I meant metaphorically."

"Thank God for that." She handed him back the paper and he replaced it in his pocket. "You're sure… about the power, I mean?"

"Yes. Go ahead. I'll go find Austin and let him know… And any other problems, just call me." She leant over the reception desk, grabbed a piece of paper and a pen, and jotted down her cell number. "Heaven knows where I'll be, but I'll pick up."

He grinned. "I wish you'd been here yesterday," he said, turning and walking away.

"So do I," she murmured to his departing figure.


Upstairs, she eventually found Austin in one of the master suites, berating a junior member of staff. The girl was cowering and looked like she was about to cry, while Austin – a man of around five-foot-eleven, with light brown hair and a sallow complexion – leant over her, his demeanor really threatening.

"Can we talk?" Becky interrupted.

"In a minute. I'm busy," he snapped without looking up.

"No. Now." He glanced up, about to scold her, then realized who he was talking to.

"I'm so sorry, Mrs Howell." He became obsequious. "I didn't know you were here. No-one informed me."

"They shouldn't need to," Becky told him. "Let's go to your office."

Austin pulled a handkerchief from his pocket and wiped his brow, then checked his watch. "I'm afraid it's going to have to wait," he said. "I've called a meeting for all staff members in five minutes."

Becky sighed. "Very well. I'll sit in on your meeting and we'll talk afterwards."

Austin seemed startled. "You're going to sit in?"

"Yes. Where's the meeting."

"In the lobby."

"The lobby?" Becky was surprised.

"Yes. It's a nice big space. I can stand on the stairs and everyone can see me…"

Becky wondered if that was the most important consideration. "I understand that, but there's a lot going on down there. Wouldn't the restaurant be better?"

"I've made the arrangements now." He sounded impatient.

"Very well." Becky knew when to fight a battle and when to give in. She was an expert on that.

As Austin's voice droned on into the twenty-fifth minute of his speech, Becky stood slightly behind him and to one side, looking at the faces gathered below. There were around sixty people gathered in the lobby, and they all looked bored to death. Austin was doing nothing to motivate them; nothing to inspire them to want to give their all for the hotel, or the company.

She'd already been feeling less than confident, but as he continued talking, her conviction waned still further. She'd hired this guy and Mark would not be pleased if she'd taken on the wrong person for the job. But it was better to face the music now, than to let it ride. She knew that much.

With as little fuss as possible, she quietly descended the steps and made her way around the edge of the room, into the manager's office, located down a corridor to the left of the reception counter, closing the door softly behind her. It was a large, comfortable office, with a dark wood desk at one end and an overstuffed brown leather couch, with a low coffee table, at the other.

Sitting down on the couch, Becky pulled her phone from her purse and looked up Mark's details, then waited for the call to connect.

He answered on the second ring.

"Tell me," he said by way of greeting. He always knew when something was wrong, because he was good at what he did... really good.

"I screwed up." She didn't see the point in beating around the bush.

"How?" He didn't sound angry, just concerned.

"I hired the wrong guy."

"For which job?"

Becky had been responsible for hiring most of the employees at the hotel, so it was a fair question.

"The big one. The manager."

"Remind me."

"Austin Lewis?"

There was a moment's silence. "Yeah, okay." She knew Mark would remember as soon as she said the name. He might employ several thousand people, but he was *that* good. "What's wrong with him?"

"Where do I start?"

"It's that bad?"

"Yeah. I'm sorry, Mark. I think you're gonna have to come down here."

"Why?" He wasn't saying 'no'. He just needed to know why his presence was required.

"Because it's a madhouse. Jake's trying to finish up, and Austin's putting up roadblocks. I've just sat in on a staff meeting and I've never come across anyone less inspirational."

"I'm sensing there's something else?"

"I... I found him in one of the master suites, telling off one of the junior staff members."

"And?"

"And I didn't like the way he was going about it."

"This was a woman he was talking to?"

"Yes. She looked scared. I might have mis-read the situation. I don't know, Mark. Maybe I'm over-sensitive—"

"No," Mark interrupted. "I know you're capable of being impartial and I trust your judgement. Where are you now?"

"In the manager's office."

"And Austin?"

"He's still delivering his speech to the staff."

"Christ. Okay. I just need to call Emma. She's meeting with the interior designer at the coffee shop today. I'll call her and tell her where I'm gonna be." There was a moment's pause. "I'll be there within the hour."

She hung up and sat back on the couch. It was really comfortable, and she let herself relax, removing her sunglasses, just for a moment, and rubbing the bridge of her nose. She'd been undecided that morning, whether to wear the sunglasses, or lots of makeup. The sunglasses had won. She didn't really like makeup – well, not in the kind of quantity that would have been required to cover the bruising around her eye. She touched it gingerly. It still hurt like hell.

There was a knock on the door and she hurriedly replaced her glasses, calling out, "Come in," at the same time.

"Hi." Jake stuck his head around the door, looking at her a little uncertainly, then came in and closed the door.

"Is there a problem?" Becky asked, getting to her feet.

"Um… No."

That was an odd answer. If there was no problem, why had he sought her out?

"Mark called me," Jake explained.

"He did?"

"Yeah. He… um… he asked me to come find you. And not let you out of my sight until he gets here."

"Oh?" She felt her eyes stinging. "Is… um… Is Austin still giving his talk outside?"

"No. Everyone's gone back to doing more useful things."

"And Austin?" she asked.

"No idea. He could be anywhere."

"I'm sure you've got better things to do than babysit me. It's really not necessary."

Jake shrugged and walked over to the desk, perching on the edge of it. "Mark thinks it is. He said Austin was being threatening toward one of the female workers?" Becky nodded her head.

"Yes. There was just something about the way he was leaning over her…" Becky didn't want to admit that seeing Austin like that had reminded her of how Tyler could be with her, but she knew that was why Mark had asked Jake to stay with her. Mark and Jake had been friends long before Jake started working for Mark. It made sense that Mark would ask Jake to watch over her if he was worried, and it was a typically considerate thing of him to do.

"Well, I'll stay with you until Mark arrives."

"But that's gonna hold you up."

"It's fine."

Becky felt guilty. "What were you doing when Mark called?"

"I was just gonna turn the power back on, and then I was gonna check the sprinkler system in the kitchen."

"Well, why don't I come with you? I'd like to take a look around, and you can get on with what you're doing."

Jake pushed himself off the desk. "Sounds like a good idea."

He went over to the door and had just opened it when they both heard a scream, followed by a thudding sound.

"What the…?" Jake turned and grabbed Becky's hand, pulling her through the door, down the corridor and around the reception counter, then into the lobby, where the cause of the noise soon became apparent to both of them. He let go of her as they stood and looked down at the prone figure of Austin Lewis, lying on the floor at the foot of the wide staircase.

"What happened?" Becky said, going over and kneeling beside him. He groaned and she sighed her relief. At least he wasn't dead.

"He fell." She looked up into the face of the deputy manager, Carter Holmes.

"Call an ambulance," she instructed.

"Already on it," Jake replied from behind her and she turned to see him standing, his phone clasped to his ear. "Don't move him."

"No." Becky stood again. "Everyone stand well back," she said, loudly enough for the gathered crowd to hear. "Carter?" He stepped forward. "Keep this area clear and send someone out to the road to watch for the ambulance."

"Yes, ma'am." He moved away, issuing instructions as he went.

Becky knelt down again. It was easy to see from the angle of Austin's right leg, that it was badly broken, and he was clearly in a lot of pain. "The paramedics will be here soon," she said, trying to sound soothing.

Jake came and knelt opposite her. "What happened?" he asked.

"I don't know. The deputy manager said he fell."

"We need to find out," Jake replied. "If it's something faulty…" He didn't finish the sentence.

"Yeah. Can you go and start asking round?"

"I'm meant to stay with you."

Becky glanced down at Austin. "I think that problem's kinda past history now." She looked up at Jake and he nodded slowly.

"Okay." He climbed to his feet. "Are you sure?"

"Yes. We need to know…"

Jake moved toward the stairs, where half a dozen or more staff members were gathered, talking.

It was only a few minutes before he returned, and gave Becky a nod, indicating they should move away from Austin. She stood and followed him.

"I've spoken to those guys over there." He pointed towards the group. "They said Austin finished his speech, and told everyone to get back to work. The woman with the blonde hair…" Jake nodded in the direction of a young woman, maybe in her late teens or early twenties. "She asked him a question and he told her to go upstairs and he'd follow her. Then someone else spoke to him for a few minutes. The blonde woman was waiting at the top of the stairs and, when he got halfway up, he started issuing her with instructions. Then someone at the bottom of the stairs called up to him, he turned…"

"And fell?" Becky finished the sentence for him.

Jake nodded. "Yeah."

"So it was just an accident?"

"Looks that way, although Mark's gonna want a full investigation."

"You bet he is." She sighed.

"It's not your fault," Jake said, sounding sympathetic.

"I know…"

They stopped talking as the ambulance crew came in through the door.

"Where's the patient?" the smaller of the two men asked.

"Over here," Jake called them over and stayed while they attended to Austin.

Becky took a step back and let the paramedics do their job, and allowed Jake to guide them. His knowledge of the hotel was far better than hers and she was grateful he was there.

Within a few minutes, Austin had been loaded into the back of the ambulance and was on his way to the hospital.

"I guess you can go back to whatever you were doing," she said to Jake, when the crowd had started to disperse.

"It'll keep."

"Really," she replied, her voice little more than a whisper. "I'm fine."

"Mark asked me to stay with you until he got here. So, I'm gonna stay."

"Okay. Well, I guess you'd better lead the way to the kitchens, then."

"Yeah, via the basement."

"The basement?"

"I've just gotta turn on the power supply again."

"Oh yes." She smiled and rolled her eyes. "I'd forgotten all about that."


They were still in the kitchen when Mark arrived.

"Hi," he said, coming in through the double doors. "I've just been told that we've got an even bigger problem than we thought."

"Yeah." Becky turned away from Jake and went over to Mark. "Austin fell down the stairs."

"And?"

"And broke his leg, by the looks of things."

"Shit..." Mark looked at her. "Why the hell are you wearing sunglasses in here?" he asked.

"I've got a headache."

He stared at her, to the point where it was beginning to feel uncomfortable, then nodded his head.

"Okay." She knew he didn't believe her. "Well, I'm not sure that is such a big problem – not for us. His leg probably hurts like a bitch, but I was almost certainly gonna fire his ass anyway. I don't have a lot of time for guys who behave like that toward women… whether they work for me or not." He looked at her again for a moment and she knew he was referring to Tyler.

"But you're still a manager down," Jake put in, coming over to join them.

Mark smiled at Becky. "How do you feel about being demoted for a couple of weeks?" he asked.

"Demoted?" She stared at him. Was he blaming her?

"I don't think we can get anyone up here in the time we've got available," he explained. "We open the day after tomorrow. I'm sorry, Becky, but can you do it?"

"You mean, manage this place?"

He nodded. "Yes. I know it's not what you're used to. Well, it's been a while, anyway… And it'd mean staying up here until I can move a few people around, but…"

"It's fine."

He stared at her again. "You're sure?" She nodded. "And Tyler won't mind?"

"No." She didn't care whether Tyler minded or not, and in any case, what could he do? He could hardly come up to a busy hotel and drag her back home. Of course, he could always threaten her with what he'd do to her when she got home, but even he'd have to see that the circumstances were exceptional, and if he did threaten her? Well, she might just have have to find the courage to tell Mark exactly what was going on, and see if he could help her. In the meantime, the idea of a few weeks away from Tyler was pure heaven.

"Okay. Let's go into your office and talk this through. You need to be up to speed for the opening."

"My office?" She glanced up at him.

"You're the manager now. That nice big office back there is yours for the time being. You'll be staying on the third floor, just like we planned, and there's a suite of offices up there too, which I'd intended you to use while you were here, but if you're gonna be the manager, you might as well get the perks that go with the title." He grinned, then turned to Jake. "Thanks, man," he said. "I'll add bodyguard to your list of credentials, shall I?"

"Hardly. The guy managed to launch himself down the stairs before I had to do anything."

"Even so, I'm grateful."

"You can buy me a beer," Jake replied. "And you can leave me alone to get on with my job."

"Gladly." Mark smiled at him and ushered Becky out of the kitchen.

"I didn't need a bodyguard," she said as she sat down at one end of the couch. Mark sat at the opposite end, facing her. "I was perfectly okay."

"Yeah, you sounded perfectly okay. I know fear when I hear it." He looked at her. "Take the damn glasses off, Becky," he said.

She shook her head. "I told you, I've got a headache."

"Hmm… I don't believe that either. Take them off."

"I really don't want to." She turned away and stared at the wall beside her. The next thing she knew, Mark had got up and come around the table to crouch down in front of her. He raised his hands, placing his fingers gently on her sunglasses and pulling them from her face.

"Jesus," he said through gritted teeth. "When did he do it?"

"Last night," she muttered. There was no point in denying the truth. Mark was her boss, but he'd also become a friend, someone she was able to talk to about Tyler; someone who'd encouraged her to leave her violent, cheating husband on more than one occasion; who'd offered to help her do so, if she wanted. God, how many times had she wished she'd taken him up on that offer?

"Why?"

"Because I told him I was going to be away for longer than usual, and he didn't like that."

"Why?" he repeated.

"The usual reason."

"Me?" he asked, and she nodded. "For fuck's sake… We're colleagues. You work for me. There's *never* been anything between us. Ever. Besides, I'm engaged. I'm getting married in less than a month."

"I know…" She looked up at him. "Hey, hang on… Did you say 'less than a month'? I didn't know you were getting married *that* soon."

"Yeah." He sat back down and turned to face her again, and she noticed the anger in his eyes when he looked at her. "Emma doesn't want to waddle down the aisle, and I don't want to wait. She's mine and I want the whole damn world to know it." He smiled, and now his eyes lit up. Becky preferred that look to his anger.

"Less than a month?"

"Yeah. In between opening this place, Emma buying the coffee shop and refurbishing it, *and* us getting married, it's gonna be a busy few weeks."

"You're not kidding."

"And you're not changing the subject that easily, either." He twisted in his seat, facing her a little better. "So this was just because of his old jealousy about me?"

"Well, yes and no."

"Okay. Care to enlighten me?"

"I told him I'd never loved him; that I'd always loved the guy I knew at college. The guy I told you about, from Somers Cove?"

Mark nodded, letting her know he'd remembered. "Was that wise?" he asked.

"In the circumstances, yes."

Mark sat forward. "What circumstances?" he asked.

She shook her head, turning away from him. "I can't tell you."

"Becky…" Mark's voice was gentle. "What did he do?"

"I can't tell you." She couldn't. There was no way she was telling Mark what Tyler had done last night, or the other times either.

There was a pause. She didn't dare turn back, afraid of what she'd see in his eyes this time. "Okay," he said eventually. "You don't have to tell me, but I think I'm kinda glad you're gonna be working here for a while." He seemed to hesitate, then spoke again: "If he contacts you and threatens you, or tries to make any trouble, I want you to let me know, and if you change your mind, and decide you do wanna talk, you know where I am."

She nodded, unable to speak for a moment. The lump in her throat got in the way.

He coughed to clear the air between them. "Right, I guess we'd better do some work..."

## *Nick*

"This isn't how I normally spend my Friday nights," Nick said, flipping through yet another magazine. "If you weren't my sister..." He was keeping Emma company while Mark spent the evening at the hotel site, getting ready for the opening the next day. Despite his grouching, he didn't really mind. He enjoyed being with Emma; he always had.

"Yeah... You'd be sitting at home, with a beer and a take-out; or in your office, buried in something boringly legal. This is so much more fun." Emma smiled across the living room at him.

He smiled back. He couldn't help it. She was so damn happy. But it hadn't always been this way. Four years ago, he'd spent a night in the hospital with her, when she'd overdosed on sleeping pills after Mark had left her the first time. And then, he'd stayed with her for weeks, until he was sure she was okay, and that she wasn't gonna harm herself again. Then, just before Thanksgiving last year, Mark had come back into her life, only to abandon her again at Christmas. Nick hadn't been sure he could ever forgive the multi-millionaire son-of-a-bitch for that. But Emma had. She'd taken him back early in the New Year, when he'd admitted his mistakes, and declared his love for her in front of most of the town. Even now, weeks later, Nick still found himself feeling slightly distrustful of Mark, despite the beautiful house he'd bought, with the top of the range security system to keep Emma safe, and the love he showed her, the time he spent with her, the understanding he seemed to display for her… and the fact that Mark had proposed and she was carrying his baby. Even now, Nick still kept an eye on his little sister… just because she was his little sister, and he was never going to forget the fear of nearly losing her.

"Going through bridal magazines?" he said. "I don't even know what I'm looking at."

"You're helping me find inspiration."

"For what?"

"The wedding."

"Yeah… I think I worked that much out for myself. What I mean is, I've got no idea what you're specifically looking for."

"Pretty much everything. We've only got three weeks and one day to go," Emma explained for the second time that evening.

"I know that. You're getting married here, in the garden – weather permitting – overlooking the ocean." He repeated her plans back to her and rolled his eyes.

"Cynic."

"That's me." He smiled. He wasn't cynical at all. He thought it sounded really romantic – for Emma and Mark. It just wasn't for him. "And I'm looking at?"

"Flowers, table decorations…"

"Flowers?" he scoffed, interrupting her. "I'm about as interested in flowers as I am in weddings. You know I don't believe in all that marriage shit."

"Except this is *my* marriage, so you have to be interested." She hurled the magazine she'd just finished flipping through across the room at him. He dodged and it missed. "You're useless."

"Of course I am. I thought you knew that already. You should get Cassie onto this. She'd be great."

"I know. But Cassie's only here at weekends."

"Jake's here though, isn't he?" Jake and Cassie were normally inseparable.

Emma nodded. "Yes." She picked up another magazine from the pile on the table in front of her. "He's here to make sure everything's okay with the hotel, but it's still school time, so Cassie couldn't come. She and Maddie are driving up from Portland tonight."

"So, you can talk to her over the weekend."

"You think there'll be time this weekend? With the opening and everything?"

"You'll have Sunday," he reasoned.

She shrugged.

"Are they both gonna be at the opening?" he asked.

"Yes. Jake's dad's gonna look after Maddie for them. Jake kinda has to be there, being as he built the place. And Cassie wouldn't miss it for the world. She's so proud of him…"

Nick closed the magazine and put it down on the table. "I'm glad it worked out for them in the end." Jake and Cassie had been high school sweethearts, but they'd split up straight after college, when Cassie mistakenly believed Jake had cheated. Then, the untimely death, the previous spring, of Cassie's mom – who was also Nick's secretary – and Jake's return to the area to oversee the construction of Mark's hotel, had brought them back together. Cassie had discovered that Jake wasn't a cheat, and Jake had been introduced to the daughter he never knew he had. Maddie was incredible and everyone who met her fell in love with her… and, because of her deafness, they'd all learned to sign, with varying degrees of success, but enough so they could communicate with her, anyway.

Emma closed her magazine too, and let out a sigh. "I'm not getting anywhere," she murmured.

"What's up?" Nick asked, leaning forward and resting his elbows on his knees, his chin on one upturned hand.

"Oh, nothing."

"I've known you all your life, Emma Woods. And I know when you're lying."

She looked at him. "I'm worried," she said.

"What about?"

"Mark."

Nick felt the hair on the back of his neck stand on end. They'd been down this road before…

"What's he done now?" he asked.

"He hasn't done anything." Emma leapt to her fiancé's defense.

"Then why are you worried?"

"Because he's working so hard." She moved her feet off the couch onto the floor and sat forward, facing him. "Take yesterday," she began. "He was working here, when his assistant called to say there was a problem at the hotel, so he had to go dashing over there to deal with it, only to discover the manager had fallen down the stairs and broken his leg. It was really late last night by the time he got back here."

"And his assistant couldn't handle this herself?"

"She was, but evidently before the guy fell, he was being a bit threatening toward the female staff, and Mark wanted to handle that part of it himself."

"Makes sense."

"Only, when Mark got there, not only was the manager injured, but his assistant had a black eye…"

"The guy had hit her?" Nick was incredulous.

"No. Her husband had hit her before she came up here."

"Jesus."

"Mark's been trying to help her for months now, but she's very private. I think the guy's beaten the soul out of her, if you want me to be honest. Mark sat and talked to her for a while, but she wouldn't tell him everything."

"I'm not surprised, Em. He's her boss, not her friend."

"Yeah…" There was a wistful note to Emma's voice.

"Em? Are you worried there's more to it between them?"

She looked up at him. "No!"

"Be honest," Nick continued. "Do you think there's something going on between Mark and his assistant. You can tell me."

"Nick…" Emma moved to the edge of the couch, leaning toward him. "There's nothing going on. I trust Mark completely."

"And his assistant?"

"She's not interested in Mark. They had plenty of opportunities to get together before I came back on the scene, if that was what they'd wanted. They don't. I've never met her, but I've spoken to her over the phone numerous times. She's a really nice person, who married an asshole."

"Em!"

Emma hardly ever swore.

"Well, he is."

Nick nodded. Based on what he'd just heard, he couldn't disagree with her appraisal.

"So, what is it that you're worried about?"

"Just that his assistant is going to step in as temporary manager of the hotel, which means Mark's got to cover her job as well as his own. He's already doing really long hours, and traveling a lot. And I'm just in the process of buying the coffee shop…"

"Which I'm handling for you," he interrupted. "And which will probably close in the next few days."

"I know, but then there's the re-design, which Mark's trying to help me with, and we're planning the wedding. I'm worried he's gonna burn himself out if he—"

"Hang on a minute," Nick interrupted. "I don't think he's the one in danger of a burn out here. You need to calm down, and slow down."

"How can I?"

"It's easy, Em. Just take a few deep breaths and remember none of this shit really matters." He waved his hand at the magazines scattered across the table between them.

"How can you say that, Nick? This is my wedding."

"Yeah, which is one day, out of the rest of your life. I may not believe in any of this, but I know that a marriage is about more than the damn wedding, Em. It's about a whole lifetime together." He got up and went across the room, sitting down beside her. "You're finally getting the man you always wanted. Who cares if the flowers and table decorations aren't perfect? It's you guys being perfect for each other that matters."

She looked up at him. "So, not such a cynic, huh? When did you get to be so romantic?" she asked, tears filling her eyes.

He leant into her. "I always was," he whispered, then wished he hadn't spoken.

"You know, whoever she was… that woman you told me about, the one you met at college, she really missed out."

He kissed the top of her head and turned away. He was the one who'd missed out… and he knew it.

A little later, Emma made them another coffee and sat back down opposite him again. He looked across at his sister and, just from the expression on her face, he could tell something was still bothering her.

Nick took a sip, and replaced his cup on the table. "Speak to Cassie," he said all of a sudden.

"What about?" Emma inquired.

"About the wedding. She'll help you."

"I know…" Her voice trailed off.

"Are you worried about that too?" he asked.

"What?"

"That Cassie won't help. She's your best friend, Em."

"I know. And I know she'll help me."

"Then is it because you're worried she'll feel put out because you're getting married before she is, even though Jake proposed first?"

"No," Emma replied. "We've talked about that already. She's fine with it. She's got most of her plans laid out already. She and Jake are having their ceremony on the beach, the last weekend in June. I'm gonna be a pregnant matron of honor."

Nick laughed. "You'll be amazing, Em."

She shook her head.

"Okay… Tell me what else is worrying at you."

"It's mom and dad," she replied, picking up her cup and letting it rest on her lap.

"What about them? What have they done this time?" Their parents had never been supportive of either of them, but while Nick let their attitude wash over him, Emma took it all to heart.

"They haven't done anything."

"Do they know about the baby?" he asked.

Emma shook her head. "I haven't plucked up the courage to tell them yet. Not about the baby, or the wedding."

"And that's what's worrying you?"

"Not exactly."

"Okay... Explain."

"I don't want them there."

"At the wedding?" She nodded her head, not looking at him. "Then don't invite them."

She raised her face, her eyes meeting his. "I wish it was that simple."

"It's your day, Em. Do whatever you want."

"And you don't think they'll have something to say, if I don't invite them."

"Probably... but you have to do whatever's right for you. You're twenty-six years old."

"So why do I feel like I'm still six?" Her voice faded to a whisper.

"Well, if you're six, then I'm ten... and I *know* I'm not ten." He smiled across at her. "But I'm still your big brother. If you want, I'll tell them for you."

She smiled and her eyes glistened again, and he wondered if this tearfulness and worry was something to do with her pregnancy. He hoped that was all it was...

She put her drink down again, without having touched it, and came and sat beside him once more. "You're the best brother," she said.

"Yeah, I know." He put his arm around her and pulled her back with him into the sofa, letting her rest her head on him, just as the front door opened. He went to move, but Emma shook her head and held onto him.

"Don't," she whispered, and he stayed exactly where he was, looking up as Mark entered the room, and raised an eyebrow, gazing down at his fiancée lying in the arms of her brother, her head resting on his chest.

"Is... Is everything okay?" he asked.

Emma nodded, but she still didn't move.

"We were just talking about mom and dad," Nick clarified. "They have this effect on Em."

"Yeah. I've noticed." Mark smiled and came to sit on the couch beside them. Emma turned and looked up at him. Nick couldn't see her face, but the look he saw on Mark's helped set his mind at rest. He didn't think he'd ever seen so much love in a man's eyes before.

"Come here, baby," Mark said quietly and Emma shifted, twisting in her seat and putting her arms around Mark's waist, her head resting on his chest instead of Nick's. It felt okay to hand her over. She was where she belonged.

Mark held her close and looked at Nick over the top of her head, raising an eyebrow again.

Nick shook his head, and nodded toward the front of the house, hoping Mark would understand that he didn't want to talk in front of Emma, but they should try and talk alone – outside.

"I'd better be going," he said, after just a few minutes.

"Really?" Emma replied, turning again to look at him.

"Yeah. You're tired, Em. You need to get some sleep."

He got to his feet, trying to catch Mark's eye again.

"I'll show Nick out," Mark said, standing and bringing Emma with him. Nick breathed out a silent sigh. Mark had understood.

"I'll come too," Emma put in.

Mark kissed her gently. "No, baby. You go on up to bed. I'll only be a minute, and I'll be right up. It's later than I thought it was, and Nick's right, you're exhausted."

She looked from one of them to the other. "Okay. If you're sure."

"I'm sure." He kissed her again and she came over to Nick, leaning up and kissing his cheek.

"Thanks for everything," she murmured.

"Anytime. You know where I am, if you need me."

She nodded and left the room.

"What's wrong?" Mark said as soon as she'd gone.

"Outside," Nick replied.

"Why do I worry whenever you say that to me?" Mark looked at him and Nick knew he was remembering the time, just after New Year, when he'd come to Somers Cove to try and win Emma back, having screwed things up with her, and Nick had pulled him outside the coffee shop and warned him to be careful with Emma. He'd told him what had happened the last time he'd let her down, and that he never wanted to go through that again. That had been a wake-up call for Mark, and Nick had known it, but the guy needed to be told. He couldn't keep messing with Emma. She was too fragile.

Nick just looked at him and shook his head, and Mark led them out through the front door, pulling it closed behind him.

"Talk to me, Nick," Mark said straight away.

"She's real stressed," Nick told him, walking toward his truck.

"Is this about your parents?"

"Partly. She's not sure whether to invite them to the wedding, or how to even tell them about it, or the baby."

"We can do that together," Mark said.

"That's not all," Nick added.

"Okay." Mark was waiting.

"She's getting wound up about the wedding itself, and about the coffee shop… and your work."

"My work?"

"Yeah. She mentioned something about your assistant?"

"What about her?"

"Just something about her having domestic problems and having to take over from the manager at the hotel, and how it's gonna impact on your work."

"Yeah, it is, but it's nothing I can't handle."

"I think she's worried she's not gonna see you."

"She said that?"

"Not in so many words, but I know Emma. She needs you, Mark. If you're not here, I think she feels kinda isolated. She's lived in the town all her life. Out here, she's a lot more cut off."

Mark stared at him for a moment.

"And that's it?"

"That's not enough?"

"Yeah, it is. I was just worried from your tone that it was something else."

"Like what?" Nick watched as Mark put his hands in his pockets and stared down at his feet for a moment. "Like what?" Nick repeated.

"Like Emma being worried there might be something going on…"

"Going on how? Between you and your assistant, you mean?"

"Yeah. Her husband accused her of sleeping with me…"

"Are you?"

"No." Mark looked him in the eye and Nick believed him. "She's good at her job. Damn good at it. But we're not attracted to each other. We never have been."

"And her husband?"

"Is a dick."

"I guessed that much. Emma told me he gave her a black eye."

"Yeah, he did." Mark hesitated and Nick thought he wanted to say more, but he didn't.

"Emma doesn't think there's anything going on," Nick explained. "I asked her outright, and she defended you to the hilt. She told me she trusts you absolutely."

Mark smiled. "Good. I'd never cheat on her, or betray her in anyway, Nick. You know that, don't you?"

"That's not for me to know," Nick said. "It's for Emma to know, and she does, so I'm okay with it." He paused for a moment. "The question is, what are you gonna do about Em? With everything that's going on, she's close to breaking."

Mark closed his eyes, tipping his head back. "Tomorrow's the opening," he said quietly, opening his eyes again and looking at Nick. "Emma's gonna be with me most of the day. I'm taking Sunday off to be with her. As far as I know she's arranged to meet Cassie to talk weddings. Then I'll work from home for as much of the time as I can, at least until after the wedding. Things should calm down a bit then."

"Well, if you have to go away at all, let me know. I'm not gonna suggest babysitting her or anything – Em wouldn't want that – but let me know if you're out of town and I'll keep in touch with her."

"You're that worried?" Mark's face paled.

Nick shrugged. "She's not gonna do anything to hurt herself, if that's what you're asking. She's happy with you, and she's not gonna do anything to jeopardize that, or harm the baby. But…"

"But what? You're scaring me."

"She's fragile, Mark."

"I know that."

"Then let me help. I get that you're real busy at the moment; so does she. All you've gotta do is remember I'm family. Let me know if you're not gonna be here. I'll call her, or come over if she wants me to."

Mark looked at him. "Thanks," he said.

"Don't thank me. Just remember what I've said." Mark nodded and Nick took a couple of steps toward his truck, before turning. "I'll see you guys tomorrow, I guess."

"Tomorrow?" Mark queried.

"The opening?"

"You're coming? I thought Tom Allen was attending."

Nick managed a half laugh. "Yeah, so did I."

Mark grinned. "And do I sense that you're not exactly pleased about this?"

"No offense, man… but a tux, lots of people, confined spaces, small talk? It's not really my thing."

"I didn't think it was." Mark smiled. "You own a tux?"

Nick gave him a long stare. "Yes. Why does that seem to surprise everyone?"

"I have no idea," Mark smirked. "So, why isn't Tom coming?"

"He's got some college buddy to catch up with. He thinks it's gonna be worth our while. I've got my doubts."

"Why?" Mark asked, looking surprised.

"I'm not sure. I've just got a feeling something's not right."

Mark shrugged. "Maybe you should go with your feeling."

"I'd love to, but Tom's not really listening to me right now."

Nick felt a shiver run down his spine and shook himself. He was overreacting. Tom wouldn't do anything to jeopardize their business…

As he lay on his bed that night, staring up at the ceiling, Nick tried to stop worrying about the bad vibes he was feeling about GHC Engineering, and turned his thoughts to Emma… and started worrying about her instead. He needed to stop that. Mark would be there for her; he knew he would.

He turned over and closed his eyes, desperate for sleep, but something kept nagging at his brain. It was something Emma had said. She'd called him romantic. It was true; he was romantic. He just didn't have anyone to be romantic with. He could still remember the feeling though – even though nine long years had passed since he'd last experienced it. Emma's words rattled around his head: 'That woman you told me about… she missed out'. It hadn't had to be that way though. If only…

He turned again and felt the familiar pang of regret, the stinging behind his eyes, the lump forming in his throat. If only he'd gone to find her sooner.

He'd gone… of course he had.

He'd made it through that final year of college, kept his distance and kept his head down, graduating top of his class. And then he'd turned down six or seven job offers in Boston and come back to Somers Cove, and started working for Tom. He'd thought he was okay, but after about three months, he'd realized he was anything but. He missed Becky. He missed her so much he'd forgotten how to live. He wanted her back and he didn't care what he had to do to get her. So, he'd taken a couple of days off and driven down to Fall River, where he'd checked into a motel and spent a day tracking her down. Scott wasn't exactly the most unusual surname…

He'd found her through a newspaper article. It was one announcing her engagement to Tyler Howell. It had been dated just five days before. He'd missed her by five days.

He'd traveled back home without even trying to see her, but for a while, he'd monitored what she was doing, just in case she broke off the engagement.

She didn't. She'd married Tyler eight months later. Nick had stopped watching after that, but he'd never stopped waiting. He never would.

# Chapter Five

## *Becky*

Becky looked at her reflection in the mirror. The makeup was ludicrously heavy by her standards… well, probably by most people's standards. But she couldn't wear sunglasses to the opening, so she had no choice. The area around her eye was a deep purple, and the concealer and foundation covered it – just about. What they couldn't hide was the slight swelling, which still hadn't gone down, but there wasn't anything she could do about that. She took a couple of steps back and looked at the whole picture. Normally, for an event like this, she'd have put her hair up, but she hoped that leaving it long might help to hide her bruise a little better, so it hung loose around her exposed shoulders. The red dress was fitted in the bodice and hung from her waist, the full skirt just touching the floor. The silver locket completed her outfit. She shrugged. She'd much rather spend the evening in jeans and a casual top, curled up on the couch, listening to music and reading a book, or watching a movie, but that wasn't going to happen. Still no-one was here to see her anyway, so what did it matter? She'd just blend into the background…

Exiting the elevator into the lobby, she was surprised by how calm it was, compared to forty-five minutes earlier, when she'd gone up to her room on the third floor. There was less than thirty minutes until the guests were due to arrive and everything finally seemed to have come together. All the surfaces shone to perfection; candles were lit; fresh flowers adorned every table, a lectern had been set up, to the right of the reception counter, for Mark to make his speech, and she knew the chefs had prepared enough canapés to feed a small nation, which would be handed out, together with the chilled champagne, by uniformed staff.

Mark was standing near the main door and alongside him was a beautiful woman, wearing an elegant, black floor-length dress, with delicate gray embroidery on the bodice. Mark had his hand resting in the small of her back and was gazing down at her. From the look in his eyes, Becky guessed this must be Emma and she stood for a moment and watched them. They looked good together, clearly in love, and very happy.

She smiled to herself. Mark deserved to be happy. He'd had it tough since his parents had died, just over four years ago... Overnight, he'd had to take on the responsibility of looking after his teenage sister, as well as running his father's business, and it hadn't been easy. She watched them as Mark leant down and kissed Emma gently on the cheek, and whispered something to her. Emma nodded in reply, looking up into his eyes. The love Mark felt for her was clearly returned. It gave Becky hope that not all relationships were destined to end in pain and disappointment, and she smiled for real, then turned and took in the scene around her. The chaos of two days ago seemed a distant memory. She'd spent the intervening hours meeting all the staff personally, making sure they all knew what was expected of them, and ensuring that the opening would run smoothly. She stepped forward and Mark caught her eye, motioning that she should join him. She nodded back and walked slowly across the lobby.

"Hi," she said as she reached him.

"Becky," he replied, and pulled Emma a little closer. "You haven't met Emma."

"No," Becky said, and held out her hand. Emma returned the gesture and they shook hands.

"It's lovely to finally meet you and put a face to your voice," Emma said.

She was even more beautiful up close. Her hair was almost black, but had slightly lighter flecks running through it. She'd worn it up, leaving a few stray strands framing her face, and she wore very little makeup. Now they were this close, Becky felt sure there was something familiar about Emma, but she couldn't quite put her finger on what it was. She was absolutely certain they hadn't met, but there was definitely something about Emma's mouth, and the shape of her eyes...

"I know. We've spoken so often," Becky replied, letting go of Emma's hand.

Emma looked around. "This is all so impressive," she said. "The last time I was here, it was just a shell."

"It's come a long way since then. And it's been a little crazy." Becky followed Emma's gaze. "But we got there in the end." She turned to Mark. "Is your sister coming tonight?" she asked.

"No." His answer was blank and she stared at him. Their openness was a two-way street and she waited. He let out a sigh. "I'm not ready for that yet."

"I thought the counseling was going well."

"It is."

"But?"

He looked uncomfortable. "I'm not ready to forgive her yet."

Mark's sister, Sarah, had been the cause of the split between him and Emma just before Christmas. Mark was a very private person, who'd spent the whole of his adult life keeping himself and his image out of the press. But, in order to break up his relationship with Emma, Sarah had contacted the press, feeding them false information and releasing images of him with a previous girlfriend, implying the couple had secretly become engaged and were expecting a child. The furore had been unprecedented in her experience, and when Mark had discovered his sister's duplicity, for a while, Becky had needed to cover his job as well as her own, as he'd tried to sort out his private life, and rescue his relationship with Emma. It had caused yet more painful problems with Tyler... ones Mark didn't know about, because she hadn't wanted to burden him with anything else when he had so much going on.

"It's gonna take time," Emma put in.

Becky understood that. Sarah's actions had been damaging and hurtful. "But you'll invite her to the wedding, won't you?" she asked.

"I'm not sure," Mark replied.

"Yes," Emma said, at exactly the same time.

Mark looked down at Emma, a shadow passing over his face. "We haven't decided," he added, clearly trying to be diplomatic.

Becky glanced over at Emma, who seemed to withdraw in on herself, just a little. "I think you should," Becky told him. "She's your sister, Mark."

He glared at her. "Have you two been talking about this behind my back?" he asked.

"No," Becky replied. "But, I think you'll regret it if you don't ask her."

Emma looked up at him. "Which is exactly what I told him."

"For fuck's sake," Mark said, but Becky knew he wasn't angry. His lips twitched upwards and his tone was playful, not irritated. "Can we talk about this some other time… some other place."

"Sure," Emma replied. "But we *are* gonna talk about it." She smiled over at Becky, who returned the gesture, and knew right there and then that she and Emma were going to get along just fine.

That thought gave her some small relief. She'd grown sick and tired of Tyler's accusations over the last three years, ever since she'd started working for Mark. The last thing she needed was his future wife assuming the same thing about them. It would make things really awkward between her and Mark. She knew Mark was thought of as handsome. He was, she supposed, and like a lot of men, he looked good in a tux. At six foot five with thick brown hair and a strong jaw, he tended to dominate a room, regardless of who else was there, but to Becky, he was just her boss. Besides, she knew how much he hated the attention he received. Once the press actually got hold of those images of him, they'd referred to him in all kinds of glowing terms – some more embarrassing and inaccurate than others – and had tracked his every move, but she'd never been interested in him… not at all. She could appreciate his ability to do his job, and do it well. She was grateful for his kindness, his consideration and his generosity, but that was as far as her feelings went. And she knew Emma understood that.

If only Tyler felt the same. She swallowed hard, remembering his hurtful accusations. In a way, she didn't really care what Tyler thought of her. Nick was still the only man whose opinion really mattered… but that was a ship that had sailed a long time ago.

"Well, ladies… it looks like showtime." Mark's voice interrupted her thoughts and she looked up to see the first car entering the parking lot.

## Nick

Climbing into his truck, Nick glanced back at his trailer and wished he could spend his Saturday evening there, with a couple of beers… and his own company. He'd gotten kind of used to that over the last nine years. He wouldn't go so far as to say he was okay with it, but he'd gotten used to it. Maybe that was why he chose to live out here in this clearing in his own little piece of the forest, five miles outside of town. He could avoid the prying eyes and gossiping mouths, and just be himself.

He'd bought this piece of land a few years ago now, when his Grandpa Jonas had died and left him some money. It was enough to buy the land, but not enough to build the house he'd always wanted, so he was saving up for that. He didn't want to build something that he wouldn't be happy with; he wanted to get it right, and he didn't mind how long he had to wait. The important things in life were worth waiting for… like Becky. Even though he had nothing tangible to base his hopes on, he still believed that one day she'd work out that she belonged with him, and she'd come back. And when she did, he'd be waiting for her.

He shook his head, started the truck, and set off toward the hotel, which was about fifteen or so miles further outside of Somers Cove. He had to pass Mark and Emma's house on the way, but he knew they wouldn't be there. He was planning on arriving about forty-five minutes into the party, because there was nothing worse than being one of the first guests, and standing around on your own…

The journey took less time than he'd hoped and, when he arrived, he handed over his keys to the parking attendant and stood for a moment, admiring the building before him. Even in the half-light of the dusky evening, he could see this was exactly the kind of thing he'd been looking for. It was perfect. He was going to have to speak to Mark about this…

He approached the main door, letting another couple enter ahead of him and, as he walked through the revolving doors, he was hit by a wall of noise and heat. The temptation not to step out, but to keep going around and come back out again into the fresh air was almost too much. But Emma was standing beside Mark, greeting their guests, and he couldn't do that to her.

He stepped forward, taking the moment while Mark was shaking the hands of the couple ahead of him, to have a quick look around. Jake's dad Ben had told him a few times that this was an upscale hotel, but he'd had no idea it was going to be quite this grand. The ceiling of the lobby went right to the top of the building and, like the front wall, was constructed entirely of glass.

"Hey," He heard Mark's voice, and took a step forward.

"Hi." Nick shook Mark's offered hand.

"You're looking a little shocked," Mark said.

"Yeah. I hadn't expected this."

Mark smiled. "It's pretty amazing, isn't it?"

"It sure is." Nick looked down at Emma. Her cheeks were paler than usual. "You okay?" he asked her.

She nodded. "Just a little nauseous."

"Nauseous?" he queried.

"Emma had her first experience of morning sickness today," Mark explained, leaning closer. The pregnancy wasn't common knowledge, and although there was no-one standing nearby, Mark had dropped his voice to a whisper. "It was… interesting."

"Interesting?" Emma stared up at him. "That's not how I'd put it."

"And you're still feeling nauseous?" Nick asked.

She nodded.

"Hopefully we'll have finished this meet and greet merry-go-round fairly soon and Emma can sit down," Mark said, putting his arm around her. He turned and looked over his shoulder. "I don't think you've met my assistant…" he added. "Well, she's covering as manager here for the time being." He craned his neck. "She's just talking to her deputy. Hang on. I'll introduce you."

Nick turned and saw the back of a woman wearing a red dress. He rarely took much interest in women these days, but he had to admit, she had an amazing figure. So, this was the woman Mark spent so much time with. He looked back at his future brother-in-law and raised an eyebrow. "*That's* your assistant?"

"Officially, she's my business manager, but we've never been that hung up on titles."

Nick shrugged, then looked back to the woman in the red dress, just as she turned around… and his heart stopped beating. *Becky?* She looked incredible. She looked even more beautiful than in his dreams. Her dark hair hung long and straight around her naked shoulders, and that dress… the color was perfect for her, and the way it clung to her… Nick struggled to control his body's reactions. It was a struggle he lost.

She saw him at exactly the same moment and, although she was wearing a lot of makeup, she paled noticeably and her mouth dropped open slightly.

"Becky?" Mark called her over. She seemed to shake herself and walked over unsteadily. Nick wanted to go to her side, to help her and hold her, but he couldn't. He couldn't move – and he had no idea how she was managing to put one foot in front of the other. He'd dreamt of this moment so many times over the last nine years, but in his dreams, they'd always been alone, somewhere private, romantic and secluded, and he'd been able to hold her, smother her with kisses, cradle her in his arms, and spend hours asking her all the questions that had rattled around his head for the last nine years. They'd never met in a hotel lobby, filled with probably over two hundred other people, and his sister and her future husband watching on.

"Let me introduce you," Mark was saying, oblivious to their discomfort. "Becky, this is Nick Woods, Emma's brother, and Somers Cove's leading lawyer." Mark smiled. "Nick, this is Becky Howell, my business manager."

They stood facing each other, just staring, neither able to move, or say anything, although he longed to pull her into his arms and kiss her… hard. Nick noticed the swelling under her left eye, and then he remembered both Emma and Mark telling him how his assistant had been beaten by her husband. He clenched his fists so tight, they hurt. *Oh God… Please, no…*

"Becky?" Mark's voice intruded yet again. "Are you okay?"

Slowly, she seemed to come to her senses and blinked a few times. "Yes," she murmured, her voice quiet and soft. "I'm sorry." She held out her hand and, after looking at it for a moment, Nick took it in his. Her skin was exactly as he remembered it: like the purest silk. He couldn't speak, which was odd. In all his dreams, whenever he'd imagined their reunion, he'd never been dumbstruck. He'd always had plenty to say; an avalanche of questions, a myriad of answers. But now, there was nothing. He couldn't think of a single damn thing.

Nick suddenly became aware that there were people behind him, new guests to be greeted.

"Becky?" Mark said again, and she blinked, seeming to realize where she was. She looked at Mark and nodded. She had a job to do and Nick pulled his hand away, releasing her, just before turning and moving away. It wasn't meant to be like this. Not awkward silences and blank stares. He needed a drink… a large one.

He'd taken maybe half a dozen paces in the direction of the bar when he heard his name, and he knew it was Becky calling him.

"Nick?" He turned and came face-to-face with her. She'd followed him.

"Yeah?" He'd finally found his voice, even if it was a little gruffer than he'd wished.

"Can we talk later? I've got to greet the guests, but afterwards… Can we? Please?" There was something about her tone; a kind of pleading desperation, with a hint of fear. He didn't like it.

He made a conscious effort to soften his voice before he spoke again. "Sure. I'll be in the bar. Come find me."

She nodded her head just once, then turned and moved away from him.

# Chapter Six

## *Becky*

The room became a haze. Guests, staff, flowers, lights… all merging into one indistinct muddle of sound and movement.

She just hoped she was heading back in the vague direction of the main door, although she couldn't be entirely sure.

"Becky?" That was a female voice. Who was it? She looked up and saw it was Emma. "You're not well. Come with me."

Emma ushered her toward a chair and sat her down.

"What's wrong?" she asked.

"It's nothing," Becky murmured.

"It's not nothing." Becky saw Emma searching around the room, clearly trying to find someone… Nick was her brother? How could that be?

"I'll be fine," Becky managed to say. She saw Emma gesturing.

One of the waitresses appeared beside her. "Bring Mrs Howell some water, please," Emma said, and the waitress disappeared again, only to reappear within moments with a tumbler filled with ice-cold water. Becky took a sip, holding the glass with both hands to steady it.

Emma crouched down in front of her and came into better focus. "I —I know we don't really know each other very well, but I'd like to help, if I can?"

Could anyone help? Yes… Nick. Nick could help. He could hold her and tell her it would all be okay. Except he probably hated her, so that was never going to happen…

Becky shook her head, then became aware of a pair of men's black shoes standing off to one side, and the bottom of a pair of men's pants... also black. She looked up slowly and saw Mark staring down at her.

"Are you unwell?" he asked. It would be so easy to say 'yes', but she shook her head.

He took a moment, glancing around the room. "Okay. Come with me, both of you." Emma helped her to her feet and guided her across the room, following Mark into the manager's office. Her own office.

Once the door was closed and silence had descended, she felt a little better and allowed Emma to sit her on the couch, and take a seat beside her. Mark crouched before her now, looking up into her eyes.

"Tell me," he said quietly. "You know Nick, don't you?" She nodded and Mark's head dropped into his heads. "Please tell me he's not the guy," he continued. "He's not the guy you knew at college..."

Becky nodded. "Yes," she said, "he is."

She heard Emma's gasp. "Oh God. You're the girl..."

Becky turned to look at her. "The girl?"

"Nick told me about a girl he dated. He told me he..." Emma stopped talking suddenly, her cheeks flushing and Becky found herself wishing she'd carried on. She wanted to know what Nick had said about her. It might make all the difference.

"He what?" Mark asked the question for her.

"It's not for me to say," Emma replied. "If Nick wants to tell Becky about it, that's up to him."

Becky wasn't sure what that meant.

"I—I don't know what Nick told you," she said, turning to Emma. "But yes, we dated for a while, and then we broke up. It was my fault. I hurt him." She looked at the door, suddenly feeling panicked. "I need to go and find him."

"Then go," Mark got to his feet.

Becky stood and Emma followed suit. "He said he'd be at the bar, but I don't want him to change his mind and leave."

"He won't," Emma said, putting her hand on Becky's arm. "If he said he'd wait for you in the bar, then he'll be there."

Becky took a calming breath. She knew that was true.

"Do you still need me?" she asked Mark.

"No. I can handle everything for the time being. I'll send someone to find you when it's speech time. Go and talk to him."

"You're sure? I know I should be doing my job…" her voice faded.

"Fuck the job," Mark raised his voice, just a little. "There are more important things than the job. Go."

She looked at him for a moment, then headed for the door, uncertain what she was going to say, or how Nick would react.

As she got to the door, she turned back and saw Mark pulling Emma into a hug, holding her close.

There was still hope, wasn't there? There had to be.


Still shaky, she made her way back through the crowded lobby and into the bar area. It was just as busy in here, but as she started to move forward, a few people stepped to one side and she saw him. He had his back to her, but she knew it was him. There was no mistaking his broad shoulders and muscular back, or the collar-length, tousled hair. She smiled to herself. Nick didn't change – thank God – although he did look different in a tux. Most six foot four, muscular, handsome men could wear a tux well, and many could be improved by it. In her experience, a tux could often turn the most average looking man into something a little bit special. None of that applied to Nick. He looked gorgeous, of course he did, but he also looked really uncomfortable, and she knew he'd prefer to be anywhere but here, and right now, so would she. She needed to be somewhere quiet with him so they could talk properly.

She came and stood beside him, noticing that the glass in front of him appeared to contain scotch. That made her stomach churn. Tyler drank scotch. He drank it a lot. She'd never known Nick to drink strong liquor though.

He turned and looked at her, his steel gray eyes filled with uncertainty, hurt, and nine years of questions.

"I—I'm sorry," she mumbled.

His expression changed, his eyes softened. He looked concerned and a little confused now, and got up from his bar stool, standing to one side. "Sit," he said, "before you fall." His voice was just the same as she remembered it; deep and very masculine, just like the rest of him.

She gratefully accepted the seat and felt the heat from his body as he stood right beside her, so close they were almost touching. He pushed the tumbler of scotch to one side and caught the attention of the barman.

"Can I have two glasses of the best red wine you've got, please."

The barman nodded and turned away.

"You still drink red, right?" He looked down at her and Becky nodded.

"Yes, thank you."

The barman placed two glasses of deep-ruby colored wine before them. Nick picked up both of them and handed one to Becky, waiting for her to take it.

"Now," he said calmly, once she had, "do you wanna tell me what the hell you're apologizing for?"

## Nick

The scotch had felt like a good idea – to steady his nerves, if nothing else – but on reflection, Nick didn't really know why. He'd never really enjoyed strong liquor. He was a beer and wine man; always had been. He'd felt Becky's presence in the room long before she came to stand beside him, but when she did, seeing how close she looked to collapsing, all his confusion, all the hurt and uncertainty about her, and about what they now meant to each other, faded to nothing. He just wanted to help her – and hold her.

She took a sip of wine and put the glass back down on the bar.

"Why are you apologizing, Bex?" he repeated and she turned to look at him. In this light, the swelling under her eye was less visible, but it was still there, and he felt his anger simmering beneath the surface. Then her lips twitched up at the corners, although he didn't know why.

"No-one else has ever called me that," she whispered, and he got it, and returned her smile.

"Good," he said. He liked that. "But I still don't understand. Why the apology?"

She looked down at her hands, clasped in her lap. "I'm sorry for what I did at that party," she mumbled, so quietly he had to lean in even closer to hear her. "It wasn't like me to do something like that. And I'm so sorry I did; and for everything that followed. It was my fault... all of it."

She looked so damned sad, and it was wrong for her to be taking all the blame on herself. "No, Bex," he said softly. "It wasn't all your fault. We were played – both of us." He took a deep breath. "Tyler wanted you and he used Kelly to get to me. I'll admit I blamed you at the time. I was mad as hell at you for doing what you did with him. I felt angry and bitter, and hurt. But later, I realized I could've stopped it. I could've told Kelly to leave me alone. It wasn't like I wanted to be with her. I could've made Tyler leave you alone, instead of just standing there and watching you with him. And I sure as hell shouldn't have tried to get cheap revenge the way I did, by kissing Kelly like that. It was dumb. I think I knew it, even then, but I was too hurt to realize it. I only worked it out properly afterwards, and by then it was too late."

"Yes, it was." A single tear fell onto her cheek.

"Don't blame yourself," he said. "I should've done something."

"I wish you had." She started to cry.

"Bex," he murmured. "Please don't."

"I can't do this..." She looked up at him, her eyes filled with sorrow and pain, and jumped down from the bar stool, running through the crowded room and back into the lobby.

Nick didn't hesitate for a second, but went straight after her, following her through the throngs of chattering people into the well-lit foyer, past the reception counter and down a short corridor. She ducked into a room, with the single word 'Manager' engraved on the frosted glass. Nick paused for a moment, then knocked just once and opened the door, passing inside and closing it behind him.

Becky was standing in the middle of the room, her back to him, her shoulders shaking as she wept.

He went over to her, turned her to face him and pulled her into his arms, as her cries became heart-wrenching sobs. She was falling apart as he held her, and it was up to him to keep her together. His body didn't respond to her this time – not because he didn't want her, but because it was taking all his concentration to control his own emotions, and not fall apart with her.

He had no idea how long they stood like that, but eventually Becky's breathing returned to normal and the crying lessened as she began to calm.

He waited a little longer, then pulled back slightly. She kept her head bowed, so he placed a single finger beneath her chin, and raised her face to his. Tears had tracked down her cheeks, leaving stained trails through her makeup. Her eyes were puffy, her nose red and, despite all that, she was still the most achingly beautiful woman he'd ever seen. He reached into his pocket for a handkerchief, using it to gently wipe her eyes, taking care to avoid the now obvious bruise and swelling.

He wanted to ask her about it, but now wasn't the best time. They both probably needed to be calmer before they started talking about that.

"I wish you'd done something," she repeated, sniffing and stepping away from him.

"So do I."

"That party marked the night when my life started to go wrong. Literally nothing went right for me after that."

That confused him a little. "The party? I don't understand. You *married* him, Becky." She must've wanted Tyler and been happy with him for a while. She'd accepted his damn proposal.

"How do you know that?"

"Well, the wedding ring's a huge giveaway. But Mark introduced you as Becky Howell, and he and Emma have talked about you in the past… They didn't mention your name, but they said you had a husband."

She nodded, swallowing.

"So, you married him?"

"Yes," she whispered. "I married him."

The regret in her voice was obvious. The black eye was enough of a clue. Her marriage must be hell, and he was sure she rued the day she'd gone off with Tyler. Still, it had been her decision… "Why did you do it, Bex?" he asked.

"Do what?"

"Kiss him."

She looked at him, her eyes darkening a little. "I watched you with Kelly all evening. You seemed to find it quite easy to forget I even existed…"

Had she really just said that? "No, I didn't."

"Yes, you did." Becky sniffled. "All you did, all evening, was talk to her, and fawn over her. I'd always known you wanted her, I just never thought you'd be that blatant about it."

*Blatant?* What was she talking about? "I didn't lay a finger on Kelly, not until *after* I'd come back into the room and seen you with your tongue down Howell's fucking throat."

"I didn't have my tongue down his throat." She kept her voice quiet, but he could feel the emotion pouring off of her.

"Really? That's not how it looked to me."

"Well, I'm surprised you noticed. You were so busy with Kelly."

"For fuck's sake, Bex." He tried to calm down. This wasn't getting them anywhere. "I'm sorry. I made mistakes. I got it wrong. I could've done things very differently." He took a step closer. "But you have to understand how much it hurt, seeing you kissing Tyler like that."

"I *wasn't* kissing him."

"You were, Becky."

"He was kissing me."

"That's just semantics."

"No, it's not."

They stared at each other, neither saying a word, until Becky broke the silence.

"It's not," she repeated and he saw tears brimming in her eyes again. "It's different for guys," she said. "If a woman kisses you and you don't want it, you can make her stop. You can push her away if you have to. You're stronger. But, when a guy does that to a woman, it's harder for her to stop him." She curled herself up a little, her arms bent across in front of her, almost like she was demonstrating, showing him how she would've been that night, when Tyler held onto her. Nick thought back. He didn't remember seeing Becky's hands, or arms. They must've been tucked inside Tyler's. He'd trapped her.

"He forced you?" Nick whispered.

She nodded, and shrugged at the same time. "I probably made it easier for him."

"Don't make excuses for him, Bex."

She looked him right in the eye. The look he saw made him fearful. "He'd told me you wanted Kelly. He said you were cheating on me."

Within an instant, Nick felt like he was going to explode with anger. "He said what?"

"He said you and Kelly were meant to be together."

"No. You and *I* were meant to be together."

She stared at him. "So is that why *you* had *your* tongue down Kelly's throat?" Her voice was still alarmingly quiet.

He sighed deeply. "I saw you kissing Tyler, Bex. What was I supposed to think?"

She shook her head and started to cry again, just as someone knocked on the door. Frozen to the spot, Becky did nothing, so Nick went over and opened it. A youngish man stood the other side, the hotel uniform sitting uneasy on his under-developed shoulders.

"Mr Gardner sent me to find Mrs Howell," he said, looking sheepish.

"Okay," Nick replied, trying to sound as normal as possible. "Tell him she'll be there in a minute." He closed the door without waiting for an answer, and turned back into the room.

Becky was still sobbing, his handkerchief held to her face. He walked straight over to her.

"Mark needs you," he said quietly.

She nodded and sucked in a breath, squaring her shoulders. "Okay"

"And we need to talk."

"We do?" She looked at him, seemingly uncertain.

"Yeah, of course we do." He raised his hand to her face, caressing her cheek gently. "We're a long way from done here. I got it so wrong, Bex. And I'm sorry. I'm more sorry than you'll ever know." He swallowed hard. "I've dreamt of seeing you again so many times, and it's never been like this." In his dreams, she'd never been this subdued. "Can we meet up later on?" he asked.

"I've gotta work."

"I know. I'll wait." He'd waited nine years, what were a few more hours? "I'll stay until you're finished. There's a private beach here, isn't there?" The thought of being outside, in the fresh air appealed to him. She nodded. "Meet me down there when you're finished?"

"It's gonna be really late, and it's freezing."

"I don't care how late it is, and you can change into something warmer, can't you? I need to talk to you, properly."

"Okay."

*Thank God for that.*

# Chapter Seven

## *Becky*

Becky left Nick in her office and ducked into the powder room. Luckily there was only one other woman in there, and she took the chance to try and rescue her makeup.

Her talk with Nick hadn't gone anything like she'd hoped. She'd just wanted to apologize for behaving the way she had at the party, for letting Tyler kiss her, and going home with him. She hadn't expected to get so emotional, so tearful and upset. Seeing Nick again just brought back all the memories of how good they'd been together, and how different her life could have been... if only...

She touched up her lipstick, and did her best to disguise the bruise, then stared at her reflection. There wasn't much more she could do, even though it was obvious she'd been crying. Still, Mark was the one making the speech. She just had to stand behind him, looking dutiful. She was good at that. She'd had years of practice with Tyler.

She went back out into the lobby and found Mark.

"What the hell happened?" he asked, looking down at her.

"Nothing."

"Bullshit, Becky. You've been crying."

"Okay... it wasn't nothing. But I don't want to talk about it."

"Did he hurt you?"

"Nick? Of course he didn't. How could you even ask that?"

"Okay, I'm sorry." He held up his hands. "But it didn't end well?"

"I don't know yet. We're gonna talk some more later. I'm meeting him on the beach."

Mark raised his eyebrows. "The beach? It's freezing out there."

"I'm gonna change."

"Okay. Well, you know where I am, if you wanna talk." He didn't wait for her to reply, but looked around. "I guess it's speech time," he said.

Becky followed him to the lectern, glancing around the room. There was no sign of Nick anywhere, and she started to wonder if he'd changed his mind and left already…

It was a little after midnight by the time everyone had left. Becky hadn't seen Nick again all evening, but she'd been kept busy. She tried not to wonder whether he was avoiding her. He wouldn't have asked to see her on the beach if that wasn't what he wanted, would he?

It took just a few minutes to go up to her room, throw off her dress and change into jeans, a pale pink v-neck sweater, black knee-high boots, and her navy blue thick quilted jacket, before going back downstairs again.

"You're still gonna meet him on the beach?" Mark asked her, as she went out through the main door. He already outside, helping Emma into his Aston Martin.

"Yes."

"And if he's not there?"

"Then he's not there."

Mark sighed and leant down, whispering something to Emma. She nodded and looked up to him, shutting her eyes as Mark closed the door.

"Come with me," he said to Becky, taking her arm and steering her around to the other side of the car.

"Where are we going?"

"I'll take you down to the beach," he said and, when she was about to protest, he continued, "I'm sure as hell not letting you walk down there alone at this time of night."

"But you need to get Emma home…"

"Yeah... which is why you're gonna squeeze into the back of my car." He smiled at her and shrugged, then he opened the driver's door and pulled forward the seat. Becky leant down and started to climb in, looking up at Emma as she did so. "Sorry about this," she muttered.

"Don't be... I'm blaming Nick. He should've waited for you here, not asked you to meet him down there."

"It's not Nick's fault," Becky replied. "I didn't make it clear I was going to walk. I can't drive... I've had too much to drink. Mark really doesn't need to do this..."

"Stop chattering and get your ass sat down," Mark said from behind her. Becky smiled and did as she was told.

Mark climbed into the driver's seat, closed the door and started the engine, driving them slowly down the private lane to the beach. There was no sign of any other vehicle.

"You're sure he said to meet you down here?" Mark asked, parking up.

"Yes." Becky's fears that he'd changed his mind started to resurface.

"Okay." Mark put the car into 'park' and got out, leaving the engine running. He pulled the seat forward again and held out his hand, which Becky took and climbed out of the rear of the car.

"Thank you," she said, with as much grace as she could muster.

"You're welcome," he replied. "I'll just make sure he's here, before I abandon you."

Mark walked the last few steps onto the sand, while Becky said goodnight to Emma. When she looked up again, he was walking back toward her.

"He's here," Mark said. "Around to the left."

Becky thanked him and, without looking back, she set off.

Luckily, they'd lit up the beach with strings of lights running all the way along the base of the cliffs, so she could see quite clearly where she was going as she walked over the soft sand and, when she looked up, she saw Nick coming toward her. He'd undone his bow tie, leaving it hanging around his neck, and the top two buttons of his shirt were also unfastened. He looked a little more crumpled now. More like the Nick she used to know.

"Hi," he said as she approached.

"Hello."

"Thanks for coming," he murmured.

"Thanks for waiting. It's a lot later than I thought it would be."

"Is that why the boss gave you a ride?"

She turned around, looking back to where Mark was still standing by his car. "He didn't want me to walk down here on my own."

"You were gonna walk?"

She nodded and gave Mark a quick wave. He returned the gesture and got back behind the wheel, driving slowly away.

Becky turned back to Nick.

"If I'd known that, I'd have waited for you," he said. "I'd assumed you'd drive."

"I've had too much to drink." *To calm my nerves.* "Besides, you didn't drive."

"No, I needed some air."

"How long have you been down here?" she asked.

"Since I left your office."

She looked up at him. "But that was hours ago, Nick. You must be freezing."

He shrugged. "Not really."

"Were you… were you avoiding me?"

His eyes opened wider, like he was surprised. "No," he said. "Of course not. I just needed to get out of there. I needed some time to myself… to think. I wasn't expecting any of this, Bex." He looked back to where Mark's car had been parked. "Mark's very protective of you," he said, evidently wanting to change the subject.

She felt her heart sink. "Oh please, not you as well. I get enough of that from Tyler."

Nick held up his hands. "I'm not accusing anyone of anything," he said. "I'm just making an observation. I get the feeling Mark likes to take care of the people who work for him."

She nodded. "He does."

"Shall we walk?" he suggested.

She nodded again and they turned and started to walk down toward, and then along, the shoreline.

"I think I forgot to mention it earlier," he murmured after a few minutes, "but you're beautiful. That dress you were wearing before was stunning, although I like this look just as much." Becky felt herself blush and was grateful the light was more muted away from the cliffs.

"Thank you," she muttered, feeling self-conscious. When was the last time anyone had called her beautiful? She honestly couldn't remember.

"And I'm sorry about what happened."

"When?"

"Nine years ago. I got it so wrong."

"No, Nick. I'm the one who got it wrong. Tyler lied to me, and I was dumb enough to believe him."

He stopped suddenly and Becky took a couple of paces to realize. She turned around to face him. Even in the dim light, she could see the dark shadows crossing his eyes. "What's wrong?" she asked.

"Why did you do it?" he asked.

"Do what?"

He sighed. "I get that you couldn't stop him kissing you. I get that he forced you into that, but why did you leave the party with him? Even if you were mad at me for talking to Kelly and then kissing her, why didn't you just come and ask me what the hell I was doing?"

She stared down at the sand between them for a moment. She had to tell him the truth; she owed him that much. "Seeing you with Kelly," she whispered, "it hurt."

"I'm sorry."

"Let me finish, please?"

"Okay."

"It hurt," she repeated. "But it also made me realize that I could never hope to compete. I knew you'd wanted her for a long time before we got together. You even told me about your infatuation with her yourself. I knew I could never be good enough, not when you really wanted her. I think that was when it dawned on me that you'd only asked me to go out with you because I was her friend, and being with me meant you could spend more time with her…"

She looked up, just as he reached out for her, pulling her into his arms. His body felt hard against hers.

"You really thought that?" he murmured, staring down into her eyes.

She nodded. "What else was I supposed to think?"

"That I wanted you, of course." He looked up at the sky just for a moment, before fixing his eyes on hers again. "I asked you to go out with me because I wanted to be with you, Bex. Being with you was magical. It was beyond anything I'd ever dreamt it could be, and seeing you like that with Tyler, losing you to him… it cut so damn deep."

Becky stared up at him. His words were so heartfelt, so believable. Except…

"I don't understand. If being with me was so magical, why did you sleep with Kelly that night?" she asked.

His mouth dropped open. "Sleep with Kelly?" he repeated. "I didn't sleep with her. I've never slept with her."

"But, she came back to the apartment with a man. They had sex… real noisy sex. I assumed…"

"You assumed it was me?" She nodded. "Then you assumed wrong, baby." Did he just call her 'baby'? A long-buried spark ignited deep inside her and, for a moment, she basked in the memory of being really, truly wanted by him. "I left Kelly at the party," Nick was saying, bringing her thoughts back to reality, "probably a couple of minutes after you went home with Tyler." He stopped and took a deep breath. "I assumed you were going back to your place – or his – and that you'd be spending the night with him. That really hurt. You can guess why…"

"Because we'd never spent a whole night together?" she whispered.

He nodded. "Yeah. That was real difficult for me." He pulled her closer. "But I swear – on Emma's life – that I never slept with Kelly."

Becky looked into his eyes, even though she didn't really need to. She believed him. And, as the realization dawned on her, she felt her legs buckle.

"Hey." Nick tightened his grip and she clung onto him for support. "Bex? What's wrong?" His voice was filled with concern.

"You didn't sleep with her…"

"No. I didn't."

"But, so much of what I did afterwards was based on me thinking you had." He held her closer.

"It's okay," he murmured.

"No it's not."

"Yeah it is. I know you slept with him. I've always known that."

"But I didn't. I—I didn't sleep with Tyler that night," she said, her voice barely audible, even to herself. "He took me back to the apartment, and he tried to come in with me, but I wouldn't let him. I just wanted to be by myself to think through what had happened. He was persistent, but eventually he went away. I didn't sleep with him that night," she reiterated, looking up at Nick.

"I believe you," he said and she saw the hurt deepen in his eyes. They both knew things could've been so different, if they'd just taken the time to talk, instead of jumping to conclusions.

"He pursued me… relentlessly," she continued. "He came to Fall River during the summer vacation. Somehow, he managed to charm my parents, and he didn't let up, and I eventually agreed to start seeing him at the end of the summer."

"I know…"

"You do?" She was surprised.

"Yeah. Tyler didn't exactly hold back with the gloating. When we got back to college in the fall, he took great delight in telling me that you'd moved in with him."

"But that's not true. I didn't move in with him." She couldn't disguise the shock in her voice. "I moved out of Kelly's apartment, because I was afraid you'd be there… sleeping with her. But I moved in with Anne-Marie, not Tyler."

She could see the anger in his eyes and she tensed slightly. "He told me you were living together."

"Then he lied." Tyler was good at that.

Nick shook his head. "Tell me, Bex… what really happened?"

"He… he tried to get me to sleep with him for the whole of that last year, but I didn't want to. I wasn't ready to move on from you. I was still hoping you'd come back for me."

"God, I wish I'd known."

"So do I…"

## Nick

He let her go and they carried on walking.

"Why didn't you come to me?" he asked. "If you wanted me back, you could've come to me…"

"How?" She turned to him. "I thought you were with Kelly. I've never had the self-confidence for that kind of thing. There's no way I could've faced a situation like that. I was too scared you'd reject me, because of what I'd done, or because you wanted Kelly and not me."

He was stunned. She was all he'd ever wanted. She was everything – why the hell would she lack confidence? Saying that out loud probably wasn't gonna help though, not right now.

"Okay. I'll admit I might well have been angry with you at the time, but I always felt partly to blame myself." He sucked in a breath. "I'd never have chosen Kelly – or anyone else – over you though, and I never stopped wanting you, no matter what had happened. If you'd have come to me, I'd have taken you back, in a heartbeat."

She stopped now, and looked up at him. "Really?"

"Yes, really."

"And yet you never thought of coming to look for me?"

"Yes. I did." He heard her gasp. "I went to Fall River a couple of months after we graduated."

"You did?"

"Yeah. I knew you were probably still with Tyler, but I didn't care. I had a kind of plan… which was to find you and beg you to try again with me. I wasn't above begging, Bex. I wasn't above doing anything to get you back."

"Then why didn't you?"

"Because I found out you'd just got engaged to him," he explained. "I traced you through a newspaper announcement about your engagement."

"And you just gave up?"

"Yeah. I could fight a boyfriend, but not a fiancé. Don't you see?"

"No." She shook her head, but he'd already heard the crack in her voice.

"Bex, getting engaged… accepting his proposal… it meant you loved him. I couldn't fight that." He took a step closer. "The worst thing was, I only missed you by five days."

"No. Oh, God… No." She started crying again and he pulled her into his arms, letting her sob into his chest.

"It's okay, Bex. I get that you loved him." Even if it had all gone sour, even if the marriage wasn't what it once had been, she had to have loved him once. She'd agreed to marry him. It hurt to think of her loving another man, but…

"I didn't," she murmured. "I didn't love him."

She pulled away from him, and he stared down at her. "You didn't?"

"No…"

"Then why did you accept him?"

"Because I'd lost you, and because he asked me, completely out of the blue. My parents were standing there, willing me to say yes. He dressed it up with hearts and flowers and told me how much he loved me. I thought loving him would come later, I thought things would get better."

He was scared to ask his next question, because he already knew the answer, but even so, he had to hear it from her.

"And did they?"

"For a while, I guess it was okay."

"Okay?"

"Yes."

"Just okay?" She shrugged, but didn't say anything more. "And then?" he prompted.

"It's not your problem, Nick."

"It damn well is."

"Can we walk again?" she said. "It's easier."

"Sure." He got it. She didn't want to face the scrutiny of his gaze. It was fair enough.

After a few paces, she started talking again. "I guess we had about seven or eight months where it was okay." She'd used that word again. It had never been 'magical', or 'great', or even 'good', just 'okay'. She looked away from him across the dark blanket of deep blue ocean and he had to strain to hear her voice. "I found out at a party at his office, the Christmas after we were married, that he'd only really proposed to me because it meant he was more likely to get his job in the first place and then be promoted."

"Where does he work?" Nick asked. This was sounding really familiar.

"Jenkins, Small and Wright."

He wanted to laugh, except it wasn't very funny.

"I interviewed there," he said. "They're very particular about the marital status of their employees." He let his eyes rest on the dim, distant horizon as they walked slowly on along the shore. "They told me they expected their associates to be settled, and engaged, or – better still – married, preferably with children—"

"I know," Becky interrupted. "Well, I didn't at the time, but that's what I found out later, at that party. One of the other wives told me."

He smiled.

"What's funny?"

"I was just remembering the look on their faces when I told them what they could do with their job offer." He glanced down at her. "That kind of thing was never gonna work for me. Besides, no-one dictates my private life to that extent – except me."

"Well, Tyler didn't have your convictions – clearly. He'd been turned down by nine or ten companies by then, and was getting desperate. But he came back from that interview much more hopeful than he'd been after any of the others. And then he proposed that evening, because it transpired, he'd told them he was engaged, and he needed a fiancée to back up his lie."

"And what happened after you'd found out his reason? After the Christmas party?"

"Then I discovered what he was really like…"

Nick stopped, but Becky kept walking and, after a moment, he jogged forward and caught up with her.

"Do you wanna explain that?" he asked.

She shook her head. "No, not really. It's not your problem."

"That's the second time you've said that. I'll repeat… It *is* my problem."

"I don't see why."

"I told you – I never stopped wanting you." He wasn't sure that now was the time to say he'd never stopped loving her, being as he'd never told her he loved her in the first place, but he hoped she might get the message.

Her shoulders fell and she turned to face him. "That was the first time he hit me," she said, her tone matter-of-fact. "It wasn't the last." She raised her hand toward her eye. "Clearly."

He gently placed his hand just under the bruise on her face, rubbing her skin tenderly with the side of his thumb. "He did this…" It wasn't a question, because he already knew the answer. Even so, she nodded her head. "And you stay with him?" He could have taken back the words before they'd even fully left his lips. He knew how lives like Becky's played out. He'd handled a few domestic abuse cases in his time… and he knew better than to ask that question. He'd made the mistake of asking it of a client once – years ago – and he could still remember the reply he'd received, the look of utter contempt on his client's face, when she'd told him he had no idea what it felt like to be undermined, hurt, threatened, abused, beaten, belittled, to live with fear every minute of the day, in your own home, to try and protect your children by putting yourself in harm's way on a nightly basis. The shame he'd felt on hearing her words lived on in him. "I'm sorry," he said quickly. "That was a really dumb thing to say."

"I tried leaving him once," she said, surprising him. "I went back to my mom's once, after he…" She stopped speaking suddenly, then continued, "But he came after me." She swallowed hard, then whispered, "I went back with him."

Nick put an arm around her as they walked, pulling her into him.

"There's something else," he said. "Something you're not telling me."

She managed a half smile. "Yes, there is."

"Then tell me."

"There's so much…" she whispered.

"Okay. I'm not going anywhere," he urged.

She turned and stared up at him, as though making a decision, then she looked away again before she started to speak. "When we'd been married about two years," she said softly, "I discovered he was having an affair." She shook her head. "And then I found out it wasn't the first time…"

"How did you find that out?"

"When I confronted him, he told me. He said he'd got bored waiting for me before we were married, and he'd been seeing her then too." She looked up at him. "I was so dumb," she said simply. "When we were engaged, I thought it was romantic that he was prepared to wait for me. And all the time, he was with this other woman."

Nick sucked down his anger. "And then he started seeing her again after you got married?"

"Yes. He told me he'd end it, but he didn't. I discovered about eighteen months ago that he was still seeing her. As far as I know, he still is…"

"You sound like you know who she is?"

"No. I just know it's someone from his law firm. I don't want to know the details." She shook her head again, more slowly. "It's ironic, isn't it? The company places so much importance on the stability of their employees' relationships, and Tyler's having an long-standing affair with one of his co-workers." She started to laugh, just softly, and then her laughter became tears as sobs wrenched through her body. Again, he stopped and pulled her into him, holding her body close to his and waiting, while the storm of her emotions washed over her.

"God," she said eventually. "I don't think I've cried this much in… well, forever."

"If it helps, then cry it out."

"I'm not sure it does. Crying doesn't solve anything."

"What would?" he asked. She looked up at him, seemingly confused. "What would solve it?" he asked again.

"I wish I knew." She gulped down her tears. "Ever since I found out he didn't end the affair, I've been asking Tyler for a divorce, but he won't listen me." She closed her eyes, and he saw a look of pure pain cross her face. He held her closer. "He ranted at me that it can't happen," she continued, "and now he won't even talk about it anymore, not that I'm brave enough to bring it up very often."

Nick swallowed down his anger again. Getting mad wasn't going to help her, and it wasn't Becky he was mad at. "I don't get why he'd refuse," Nick said, trying to sound calm. "If he's seeing someone else, and has been seeing her for some time, surely a divorce would suit him, wouldn't it?"

"You'd think so. But he's going for a partnership in the firm now. A divorce would ruin his chances. There's no way he's gonna agree."

"But he doesn't have to agree, Bex."

She sighed. "Yes, he does. He explained it to me. Well, he yelled it at me, while he…" She shuddered and he dreaded to think what memories she was reliving. "He said we can only divorce by mutual consent, because I can't use his affair as grounds, being as I continued to live with him after I found out about it. He said that under Massachusetts law, it's not permitted for me to use it as grounds in those circumstances, because I'm deemed to have condoned it."

*Son-of-a-bitch.* "That's not true," Nick told her, stepping back and taking her hands in his. "In fact, it's bullshit. His adultery can be used as grounds. The court might take into consideration the fact that you stayed on in the marital home, and therefore seemingly condoned his behavior, but that only applies in considering alimony and custody of any children of the marriage." He paused. "Sorry," he added, "I'm starting to sound way too much like a lawyer."

"But we don't have any children, and I don't care about alimony," Becky said, ignoring his last remark.

"Somehow I didn't think you would." He smiled. "Do you want me to carry on sounding like a lawyer for the time being?" he asked, and she nodded. "Okay… well, the fact that you stayed on in the house has no bearing on your ability to file for divorce and use his adultery against him."

"But he told me that, because I'd stayed in the house, I'd condoned it."

"Even if you did stay on in the house, that doesn't mean you condoned anything. And it doesn't mean you can't use the adultery." He paused. "The only time it can possibly count against you is if you continued to live as man and wife…" He left his sentence open.

"You mean, if I'd continued to sleep with him?"

"Yes. The court would still allow his adultery to be used as grounds, but they'd say that, if you continued to have… marital relations…" He paused again for a moment, trying to rein in his feelings, and control his thoughts. "Then your claim against him is limited. It still only affects your alimony claim though, not your right to file for divorce in the first place."

She looked confused. "I'm really tired, Nick. Can I just get this straight? If we continued to have marital relations after I knew about the affair, then can I still divorce him?" she asked.

"Yes. It can just limit your claim in certain circumstances," he clarified, feeling disappointed in the knowledge that she'd obviously slept with Tyler since discovering his infidelity.

She nodded her head slowly and looked down at her feet. "And, in the eyes of the law, does attempted rape count as having marital relations?" she whispered.

He felt the air being sucked from his lungs. "Did… Did you just say rape?"

She didn't look up. "No, I said *attempted* rape."

"Becky?" He ran his fingers through his hair. "What the fuck?"

Her head darted up and he saw the tears in her eyes, just before she turned and started running. He took off after her, and she hadn't gone more than a few yards before he grabbed her and turned her around.

"Don't," he said. "Please don't run away from me."

"You're angry," she mumbled and he saw fear in her eyes again.

"Not with you, Bex." He held her in his arms. She was stiff, unrelenting. "I promise you, I'm not angry with you," he whispered into her hair, and understood why she'd run. "Don't be scared of me," he murmured.

"Why are you angry…?"

"I'm not."

"Yes you are. It's written all over your face."

"Okay. I'm angry. But it's not you I'm angry with. I'm livid with him, and I'm angry with myself, but none of that means I'd do anything to you."

"Why are you angry with yourself?" He could hear the confusion in her voice.

"Because I let you go. I could've stopped it, and I let you go… to him. And he did that to you."

She pulled back and looked up at him. "It's not your fault, Nick."

"No, it's his." He held her face in his hands, staring into her eyes. "But if I hadn't let you go…" He could hear the regret in his own voice.

"Please don't think like that. I know how it feels. It's torture and it just makes it worse." Her voice cracked and he pulled her close again, holding onto her for ages, before she leant back in his arms.

"Let me help you," he said quietly.

"How?"

"Well, for a start… I'm a lawyer. I'll help you divorce him."

"He's gonna make it impossible, Nick. I don't want you getting involved."

"I'm already involved, baby."

She smiled up at him, just gently.

"He won't like it."

"Do I look like I give a damn?"

"No, but…"

"I won't let him hurt you, Bex, if that's what you're worried about. You're safe with me."

She leant into him again and he felt her relax.

"Can you really help?" she whispered.

"Of course I can."

# Chapter Eight

*Becky*

She pulled away eventually and looked into his eyes. Even in the darkness, they shone with that light that seemed to come from within him. It gave her hope.

"What can we do?" she asked, and he smiled.

"You said 'we'," he said, his smile becoming a grin. "I like that."

"So do I." She let her forehead rest against his chest for a moment. "So... what can we do?" she repeated.

"You've got options," he replied, keeping hold of her. She was glad of that. It felt comfortable and safe being in his arms. "You can divorce him on the grounds of adultery..." He paused for a moment. "Or cruelty." She lowered her face. "There are plenty of people who'll willingly testify that he's hit you, Bex. Me. Mark..."

She shook her head. "It's bad enough dragging you into this. I don't want to involve Mark as well."

"Does he know?" Nick asked, seeming to hold his breath.

"Know what?"

"About the attempted rape." He stopped. "Or is it rapes? Was it more than once?" he asked.

She paused before replying. "He tried it three times, on separate occasions." She took a deep breath. "I'm sorry, Nick. I don't wanna talk about that right now," she added, then placed her hand on his chest. "I will tell you about it, but just not right now."

"It's okay." His voice was so soft, so understanding and kind. "I'm here, whenever you want to talk." He gazed down at her. "So, does Mark know?"

She shook her head. "No. He knows Tyler hit me, because he saw the bruises."

"How do you feel about him knowing?"

"What do you mean?" she asked.

"About what Tyler did. How do you feel about him knowing? This could get messy," Nick said, his voice more serious. "Who knows what Tyler will accuse you of in retaliation. You need to be prepared, and so does Mark, being as he's the one Tyler's so paranoid about."

"Do you think I should tell Mark then?"

"I think *we* might have to," Nick clarified. "But we don't have to worry about it just yet. Let's see what happens."

She felt herself deflate.

"Bex," he said, bringing his hands up to her shoulders and letting them rest there. "Look at me, baby." She did. The expression on his beautiful face reminded her of how much she loved him, and why. "I'll do everything I can to help you. And the first thing I'm gonna suggest is that you file for a no fault divorce and cite irreconcilable differences. You don't have to mention the adultery, or the abuse. I think it'll be a lot less messy…"

She felt the familiar chill of defeat settling over her. "I already suggested that to Tyler in one of our many arguments. He said it was impossible."

"Why?" Nick asked, looking confused.

"Because he said he wouldn't agree to it." She swallowed down the lump in her throat. "He said he had to agree."

"That's bullshit – again. He doesn't have to agree. You can file for what's called a contested no fault divorce. That way he doesn't have to agree to anything. It takes a little longer than if he does agree, but there's nothing whatsoever to stop you from filing the papers."

"And you think that'll avoid Tyler making trouble?"

"I seriously doubt it. But I'm hoping he's less likely to be difficult if you're not citing his adultery."

She nodded. "Are you saying I can actually divorce him? I can be free of him?" It seemed almost too much to hope for.

"You're already free of him, Bex. I'm not letting you go back to him, ever again." He pulled her close again and she hung on.

When she leant back, he looked down into her eyes.

"You're exhausted," he said quietly.

She nodded her head. She'd passed exhausted some while back. She had nothing left…

"Come here." He bent down and picked her up, holding her in his arms, and slowly started to walk back along the beach toward the lane that led up to the hotel. She put her arms around his neck and nestled into his shoulder, savoring the feeling of safety, for the first time in nine years.

"I can walk," she whispered.

"You don't have to," he replied, smiling. "Besides, I like carrying you."

She looked up at him and snuggled in a little closer.

"Where's your car?" she asked as Nick gently deposited her on the ground outside the hotel's main entrance. The area was well lit and she could see him more clearly now. He looked beautiful.

"Around the back," he replied.

"I'll walk round with you," she said. "I can go in the staff entrance."

"You sure?" he asked, and she nodded. He took her hand, and they walked around the corner of the hotel.

"Are you sure you want to get involved in this?" she asked him quietly.

"Absolutely positive. Anyway, I keep telling you, I'm already involved." His reply was adamant. He seemed to hesitate for a moment, and then continued, "I'm not saying it's necessarily a good idea for me to represent you though…"

"Oh?"

"You need advice from someone more impartial."

"And you're not impartial?" What was he saying?

He stopped and pulled her back to him. "No, Bex. I'm a long way from being impartial." His eyes pierced hers and she sucked down a gasp at what she thought she saw there. It looked like love, but that was impossible. He hadn't loved her before, so why would he now?

"But, if you can't represent me…" She tried to focus on something other than his eyes, and her own feelings.

"I'll ask Tom to advise you," he said.

"Who's Tom?"

"My business partner…"

"You're a partner?"

"Yeah. Don't sound too impressed though." He smiled. "It's just the two of us."

He led her toward the rear of the parking lot. "This is me," he said quietly.

"You're still driving a Dodge Ram?" She looked up at him, and a smile formed on her lips.

"Yeah. Some things never change, Bex."

"No, I guess they don't," she murmured.

"I'll speak to Tom on Monday," he said. "I'll arrange for you to meet with him… hopefully sometime next week."

She nodded. "I'm gonna be around for a while," she said. "It's gonna take time to find a permanent manager for this place, so I think I'll be here for at least three or four weeks."

"Good," he replied.

"Good?" she repeated, wanting an explanation.

He nodded, but offered nothing more. She had no idea what he meant or where she stood. He'd said he wasn't going to let her go back to Tyler, but what did that mean? What was he really offering her? Was it more than his help and protection? She needed to know, but she was scared to ask outright.

"So, you practice law in Somers Cove?" she asked, fishing a little. He nodded. "You were never tempted by the bright lights of the city then?"

"No. I wanted to help make the law work for people, not just let it work for me," he told her. She nodded. That sounded just like the Nick she remembered.

"And you still live there? In Somers Cove, I mean?"

He shook his head. "No, I bought a plot of land a few years ago."

"You built your own house?" she asked.

"Well, I haven't exactly gotten around to the house building part yet…" He smiled down at her.

"Then where do you live?"

"I've got a trailer… a very nice trailer." She laughed. "And I'll build the house one day," he added.

"And your family?" Now she was really fishing. Did he realize?

"Well, mom and dad still own the boat yard, although they don't spend much time there these days. And you know all about Emma…" He paused. "But that's not what you're asking, is it?"

She shook her head, blushing. He'd realized.

"I live alone, Bex," he said quietly. "I've lived alone since we split up."

She looked up at him, unable to believe what he'd just said.

"There's never been anyone but you," he added.

She took a moment to process his statement. "Never?"

"No. Never."

"You mean, you've been on your own all this time?"

"Yep. I haven't even dated anyone."

She struggled to take in what he was saying. "But that's wrong, Nick. That's all wrong." She reached up and placed her hand gently on his cheek, feeling his stubble against her skin. "You're a handsome, romantic, sexy, gentle man. Any woman would love to be with you. And I'm sure you haven't been short of offers…"

"I haven't," he admitted.

"Then I don't understand why you'd choose to be on your own. Nine years, Nick… It's a long time."

"Yeah, I know it is."

"Then why? I mean, you can't have—"

"You broke my heart, Bex." He said the words simply and calmly.

She froze and stared up at him, her own hurt reflected back at her. He'd lived alone for all this time, because of her? No… That was too much.

"I'm sorry," she mumbled. "I'm sorry. I'm sorry." She couldn't bare to look at him anymore and, without thinking, she turned and started to run away again.

After just a few yards she felt his hand on her arm, pulling her to a stop, and turning her around. Then he was holding her, one hand behind her head, the other in the small of her back, his body pressed hard against hers, his eyes boring into her.

"Again?" he said. "Stop this. Please don't keep running from me." He hesitated just for a moment, then lowered his lips to hers, kissing her gently, demanding nothing. It was a brief kiss, but it gave her just the reassurance she needed and, as he pulled away, he stared at her for a moment, then nodded slowly and she wondered if he understood how she felt, how scared and confused she was. Was that even possible? How could he ever understand? "Don't ever do that again," he said.

"Do what?"

"Run away from me," he explained. "I'll never hurt you, Bex."

She'd thought she was all cried out, but more tears started to fall. He pulled her head down onto his chest, stroking her hair gently.

After a while, her tears subsided and she leant back and looked up at him. His eyes dropped to her lips, then neck, then lower still. "Oh… You kept it," he said, sounding surprised.

"Kept what?"

"The locket." She'd left it on when she'd changed.

"Of course I kept it. You gave it to me. That night… it was so special." She choked back another sob. "I wish…" she stuttered, "I wish so much we could turn back the clock, and we could get it right…"

He smiled at her. "Well, we can't turn back the clock, but it's not too late to make it special again, or to get it right," he added. "I never gave up hoping we'd get back together. That's why I've been on my own all these years. I knew you were worth waiting for." He kissed her gently again, letting his lips rest on hers.

"You've been waiting for me?"

"Yes."

"Why?"

He smiled. "Because I love you, Bex. I always loved you."

# Nick

There was a pause, which probably only lasted a few seconds, but to Nick it seemed to go on for a lifetime.

"You love me?"

"Yes, of course I do." He smiled and caressed her cheek with the backs of his fingers.

She closed her eyes again and, when she opened them, a single tear slid down each cheek. "I love you too, Nick," she murmured softly and he felt the pieces of his long-shattered heart locking back together again. "I love you so much. And I'm sorry I hurt you," she whispered. "I'm sorry it all went so wrong. I'm so, so sorry."

He leant back, looking down at her. "Don't," he said firmly. "Stop apologizing. We both fucked up fairly spectacularly. If I hadn't been so scared, I'd have told you I loved you back then."

"What were you scared of?" she asked.

"That it was too soon."

She shook her head. "I—I felt the same," she whispered. "I wanted to tell you so much. I thought you'd run a mile if I said it."

He smiled and pulled her close again. "Like I said, we both fucked up…" He stroked her hair. "And you paid such a high price…"

"Please," she whispered into him. "I don't want to talk about him at the moment."

"Neither do I." Thinking about what she'd had to deal with during the intervening years, Nick wasn't sure he'd ever be able to talk about it calmly.

They stood in silence for a long moment, holding each other.

"It's late," he said eventually.

"It's early," she replied, leaning back and smiling up at him.

He checked his watch. It was a few minutes after two thirty. "Yeah, it is."

"I've got to work tomorrow… well, today," she said, a little wistfully.

"You have?" He was surprised. "Even though it's Sunday?"

She nodded. "We're fully booked, and I'm the manager."

"Then you'd better get some sleep." He looked around. "Where's this staff entrance you were telling me about?"

She pointed to the left hand side of the building. "Over there."

"Okay." He released her, but took her hand in his and started walking slowly toward the door. "Can we agree on one thing?" he asked.

"I think we can probably agree on lots of things," she replied and he looked down at her. She was smiling up at him and he felt his heart swell in his chest.

"Okay, but can we agree on one specific thing?" She nodded. "The past is the past. Whatever we did back then, we leave it there." They'd reached the door and he pulled her into his arms again. "I don't want to keep dwelling on what either of us did wrong," he said. "I just wanna be with you – now." She went to speak, but he put a finger gently on her lips. "If you want to tell me about what happened with Tyler, then I'm here and I'll listen, but if you don't, then that's okay."

She leant back and stared up at him. "I'm gonna have to tell you, Nick," she whispered. He wasn't sure what she meant by that, but he nodded his head.

"Okay," he replied. "And before you say anything else, I know this is gonna be tough, I know we'll have to take it slow. And I know the road ahead isn't gonna be exactly plain sailing." Her lips twitched upwards. "*And* I know I just did something really horrible with my metaphors," he added, a grin breaking out on his face. "The point is, I've got you back."

"You have," she whispered. "I'm yours, Nick. Deep down, I always was"

He closed his eyes and sighed, letting her words wash over him and soak into his soul. "And no matter what happens," he said, opening them again, "I'm not letting you go again."

He had let her go, even though it was tough to do so. He'd watched her go inside and stood staring at the door as it closed behind her. But he wasn't letting her go for long. And that was why he'd driven home at three in the morning, with a dumb smile on his face.

He woke late the next morning, his cock hard and aching, wondering whether it had all been just another dream. This wasn't that unusual. He always woke like this when he'd dreamt about Becky, and it took a while for that sense of longing and disappointment to go away. He sat up, running his hands down his face. He was sure he'd kissed her. He hadn't dreamed it, had he? He looked around his bedroom. Everything was exactly as it usually was. *Shit*. Was it really just another dream? He swung his legs over the side of the bed and smiled.

There, on the floor beside the bed, were his clothes. His black pants, his white dress shirt and bow tie, and his shoes, caked in sand.

"Well, thank fuck for that," he said out loud. It hadn't been a dream. It was real. She was back. And she was his. She'd said so.

His smile fell. He remembered their kisses. He'd kept them brief because of what Tyler had done to her. Nick gripped the edge of the mattress... hard. "She's still married to that fucker," he muttered to himself. "But not for long." Nick was going to do whatever it took to get her away from him, and not just because he wanted her, but because it was the right thing to do. And if he had to wait for her to be ready, for her to be free? Well, he'd already waited nine years, he could wait a few more months. In the meantime though, he needed to see her again, just to be absolutely sure it hadn't been a dream.


Once he'd showered and dressed, and had two cups of hot black coffee, Nick drove back to the hotel. It was late morning, and the place looked busy, even from the outside.

He handed his keys over to the parking attendant and walked in through the main door. It was very different to the previous evening – more businesslike, more organized. He looked around. He had no idea where Becky would be, but he guessed he could just ask at reception and they'd find her.

He started walking toward the glass-topped counter, when he caught sight of her. She was talking to a young guy, who was wearing the hotel uniform, and filling it out a little better than the youth who'd come searching for Becky the previous evening. He was nodding attentively, looking maybe a little smitten, Nick thought, and he smiled and went and sat down on one of the large pale gray leather couches, his eyes not leaving Becky.

"Can I get you something, sir?"

The young female voice caught his attention and he looked up to see a wide-eyed, uniformed blonde looking down at him.

"Sorry?" he asked.

"Would you like anything from the bar… or a coffee?" *Anything from the bar?* At this time of the morning?

"A coffee would be great, thanks." He returned her smile, and she nodded before turning away. He looked back at Becky. She was still talking to the young man, pointing at something on the sheet of paper she was holding. The youth moved closer and tilted his head toward hers, and Nick smiled again, feeling a little sorry for the guy. He couldn't blame him for his infatuation. Becky was breathtaking. Nick let his eyes wander up her body, starting at her feet, encased in navy, high-heeled pumps, then he moved higher and took in the tight, dark blue skirt that came to just above her knee, then the fitted jacket, and white open-neck blouse. She'd worn her hair long, and she'd used a lot of makeup again, but Nick understood why, and from this distance, he couldn't really notice the swelling, or the bruise that he knew would still disfigure her beautiful face. Her appearance gave away nothing. It was impersonal. She exuded professionalism and was the image of organized sophistication.

Nick let out a long sigh. What the hell did she see in him?

She finally finished her conversation and the young man moved away, with noticeable reluctance, just as Becky's phone seemed to ring and she took the call, walking quickly toward the reception counter and talking at the same time. She still hadn't seen him, and Nick watched her, fascinated. She leant over the desk, and he felt himself harden at the sight of her perfect ass, as she reached for something on the other side of the counter… a pen, evidently, as she then started to write something down on the back of the piece of paper she'd just been studying with the young man. She talked for a moment longer, laughed lightly, then hung up and spoke to the woman behind the counter, giving her back the pen before turning around, and finally making eye contact with Nick.

"Your coffee, sir." The blonde waitress stepped in front of him and he leaned to one side, trying to keep Becky in his sights.

"Thanks," he mumbled.

"You're welcome," she chimed and he heard the smile in her voice, even though he wasn't looking at her. "Will there be anything else?" she asked.

"No, thanks," he said, willing her to move away.

She obliged, after just a moment's hesitation, and Nick noticed Becky was now talking to a slightly older man. He remembered this guy from the previous evening. Becky had been speaking with him just before Mark had introduced them. He was the deputy manager. He had a notebook in his hand and was showing Becky something. She pointed upwards, toward the roof of the building. He nodded and walked away, and again, Becky made eye contact with Nick, and he smiled. She smiled back, then blushed, lowering her eyes and took a step toward him, just as the woman behind the reception desk seemed to call her name. Becky turned and the woman handed Becky a telephone. She spoke for a few minutes, then handed back the receiver and walked quickly away, down the corridor that Nick knew led to her office.

He sighed. He was starting to wonder whether this was a dumb idea after all. He'd come over here to see her, but she was working, and she was busy. Maybe he should ask someone what time she finished and come back later, or get them to give him her phone number, so he could at least call, or text her. He took a sip of coffee. He'd wait a little longer. He wasn't in any rush and, besides, the coffee was good.

Two hours and three more cups of coffee drifted by. He caught glimpses of Becky as she went about her job, but whenever she tried to come over, something – or someone – seemed to get in the way.

He was walking back from the men's room when he looked up and saw her standing right next to the seat he'd been occupying all morning, looking around, a worried expression on her face.

"Becky?" he called as he approached, concerned she might disappear again.

She turned. "I'm sorry," she said quickly. "I wasn't ignoring you. I honestly wasn't. It's just been crazy here this morning. But I promise I'd have come over sooner, if I could, I'm so sorry—" She sounded panicked, fearful.

"Stop it," he interrupted, noticing the look of alarm in her eyes. He glanced around quickly. "Let's go to your office, Bex," he said softly.

"Um… okay." She seemed to hesitate.

"You're safe," he whispered, leaning into her a little. "Come with me." He placed his hand on her lower back and guided her toward the corridor.

"Excuse me?" A suited man stepped in their path, looking at Becky. "Are you the manager?"

"I'm sorry," Nick said, with authority, moving Becky behind him slightly. "Mrs Howell just has something to attend to. She'll be right back. Maybe someone at reception can help you?"

The man smiled and nodded, moving away toward the counter and Nick directed Becky onward to her office. She opened the door and he let her pass through, closing it behind them. When he turned, she was standing in the middle of the room, staring at him.

"I'm sorry," she said again. Tyler had done this to her. He'd crushed her spirit as well as her body.

"Will you stop apologizing to me," he replied, keeping his voice as calm as he could. "You've got nothing to be sorry for."

"But I made you wait."

"So what? You weren't expecting me to be here. You're busy. I get it."

"But…"

He took three steps forward and stood right in front of her. "I'm not Tyler," he said quietly. "I know it's hard for you, but please try and remember, I'm not gonna get mad at you just because you're doing your job, or because there's a hair out of place, or something's a little less than perfect." He cupped her face in his hands and smiled. "Bex, to be honest, I'm so damn happy to have you back, I'm unlikely to get mad at you at all – ever – so please, please don't be scared of me." He placed his lips gently over hers and kissed her, just lightly. "I won't hurt you," he whispered. "I promise."

"I'm sorry," she repeated. He looked at her, raising an eyebrow, and she smiled. "I mean I'm sorry for apologizing, and for thinking you could ever be like him. You're right; it's hard."

"Hey, it's okay. He's worn you down. I get that." He leant back a little. "You just need to remember, you're safe with me… okay?"

She nodded. "I'll try."

"Besides," he added, pulling her into his arms, "I've had a great morning."

"You have?" Her brow furrowed and a look of confusion clouded her eyes. "Doing what?"

"Watching you. You're very beautiful and *very* organized."

She blushed, and smiled. "I have to be – organized, that is," she said. "Have you tried working for Mark?"

He laughed. "No. I'll leave that to you. You do it very well." Her cheeks flushed an even deeper red and she lowered her eyes. "I guess I'd better tell you why I'm here," he said.

She looked up again, the blush fading.

"I've got three reasons for coming over to see you," he announced, smiling down at her.

"You have?"

He nodded. "Yeah. Firstly, I woke up this morning in a state of panic," he explained.

"You did?" She seemed surprised.

"Yeah." He moved a little closer, but kept his body slightly away from hers. He was hard… bone hard, but he didn't want her to feel his erection and be scared, which he had a suspicion she might be. "I've dreamt about us being together again for such a long time," he said, "and when I woke up, I was so afraid that last night was just that… another dream."

"It wasn't," she whispered.

"Yeah, I know. But I just had to come over and see you for myself, to make sure you're real and you're here." She smiled, blushing again.

"The second reason is that I wanted to ask you to have dinner with me tonight, at my place," he said.

"Your place? Your trailer?" Was he asking too much?

"Yeah… I told you, it's a very nice trailer." He grinned.

Her eyes lit up again and she smiled. "I'd love to."

He didn't reply. Instead, he leant down and kissed her, gently again, his lips caressing hers, just for a moment. He knew he was going to have to take it slow with her… real slow. And he was okay with that.

"What's the third reason?" she asked when he broke the kiss.

"I needed to tell you I love you." A really slow smile formed on her lips, spreading to her eyes, which sparkled up at him. "I've got nine years to make up for," he whispered. "I'm gonna be saying it a lot." He leant forward. "I love you, Bex."


It was only as he drove back home again that the reality of the situation dawned on him. It was a little before two in the afternoon, which meant he had roughly six hours to straighten up the trailer, and himself. Well, he could manage that, but then he also had to cook, and cook something suitably impressive. Shit…

He didn't even bother waiting until he got home. He pulled over to the side of the road, grabbed his phone, and made a call.

"Emma?" he said as soon as she picked up. "I've got a problem…"

# Chapter Nine

*Becky*

For the next couple of hours, Becky kept finding herself standing, staring into space.

Nick's words had left her a little speechless. He was so confident and self-assured, and she found it hard to believe he'd woken up in such a state of anxiety, imagining that their time together the previous night had been a dream. She smiled, remembering his arms around her. It had felt so good to be held again, and to know that his arms posed no threat, and carried no danger. He felt comfortable, and safe. And she liked that.

But more than anything, she liked the fact that he'd come over to tell her he loved her. It was so sweet, so romantic. So Nick.

He'd programmed his number into her phone, and given her directions to his trailer, and as the afternoon progressed, she was finding it harder and harder to concentrate, as she thought more and more about their evening together. What would Nick expect from her? Would he want them to be intimate? Maybe he'd want to have sex? She swallowed down the bile that rose in her throat when she thought about sex... about what Tyler had done, then she shook her head. She needed to stop thinking about Tyler. Nick wasn't Tyler. He was nowhere close to being Tyler.

Somewhere in the depths of her memory she could still remember the way it had felt when Nick made love to her. There was no comparison between that and Tyler's assaults. What he did had hurt badly… physically and emotionally. Nick had never done anything like that. He'd treated her gently, kindly, with respect. He'd pleasured her, and enjoyed her pleasure. He'd taken his time with her, guided her, touched her, tasted her, made *love* to her. And, deep down, she knew she wanted to have those feelings again. Somehow.

She also knew he wouldn't have any expectations. He wouldn't push her. He'd wait until she was ready. But if she was going to stand a chance of regaining that tenderness with him, she was going to have to tell him what Tyler had done. She was going to have to share it with him, and hope he'd understand and help her to get over her worst fears; that he'd be patient, kind and tolerant while she worked things out with him. Of course he would – she knew he would. This was Nick.

She let herself into her room on the third floor at just after eight-fifteen, threw her purse onto the bed and shrugged off her jacket, slinging it on top. She was running late, but she'd had to take that last call. Even so, she'd told Nick she'd be at his place by eight-thirty and there was no way she was going to make that now. He'd been really laid back and had told her not to worry and just to get there whenever she was ready, but she didn't want to be late. Tyler had always gotten real mad at her if she was late…

'I'm not Tyler… I'm unlikely to get mad at you at all…' Nick's words echoed around her head and she took a deep breath. She needed to calm down and stop this.

Slipping off her blouse and skirt, she reached into the closet and pulled out the black sheath dress, stepping into it and pulling it up past her hips, before she stopped and stared at her reflection in the full-length mirror. Why was she even thinking of wearing this dress? It was very smart, sleeveless, knee-length, and skin tight. Tyler had chosen it for her, but then Tyler chose most of her clothes, because he wanted her to look 'right'. She had to look 'right' all the time. Even at home in the evenings and at weekends, he expected her to dress a certain way. Four of his work colleagues lived in the same housing complex as them and he didn't want them to see her looking anything but 'right'.

*Dammit!*

She let the dress drop to the floor and stepped out of it, leaving it where it fell as she walked across to the dresser, pulling out a pair of jeans and a purple boho-style top, with an embroidered panel at the front. It was a couple of years old now, but she loved it. She layered it with a navy longline cardigan and, as she turned, she caught sight of herself in the full length mirror again. This was the real Becky. These clothes were reserved for when she was away from home, off duty and relaxed. They were hers, and they were 'her'… except… She moved closer to the mirror and shook her head before going quickly into the bathroom.

She turned her BMW into the track Nick had told her about, opposite the signpost to Somers Cove, then slowed down and drove carefully about fifty yards down the bumpy lane, to the clearing, pulling up outside Nick's trailer, and parking beside his black Dodge.

His home was larger than she'd expected, and more modern. She opened the car door and started to climb out, just as Nick stepped out from the trailer. Like this morning, he was wearing jeans – although these were black instead of blue – and had on a white shirt, open at the neck, with a dark gray waistcoat. This was the Nick she remembered. Even in the dusk she could see his hair was tousled and looked damp at the ends, and she guessed he'd probably showered recently. He looked comfortable in himself, much more so than he had in a tux, anyway.

"Hi," he called to her.

"Hello. I'm sorry I'm late."

"You're not." He wandered over, his hands in his pockets. "You're exactly on time."

"I am?"

"Yeah. Anytime you arrive is the perfect time," he whispered, and took her hand. "Wanna have a look around?" he asked.

"I'd love to."

"It doesn't take long." He smiled down at her and waved his arm around them at the dense forest, still just about visible in the evening twilight. "This is my back garden – and my front garden."

"You own all of this?" she asked, twisting around.

He nodded his head. "I own the bit you can see from here," he said.

"It's beautiful."

"It is. But you should see it when it snows," he replied. "That's when it's really breathtaking."

"I can imagine."

"Come inside," he said and led her to the door of the trailer. "Mind the step. It's kinda steep." He helped her up, and followed her inside.

The space was so much larger than she'd expected, and better furnished. She turned to face him.

"Fucking hell, Bex… I'm sorry," he added quickly.

"What's wrong?" she asked.

He raised his hand and gently caressed the side of her face, just below the bruise. "You need to ask?"

"Oh… I forgot. I took my makeup off."

"So I can see."

"I hate wearing it. It's not me at all."

"I know." He leant down and studied her. She knew what he was seeing; the angry, deep reddish-purple bruising above and below her eye, the swelling over her cheekbone. "He did *this*?" She nodded. He ran his hand down and behind her neck, pulling her close to him, his mouth next to her ear. "I don't care what happens. Whatever he says, or does, Bex, you're never going back to him. Do you understand? He'll have to go through me first." He leant back and looked down at her.

She stared up at him. His eyes were glistening, his lips drawn in a thin line. She nodded, just once.

"He's never gonna touch you again," he murmured and she rested her head on his chest, and let him stroke her hair and, despite her previous bitter experiences with Tyler, she believed every word Nick said.

They stood for a long moment, before Nick took a deep breath and pulled back. "I think we both need a glass of wine," he said.

"I'm driving," she pointed out, feeling disappointed. She could have done with a glass of wine right about now.

He hesitated, like he wanted to say something, then changed his mind, and she wondered just for a moment if he'd been going to suggest she could stay the night. She also wondered what her answer might have been. "Good point," he replied eventually. "Do you want a glass?" he asked. "I've got a really good Pinot Noir."

"You have? That sounds delicious."

"Okay. Then I won't drink, and I'll take you back to the hotel later. You can leave your car here and pick it up tomorrow."

"Really?"

"Yeah. I think you could do with letting your hair down a little, and besides, it means you have to come back here for your car." He grinned at her.

"I think..." she started to say, then stopped herself, feeling embarrassed.

"You think what?"

"Nothing."

"Tell me."

She stared up at him. "I was just going to say that I think I'd have come back anyway," she whispered.

He leant down and very gently kissed her lips. "I'm glad to hear it," he murmured and pulled her further into the room, toward the kitchen. "Have a seat," he said, leading her to the breakfast bar and pulling out a stool for her. She sat and pulled her cardigan from her shoulders, laying it across her lap, as Nick poured her a large glass of red wine, passing it across the wide countertop, before helping himself to a glass of chilled San Pellegrino. "Cheers," he said, coming back over to her.

"I feel kinda guilty," she said, taking a sip of wine. "This is lovely, and you're not having any."

"You're planning on drinking the whole bottle?" he teased.

"Well, no."

"Then I'll have some later. After I've taken you back to the hotel."

She took another sip. "This is an amazing kitchen." She looked around. "Actually, the whole trailer's pretty cool," she added.

It really was. The living area had an overstuffed full-size black leather couch along one wall, with a low table set in front. On the other side of the room was an old-looking dining table, which had been laid for two people, and was surrounded by four ladder backed chairs, and at the end of the room was a roll-top desk, with an antique oak swivel chair sat in front. The place summed Nick up to a tee. A little unconventional, a bit worn looking, and really comfortable. Becky smiled.

"You okay?" he asked, taking the lid off one of two pans on the stovetop, and dropping fresh pasta into it, before adding what looked like a handful of spinach to the other one.

"Yes. I was just thinking… This place suits you perfectly."

He turned and looked at her, his head tilted on one side. "How?" he said.

"It's kinda unexpected, unconventional… comfy, cosy, and a little worn around the edges," she said, smirking.

He came around the breakfast bar and stood beside her, twisting her seat so she was facing him. "I'm worn around the edges, am I?"

She nodded. "In a good way," she whispered.

"Well, I'm real glad you cleared that up." He leant down and they both smiled into his gentle, brief kiss.

## Nick

It felt good that she was so comfortable she could even make a joke with him. He imagined jokes had been fairly few and far between in Becky's life over the last nine years and, although he'd often felt lonely, dejected, and heart-broken, he realized now how lucky he'd been.

Looking down at her, his eye was drawn to the the bruise once more. Seeing it for the first time without any makeup to disguise it had shocked the hell out of him. He'd seen a fair few black eyes in his time, he'd even seen them on women; victims he'd represented in abuse cases. But he'd never seen one on someone who mattered to him. It made him want to punch Tyler, and hold Becky close all at the same time. His conflicting emotions were hard to control, but he needed to, for her sake.

One thing was for sure… Now he'd seen that, there was no way on earth he was letting her go. Hell would have to freeze over first.

"What are we eating?" Becky asked, and he dragged himself him back to the here and now.

"Pasta," he replied, "with mushrooms, wilted spinach and pancetta."

"Sounds nice."

"It's a recipe of Emma's," he admitted. "She's an incredible cook."

"I know. Mark told me."

Nick went back over to the stove and turned off the heat. "It's ready," he announced. "Do you want to go sit at the table?"

"There's nothing you want me to do?" Becky offered.

"No. I've got it."

Becky went over and sat down, taking her wine glass with her, and Nick finished preparing the food, stirring the mushroom mixture into the pasta, and pouring it all into two dishes.

He carried them over to the table, then went back for the parmesan and the bread, before sitting opposite Becky. It felt so good to have her here, he almost wanted to pinch himself, just to make sure this wasn't another dream.

"It smells good too," Becky said, leaning over the steaming dish of pasta.

"I claim no credit," Nick replied, holding up his hands. "Like I say, Emma's real good at this kind of thing."

Becky tilted her head to one side. "You cooked it, Nick."

He smiled. "With very strict instructions."

She nodded and smiled. "I see."

They ate, and talked, and Becky explained how she'd met Mark when he'd visited the hotel she was managing in Boston.

"You were young to be managing a hotel, weren't you?" Nick said.

"It was my first job out of college," Becky explained. "I started there as an assistant manager; did about three years and, when the manager left, I was promoted by the owner."

"At the age of… twenty-five?"

She nodded, twirling a little pasta onto her fork. "I'd been manager there for just over eighteen months, when Mark showed up."

"As a guest?"

She shook her head. "No, he was looking to buy the place. It was about a year after he'd taken over the company, and it would have been his first acquisition, but the owner didn't want to sell. Mark wasn't into making aggressive purchases, so he left it alone."

"But he came back for you?"

"Well, yes." She seemed shy. "He left me his card and asked me to call him. I did, and the rest, as they say, is history."

"What made you decide to start working for him?"

"He offered me a very good deal." She put her fork down on the side of her plate. "And the job meant I was traveling for two or three days a week…" She left the sentence unfinished.

"Which meant you were away from Tyler?" Nick did it for her.

She nodded. "He didn't like it. Mark pays me very well…" She paused, like she wanted to say something else, but then changed her mind and continued, "Tyler accused me of sleeping my way into the job, and the salary, but I've never been interested in Mark like that – honestly. And he's not interested in me either. There's nothing between us; we're colleagues, nothing else." Nick heard the panic rising in her voice and put down his fork quickly, reaching over and taking her hands in his, holding them in the center of the table.

"Bex," he said softly, "I know. It's okay."

"But…"

"It's okay. I know there's nothing going on between you and Mark. I know you're not the kind of person who'd cheat. I trust you, and I trust him. He loves Emma." He held her gaze. "And you love me."

She stared at him and nodded. "Yes, I do."

"Then stop worrying. I know your relationship with Mark is just professional. I promise, you've got nothing to fear around me, okay?"

She nodded once more. "I'm sorry," she whispered.

"Don't be." He released her hands. "Let's finish eating, and then we can sit down and talk."

"Okay." She picked up her fork again and started to eat. He'd already noticed she ate very little, but she was eating even less now.

What was that about? And what was she so scared of?

After they'd finished, Nick made them both a coffee and they sat together on the couch, where he pulled Becky into his arms and she rested her head on his chest. He'd hoped the wine would relax her, but it hadn't and he could do with some himself now. When she'd arrived, he'd thought about suggesting she stay the night, but had changed his mind, knowing she wasn't ready for that yet. She felt stiff in his arms; their earlier conversation had put her even more on edge, and he decided he needed to find something neutral to talk about.

"I'm gonna need to speak to Mark," he said.

"Why?" Becky looked up at him, seemingly a little startled.

"Because I want to talk to him about the hotel design."

She sat up, her face giving away her confusion. "The hotel design?"

"Yeah. I really liked it. It's exactly what I'm looking for."

"In what way?"

"For my house."

"You want your house to look like a hotel?" She smiled just lightly.

"No, not exactly. But, I would like to have lots of glass incorporated, like there is at the hotel. I'm in the middle of the forest. I wanna be able to see it, not shut it out. The thing is, I don't want to lose all the heat through the glass."

Becky nodded. "I see. Well, it's not really Mark you want to speak to. It's Jake Hunter."

"Jake? I know he built the hotel, but I'm still at the design stage."

"Exactly. Jake didn't just build it, he designed it too."

"He did? I had no idea."

"Do you know Jake then?"

"Oh, yeah. We go way back. He's one of Emma's oldest friends."

"Then call him. I'm sure he'll help you out."

"I will."

Becky rested back on him again and he stroked her hair gently.

"Can I talk to you?" she asked.

"Of course you can. What do you want to talk about?"

She didn't reply and a short silence followed. Nick was just wondering if he should ask again, when Becky let out a long sigh. "It's hard, but I need to tell you what Tyler did to me."

Nick tensed. "You don't have to." He wasn't entirely sure he was ready for this.

Becky straightened and looked up at him. "Yes, I do." She rested her hand gently on his chest, just over his heart, where her head had been. "I love you," she whispered.

"I love you too." He smiled down at her.

"And I want us to be together."

"So do I."

"Do you understand what I mean by that?" she asked.

"I think so. You want us to make love." He wanted that too, more than anything.

She blushed and nodded. "At some point, yes, I think I do. But I'm not sure I can."

Nick took a deep breath. "Because of what he did to you?" he asked.

"I'm frightened the memories of what he did will haunt me forever. I'm worried that, if we don't face up to it, what he did is gonna be a barrier between us; that it'll make it impossible for us to be together properly, and could maybe even break us up—"

"It won't," he interrupted, caressing her cheek with his fingertips. "Nothing's gonna break us up."

"Please, Nick," she continued, "I need to get it out in the open. I don't want to have any secrets from you." She swallowed. "I can still remember what it felt like to be with you and, deep down, I know I want that back, but I need you to understand that it's gonna be hard for me. I can't expect you to understand that, if you don't know why."

Nick nodded. At that moment, he was struggling to speak. He felt the trust she was placing in him, but he didn't know if he wanted to hear the detail. He wasn't sure he could control his emotions if she told him exactly what Tyler had done. He looked into her glistening eyes and mentally shook himself. This wasn't about him. None of this was about him.

"Tell me whatever you need to," he said, his voice much clearer than he'd expected.

"Thank you," she whispered and leant back on his chest again. He couldn't see her face, but he thought that was probably a good thing. It'd be easier for both of them.

"Do you remember, I told you that about eighteen months ago, I found out that Tyler was still having an affair?"

"Yeah."

"Well, the night I found out, I confronted him. We had a really horrible row. He called me lots of awful names and, when I could see he wasn't gonna calm down, I went upstairs to my room."

"*Your* room?" Nick queried.

"Yes. We hadn't shared a bed, or a bedroom, or had any kind of physical relationship since I found out about the affair the first time."

"I see." She'd said that was two years into her marriage. That was a long time ago…

"He barged in behind me," Becky continued and Nick heard the crack in her voice and pulled her a little closer in his arms. "I turned on him and told him I wanted a divorce and he laughed, and said it would never happen. And then…" She let out a small sob. "And then he pushed me down on the bed, on my front, and told me I needed reminding that I was his wife. He… he ripped off my skirt and panties and…"

"You don't have to tell me, Bex. I understand."

She shook her head. "No. I don't think you do…" She took a deep breath. "Let me try and finish, please." He tightened his grip on her, wondering what she was going to say. "Before I knew what was happening, he was inside me," she whispered. Nick felt his muscles clench and tried to relax. She was describing a rape, not an attempted one, even though that's what she'd called it. "But he couldn't stay hard," she continued. "He said it was my fault. He said I didn't turn him on, or words to that effect." She curled in on herself a little. "He pulled out and I thought he was going away. I was about to get up, but then I felt him pushing himself into me."

"He tried again?"

There was just a moment's pause, then Becky nodded her head. "Yes, but not in the same place."

Nick heard the blood rushing through his ears, pounding through his head. He needed to be sure he'd understood, but he didn't think she could say the words. "He forced you to have anal sex?" he whispered.

"He tried to, but he still couldn't stay hard, so he beat me." She let out a small sob. "He beat me really badly."

Nick felt enraged, but he had to keep his emotions under control. She needed love, not anger.

"It was such a shock," she murmured. "It was the worst he'd ever been, and it hurt. It really hurt." She hesitated. "Afterwards, he left and locked me in. He took my phone with him, so I couldn't even call anyone for help. I just lay there, feeling used, and dirty, and in so much pain."

He leant down and kissed the top of her head gently, stroking her hair still.

"The next day, he let me go."

"What did you do?"

"I went to the hospital." She looked up at him. "I had no choice. He'd broken two of my ribs." Nick fought every instinct in his body to try and stay calm.

"What happened?"

"They wanted to call the cops, but I wouldn't let them."

"Why not?" He slowly uncurled her and pulled her up his body, looking down at her face. She looked shocked, still disturbed by the memories.

"Not because I didn't want him punished for what he'd done, but because he's always made a point of telling me he's got friends in high places, and no-one would believe me."

"I believe you," Nick whispered.

"Thank you." She smiled up at him.

"So you went back to him?" Nick asked

"No, I went to my mom's."

"Your mom's?"

She looked up at him. "Yeah, my dad died about six months before this all happened."

"I'm sorry. I didn't know." He paused. "What happened at your mom's? Didn't she notice your injuries?"

"Yeah, but I told her I'd been in a car accident. I didn't want her getting involved."

"So you were safe?"

"No. He found me there that same night. I didn't exactly make it hard for him, did I? But then, I didn't really have anywhere else to go. Of course, my mom thought everything was fine between us, so when Tyler arrived, she cooked him dinner and he sat there at the table, talking to her, just like nothing had happened. Then later, he took me out on the porch and told me that, if I didn't go back home with him, he'd make it so much worse for me the next time." She started to sob. "I went back," she muttered through her tears.

"Come here, baby." Nick enclosed her in his arms and, thank God, she clung onto him, letting him comfort her.

They sat for a while, until Becky took a shuddering breath and sat up a little. "Do you remember, just before Christmas there was a fire at one of Mark's hotels?" she asked. "I think Mark was with Emma at the time."

"Yeah, I remember it."

"Well, Mark got a call from the police, letting him know about the fire, and that the manager had been injured, and he phoned me and asked me to drive up there. It was still early; I hadn't left the house yet, and neither had Tyler."

Nick closed his eyes, but felt Becky's fingers caressing his cheek and opened them again. "Just bear with me a little longer," she said. "I'm nearly done."

"I'm sorry," he said. "I just think I know what you're gonna tell me."

She nodded. "He didn't like the idea of me going away for an indefinite period. Mark couldn't tell me how long I'd be needed for, so I packed for a week. Tyler hit the roof and accused me of seeing Mark behind his back. He threw me down on the floor this time, tore my panties off and was about to… you know… when the doorbell rang."

"Who was it?"

She looked up at him. "It was one of his colleagues," she explained. "There are four of them who live in the same housing complex, and this guy's car wouldn't start. He needed Tyler to give him a ride to work. Tyler acted like nothing was wrong – naturally."

"And he left you there?"

"Yes. I drove up to Vermont that morning. Mark guessed something was wrong, but I couldn't tell him what. I just said things were bad. He knew Tyler hit me, so he assumed it was more of the same. He was very kind and offered to help me leave, or get a divorce. I thought about it, I really did."

"But?" He sensed there was more to come.

"But Tyler called me. He said if I told anyone what had happened, or if I did anything with Mark, or didn't get home as quickly as possible, he'd introduce me to some of his golfing buddies. He went into graphic detail about what they'd do to me… and how he was gonna watch. I was so scared, Nick. I had to stay up in Vermont for that weekend, but he made me promise to go back to him by the end of the next week. I did," she added. "I had no choice."

She shuddered in his arms and he rubbed her back and shoulders, just gently. "And then… there was this last time," she said, sounding really tired.

"This last time?"

She nodded her head. "Just before I came up here."

He sat up a little. "What happened?" he asked.

"It was kinda similar to the time before, really," she explained. "Mark had asked me to come up for the opening and to stay on while the staff got settled in. I packed a suitcase for a couple of weeks and was just trying to decide whether to leave there and then, or wait until the morning, when Tyler came home. I'd locked myself in my room, but he threatened to break the door down. I didn't want to make him mad; I knew the consequences of doing that." Tears formed in her eyes. "I let him in." She looked at him. "I shouldn't have done that, should I?"

"You did the right thing," Nick reassured her. "He'd have broken the door down anyway, and been really mad at you. At least letting him in, you probably diffused the situation a little. Don't blame yourself, baby."

"It didn't help much." She sniffed. "He saw the size of my bag and knew I'd be going away for more than a couple of days, and then he started hurling accusations about Mark again. He pushed me down onto the bed and he tore my clothes. I tried to get away, but he threatened me with his golfing buddies – just like the last time. He told me he'd actually spoken to them, and that they were interested. Well, he said 'keen', to be precise. He said he wanted to watch them both take me at the same time, and that idea seemed to really turn him on. There was absolutely no chance of him not staying hard, not while he was thinking about that, and he was just about to… to force himself inside me… when a switch just kinda flicked inside my head. I got so damn mad at him." She almost smiled. Almost. "I'd had enough."

"What did you do?"

"I—I told him that I didn't care what he did to me."

"Seriously?" Nick was shocked.

"Well, I did care, obviously, but I wanted to hurt him, and I suddenly realized a good way to do it." She stared up into his eyes. "I told him he could rape my body if he wanted to, but it didn't matter, because my heart had always belonged to you…"

Nick stared at her. "You told him that?"

She nodded. "It was a risk, but I couldn't just lie there and let him do that to me. I was sick to death of being a victim. I knew you couldn't save me – not in person," she murmured. "But I thought maybe your name might."

"He stopped?"

"Oh yes, he stopped. That's when he hit me."

"Jesus, Bex." He spoke through gritted teeth.

"This will heal," she said, gently touching her bruised cheek and eye.

"I know." He held her. "I think you're an incredible person," he said after just a moment's pause. "You're so strong, and so brave."

"I don't feel very brave."

"You took such a risk, mentioning my name."

"Especially as he'd always told me that he didn't ever want to hear your name on my lips. Up until the other night, he had no idea how I felt about you, but he always hated the fact that you were my first, and not him. I guess that's how I knew it would work. I knew he'd hate to think that I'd always loved you. He still tried to get his revenge, even after he'd hit me."

"How?" Nick asked. "What did he do?"

"He didn't *do* anything. He told me you'd never loved me." Nick snorted out a laugh and went to speak, but she covered his mouth with her fingers. "He said you'd slept with me and realized how useless I was, and that was why you went with Kelly."

Nick pulled her hand away from his mouth. "Okay. That's enough." He kissed her fingers, one by one. "I always loved you, Bex. Always. Making love with you was beautiful, baby, just beautiful. I've lived on those memories for nine years. If you'd been anything but perfect for me, I wouldn't have waited, would I?" Becky shook her head slowly. He placed his finger under her chin and raised her face to his, looking into her eyes. "I didn't sleep with Kelly. I didn't want to. I kissed her. That's all. It was a dumb thing to do and I've regretted it every single day for the last nine years. But I need you to believe me… I've never wanted or loved anyone but you."

He leant down and kissed her, tenderly covering her lips with his, then quickly pulled away again.

"I'm kinda relieved my name saved you, Bex. I just wish I could have been there to do it in person."

"So do I." She snuggled into him and a silence descended over them both.

"Is there anything else you wanna tell me?" he asked eventually.

"No, that's all of it." She sighed. "I'm sorry if that was hard for you to hear. It was hard for me to tell, but I needed to."

"I know. And don't be sorry. I'm honored that you trust me enough to tell me." She looked up at him and he sensed she was waiting her him to tell her how he felt about her revelations. He wasn't sure he could do that, not without getting mad, and maybe scaring her. But the point of her telling her story had been to clear the air between them, to avoid them having secrets, and to try and help them have a full, intimate, loving relationship, and he *could* respond to that. He sat her forward a little so he could see her face, which he clasped in his hands, so she was forced to look at him. "Thank you for telling me," he whispered. "I understand how tough that must've been for you." He stopped and shook his head. "Actually, I don't have a clue how tough that was. I've never experienced anything like that, so it's real patronizing of me to say I have even the vaguest understanding of what you've been through, or how difficult it must've been for you to tell me about it." He paused for a moment. "I do understand why you told me. I get that you want us to be able to touch each other and taste each other and make love again one day, but that it's gonna be hard for you to forget what he did to you." She nodded her head and Nick saw her eyes glistening. "Don't cry, Bex," he murmured. "It's gonna be just fine. I want exactly the same things as you do. I want to touch your beautiful body, to feel your soft skin next to mine, to hold you naked in my arms. I want you so much, baby, it hurts. My body aches for you. But I'll wait as long as it takes for you to be ready." He shifted in his seat, not letting go of her, his eyes piercing hers. "I want you to listen real carefully to what I'm gonna say next," he said. She nodded. "Everything we do from now on is your choice. You make the decisions. You dictate the pace… for everything."

"How?" Her voice was barely audible. "I'm a different person now. I don't know how to do that anymore."

"You're not a different person. Deep inside, you're the same as you always were. We've just gotta bring you out of yourself again."

"How?"

"By reminding you how good it can be. By making you feel safe. By getting you to understand that you never have to do anything you don't want to… You've just gotta relax, and trust me, and allow your body to guide you."

"But how?" she repeated, a little desperately.

He smiled. She needed specifics… "It's easy, baby. If you want me to kiss you more deeply, then just use your tongue. I'll respond to you." He saw her cheeks flush slightly, and he continued, "If you want me to touch you, and you don't want to say that out loud, just take my hand and put it wherever you want it to be. I'll work it out. If you want to touch me, then just do it. And, if you want to make love, then you can take me. I'll do whatever you want, wherever and whenever you want, entirely at your pace." He kissed her very gently. "I don't care how long it takes, Bex. I've waited so long for you to come back to me, now you're here, nothing else matters. Just seeing you, holding you, talking to you, spending time with you and knowing you're safe is enough for me. You take as long as you need to feel comfortable, and I'll wait. I promised myself once that I'd never stop waiting for you, and I've never broken a promise in my life."

# Chapter Ten

## *Becky*

"You okay?" Nick looked across at her as he started the engine.

"Yes, thank you." She smiled, and he reversed his truck around and drove onto the bumpy lane, heading toward the main road. "I'm just really tired," she added.

"You've had two late nights," he said, looking at the clock on the dashboard. "It's gone midnight. I'm sorry, I didn't mean to keep you so late."

"It's fine. We had things to talk about. And don't apologize, it was me doing most of the talking."

He glanced across at her. "Close your eyes if you want to. I'll wake you up when we get there."

Becky knew she wouldn't sleep, but she was struggling to keep her eyes open and let them close softly. Nick's kindness and understanding had been almost overwhelming. He'd accepted everything she'd told him, although she'd felt his muscles tensing around her when she'd revealed what Tyler had done, but that was hardly surprising, really. She sighed out a breath, feeling a sense of relief wash over her. The freedom he was giving her to dictate the course and speed of their relationship felt liberating and she was grateful, but she had no idea how to go about communicating her own needs and desires to him. Despite everything he'd said, and how easy, and even exciting he'd made it sound, she wasn't sure she could take control like that. And did he really want her to? Long forgotten memories of how Nick used to be crossed her mind and she shifted in her seat as the thought crossed her mind that, regardless of what he'd said, Nick might end up feeling belittled by his suggestions.

She felt the car stop and opened her eyes again. They were parked out the front of the hotel and Nick climbed down and walked around to her side of the truck, opening her door and helping her out.

"I'd offer to carry you," he whispered, "but I think your staff might get the wrong idea."

"Yeah. I'm sure they'd like nothing more than something to gossip about."

"Sounds just like Somers Cove," he replied, smiling. "Come on." He held out his hand and she took it, letting him lead her through the revolving doors to the elevator.

"It's late," she whispered as they waited. "You don't have to see me upstairs."

He looked down at her. "Yeah, I do."

The elevator doors opened silently and she felt his hand in the small of her back, guiding her inside. As the doors closed again, he took a step closer. "You're not going to your room by yourself," he said firmly and she leant into him and felt his arm come around her.

"That's the office," Becky said, nodding to the frosted double doors opposite the elevator on the third floor.

"And your room?" Nick asked.

She turned to the left. "Just down here."

He took her hand again and they walked slowly down the corridor, their feet falling silently into the deep carpet. Becky stopped at the first door on the left and pulled a card from the pocket in her purse, holding it over a scanner to the right of the door, which released the lock.

She went to go in, but Nick put his hand across her. "Just let me check it out," he said and she waited while he went in, turning on the lights and looking around. "Nice room," he said as he came back out, smiling down at her.

"Can I go in now?" she asked.

He stood to one side. "Sure. Just call me paranoid."

She turned as she was crossing the threshold and placed her hand on his chest. "I'll just call you caring, if it's all the same to you."

He rewarded her with a broad smile, his eyes lighting up. It felt so good to know he loved her.

He followed her into the room and pushed the door closed behind him. "I'll speak to Tom in the morning, and set up a time for you to meet with him, and then I'll call you?" he suggested. "And we'll need to arrange for you to pick up your car." She nodded.

"Thank you for this evening," she murmured, putting her bag down on the bed and coming back over to him. "You were very kind."

He reached out and ran the backs of his fingers down her cheek. "I wasn't being kind, Bex," he murmured.

"No, you were just being you." She saw his cheeks redden. She wasn't sure she'd ever seen him blush before. He looked even more adorable than normal.

"I guess I'd better be going," he said quietly. "You're tired, and we've both got work tomorrow."

She nodded, and he took a step nearer, his hands resting on her waist, and leant down to place his lips gently against hers. In that second, she decided to take a chance. She wanted just a little bit more of him, and she very hesitantly touched the tip of her tongue against his lips. She heard his rumbling groan as he opened to her and she delved inside, just a little. He let her find his tongue with ease, but kept his movements light, just teasing back with his own and letting her set the pace, exactly as he'd promised. She had all the power, and it felt great.

She moved closer, her breasts brushing against his hard chest, and heard him groan again as her tongue roamed a little deeper. He kept his hands still, even as hers began to slide up his arms and around his neck, then into his hair. Her breathing was heavier, more ragged, and she decided she needed to stop, before she got carried away. Reluctantly, she pulled back and looked up into his face. His eyes were closed, but he slowly opened them and smiled down at her.

"That was perfect," he whispered.

"It was?"

He nodded. Becky's thoughts from the journey home began to crowd into her head and, before she knew it, they'd formed into words which started to flow from her mouth…

"Is it enough?" she asked.

"Is what enough?" He seemed confused.

"This. Us, being like this? I appreciate you giving control to me, Nick, but doesn't it feel like you're being a little – I don't know – emasculated by the whole thing?"

His smile broadened. "No," he said simply. "That kind of thing doesn't matter… not really." She studied his face. "Okay," he continued, and she knew he'd seen the doubt in her eyes. "Let me put it this way… Sure, I'd love to remove your clothes, piece by piece, lay you down on the bed, kiss your whole body, and make love to you real long and hard, and slow, I'm not gonna deny that." She felt herself blush, but she also felt a warm glow deep inside. "The thing is, I know we'll get there one day… and in the meantime, I wanna concentrate on making you feel happy, and safe, and satisfied." His voice dropped a note on the last word and he kissed her again, very gently. "Besides," he added, "do I look emasculated to you?" He grinned and stood back a little so she could take him in.

She let her eyes roam over his body… he fit his jeans to perfection, his shirt clung to his muscular arms and chest and his eyes were sparkling at her in a way she remembered oh so well. He exuded masculinity.

She shook her head. "I guess not."

"Then don't sweat it, Bex."


So far, the morning had been slow, probably not helped by the fact that she'd been waiting nervously for Nick to call, and he hadn't. He'd texted her first thing, to say hello and check she'd slept okay, but she'd heard nothing about the appointment with Tom and she was starting to wonder if something was wrong.

A single tap on her door was followed by it opening and Mark appeared, saying, "Hi."

"Good morning. I wasn't expecting you today, was I?"

Mark shook his head and came and sat down on one of the chairs facing her. "No," he said. "but I needed to talk to you and it seemed easier to do it face-to-face, rather than over the phone."

Becky put down her pen. "That sounds ominous."

"It's not." He sat back, looking relaxed, put his legs out straight and crossed them at the ankles. "It's good just to sit down for ten minutes."

She stared at him. "Have you been busy then?"

"I've been holding Emma's hair back while she's been being sick. Does that count?" He smirked.

"Stop grinning. I imagine morning sickness is horrible."

"It is."

"I meant for Emma."

"So did I." He tried to sound genuine.

"Have you left her at home by herself?" Becky asked, a little surprised.

"No. I've just dropped her off at the coffee shop."

"She's gone to work?"

Mark nodded. "Yeah. It's weird. It seems she gets to about ten-thirty and she starts to feel a little better, so she felt like she should go in. I'm gonna go back and check on her in a couple of hours." He glanced at his watch. "For the time being, Patsy has agreed to open up the shop each morning, which makes things easier, and when I left, she'd even agreed to start learning the basics on the barista machine – wonders will never cease. Still, at least the morning sickness probably won't go on for too long, so the doc says…" His voice faded to a whisper.

"Yeah. It's only a couple of weeks until the wedding now. The last thing Emma needs is to spend the day being sick."

Mark nodded. "Luckily, the ceremony itself isn't until the afternoon. The timing should be fine. We've worked out that if she eats little and often, she can keep the nausea at bay. She's worried about putting on weight now though." He smiled.

"Then I hope you're being suitably reassuring," Becky warned.

"Of course."

"Good. Make sure it stays that way." Becky wagged a finger at him, jokingly. She felt a certain solidarity with Emma, now she'd met her.

"Now, did you have a reason for coming over here and disturbing my day?"

"Yeah, I did." Mark sat up and moved his chair a little closer to her desk. "I've been thinking…"

"Really? They make pills for that, don't they?"

"Haha." He gave her a mocking look. "I could demote you to chamber maid, you know."

"Go ahead. See how long you can last without me." She smirked at him.

"Yeah." He shook his head. "That's why I'm here."

"You're gonna make me a chamber maid?"

"No. But Emma needs me right now, which means I need you back doing your real job, Becky. Sooner rather than later."

"And what about this place?" She gestured at the paperwork scattered across her desk. "I don't see—"

"I know," Mark interrupted, "but I've had an idea…"

"You have?"

"Yeah. Remember Kyle?"

"Kyle Langton?" Mark nodded. "The guy who was managing the Vermont hotel when it burned down?"

"Yeah, but that wasn't his fault, was it? We can't hold that against him."

"No…" Becky shook her head, suddenly fearful about what Mark was going to suggest.

"Well," he began, "he's been back at work for a couple of weeks, but the best position I could find for him was assistant manager at Bridgeport…"

"But that's a really small hotel. He's a bit wasted there, isn't he?" Becky queried.

"Yeah." Mark rested his hands on Becky's desk. "It's not ideal, but I didn't want Kyle to leave."

"No, I understand that."

"Which brings me to my idea. He could come and take over from you here." Mark gestured around her office. "I don't know why I didn't think of it before. It's perfect. He's ideal for this place."

"He's really good at his job," Becky said, being fair. "And me?" she added.

"You'd stay on until the end of the week as we planned, just to make sure everything's running smoothly, and then go back to Boston," Mark said.

Becky felt the blood drain from her face. "Boston?" she whispered.

"Yeah. You could handle my Boston meetings for me, and obviously go back to doing your old job again…" His voice faded. "Becky?" He got up and came around to her side of the desk. "What's wrong?"

"Nothing."

"Bullshit. You might have plastered makeup all over your face again, but you've gone real pale."

She looked down at her hands, which were clasped in her lap to stop them from shaking.

"I—I don't want to go back," she murmured.

"Back to Boston?"

She nodded.

He leant against the edge of her desk, looking down at her.

"Wanna tell me why?" he asked.

The words were caught in her throat. How much could she tell him?

"I take it this is to do with that piece of shit you're married to?"

"Partly," she murmured.

"Okay," he said softly. "I've said it before and I'll say it again no doubt, but why don't you just leave the son-of-a-bitch? You know I'll help you. You've just gotta ask…"

"It's not just about Tyler."

"Then what?" he asked.

"I really want to stay here," she said quietly, lowering her head again. "I—I spent a lot of the weekend with Nick…"

"You did?" She didn't have to look up to know he was smiling; she could hear it in his voice.

"Yes," she said. "We talked. We talked a lot, and he knows all about Tyler." She looked up at him again. She was right, he was smiling. "He knows *everything*." A look of confusion clouded his eyes, but it passed quickly. "We're back together," she murmured. "And I know that's weird, considering I'm still married, but—"

"I think it's great." Mark interrupted.

"Nick's gonna help me," she continued. "He's gonna speak with the man he works with about helping me file for a divorce."

"About fucking time!" She glanced up and couldn't help but smile.

"Yeah, I know. The thing is, Tyler was telling me I couldn't divorce him. He said it was impossible because the law was on his side, but I spoke to Nick and he said that wasn't true. He explained it all, and he's gonna help me work it out."

"He's a good guy, Becky."

She nodded. "I know. He makes me feel safe, for the first time in years." She heard him sigh quietly. "But you still need me to do my job, don't you?" she said, looking up again.

She was surprised to see Mark shaking his head. "Not that much, I don't." He ran his hand across his chin, clearly thinking, then pushed himself off the table and walked around the other side again, sitting back down in the seat. "I want you to stay on here," he announced.

"But—"

He held up a hand and she stopped speaking.

"But nothing. I'm still gonna bring Kyle in," he continued. "You can do your job out of the offices upstairs for the time being."

"And what about the Boston meetings?"

"I'll take those."

"And Emma?"

"I'll work it out."

"Mark. That's not fair…"

"I said, I'll work it out. It won't be forever. Just until your divorce gets underway. Once Tyler realizes your marriage is over and he's got no way back with you, I'm sure things will quieten down and you'll feel safer going back to the city for the odd day here and there. You'll still have to travel around, just like you used to, and I'll get you to cover some of the other meetings around the area, if that's okay, but I'll keep you out of Boston."

She nodded. It would mean being away from Nick for a couple of nights a week, but at least she'd be nowhere near Tyler.

"Are you sure you don't mind?" she asked.

"Absolutely."

He got to his feet.

"Thank you, Mark," she said quietly. "I didn't realize until I met up with Nick again, how scared I really was of Tyler."

"Didn't you?" He looked down at her. "That's weird. I did."

## Nick

Nick ran his fingers through his hair and stared across the desk at Tom.

"Why?" he asked.

Tom shook his head. "Because you went to college with her." Tom sounded as though he thought Nick was being more than a little dumb. "You're hardly impartial."

"Which is why I'm asking you to take the case. And anyway, so what if I went to college with her? You were at college with the CEO of GHC Engineering. That hasn't stopped you from taking on their work." They'd spent the first hour of the morning arguing over the result of Tom's weekend, which was that he'd agreed to take on his old friend's account – without consulting Nick. Nick wasn't happy about it, but he'd accepted it, and they'd spent the next hour re-arranging their work schedules to accommodate GHC's cases, which basically meant Nick taking over everything else that Tom had been dealing with. Now he'd finally been able to move the conversation on to Becky's divorce, only Tom didn't seem willing to help. "This is just a divorce. We've handled lots of them in the past for people we've known."

Tom looked down at the file in front of him, not that Nick knew what it was. "We've got a lot of work on," Tom said, trying to sound reasonable.

"Yeah, I know we have. But this should just be a simple contested no fault divorce."

"Contested?" Tom queried. "So maybe not as simple as you think?"

"A lot less complicated than if Becky was using her husband's adultery," Nick pointed out. He wasn't going to mention Tyler's assaults, not yet. "And we've dealt with a lot worse."

"I still don't think we've got time." Tom closed the file now, moving it to one side of his desk. "Wouldn't she be better off employing a lawyer in Boston?"

Nick shook his head. "She's gonna be here for a while. And her husband works for a Boston firm…"

"He's a lawyer?"

Nick nodded. "Yeah. I think it's best she avoids any companies that he might be involved with."

"I didn't realize the husband was a lawyer," Tom said, his voice a little distant.

"What difference does it make?"

Tom looked up. To Nick, it seemed as though he'd just come back from somewhere far away. "Are we sure she can afford our fees?" Tom asked.

"I imagine so. But if she can't, then I'll pay."

Tom raised an eyebrow and Nick wondered if he'd gone too far. He'd spent the last half hour convincing Tom there was nothing going on between him and Becky. "Why are you being like this?" he asked, deflecting Tom's attention.

"Like what?"

"So negative, so interested in money all of a sudden. I've done favors for several of your friends over the years. I've never asked for anything in return, until now."

"I'm just not sure it's a good idea," Tom persevered.

"I wasn't sure it was a good idea for you to bring in all that work from GHC, but you've gone ahead and done it anyway. All I'm asking is that you take on this simple divorce for an old friend of mine, and you won't even see her and talk it through? Jesus, Tom…" Nick raised his voice and got up, turning toward the door. "I don't know what's wrong with you, but I think you'd better start looking around for a new partner. I'm really not sure I wanna work with you anymore."

Nick hadn't even taken two paces before Tom was at his side.

"What do you mean?" he asked, his voice unsteady.

"Exactly what I say, Tom. This is meant to be an equal partnership, but you seem to think you can dictate what we do, and who we do it for." Nick stepped forward again.

"Wait!" Tom called. Nick turned and saw the sallow complexion on his friend's face. His eyes seemed to have sunk and his mouth had an almost blue tinge. "I can't afford to lose you," Tom whispered. "I can't handle all this work by myself."

"I know you can't," Nick said.

They stared at each other for a moment before Nick saw Tom's shoulders drop.

"Okay, I'll see your friend," he offered.

"Thank you," Nick conceded.

"I'm not making any promises," Tom continued. "I'll see her, but I'm not committing to taking her case."

Nick shrugged. "Okay."

"I can't fit her in until next Monday morning," Tom added, going back around to his side of the desk again, and looking in his appointment diary. "I've got a slot at ten-thirty."

"That's the earliest you can see her? A week from today?" Nick was surprised. He was more than surprised; he was incredulous. Becky only needed an hour of Tom's time. This was obviously another stalling tactic, in the hope that Becky wouldn't want to wait and would go elsewhere.

"Yes. Take it or leave it."

"She'll take it."

Tom shrugged and made a note in his diary.

Nick went back into his office and slumped down in his chair, letting his head fall into his hands. He'd genuinely thought that getting Tom to help out with Becky's divorce was going to be a formality, except nothing with Tom seemed to be simple these days.

His grumbling stomach told him it must be nearly lunchtime and he remembered he'd promised to call Becky as soon as he'd spoken to Tom. She'd probably be worried by now. He pulled his phone from his pocket. He had several missed calls; none of them were from Becky, but two were from Mark, which was unusual. He toyed with the idea of calling Mark first, but decided he could wait until after he'd spoken to Becky. He called up her details, waiting for the phone to connect.

"Hello." She answered on the second ring, sounding wary.

"Hi," he replied. "How are you?"

"I'm okay." That didn't sound like she was too certain.

"I've spoken to Tom," he said, hoping to reassure her.

"And?"

"And he's gonna see you next Monday at ten-thirty. I'm sorry it can't be before then, but he's slammed at the moment."

"That's fine." She didn't sound as relieved as he'd hoped she would.

"Are you sure?" he said. "You don't sound too happy about it."

"I'm sorry," she murmured and he struggled to hear her. "I've just had a difficult morning."

"Why? Tell me about it."

He heard her sigh and waited. "Mark came over," she began. "He's going to bring in a permanent manager here later this week…"

Nick felt his blood turn to ice. She was leaving? Already?

"You're going?" he managed to say.

"No."

*Thank fuck for that.* "Then I don't understand. I thought…"

"He wanted me to go back to Boston."

"You can't." There was no way she was going anywhere near Boston.

"I know. I told him."

"You told him what?"

"I told him I can't go back. I told him I want to say here, and I told him about us," she whispered. He could imagine her blushing. The thought made him smile a little.

"You did?"

"Yes." There was a pause. "Are you okay with that?"

"Of course I'm okay with that."

"It's just, I realized afterwards that I should probably have kept quiet about us being together, what with the divorce and everything. I'm sure it's not—" He could hear the panic rising in her voice.

"Bex, it's fine. Stop worrying. Mark's hardly likely to tell Tyler about us."

"No… I guess."

"So, what did he say?"

"He said you're a good guy."

"Well, that's real nice of him." Nick smiled. "I meant, what did he say about you staying on here?"

"Oh, I see. He was fine with it. Part of my job has always been to go around to the hotels, do spot checks, make sure they don't have any problems, just remind them we're there if they need us. He still wants me to do that."

"So you *are* going?" He heard his own fear.

"No. I'll just have to be away for a couple of nights a week. The rest of the time I'll be here."

"And will you have to go to Boston as part of this traveling?" He really didn't like that thought.

"No. Ordinarily I would, but in the circumstances, Mark said he'd cover any Boston appointments."

"He did?"

"Yes. Is that a problem?" Becky must have sensed something was wrong from the tone of his voice.

"No. But it might make sense of why Mark called me twice this morning. I'll phone him back and see what his plans are."

"I don't understand."

"I'm sorry, I'm not making sense, am I?"

"Not really, no."

"I have to think about Emma as well in all this."

"Oh, I see." He could hear the disappointed tone in Becky's voice.

"Hey… You come first, baby," he whispered. "You always come first."

"I'm sensing a but, Nick."

He paused. "There isn't really. I just need to check with Nick that he's remembered to let me know when he's going to be out of town, so I can keep an eye on Emma, that's all."

"Oh, okay." That note of sadness still lay behind her voice and Nick knew he needed to explain the situation with Emma, but not over the phone.

"Where are you gonna be working from, when you're here?" he asked, trying to change the subject a little.

"The offices here at the hotel," she replied. "At least for the time being…"

"And you'll only be away a couple of nights a week?"

"Yes, at most."

"Good. I've only just got you back. I don't like the idea of you leaving again."

"Neither do I." He wondered if she was feeling sad about that too, not just about his unexplained attitude toward Emma.

"What do you want to do tonight?" he asked.

"I'm really tired." Hell, was she saying she didn't want to see him? "I was wondering…" He held his breath. "Would you mind if we had dinner at the hotel? There's no charge."

He sighed out his relief. "I don't care if there is a charge. I'd love to have dinner with you at the hotel." He'd have dinner with her anywhere, as long as she was still happy to see him. "What time do you finish work?" he asked.

"I'll be done around seven…"

"Okay. And do we need to work out getting your car back over to you?"

"No. We can deal with it another day."

"Great. I'll just come straight over after work then."

"Okay. Come up to my room."

"With pleasure, baby." He smiled and heard what sounded like a sigh on the end of the phone.

Mark answered his phone on the fourth ring.

"What on earth is that noise?" Nick asked.

"I'm at the coffee shop. It's lunchtime," Mark explained. "And it's really busy."

"Oh. Well, why don't I come over there and we can talk and eat at the same time," Nick suggested. His stomach was growling even more now.

"Because we need to talk in private; away from my future wife."

"Okay. Come over to the office then, and can you get Noah to put together a turkey sandwich for me, and bring it with you? Tell Emma I'll pay her back later. I'm starving."

"Sure. I'll see you in ten minutes."

Nick took a bite from his sandwich and listened to Mark explaining how he was going to bring in a guy called Kyle Langton to take over as the permanent manager of the hotel, which would free up Becky to do her normal job.

"I know," Nick said, swallowing. "Bex told me."

"Bex?" Mark grinned. "You call her Bex?"

"Yeah. Always did." He put down his half-eaten sandwich. "And don't get any ideas. She's still Becky to you. Okay?"

Mark held up his hands. "Okay. I know better than to argue with you."

Nick nodded his head. "She also told me that you're gonna be going to Boston more often."

"Well, she doesn't want to go there. I understand why, but one of us has to."

Nick looked at him. "Is that why you were trying to call me?"

"Yeah. I wanted to let you know that I'm gonna be away for maybe one night a week, probably starting next Wednesday. I'm gonna try and work from home for this week, but I know there's a meeting next Thursday morning that someone has to cover, and it can't be Becky."

"No. I'll make sure to keep in touch with Emma while you're away, and I'll go and see her if she needs me to."

"Thanks. I appreciate it."

"Don't thank me. You're helping Becky out. It's the least I can do. Besides, Emma's my sister and…"

"I know… we're family." Mark smiled.

"Bex said that she'd told you about us," Nick said, after just a moment's pause.

"Yeah. And she said something else that had me kinda worried."

Nick looked across the table, his brow furrowing.

"What was that?"

"She said that you know everything, with an emphasis on the 'everything', which implied that I don't." Mark leant forward and lowered his voice, even though they were alone in the office. "I've known for years that her excuse of a husband beats the shit out of her whenever he gets the chance. I've been trying to persuade her to leave him for ages."

"I know."

"She told you that?"

"Yeah."

"So, what did she mean when she said you know everything, Nick? I'm not prying, but I spend a lot of time with Becky and, if there's anything I can do…"

"I don't think there is. Just knowing she doesn't have to go back there is really helping her."

"I think getting back with you is what's *really* helping."

Nick felt his cheeks flush. "It's been a damn long wait," he murmured.

"Wait?"

Nick raised his head. "Yeah. Nine years. It's a fucking long time to wait."

"You mean…?" Mark stared at him. "You mean you've been on your own for nine years, waiting for her?"

Nick nodded.

"Jeez." Mark shook his head. "You and Emma. You're like peas in a pod, you really are."

Nick raised an eyebrow. "I'm not even gonna ask what that means," he said. He thought he could guess though. He knew Emma hadn't seen anyone when she'd been apart from Mark for four years, and he thought maybe Mark had a point.

"Can I ask you something?" Mark said eventually.

"Sure."

"Is there more to it with Becky than hitting? Is that what she meant about you knowing everything?"

Nick huffed out a breath. "Yes, but I can't tell you about it. She might tell you all of it herself, one day, when she's feeling stronger. For now, you're just gonna have to use your imagination." He leant forward. "And let it go dark…"

"Fuck." Mark whispered.

Nick sighed. "She's terrified of him. And she's right to be. I can keep her safe when she's with me, but she's not with me all the time." He paused. "We're not at the stage of spending the night together yet, and I don't know how long it's gonna take for Bex to get there." He ran his finger along the edge of his desk. "So, can I ask a favor?"

"Of course."

"Can you tell the people at your hotel not to let Tyler into her office, or her room, or anywhere near her? Can you ask them to call me – or you – if he goes anywhere near the place? Give them my cell number. I don't care what time of the day or night it is, I want them to call me if he turns up."

"I don't know what he looks like," Mark said. "I've never met him."

"There's a photograph of him on his company's website. I'll send you the link to it."

Mark nodded. "Okay. I'll send that out, with a message to call you or me if he shows up." He looked up at Nick. "Do you think he will?"

Nick shrugged. "Who knows? Tyler isn't renowned for being rational."

"No, I guess not."

# Chapter Eleven

## *Becky*

Becky stood in her underwear and stared at the clothes hanging in the closet. She was being indecisive, and she knew it. The restaurant at the hotel didn't have a strict dress code, so she could wear jeans, if she felt like it. She was fairly sure Nick would be. But she felt like getting a little bit dressed up. Not dressed up in the way that Tyler would expect; nothing fitted, nothing fancy, but just something a little smarter than jeans. She'd kept her makeup on, because she didn't want the hotel staff to see her bruises, but other than that, she wanted to be herself. She pulled out the wine-colored dress and held it up. She'd had it for a few months, but never had the opportunity to wear it. The neckline was daring and she hesitated, then shrugged her shoulders and pulled it from the hanger. Just as she was about to lower it over her head, she realized she couldn't wear a bra, not with that neckline, so she unclipped her lacy white bra, threw it on the bed, alongside her work suit, and put on the dress. Straightening it, she looked up into the full-length mirror and tilted her head from one side to the other. The skirt was full and, as she swung about, it moved with her, the long sleeves touching just below her wrists. The waistband was wide and featured embroidered flowers in shades of pink, white, and pale green, which were mirrored on the edges of the plunging v-neckline that ended just between her breasts. She'd fallen in love with this dress the moment she'd seen it. She'd known Tyler would hate it, but she'd figured he'd never even know about it, and she could just about afford it, so she'd bought it and kept it hidden from him, saving it for one of her trips away… like this. Now, she wondered whether Nick would like it.

Becky checked her watch. He was due any minute. She didn't have time to change again anyway. She pulled out her black knee-high boots – another thing Tyler hated – and sat down on the edge of the bed to put them on, just as she heard the knock on her door.

Leaving her boots aside, Becky crossed the room and pulled the door open, and her breath caught in her throat. Nick was leaning against the wall opposite, and he looked spectacular – as ever. He'd obviously been home and showered. His hair was damp at the ends. He was wearing his 'uniform', but with dark blue jeans, a white shirt, undone at the neck and a gray tie, and waistcoat. And over the top, he wore a navy blue pea coat.

His eyes wandered down her body and back up to her face again.

"That is one amazing dress," he murmured, pushing himself off the wall. "You look beautiful."

She wondered if he could sense her relief. "Thank you," she whispered. "Come in for a minute while I put my boots on."

"Sure."

He followed her into the room, closing the door behind him and stood waiting while she sat down again, pulling her boots on and zipping them up.

"Ready?" he asked, as she stood.

"I think so." She turned and noticed her clothes and bra still lying on the bed. "Sorry," she mumbled. "Forgive me. I should have cleaned up. I'm sorry." She started to pick up her clothes, folding them over her arm. "I'll just put these in the laundry."

"Bex." Nick moved further into the room, coming closer and standing in front of her. "You're doing it again."

"What?" She looked up at him, feeling flustered.

"Apologizing when you haven't done anything wrong. Remember? I said I'm unlikely to ever get mad at you." She nodded slowly. "Well…" He reached out and took her clothes from her, dropping them on the floor. "I don't give a damn whether you leave your clothes on your bed, on the floor, scattered around the room, or if you're a complete neat freak." He placed his hands on her cheeks. "None of that matters. Okay?"

"Okay. I'm sorry."

He sighed. "Stop it." He looked deep into her eyes, moving closer, so their bodies were touching. "The only thing that matters is that I love you."

She felt a lump in her throat, tears pricking behind her eyes. "Oh, Nick," she whispered.

"Shh, baby… It's gonna be okay."

He bent down and, as he kissed her gently, she'd never felt more sure of anything in her life.

As they waited for the elevator, Nick turned to her.

"I had a long conversation with Mark earlier," he said.

"Oh?"

"Yeah. You know I said I wouldn't get mad at you?" He looked down at her a little warily and she felt nervous.

"Yes."

"Can you promise me that for at least the next five minutes, you won't get mad at me?"

She felt her shoulders relax and smiled up at him. "I'll do my best," she said and he nodded.

"Okay." He took a deep breath and she wondered what he was going to say next. "I've asked Mark to get the staff here to look out for you."

She felt the hairs on the back of her neck stand on end and pulled her hand away from his, although he grabbed it back quickly. "You promised," he said.

"No, I didn't. I said I'd do my best."

"Okay, then keep trying."

"Why would you do that, Nick?" The last thing she needed was to become a subject of speculation and gossip.

"Because I can't be here all the time, baby." His voice softened just as the elevator arrived and they stepped on board. Becky took the opportunity to pull her hand away, as Nick pressed the button for the lobby, and the doors slowly closed. They stood side by side, neither touching the other.

"Did you tell Mark what Tyler did?" Becky asked, feeling sick.

"No, of course not. I think he's guessed, if you want me to be honest, but I didn't tell him. Only you can decide who knows about that. The point is, I can't be with you all the time and we've got no idea what Tyler's gonna do, so I've just asked Mark to issue an instruction that, if Tyler comes here looking for you, they should contact me, or Mark – that's all."

"You're sure?"

"Yes, I'm sure." He moved so he was facing her, taking both her hands in his. "I'd never do anything to undermine your position in Mark's company, or at this hotel," he said quietly, "but I have to know you're safe. I have to know that, when I'm not around, there are other people to look out for you." His voice faded to a whisper as the doors opened again.

Becky didn't hesitate for a moment, but leant up and kissed him on the lips. He didn't have time to respond before she moved away again, smiling. "Thank you," she murmured. "I'm sorry if I overreacted."

"You didn't." He turned and, keeping hold of one of her hands, he led her to the restaurant.

"It's not long to go now, is it?" Becky said, glancing at the menu. They were talking about Mark and Emma's wedding, which was less than three weeks away.

"No. And things are hotting up."

"Really?" Becky put the menu down again, looking across at him. In the dimmed candlelight of the restaurant, he looked even more handsome than normal. His tousled hair hung down to just below his chin line, his gray eyes glinted and shone, his chin looked stubbled and rugged, and his muscles flexed every time he moved. There was something a little wild about Nick, something kind of untamable, and yet she'd never felt in any way scared of, or threatened by him. She just felt safe. Safe and loved.

"Yeah. Emma called just before I left work. She's finally decided what to do about inviting our parents."

"There was a doubt about it?" Becky couldn't hide her surprise.

"Oh yeah." Nick smiled. "You never met our parents, did you?"

Becky shook her head.

"If you had, you'd have understood Emma's reservations." Nick glanced at his watch. "She and Mark will be at my parents' house now," he said.

"So, she decided to invite them?"

"Yeah. She couldn't handle the hassle of not doing it."

"And why is them being there going to be so much trouble?"

Nick laughed. "Because they're a royal pain in the ass." He shook his head. "Or to be more precise, they're Mr and Mrs Perfect – in their own eyes, anyway. They've never let Emma forget any of her shortcomings."

"I wasn't aware Emma had any." Becky tried to hide her lingering resentment that Nick had seemed more concerned about Emma's wellbeing than anything else during their telephone conversation earlier. She'd spent the whole afternoon trying to forget it, but it wasn't working.

"She doesn't," Nick replied. "Not major ones, anyway, but they like to remind her that she only lasted one semester at college and that she works in a coffee shop."

"She practically *owns* a coffee shop," Becky put in.

"She does now. But trust me, even marrying a multi-millionaire won't be enough for them. I'm sure they'll manage to find some fault with Mark."

"And they just do this to Emma?" Becky asked.

"No. They do it to me too. The difference is, I don't give a fuck." He grinned. "I've always been a bit rebellious. They didn't like it. So, I came first in my year at college, was offered a handful of top jobs in Boston, but decided to come back here instead of making it big in the city. They were real disappointed in me and didn't hold back in letting me know."

"You're kidding."

Nick shook his head and opened his mouth to say more when the waiter arrived to take their order.

"Are we ready?" Nick asked, looking at Becky.

"Well, I'm already familiar with the menu, so I am."

"Okay. You go first and I'll have a quick look."

Becky glanced up at the waiter. His name was James, but she knew he preferred to be called Jimmy and she gave him a smile.

"Hi, Jimmy," she said. He smiled back.

"Hello, Mrs Howell."

"I'll have the New England Cobb Salad, please," she said, "but without the bacon and no dressing."

Jimmy nodded, entering her order onto a hand held device.

"No appetizer?" he asked.

Becky shook her head, then looked at Nick. "You can have one, if you want."

"No, I'm fine," he said, staring at her for a moment before turning to Jimmy. "I'll have the Filet Mignon, please."

"How would you like that cooked?" Jimmy asked.

"Rare," Nick replied, as though he saw little point in the question. He returned his gaze to Becky. "Do you want wine?" he asked her.

"Yes, please."

"Pinot Noir?" he suggested and she nodded her head. "Better make it two glasses," he said to Jimmy. "I'm driving, and we don't want Mrs Howell to drink the rest of the bottle all to herself." Jimmy smiled and went to turn away.

"Before you go," Nick said and Jimmy held his ground, "can we order desserts?"

"Now?" Becky asked. "We might not want them."

"We will," Nick smiled, still holding her gaze. "There's New York Style Cheesecake on the menu. I know it's your favorite."

"Even so," Becky said quietly, "we can order later."

Nick looked up at Jimmy. "We'll order it now. Two of them."

Jimmy nodded, made the entry and left.

Nick stared at her a little longer, then sighed and said, "Anything you wanna tell me?"

Becky shook her head. "No. What's wrong? I—I don't understand…"

"You ordered a real boring salad, Bex," he said quietly, leaning toward her, "and then made it even more boring by taking the bacon and dressing out of it. You said you knew the menu, which means you must've seen the lobster. You always used to love lobster. So why order the salad?"

"People change, Nick," she replied. "The lobster dish comes with a creamy bisque, and I don't eat high fat foods anymore. That's why I didn't want the cheesecake. I—"

He shrugged, holding up his hands. "Okay. I'm sorry. I just thought…"

Becky felt awful. "No," she muttered, "I'm the one who's sorry."

"It's fine," he said, attempting a smile that didn't reach his eyes. "I shouldn't have behaved like that. It was a little autocratic of me. You're perfectly entitled to eat whatever you want—"

"Stop being so nice," Becky interrupted.

"I'm not."

"Yes you are." She sat back and sighed. "You're right as well."

"Right about what?"

"I did want the lobster."

"Then why didn't you order it?" He looked around the restaurant and raised his hand, beckoning someone – Jimmy she guessed.

"B—because Tyler had rules. He didn't like me gaining weight," she whispered. "He got mad if I didn't look the way he wanted. I guess I got used to eating light and not having the foods I enjoyed anymore."

Nick's eyes glinted into hers and he took her hand in his. "Do you want the lobster?" he asked. She nodded. "And do you want the cheesecake?" Again she nodded. "Right, then go ahead and have them. Ideally, I'd prefer you to not eat them from the same plate, at the same time, but…" He smirked and she couldn't stifle her giggle.

Jimmy arrived at that moment.

"Hi again, Jimmy," Nick said. "I know this is a pain, but can we change Mrs Howell's order?"

"Sure," Jimmy replied.

155

"She'd like to have the Maine Lobster instead of the salad, if that's okay?"

Jimmy nodded. "That's fine," he said, typing into his device. "Anything else?" He glanced from Becky to Nick and back again.

"I guess a Chablis might go better with your lobster?" Nick suggested, looking at her, and Becky nodded in agreement. Nick looked up. "Sorry, Jimmy," he said, smiling. "Can you change Mrs Howell's Pinot Noir for a Chablis?"

"No problem." He made the amendment. "I'll bring the wine over in a minute," he added.

"Thanks," Nick said, and Jimmy left.

Nick reached across the table and took her hand. "I want you to always be yourself with me," he said quietly. "His rules don't mean a thing anymore, Bex. Go crazy, gain a few pounds. It won't stop me loving you, or wanting you."

Becky wanted to cry, but she managed a smile.

"Forget him," Nick added. "Forget everything about him. And just be you."


Between the main course and dessert, they took a few minutes' break. They were both feeling full, but they were equally determined to have the cheesecake – and enjoy it.

"Something happened earlier," Nick said, taking Becky's hand in his again, "and I think I owe you an explanation. And maybe an apology."

"Oh?" Becky felt confused.

"Yeah. When we spoke this morning, I told you I needed to speak to Mark about Emma, about being there for her when he's away."

Becky nodded her head. It was the thing that had been troubling her all day, and she wondered if she was so transparent that Nick had seen through her insecurity.

"I don't want you to think that Emma comes first," Nick explained. "She doesn't." He stared into her eyes. "You do. You always will. Every time. But, I have a sort of arrangement with Mark."

"What kind of arrangement?"

"One whereby he lets me know when he's going away, so I can keep an eye on Emma."

"Is this because of her morning sickness?" Becky asked. She guessed that might make sense. Emma really was quite unwell.

"No. This goes back a lot further than that." He leant forward a little further and she felt his hand grip her fingers. "I'm gonna tell you something that only Emma, Mark and I know about. That said, I know you won't repeat it."

Becky nodded again.

"I don't know if you're aware," Nick began, "that Emma and Mark were together a few years ago."

"Yes," Becky said. "Mark mentioned it."

"Okay," Nick replied, lowering his eyes to the table. "Well, that time around it didn't last. Mark stayed here for a while, but then went home to his family, the accident happened and, for one reason or another, he chose not to contact Emma again. She was devastated. I know it was tough for him too, but Emma was… well, she was wrecked. She…" He paused and Becky sensed he was struggling to tell her whatever it was he needed to say. "She took an overdose," he muttered.

"Oh my God." Becky put her other hand – the one Nick wasn't gripping – up to her mouth.

"I found her," Nick continued. "Well, I broke down the door of her apartment first, and then I found her."

"That must've been awful for you."

"It wasn't exactly a party." Nick looked at her again. "I stayed with her, once she was out of the hospital, until I knew she was okay. It took a while." He paused. "Then, just before Christmas, when Mark broke up with Emma again – because he is, essentially, an idiot – Emma had another breakdown."

"She did it again?"

"No. I got to her in time. I think she was going to though." He sighed. "No, I *know* she was going to. She knew it too. I stayed with her again, just to make sure she…" He left the sentence hanging. Then after a moment, he sat up straighter and sucked in a breath. "I just wanted to explain," he said. "I wanted you to know that, if I sometimes seem to be a little protective of Emma, there are reasons for that."

Becky brought his hand up to her lips and gently kissed his fingers.

"I understand," she whispered, feeling a little ashamed of her earlier resentment.

"I'm sorry if you felt like I was putting Emma before you. I'm not. I just have to be there for her sometimes."

"Please, Nick… don't apologize to me. I think Emma's very lucky to have you. You're a pretty amazing brother."

Nick smiled. "I'm not always. I can be an overbearing, interfering, pain in the ass too." His smile turned to a grin. "Ask Mark."

"Next time we eat here, we're splitting the dessert," Nick said, as he held Becky's hand on the walk down to the beach. They'd skipped coffee and had decided to take a stroll in the moonlight.

"Definitely," Becky agreed.

"Are you cold?" Nick asked, feeling a gust of wind.

"A little. I should have thought about it and gone up to my room for a jacket."

Nick shrugged his off and placed it around Becky's shoulders. "Take mine," he said.

"But you'll get cold."

"No I won't." Nick smiled down at her and they walked on. He took her hand again, then suddenly stopped in his tracks. "Your wedding ring," he said, lifting her bare left hand.

"I took it off earlier."

"I didn't notice."

"We've been sitting in a candlelit restaurant and you only held my right hand at the table."

"Yeah." He smiled. "And I was more interested in looking at your face than your hands, if I'm being honest." He turned to her. "Why did you take it off?"

"Because I finally feel like I'm gonna be free of him. I feel like I've got hope at last."

"You have, baby." He pulled her in close, kissed her gently, then started walking again.

Becky leant into him a little. "Going back to your sister," she said, after a short while. "You said only you, Emma, and Mark know about what happened. But how did Mark find out? He wasn't here at the time, was he? So, did Emma tell him?" She thought that would have been a very difficult and brave conversation, if Emma had.

"No, he wasn't here," Nick confirmed, looking up at the clear sky, the stars twinkling brightly. "He was sitting at his sister's bedside at the time." He coughed. "Obviously Emma didn't know that."

"Why not? The death of Mark's parents made headlines everywhere. It was even on the TV news. How could she not have known about the accident?"

"Because she didn't know who Mark was."

Becky looked up at Nick's face. There was something behind his eyes she'd never seen before. She wasn't sure what it was.

"He lied to her," Nick explained. "He didn't use his own name when they first met."

"Really?" Becky was surprised. Mark had always seemed to her like such an honest person.

"Yeah. But don't think too badly of him. I did to start with, but once he explained and I got to know him a bit better, I did kind of understand. He just wanted to be anonymous for a few days. He didn't expect to meet someone and fall in love, but by the time he did, the lie had already been told and he didn't really know how to un-tell it."

Becky nodded. "I see."

"So, when Emma sent him a last text message—"

"What? Like a kind of suicide note?" Becky was astounded.

"I guess. It was very brief; she didn't say what she was going to do, or say goodbye, or anything like that, so he probably wouldn't have guessed what she had in mind." Nick went quiet for a moment. "Anyway," he continued, "when she sent that, he was none the wiser, and he was preoccupied with his sister, and his parents' funerals."

"I'm sure he'd have come back to Emma, if he'd realized."

Nick turned to her. "Yeah. I know he would… well, I do now. At the time, I was about ready to punch him from here into next year."

Becky shuddered, and Nick clasped her hand just a little tighter.

"I didn't, Bex," he clarified. "Even when I saw Mark again, I didn't do anything to him. I won't say I wasn't tempted, but some of us can control ourselves…"

She knew what they were both thinking about. "I know you're not like Tyler," she whispered.

"No, I'm not…"

They carried on in silence for a moment. "So, did Emma tell him what had happened when they got back together?" Becky asked.

"No," Nick replied. "I told him, when he came back for her after New Year. He'd let her down really badly, over that business to do with his sister and those press stories. Like I said earlier, she'd come close to doing it a second time and I wasn't about to let him do her any more damage. He turned up at the coffee shop and I… well, I removed him from the scene."

"You did?" Becky smiled, just a little. Nick was tall; probably six foot four, but Mark was taller by maybe an inch or so, although he was perhaps more athletic than muscular in build – and Nick was definitely muscular.

"Yeah. I think I caught him off guard. And I don't think he wanted to create a scene, so he let me." Nick smiled back, and Becky wondered if that was how it had really been. "We talked. That's to say, I talked. I shocked the hell out of him and, to start with, I really wasn't gonna let him anywhere near her, but he convinced me he loved her, and that I should give him one more chance. So I did."

Becky sighed and was about to reiterate what an amazing brother she thought he was, when his phone rang in his back pocket. He pulled it out and checked the screen.

"It's Emma," he said, looking down at her. "I'm sorry, I'd better take it."

"Go ahead."

He connected the call and Becky walked a short distance away. They were right down by the beach now, and she stood at the point where the road became sand and looked out at the moon's sparkling reflection in the otherwise inky black ocean. She turned back and watched Nick as he paced, the phone held to his ear. She could vaguely hear the tone of his voice, if not the words he was saying and he sounded surprised to start with, then a little angry, and then pleased. Finally, after listening for a long time, he went silent. She could feel him staring at her and wondered what was being said, before he ended the call, replaced his phone in his pocket, and walked over to her, taking her hand in his, and stepping onto the sand.

They walked for a short while in silence. The lights along the cliff edge illuminated Nick's face enough for her to see he was deep in thought.

"Is everything okay?" Becky asked eventually.

He startled, as though he'd forgotten she was there, even though he was still holding her hand.

"Yeah. Sorry," he said. "I was just thinking."

"Anything you want to talk about?"

He stopped walking and turned to face her. She looked up into his eyes, which seemed to be glistening. "Em's asked me to give her away," he said quietly.

"Really? But that's lovely," she replied.

"I know." He ran his fingers through his hair. "I just can't believe she asked me."

"Why not? She obviously loves you."

He looked at her for a long moment. "Why me, though?"

She heard the crack in his voice and, leaning forward a little, put her arms around his waist.

"Of course she'd ask you," she said. "You've done so much for her. I'm sure she appreciates it – and you. She's just showing that appreciation."

Nick brought his arms around Becky, over the top of his coat. "That's what she said," he replied.

Becky smiled. "Then maybe you should listen to her."

He grinned back, his eyes still shining. She was surprised by how emotional he was.

"I assume this means your parents aren't going to be at the wedding."

Nick shook his head, his smile fading. "No."

"The meeting didn't go well?" Becky asked, and they started walking again.

"You could put it that way," Nick replied. "Emma invited them as planned, but they told her they couldn't come. They've booked themselves on a Caribbean cruise, or something, and they don't wanna cancel it. They criticized Emma for not giving them more notice, and then they suggested she change the date of the wedding "

"Seriously? She can't do that. Everything's booked."

"I know. That's when Mark stepped in, evidently. Emma told me he stood up to them, and in the end, they backed down and said they wouldn't come."

"It's their loss," Becky said quietly.

"Exactly. The good thing is that Emma feels much better about the whole thing now. She knows she did the right thing by inviting them, but she doesn't have to actually face having them there. To be honest, she's sounding a lot less stressed about it already."

"That's good."

"And that's why she asked me to walk her down the aisle and give her away."

"You think?" Becky looked up at him. "You think she only asked you because your father isn't gonna be there?"

"Well, I think if dad had been there, he'd be doing it…"

"Maybe. But only because it's traditional. I think Emma would have always *wanted* you to do it. I think she'll much prefer it this way." She took a deep breath, banishing for a moment the memories of her own wedding day. "And I think she asked you because she wants you to be there for her – just like you've always been. Sure, she's marrying Mark and, in effect, your role means you're giving her to him, but I think she wants you to understand just how much you mean to her."

# Nick

"And how exactly do you work that out?" he asked, looking down at her again.

"Because I know how it feels to walk down that aisle and feel like you're leaving one life behind and starting a new one." She paused and he wondered what was coming next. "I know that feeling of going into the unknown, I remember the uncertainty, and how much it means to have someone you love to cling onto."

God, had it really felt like that for her? He got that, for some people, there might be an element of nerves on their wedding day, but 'uncertainty'? That sounded all wrong. Had there been no joy? Were there no hopes, no dreams, no excitement? Had there been nothing to look forward to?

"Was it that bad, Bex? Even then?" he asked quietly.

"Yes," she whispered, then took a deep breath. "But we weren't talking about me. We were talking about Emma. She's looking for your support, just like she always has."

"I know," he replied. "But it's very different for Emma. She's not walking into the unknown and there's no uncertainty for her. She's so in love with Mark—"

"And he is with her," Becky added.

"Yeah, he is." He let out a long sigh. "I don't know," he said, "This 'giving away' thing seems real old fashioned, but I feel like it's completely redundant in their case. She's already his – so why does she need me?"

"That's the whole point. She doesn't, but she's asking you to do it anyway." She looked up at him. "Why? You're not thinking of saying no, are you?"

"Of course not. I've already said yes." He smiled. "I'd never do that to her."

"Then why are we having this discussion?"

His smile became a grin. "I don't know. I guess it just blew me away a little, that's all."

She stared up into his face. "You're a beautiful man, Nick – inside and out." He noticed the change in her eyes just as she stopped, leant up and kissed him gently on the lips. He held his breath, waiting to see what she'd do next, unsure whether she'd try and take it further. Then he felt her tongue touching his lips and he opened up to her, letting her feel her way inside. She was tentative and inquisitive as she explored him, and he fought his instincts to explore back, letting her call the shots, exactly as he'd promised. Her breathing changed, becoming more urgent. But then suddenly, she pulled back and took a step away from him. Something was wrong.

"Bex?" he said softly. "What did I do?"

She shook her head, looking at his chest, not his face, and he stepped toward her, taking her hands.

"Tell me," he urged. "Please."

He could feel her hands shaking in his and pulled her into his arms. Whatever was wrong, it was bothering her. A lot.

"I—I don't want it to be like this," Becky whispered. "I can't see how this is ever gonna work, Nick." Her voice faded to silence.

Nick felt a pain deep in his chest.

"I don't understand," he replied. "Are you saying you don't want me?"

"No," she said immediately, pulling back and looking up into his eyes. "No, that's not what I'm saying."

"Then please can you try and explain, baby. I'm dying here."

She took a breath, opened her mouth, closed it again, then sighed and said, "I—I appreciate you giving me control, but I'm not sure I want it." She blinked rapidly a few times and he wondered if she was about to cry. In this light it was hard to tell. "I want you to feel like you can take the lead," she continued, "but I don't know how that's gonna work."

He laughed, purely out of relief. "We need to learn to walk before we worry about running," he told her, brushing the backs of his fingers gently down her cheek. "We'll get there."

"But how, Nick? How?" She sounded a little desperate and he cupped her face in his hand, tilting it up toward his.

"I'll work it out," he murmured. "Nothing's changed, baby. I can still read your body, just like I always could." He heard her suck in a breath. "I know what you want, even now."

"You do?" She was wide-eyed.

"Yeah." He smiled. "But I also know you're still feeling scared and uncertain." He moved closer, their bodies fused. "You just need to relax, and trust me, and get used to feeling safe again."

She nodded her head.

"And," he added, "you need to remember that love is about pleasure, not pain."

"Pleasure?"

"Yeah. You remember. The kind of pleasure that makes you scream in ecstasy, makes you beg for more. The kind of pleasure you never want to stop."

She was breathing hard again now.

"See? You *do* remember," he whispered, and she nodded her head. "Then trust me to get you back there."

He felt her shiver in his arms.

"It's cold," he said, although he didn't think for one minute she was shivering because of the temperature.

"Yes," she whispered.

"Shall we go back?"

She nodded and they turned and started back up the beach.

"Do you want to come in?" Becky asked, looking up into his eyes. They were standing outside her room. She had the entry card poised in her hand. "I could make us that coffee we didn't have earlier."

Nick stared at her for a minute, wondering if she really meant it about the coffee. "Sure," he said. She seemed to want him to stay a little longer, and that was fine by him.

She let them in, flicking on the dim lights, and he followed, closing the door behind him. As he turned into the room, Becky was there, right in front of him. She gazed up into his face, her eyes fixed on his. She bit her bottom lip and he felt her sigh, just as he pulled her close and claimed her mouth. Hard. She moaned into him and he explored her with his tongue, tasting her. She responded, bringing her arms up around his neck, her fingers twisting in his hair, his coat falling from her shoulders to the floor as she did so. He groaned at her touch and delved deeper, feeling her breasts pressed against his chest. He was bone hard, but tried to keep a distance between their lower bodies, not wanting to scare her into thinking they had to do anything but kiss. Even though her body was telling him she wanted him to take her, and had been for most of the evening, he wasn't entirely sure her mind – her emotions – had caught up yet. And if kissing was going to be like this, he'd happily wait.

# Chapter Twelve

## *Becky*

His kiss felt so good and Becky wanted it to go on forever. Well, that wasn't strictly true. What she really wanted was for him to take her to bed and help her forget all the bad things that had happened in the nine years they'd been apart, but she wasn't sure she was really ready for that – not yet. Her body definitely was. She craved the release of the mind-blowing orgasms she knew only Nick could give her, but she was scared the memories of her time with Tyler would haunt her.

He moved his feet, just fractionally, coming slightly closer and she was almost sure she could feel his erection against her hip. He must be really turned on and the thought made her breath catch in her throat. Was that fear, or excitement? She wasn't entirely sure and thought it might be a little of both. She tried to calm her breathing, even through his kiss and, as his fingers moved gently up and down her spine, she realized that Nick would never hurt her. It would be a cold day in hell before he would hurt her – or let anyone else harm her either. She shivered to his touch and, as he deepened the kiss, she felt a pool of heat gathering right at her core. It hadn't been like this since the last time she was with Nick. She wanted more. How much more, she wasn't sure, but she wanted the chance to find out.

She pulled back, breaking the kiss, and looked up at him.

"You felt good," he whispered.

"So did you."

He smiled and bent to kiss her again, just briefly. Could she ask him? Was she brave enough? She looked up into his eyes.

"Can... can you...?"

"Can I what?" he asked.

"Can you stay?" she asked.

"Of course I can."

He hadn't understood.

"I don't mean just for coffee. I mean, can you stay the night?" Her voice was so quiet, she wasn't sure he would have heard.

"I know that's what you mean," he said. So he'd heard her then; and he'd understood. "I told you, Bex, I can read your body." He smiled. "And I'd love to stay the night with you."

She put her hand on his chest. "I—I'm not sure I'm ready to do anything..."

"I get that," he replied.

"Well, I am ready..." she clarified.

"Hey," he said. "You don't have to explain. I understand." He sighed. "You're ready physically, but you're not quite there yet emotionally. Is that right?"

She nodded. "Yes. Thank you for saying it for me."

"No problem, baby." He smiled.

"And you don't mind staying the night? Even if we don't..."

"There's nothing I'd love more." He let out a slight laugh. "Although I can't promise to be very good at it."

She tilted her head to one side, confused.

"I've never spent the night with anyone, Bex," he explained.

"Never? Not even before me?" She'd always known she wasn't his first, even back then. "I assumed..."

"Well, you assumed wrong." He pulled her close, looking down into her eyes. "I had sex a few times before we got together," he said, "but I didn't spend the night with any of them. And after you... well, you know about that." He closed his eyes.

She raised her hand and held it against his cheek.

"Yes," she whispered. "It's just, I'll feel safer with you here. And I'll sleep better."

"You have trouble sleeping?" he asked.

"I may have had a lock on the door, but I always knew he could break it down, if he wanted to. It turned me into a very light sleeper."

She felt his muscles tighten around her. "Well, I promise to keep you safe," he said gently. "And you've got nothing to fear, so sleep easy, baby." He bent down and kissed her. "There is one problem though – apart from the fact that I might well hog all the covers, and I have a tendency to throw my pillows around a little…" He grinned.

"What's that?" She smiled up at him, feeling more relieved and light of heart already.

"I've got nothing to wear." He lowered his voice. "I'll be naked. Are you okay with that?"

She swallowed hard at the thought, that pool of heat lighting up a little more. "I guess you could keep your underwear on…" she suggested, half-heartedly.

"Um… don't you remember?" A slight smile formed at the corner of his lips. "I don't wear any."

"Oh yes." She recalled her surprise the first time she'd found out he wasn't wearing anything under his jeans, and how much she'd enjoyed taking advantage of that at any and every opportunity. She smiled back at him. "Yes, I remember."

"I thought you might." He stared at her. "So, are you okay with that?"

She nodded slowly. "Are you?" she asked.

"Okay with being naked?" he enquired. "Sure. I always sleep naked." He seemed confused.

She shook her head. "No. I meant are you okay with me being naked? I don't wear anything in bed either. I never did…"

There was a moment's silence and she started to wonder what he was going to say. "I—I'm fine with it," he stammered. Then he paused and took a deep breath. "Sorry," he said, "I was just having trouble focusing then." He smiled and leant a little closer. "We're gonna have one other problem though…"

"We are?" She had no idea what he was talking about.

"Yeah." He kissed her gently again and leant back a little. "I'm real hard right now, Bex," he said simply. She felt herself blush. "I can't help it," he added. "I never could around you. You always did that to me." He paused. "The thing is, I'm hard… and you're still fully clothed. My erection won't be going anywhere if you're naked. I need to know if that's a problem for you? I'm not saying I'm gonna do anything, but it's gonna be there, because I promise you, there's damn all I can do about it."

She felt the smile forming on her lips, despite her embarrassment. He was so open about everything and she wondered if she'd ever be able to be like that again.

"I trust you," she whispered, and she knew she didn't need to say any more.

"Good," he replied.

"Do you still want that coffee?" she asked.

He smiled. "No, not particularly." He pulled away. "I'd really just like to go to bed with you."

She blushed. "God," she said, touching her cheeks. "Do you think I'm gonna blush every time you say something like that?"

"I don't know," he replied, grinning. "But I guess if you are, it's gonna get boring, real soon, because I've got no intention of stopping." He cradled her face in his hands. "You go to the bathroom first. I'll keep myself amused out here."

She turned and walked over toward the bathroom door. Just as she touched the handle, he called out, "Don't worry about the blushing, Bex." She turned and looked at him. He was smiling across at her. "You look real cute when you're embarrassed." She flushed bright red again and ducked into the bathroom, hearing him laugh gently behind her.

When Becky came back out into the bedroom, still fully clothed, she noticed Nick had turned off the lamps by the bed and was standing in the darkness over by the floor-to-ceiling, wall-to-wall window, looking out across the ocean in the moonlight. She'd left the bathroom light on and, as the room lit up behind him, Nick turned to face her.

"You okay?" he asked.

She nodded.

"Sorry," he continued. "I meant to get undressed while you were in there, but the view caught my eye and I've been staring at it."

She came and stood alongside him.

"It's beautiful, isn't it?"

"Sure is." He turned to her. "I'll go to the bathroom while you get undressed," he offered. "Call me when it's okay for me to come out." She looked up at him. "I'm guessing you'd rather be tucked up in bed when I come out of there, so call me when you're ready. I'll wait until I hear your voice."

"Thank you," she whispered.

His kissed the top of her head and disappeared into the bathroom.

Becky undressed quickly, picking up her work clothes from the floor, where Nick had dropped them earlier and putting all the laundry in the bag in the closet. Then she climbed into bed, pulled the covers up to her chin, and called out to Nick.

"Won't be long," he replied from the other side of the bathroom door.

A few minutes later, he came out. He'd already turned off the bathroom light and, for a moment, she panicked.

"Sorry, Nick." She sat up in bed, ignoring the fact that the covers fell down a little. "Can you turn the light back on, and leave the door open."

He glanced across at her and she gasped. In her panic, she'd somehow missed the fact that he was naked but now, in the moonlight she could see his firm body outlined against the window.

"Sure," he said, seemingly confused. He opened the door and switched the light back on. Now she could see him even more clearly; his strong shoulders, muscular arms, and hard, toned abs. She let her eyes roam southwards. He hadn't been kidding. He was hard – and a *lot* bigger than she remembered. She drew in a sharp breath, then choked. Had that ever actually been inside her? Surely not… It wasn't possible, was it?

"You okay?" he asked, dumping his folded clothes on the chair by the window and coming over to the bed.

She nodded. "I'm fine," she managed to whisper. Close up, he seemed even bigger and she dragged her eyes up to his face. He was smiling down at her.

"Why the light?" he asked, trying to put her at ease, she thought.

"Oh, I just don't like the dark."

"Is that a childhood thing?" he enquired, still standing and looking down at her.

"No… it's a Tyler thing."

His smile disappeared, but he nodded his head.

"Are you okay… sleeping with the light on, I mean?" she asked.

"Sure." He pulled back the covers on his side of the bed and, as he leant forward, she noticed the tattoo on his chest and shoulder.

"That's new," she remarked, pointing. He'd definitely not had a tattoo before – anywhere.

On the left side of his chest, was a large, ornate letter 'B' surrounded by and decorated with roses, twisted around ivy stems. It was placed right over his heart, the tendrils of the flowers and leaves going up to his shoulder, and down onto his arm. It was absolutely beautiful.

"Yeah," he said, sitting down on the edge of the bed.

"Can I see it properly?" she asked.

He leant over and turned the light back on beside the bed, then twisted around so she could get a better look. She leant across, oblivious to the fact that, in doing so, she'd exposed her breasts. He groaned quietly, but she was absorbed in looking at his chest. "It's beautiful," she said, reaching out and gently touching his soft skin, tracing the lines of the letter.

"Is the 'B' for…?" She was scared to ask, just in case.

"It's for 'Bex'." He reassured her.

"You do know my real name is Rebecca, don't you?"

He smiled. "You'll always be 'Bex' to me."

She smiled back. "I like that." She looked up at him. "When did you have it done?" she asked.

"While we were still at college," he replied. "It was at the beginning of that next semester, a few days after Tyler told me you were living with him."

"Were you drunk?" she asked, smiling.

"Nope. Stone cold sober." He twisted round a little further, and very gently ran his thumb across her bottom lip. "My heart was always yours, even if you didn't know it," he whispered. "This was just the nearest I could get to keeping you there."

She struggled to swallow down the lump in her throat. "Not any more," she whispered.

"No. Not any more." He leant down a little, his lips just an inch from hers. "I love you, Bex," he murmured.

"I love you too." She looked up into his eyes and wondered if he was going to kiss her. She wanted him to… and yet she didn't, because she knew if he did, she'd want more. Much more.

As if he could read her mind, he pulled away again. And it was only then, as she went to lie down, that she realized how exposed she was. She panicked, trying desperately to grab for the covers, but then she felt him gently raise the comforter, screening her again. "I'm sorry," she whispered.

"Don't be," he said. "It's fine." He turned off the bedside lamp again, then lay down beside her, on his back.

"It's not fine though, is it?" she said quietly, staring at the ceiling.

He turned to face her, leaning up on one elbow. "Look at me," he whispered and she twisted her head around to look up into his eyes. "It's fine," he repeated. "We go at your pace, Bex." He ran a finger down her cheek. "You can't help feeling apprehensive any more than I can help feeling aroused."

"But I don't want to be feel apprehensive," she whispered, feeling tears welling in her eyes.

"I know you don't." He paused for a moment. "I think you could use a hug," he murmured. "Would it be okay if I held you?"

She stared up at him, then blinked and a lone tear fell down her cheek. "Yes," she whispered. "Oh, yes please." There was nothing she needed more.

He put his arms around her and pulled her close, turning her so they faced each other and she rested her head against him. After a moment, he wrapped a leg around her and she felt his long, thick erection pressing into her. She didn't care... It was good to lie there, wrapped up in him. Safe.

Becky woke with the sunrise and she stretched her arms above her head, curling her fingers into fists. She hadn't slept so well in years; not since before Tyler... She banished that thought and twisted her head around, squinting at the clock beside the bed. It was ten after six. She smiled. They had at least two hours before she needed to be in the office. Plenty of time to shower and order up some breakfast. She turned onto her side, where she came up against Nick's chest.

"Good morning," he muttered, his voice full of sleep.

"Good morning," she replied and opened her eyes properly. He filled the space beside her. He'd been right, he had stolen a lot of the covers, and wrapped them around himself, and his pillows were nowhere to be seen; in fact he seemed to have taken one of hers. She smiled.

"What?" he asked, pulling her close.

"You're a pillow thief," she said.

"I am?" He looked around a little. "What did I do with mine?"

"Who knows?"

"Hmm..." He turned back to her. "Who cares?" He smiled and kissed her briefly. "How did you sleep?" he asked.

"The best I have in years," she replied.

"Good." He turned away and went to get up. "Well," he said, bending over the side of the bed, "at least we found the pillows." He replaced them at the head of the mattress.

"They were on the floor?"

"Yeah..." He got up.

"Where are you going?" she asked, confused.

"To the bathroom."

"Oh..." She watched as he walked away, taking in his broad back, perfect firm ass, and strong, muscular thighs. She sighed.

He returned a few minutes later, switching off the bathroom light as he closed the door behind him, then turned to her and she once again gasped. This time he heard her and smiled.

"I did warn you," he said, glancing down at his erection.

"I know," she murmured. "I'd just forgotten."

"Forgotten what?" he asked, coming back over to the bed and sitting down again. He seemed a little on edge, but she couldn't work out why. It wasn't like Nick at all… he'd been so calm and natural about everything until now. "Forgotten what?" he repeated when she didn't reply.

"I—I just don't remember it being like that."

"How do you remember it then?"

"Not that big." She felt herself blushing again.

He smirked. "Well, I don't think it's grown in the last nine years…"

She looked up at him. "Did it really fit?" she asked, feeling shy.

He leant over to her, kissing her lightly. "In you, you mean?" She nodded. "Oh yeah," he said. "It fitted perfectly."

He got up again and walked over to the window, taking a few deep breaths. He seemed so tense.

"Is something wrong?" Becky asked, sitting up and taking care to bring the comforter with her this time.

"No." He continued to stare out the window.

"Nick…"

He turned and looked at her.

"It's nothing to do with you," he said.

"And that's meant to make me feel better?"

He shook his head. "I'm sorry," he said. "I just don't like hotels very much."

She let out a laugh. "Well, that's not a very good start," she said, "considering what I do for a living."

"Don't take it personally. I've never liked hotels – any of them, not just ones that are as upmarket as this." He glanced around the beautifully furnished room. "I always feel restricted… and I hate being restricted, or tied down, or imposed on in any way."

Becky felt herself stiffen. What was he trying to tell her? He must have seen the look on her face, because he walked quickly across to her and crawled up the bed, leaning over her.

"Please don't misunderstand what I just said," he murmured. "It probably came out all wrong. What I meant to say was, I hate routine. I hate being told when to eat, or what to eat, come to that. I hate knowing that someone can come and knock on my door at any time." He sighed. "I've gotten kinda used to doing things my own way," he said. "I like open spaces – that's why I like the view out the window. It's also why a bought a plot of land in the middle of a forest. I like to be able to see the sky and feel the sun on my face and the wind in my hair." She nodded. "But," he added, leaning in a little closer, "please don't think I ever want to be free of you. I don't. Not ever."

"Ever?" She was surprised by how that sounded. The permanence of it. Did he mean what she thought he meant?

"Yeah, ever," he repeated. "I want you in my life always, Bex. I told you already, I'm never gonna let you go."

He closed the gap between them and covered her mouth with his. She let herself sink back into the pillow and felt him move his legs either side of her, his arms supporting his weight above her as his tongue delved deep into her already open mouth. She moaned and, letting go of the comforter so it slid down a little, she snaked her arms around his neck, her fingers playing in his hair. His groan hummed into her throat, and brought the heat deep inside her to boiling point. Instinctively, she raised her hips toward him – the comforter being all that separated them from each other – and felt him grind his erection into her. His breathing altered, as did hers and, within seconds, they were both frantic, their kisses harder, their hunger mutual and matched.

Suddenly, he pulled back, kneeling up and looking down at her, a pained expression on his face.

"We have to stop," he said, "or I'm not gonna be able to."

She nodded just once, feeling grateful that at least he'd shown some common sense, even though all of hers had deserted her.

"I'll go shower," she said and he moved to one side to let her get up, groaning loudly at the sight of her naked body as she hopped off the bed and made her way to the bathroom.

"Jeez, Bex," he said, flopping down onto his back, his erection proud, his hands covering his face. "How could *I* have forgotten?"

She stopped, and looked over at him.

"Forgotten what?"

He shifted and leant up on one elbow, looking across at her. "I dream about you all the time," he explained and she felt his eyes roaming over her body. Oddly, this time she didn't want to hide away. She welcomed his gaze. "Pretty much every night for the last nine years, I've had some kind of dream about you. I thought I'd remembered every inch of you. I thought it was all firmly locked away up here." He tapped the side of his head. "And in here." He placed his hand on his chest, where the tattoo covered his heart. "But," he added, pausing for a moment, "I was so damn wrong." He clambered off the bed and walked slowly over to her, putting his hands on her bare waist. She shivered at his touch, and closed her eyes. "You're even more beautiful than I remembered," he said. "You're perfect. You're completely fucking perfect."

She felt his lips on her neck, working their way up to her jaw, then tracing a line to her ear.

"Go shower, baby," he whispered. "Please…" She heard the desperation in his voice. "I promised I wouldn't do anything you weren't ready for, but seeing you like this makes it real hard to keep that promise. Please go shower and give me a few minutes…"

She opened her eyes, staring into his, and gasped as she saw the depth of his aching need.

She took her time in the shower, washing her hair slowly, wanting to give him the chance he'd asked for, to calm down and collect himself. She needed exactly the same chance too. The problem was, even being in a separate room wasn't helping. She wanted him more than anything. Rinsing the shampoo out of her hair, she confessed to herself that she'd wanted him since the night of the hotel opening, when she'd turned around and come face to face with him, right in front of Mark and Emma. Even then, she'd recognized the familiar heat, the pull of him. But spending time with him over the last few days, she craved him, like a drug…

As she washed herself in the shower, her skin felt more sensitized than ever before, even than when they'd been together nine years ago, and she'd first experienced his expert touch. Every brush of her fingers under the running water made her gasp with need, and sigh with desire.

She climbed out of the shower, wrapping her hair in a towel, and fixing another one around her body, fastened above her breasts, her skin damp and glistening.

She opened the door and stepped out into the bedroom. Nick was standing by the window, still naked, still aroused.

"It didn't work for you either, did it?" he asked, turning toward her.

She shook her head. How did he know?

He moved across to her. "I told you. I can read your body," he whispered, and she breathed out a sigh.

"I'm gonna shower now," he said. "But I don't, for one second, think it's gonna do any good…"

She waited for the door to close then walked over to the bed and flopped down. She remembered how, all those years ago, seeing his naked body, his need, his arousal, had turned her from an inexperienced, virginal girl into a hungry, insatiable woman, not afraid or ashamed to show him and tell him what she wanted. She wondered if she'd ever be that woman again.

She shook herself. This wasn't helping in the least. She got up and went over to the dresser, opening the drawer and pulling out the hairdryer, plugging it in and releasing her hair from the towel in which it was bound. Brushing it through, she turned to the mirror and started drying it.

Once she was finished, she brushed it through again, then turned to find Nick sitting on the edge of the bed, staring at her, the towel wrapped around his hips doing a poor job of hiding his huge erection. She felt her mouth dry at the sight of his wet tousled hair dripping onto his shoulders, the water droplets running down his smooth skin. She followed one as it fell, tracking down over his hard pectoral muscle, tracing through the ornate 'B', the white roses and green ivy leaves painted there, before running down and over his taut, rippled abdominals and soaking into the thick white towel. She let her eyes drop further still to the impressive bulge. Knowing now how long, thick, and hard he was, all she could think about was that she wanted to walk over, pull away his towel, and her own, then sit on his lap, taking him deep inside her body, holding him to her. She closed her eyes, shuddering and sucking in a deep breath, thinking about how good it would feel to be stretched and filled by him again…

"Come here," Nick said and she opened her eyes. He was still staring at her, his eyes dark and shining. He held out a hand and beckoned her. "Come here, Bex," he repeated.

She walked over and stood before him, letting him take her hand in his.

"I know what you need," he whispered, looking up into her eyes..

"You do?" she said, feeling her cheeks redden.

His eyes were locked with hers. "When did you last have an orgasm?" he asked.

She felt her pussy tingle and clench, her thighs shaking at the thought.

"I'll take that as some time ago," Nick continued.

"It was nine years ago," she replied, her voice little more than a whisper. "The last time we were together."

His mouth dropped open. "You mean you didn't come at all, in all the years you were with him?" She noticed he didn't say Tyler's name.

"No."

"But…" He paused for a moment. "But you used to enjoy it so much, Bex. Watching you come was magical. You used to get so lost in it all…" His voice faded. "Did you never masturbate either?"

She shook her head.

"Really?" He seemed shocked by that.

"I never have," she confessed, her blush deepening. "When we were together, I never needed to…" She smiled. "Why would I have needed to do it to myself, when I had you?"

He grinned. "But what about before me?" he asked. "I know you were a virgin, but surely…?"

"No," she said, shrugging. "I was a complete innocent. That first time with you – when you used your fingers – that really was my first time."

"Wow." He kept his eyes fixed on hers. "And with him?"

"He took all the pleasure out of sex," she said, and she felt herself curl up a little inside. He seemed to sense her withdrawal and pulled her closer, between his legs.

"Do you trust me?" he asked, looking up at her.

"Yes," she replied without hesitating.

"I want you to let your senses guide you... and surrender yourself."

She tried to pull her hand away from his. What was he asking of her?

"I don't mean surrender to me," he clarified, pulling her back again. "I mean surrender to pleasure. You remember how good it felt, don't you?" he asked.

"Yes," she whispered.

"I can make it like that again, baby, I promise. And you won't regret it..."

## Nick

He waited, still looking up into her eyes, until she slowly nodded her head.

"Turn around," he murmured, releasing her hand. She did as he said, turning her back to him. He put his hands on her hips and moved her away, just a little. Then he inched forward, so he was right on the edge of the bed, before reaching up and pulling the towel from her body. She gasped and brought her arms up to cover herself.

"It's okay," he said. "You can trust me."

"I do trust you," she whispered. He heard the emotion in her voice, and her arms came slowly back down by her sides again, her hands shaking a little.

This was a big deal for her, much more than anything they'd done before. This was the first step on what he knew was going to be a long road to banishing her nightmares and demons.

"You weren't nervous about being naked earlier when you got out of bed," he said reassuringly. "You didn't mind me looking at you then. I can't really see you now, and I'm not gonna do anything you're not ready for."

"I know," she whispered. "But this feels so much more intimate, more intense than earlier."

"That's because it is." He paused. "Do you want to stop?" He knew she didn't, but he asked anyway.

"No." She answered immediately and a smile formed on his lips. He'd been right. She needed this.

"Okay," he said. "Close your eyes." He waited. He couldn't see her face. "Are they closed?" he asked. She nodded her head and he placed his hands gently on her hips. "Remember, I can't see you – not really. And now you can't see yourself either. So, just let your senses guide you… Now, sit back," he whispered and, with his hands on her hips again, he guided her down onto his lap, keeping his legs close together. "Trust me," he repeated and she nodded again settling back into him. He reached around her, putting his hands just above her knees and moving her legs to be either side of his own. Then, slowly, he shifted his legs further and further apart, spreading hers too, until her thighs were wide open and she was completely exposed. Her breathing quickened.

"Now," he said, tracing a line of soft kisses along her shoulder. "Give me your hand."

"Which one?" she asked.

"Your right, I guess."

She held up her hand and he took it in his, moving it slowly down between her legs, guiding her, until she was touching her clitoris.

"Oh God." She gasped loudly, then let out a long, soft moan as he pressed his fingers down against hers.

"You're wet, aren't you?" he murmured into her hair. He couldn't feel her properly, but he knew he was right.

She nodded.

"Keep your eyes closed," he said softly in her ear. Putting his left arm around her waist, holding her in place, he pressed the fingers of his right hand into hers and started to circle them around her exposed clitoris.

She tipped her head back, onto his shoulder, sighing and moaning, rotating her hips into their mutual touch. His cock strained against her, through the towel but he focused on their fingers, spreading his legs still further, taking hers with them so she was as wide as she could go.

"Yes..." she hissed between her clenched teeth, her whole body grinding against him in desperate, urgent need. "Please... Nick." He moved his left hand up a little and covered her right breast, pinching her extended nipple between his thumb and forefinger.

"It's not me, baby. It's you," he whispered into her ear. "Rub that beautiful wet clit. Make yourself come..." That was all it took. She rocked her head back a little further, then let out a long, deep moan, whispering his name gently as her body writhed and bucked in his arms. She'd lost control, the waves of pleasure washing over and over her, claiming her body. Eventually, the shuddering subsided and she calmed a little, flopping forward. He held onto her, moving their soaking hands away from her pussy. She'd come real hard, even if she had been quiet about it, and she was still breathing deep and ragged.

"Still trust me?" he asked. She nodded. "Keep your eyes closed," he said gently, "and stand up." She got shakily to her feet and he stood behind her, stepping to one side and moving her backward so she was right by the bed. "Now sit down again," he whispered. She did as he said, sitting with her legs just slightly parted, and he looked down at her flushed face, her firm rounded breasts, her rigid, deep pink nipples, her flat stomach, and her shaved pussy. She hadn't been shaved when they were together before and she looked beautiful, her slick juices glistening on her soft swollen flesh. His cock twitched and he removed the towel from his waist and knelt in front of her.

"Do you want some more?" he asked.

She nodded and bit her bottom lip.

"I thought you might." He smiled and, placing his hands on her knees, he parted her legs again, taking them as wide as he could, spreading her.

"You're beautiful," he murmured and saw the blush rise on her cheeks, even as her nipples hardened a little more.

He moved closer, knelt right down and used his fingers to open her up to him. Then he leant forward and very gently ran his tongue across her swollen clitoris. She jumped at his touch, letting out a moan of pleasure. She hadn't been expecting that and he smiled before repeating the motion, slightly harder this time, letting his tongue flick over and around her, then sucking her hardened nub into his mouth. She groaned deep in her throat and he leant back slightly, licking her, and looked up into her face. Her eyes were still closed and her face was a picture of enraptured bliss.

"Open your eyes, baby," he murmured into her, and she did, staring down at him. He stopped, just for a moment. "Watch," he whispered. "Watch my tongue on your clit."

She blushed, but didn't look away as he flicked his tongue over her once more. He saw her eyes widen, their color deepen as she took in the sight before her. She leant back a little onto her elbows, to give him better access, and rocked her hips up into his touch as he worked her harder and harder. He felt her thighs quiver, saw the flush rising on her neck and cheeks and, remembering how responsive she was, he very gently, inserted a finger into her. That was enough. She exploded a second time, letting out another moan, his name a repeated whisper on her lips as she thrashed and squirmed against him. He let her ride out her pleasure, then as it started to subside, he lay down beside her, pulling her further up onto the bed, and taking her in his arms.

"God…" She turned to him, looking up into his eyes. "That was incredible… twice." A familiar smile formed on her lips.

"Still want more?" he asked, knowing what her smile meant, remembering her insatiable appetite for pleasure.

She nodded, then lowered her head, seemingly embarrassed.

"Don't be shy," he said. "I'm happy to do all that again, if you want."

She smiled again, but shook her head.

"What's wrong?" he asked. Something wasn't right. She wanted more, and yet she didn't…

She nestled down into him, her head buried against his chest so he couldn't see her face.

"I want to be able to really let go, like I used to," she whispered into him. "I want to be able to yell and scream and cry out your name. I can't do that here, Nick."

He smiled. "Is that it?" he asked, and she raised her face and looked up at him.

"Yes."

"That's another reason I love where I live," he said. "I mean, obviously I've never had sex there, but if I want to, I can howl at the moon and there's no-one to hear me – or judge me."

She moved a little closer, her lips barely an inch from his. "Can we go to your place then?" she asked.

"What? Now?" He smirked. This was more like the Becky he remembered.

"Well…" She paused. "No. Unfortunately, I've gotta work. And I'm sure you do too."

"I'm the boss," Nick replied. "I can take the day off if I want."

"Yeah… well, I'm not the boss," Becky replied, dragging herself out of his arms. "And I've still gotta work." She went to get up, but turned back to him. "But tonight…?"

"Sure." He smiled. "I can drive over here and pick you up. Your car's still at my place anyway."

"Oh, yes." She stood and walked around to the closet. Her unashamed nakedness made him smile.

"Pack a bag for tonight, Bex," he said softly. She turned and looked at him. "I like sleeping with you."

He watched her dress, enjoying the view and taking in every inch of her as she moved easily around the room, more comfortable now.

As she sat in front of the mirror, fixing her makeup, he told her that he preferred her without any.

"So do I," she said, tipping her head back a little while she applied her mascara. "But I have to—"

"I know," he interrupted. "I get that you don't want the people you work with to see what he did to you."

She stopped what she was doing and looked at him in the mirror. "I just don't want to have to explain it to everyone," she said.

"I understand." He sat up, his knees bent, his arms resting on them. "Can I ask you something?" he said, still watching her.

"Of course."

"You weren't shaved when we were together," he said, his voice dropping to a whisper. "Is that something you chose to do? Or was it his idea?"

"It was his," she replied quietly.

He nodded. Somehow he'd thought as much. "You don't have to keep it that way, if you don't want to," he said.

She turned and looked at him. "I kinda like it as it is," she murmured, now a little shy again.

He smiled. "That's okay." He got up and went over to her. "I kinda like it too – but only if it's what you want."

She nodded. "It is." She opened her mouth as though she was about to say something else, then closed it again.

"What is it, Bex?" he asked.

"That," she said, pointing at his erection. "Don't you feel a little frustrated?"

He smiled down at her. "No," he replied. "I had a great time."

"But you didn't get anything out of it."

"Yeah, I did." She tilted her head to one side and he smiled again. "I told you earlier, watching you come is magical. I get so much pleasure, just from that." His smile widened. "I can't wait until tonight," he whispered. "I can't wait to see you really come apart… really let go." She shuddered. "You're thinking about it already, aren't you?"

She nodded and he heard the slight moan escape her open mouth.

"Don't sweat it, Bex," he continued. "I'll know when you're ready for me to make love to you." He paused and looked down into her expectant eyes, then cupped her upturned face in his hands. "And you're so nearly there, baby," he murmured.

She closed her eyes. "Yes, I am."

He leant down and kissed her, deeply.

Nick found it almost impossible to concentrate on anything at work and, by lunchtime, he was so distracted by the thought of what he and Becky could be doing – and probably would be doing, later that evening – he went for a walk, and called Jake.

"Hi." Jake answered on the third ring. "You okay?"

Nick knew it was unusual for him to call.

"Yeah. I'm fine, and Emma's fine too, before you ask."

"Good." Nick could hear the smile in Jake's voice. "And Becky? Is she okay as well?" Jake was almost laughing now.

"Yeah… How the hell—"

"Cass and I were there on Saturday night, Nick. We're not blind. We worked out that Becky meant something to you. And then Mark and Emma filled us in on the details."

"Great." Was nothing sacred?

"Hey, don't blame them. We were worried. Becky looked upset and you looked… well, weird, to be honest."

"Weird?"

"Yeah. Like you'd lost control. You're normally so together. I've never seen you look that lost."

"I know, but then it's not every day that the woman you've waited nine years for, walks back into your life."

"You waited nine years?" Jake was surprised. "She's married though, right?"

"Yeah… to a douchebag."

"So I gathered."

"A douchebag she's gonna be divorced from real soon," Nick clarified.

A short silence followed. "You waited nine years?" Jake repeated, still sounding surprised.

"Yeah."

"You mean, you *really* waited?"

"Yeah. I *really* waited."

"You didn't see anyone else in all that time?"

Did Jake need him to spell it out? "No. I didn't see, kiss, date, sleep with, or look at another woman in all that time." Nick spelt it out.

"Fucking hell."

Nick laughed. "It wasn't quite that bad," he said, and Jake laughed too.

"Yeah. I believe you."

"I did have a reason for calling," Nick said, "apart from discussing my non-existent sex life."

"Okay," Jake replied. "Although I'm sure your sex life isn't non-existent anymore."

"I wanted to talk to you about my house, and the hotel," Nick said, ignoring Jake's comment.

"The hotel?"

"Yeah." Nick explained to Jake how he liked the idea of incorporating as much glass as possible into his house. "Is that gonna cost me a lot more?" he asked.

"Just a bit," Jake replied. "It means you have to think hard about heating systems, and that kind of glass isn't the cheapest building material."

"But it's possible?"

"Sure, it's possible."

"Can we get together sometime soon and talk through my options?"

"We'll be up there at the weekend, as usual," Jake replied. "Why don't you come over to the beach house Saturday lunchtime? We can go through everything then."

"Sounds great. Is it okay if I bring Becky?"

"Of course it is. I was just about to suggest it. Cassie's dying to meet her properly. They only got to say a brief hello at the opening. Only do me a favor and make sure she doesn't mention that you waited nine years for her… I doubt Mark or I will ever hear the end of it." Nick laughed and Jake joined in before hanging up the call.

"Come on, baby," Nick whispered, his hand resting on the tiles behind her head. He had two fingers deep inside her, while his thumb rubbed over her clitoris, the water cascading over their naked bodies. She'd already come twice – the first time within minutes of their arrival at the trailer. Their kiss at the hotel, when he'd called to collect her, had set things in motion and, by the time they'd driven out to his place, he knew she was too far gone to wait a moment longer. When he'd closed the trailer door, he'd turned and kissed her again, just lightly, just once… and that was it. He had to admit, the sight of her in her black stockings and heels, her panties around one ankle, her skirt pushed up, her legs apart, while his fingers worked her over, was almost too much for him. She'd taken just a few minutes to scream his name at the top of her voice. She was still stuttering out the last breaths of that first orgasm when he'd lifted her into his arms and carried her through to his bedroom, laying her down and, without bothering to undress her, had licked her to another screaming, shattering climax. Now, she stood in the shower, her back against the cool tiles, her naked body writhing into his touch. "Come for me. I want all of you," he urged. "Give me everything you've got." She looked up into his eyes, just as he flexed his fingers inside her. Her legs buckled and he quickly moved his free arm to hold her up as she clung onto him, biting his shoulder and crying out his name over and over.

"No more," she murmured. "I can't take it."

"Are you sure about that?" he whispered, clasping her chin in his hand and raising her face to his. His fingers were still inside her and she whimpered as he started to move them again.

"Oh God," she murmured. "Please, let me rest. Or at least eat something."

"You're hungry?" He looked down at her.

She nodded. "Ravenous."

"I thought you might be," he whispered, moving back, but leaving his fingers where they were, his thumb now circling over her again.

She squirmed into him, and he felt the throb from deep inside her. "How can you be doing this to me… again?" She looked up into his eyes.

"It's not me. It's all you, baby." He smiled down at her, then knelt and, opening her up to him, he ran his tongue across her sensitized nub.

"Yes!" she screamed, and he felt her hands come around behind his head, holding him in place as she raised one leg, putting it over his shoulder and pushed herself onto him. He pumped his fingers in and out of her, licking harder and faster as she came loudly, begging him for more, screaming at him to never stop. Eventually, her standing leg gave way and she collapsed onto him. He caught her and held her shuddering body in his arms until the spasms subsided.

"I really do need to rest," she whispered into him.

"Okay," he replied, brushing the wet hair from her cheeks with his fingers. "I think you probably have had enough – at least for now." He got to his feet, taking her with him and shutting off the shower, before he carried her into the bedroom. He stood her up. "Can you stand?" he asked, still holding onto her. She nodded, sleepily, and he wrapped her in a soft bathrobe, pulling it closed around her, before backing her onto the bed and letting her sit. Then he fetched a towel from the bathroom and used it to dry her hair, before going to her bag, finding her hairbrush and slowly, gently brushing it out.

"Still hungry?" he asked, standing back just a little, putting down the brush and using the towel to wipe the last drips of water from his body.

She nodded her head and he noticed her eyes dropped to his bone hard erection. He wondered… but then dismissed the thought, even though the image of her lips around his cock had filled many of his dreams.

"I've made a chicken salad," he said softly, and she looked up at him. He thought he detected a hint of disappointment and it made him smile. He wondered if she was remembering the same thing as him. She might have only sucked his cock twice while they were together, but she'd done so with unrivaled enthusiasm. Even so, now wasn't the time. She looked tired, satisfied, contented, and so fucking beautiful. He pulled her up the bed, letting her head rest on the pillow.

"I'll only be a minute," he said. "Try not to fall asleep before I get back."

"I'll try," she murmured, and he went through to the kitchen, grabbing the two bowls of salad he'd prepared earlier, and the dressing, together with two forks and two glasses of chilled Chardonnay, which he put onto a tray, before carrying it all through to the bedroom.

"You're still awake then," he said, setting the tray down on the dresser.

"Just," she replied.

He handed her a bowl of salad, and put her glass of wine on the nightstand next to her, before joining her in bed. She ate heartily, her hunger obvious, and that thought made him smile again. Sex was clearly good for her.

Afterwards, he took the dishes out to the kitchen and returned to her. "Come on," he said quietly, "let's get you out of this." He pulled her to her feet and removed the bathrobe, letting it fall to the floor, revealing her perfect body again. "God, I love you," he murmured, pulling back the comforter and lowering her into bed. Her eyes shuttered closed. "Sleep well, baby."

"Come to bed," she whispered.

He smiled. "I'm going to." He picked up the bathrobe and hooked it up behind the door before going back across and lying down beside her. She rolled over, resting her head on his chest and he put his arm around her, as she brought hers around him, her hand on his stomach.

He heard her whisper, "My Nick," as she nestled down into him. She sounded almost drunk. It was real cute.

Becky had only brought an overnight bag with her, but the next evening, Nick met her at the hotel after he'd finished work and, at his insistence, she packed up all her belongings.

"I want you with me," he said quietly. "I don't care that you're still married or that people might talk, especially in a small town like Somers Cove."

"Are you asking me to move in with you?" Becky asked as she emptied the contents of her drawers into her case.

Nick sat on the bed watching her. "Yeah, I guess I am."

"And you don't think it's a little soon?" she asked, although he noticed she didn't stop packing.

He got up and went over to her, kissing her. "Nope. And neither do you."

Once they'd gone back to the trailer, Nick spent the rest of that evening, reminding Becky that four orgasms wasn't her limit. She could easily manage six with the right encouragement and, the following morning, while they showered together, she reached down, her hands soaped up, and placed them around his cock. He froze to start with, uncertain what to do, and then watched her glide her fingers gently back and forth along his length. He stopped her before he came. He didn't want her to jerk him off in the shower. He wanted his first time with her in nine years to be a lot more special than that.

On Thursday night, they were together, naked on the couch. Becky was sitting in the corner, while Nick lay out, his head resting in her lap. He'd already made her come three times in less than thirty minutes and was now giving her a rest, while their chicken and roasted vegetables cooked in the oven. He decided the time had come to raise an important question, one which he thought needed answering probably sooner rather than later, the way things were going.

"Bex," he said gently, "I need to ask you something."

"Hmm…" Her voice was a little sleepy.

"Should I get some condoms?" he asked. He felt her tense. "I don't mean right now, this minute," he added quickly. "I mean, should I buy some… soon."

She relaxed. "You mean you'd need to buy them?" she asked. "You don't have any already?"

"No." She was looking down at him, a slight smile on her lips. "Why would I have condoms?" he asked

She shrugged. "I don't know. I guess I thought all men had them."

"Not this one." He reached up and traced a line across her lips with his fingertip, smiling when she shivered. "I used to, obviously…"

"I remember," she said. "I wondered if you owned shares at one stage."

"Well, we did use a lot of them." They may have only had sex over the course of a week when they'd been together before, but it had been a very busy week. They both smiled to themselves, remembering. "The ones I had left expired years ago."

"Oh. I see."

"And I haven't needed to buy any since," he continued, his voice fading a little. "But now… Well, it's just, reading your body, I think we're gonna need some."

"We're not," she said softly.

"Oh, okay." He felt a little crushed. "I must've read the signs wrong. I'm sorry. I thought you were—"

She sat forward, leaning over him, and placed her hand on his cheek. "I am," she said. "I really am. I need you so damn much, Nick. You're not reading me wrong at all."

"I'm not?" He couldn't help but smile. "But in that case…"

"You don't need condoms because I'm on birth control."

"You take the pill?" he asked. He hadn't noticed her taking it over the last few days, and they'd done pretty much everything together.

"No. I get the shot every three months." She turned away, a shadow crossing her eyes. Nick sat up and moved next to her.

"What?" he said. "What's bothering you?"

"It's just that it's another thing to do with Tyler," she muttered, folding her arms across her chest.

"He didn't want kids?" Nick asked.

"No. He did."

"Oh. So you didn't?"

She shook her head and sighed out a breath. "I started getting the shot about two weeks after the wedding."

"Did he know?" Nick asked.

"No." She looked up at him. "That was the whole point. I couldn't take the pill, because I couldn't risk him finding them and realizing what I was doing. I know it was wrong of me to deceive him, especially when he wanted children, but his motives were all wrong. He only wanted kids so he could give the impression of being a settled family man at his office. It had nothing to do with me, or any child we might have had together. It was bad enough that he hurt me. There was no way I was gonna risk him hurting a child as well. So, I got the shot and kept it a secret from him."

"And he didn't guess? When you didn't get pregnant, I mean?"

"No. All the while we were still sleeping together, at the beginning, he blamed me for not getting pregnant. I guess he was entitled to that. It was my fault, after all."

"Not your fault, Bex. Your choice."

"Well, I suppose he'd have been quite right if he'd said he was entitled to a part of that choice."

"Yeah... the same as you were entitled to not be beaten and raped." Nick could hear the anger in his own voice and took a deep breath just as the timer beeped on the oven, announcing that their supper was ready. He leant over her. "Sorry," he whispered. "Even thinking about your husband gets me mad."

"Yes. I did notice that you stopped using his name a few days ago."

"I did?" Nick hadn't even realized.

"Yes." She looked at him. "I think it's best if we both try real hard not to talk about him, or even think about him, don't you?"

Nick smiled. "I'll go along with that." He touched the yellowing bruise around her eye. "It's kinda hard though."

"I know." She held his hand in hers.

He kissed her gently then pulled back. "You still get this shot, do you?" he asked, changing the subject. She nodded. "Then we don't need condoms?"

"No. I also had myself tested after I found out he was having the affair. I wanted to be sure..." She stared up at him. "At least he just left me with bad memories, and nothing else..."

"We can make those better," he murmured.

"I know." He kissed her again. Harder this time.

They didn't make love that night. Somehow the talk of Tyler had dulled the moment and, after they'd eaten, they went to bed and hugged until they drifted off to sleep, waking late and rushing off to work with a deeply satisfying kiss that promised a lot more.

Nick arrived home from work to find Becky already there. He'd given her a key earlier in the week and she'd let herself in and was chopping vegetables in the kitchen.

"Well. I could get used to this," he smirked, leaning back against the closed door. "You, in my kitchen, cooking for me."

"That sounds a bit possessive." She smiled over at him.

"Only in a good way." He came around behind her, put his arms around her and kissed her neck. She dropped her knife and twisted in his arms, leaning up and kissing him. They both deepened the kiss and, within moments, he was pulling her blouse from her skirt, feeling her soft skin beneath.

"Can we take this to the bedroom?" he asked.

"You want to…?" She looked up at him, not finishing the sentence.

"I'm happy to go on as we are," he murmured, kissing her again, and undoing the button on her skirt, pushing it down over her hips and letting it fall to her ankles.

She leant back. "And if I want more?"

He smiled. "Then I'll think I've died and gone to heaven."

"You haven't," she said softly. "What you've done for me over the last few days has been incredible and I love you so much for taking me back to myself… But I really don't want to wait any longer. I need you, Nick. I need all of you."

"Oh God," he whispered, leaning back and looking down at her, standing before him in stockings, heels and a blouse. "You've got no idea how good it feels to hear you say that. It's been a really, really long wait for this."

She giggled slightly and touched his cheek. "For me too." She paused for a moment. "I mean, I know I wasn't on my own like you were, but it wasn't the same," she whispered. "It was never the same."

"I know." He bent down and lifted her into his arms, kissing her as he carried her into the bedroom.

He set her down on her feet and slowly removed the rest of her clothes until she was naked. Then he stripped, thinking quickly. He had to make it right for her…

He took her hand and led her to the bed, feeling her shaking.

"Relax," he whispered. "If you want me to stop, you just have to say. At any time, if there's anything I'm doing that you don't want, or don't like, tell me."

She nodded.

"Okay," he murmured and, keeping hold of her hand, he sat down on the bed, his feet planted firmly on the floor, his legs together.

"You want me to sit on you again?" she asked. "Like at the hotel?" And he noticed she was looking at his face, avoiding his erection, even though her eyes were on fire.

"Kind of," he replied. He knew he had to keep eye contact with her, so she knew the connection was with him, and so that no-one else – no nightmare memories – could drift into her mind, and he'd thought of something she'd always loved doing before – or a variation of it, anyway. "Come here," he said, letting go of her hand. "Now, put your hands on my shoulders and your knees up on the bed, either side of me." She did as he told her, slowly straddling him as he brought his hands around behind her, cradling her ass and pulling her closer, his cock between them. Her breasts were hard up against his chest, her arms around his shoulders, her fingers entwined in his hair, her mouth touching his and he opened up and kissed her gently.

"We used to do this," she whispered. "Except you used to lie down, didn't you?"

"Yeah, but I want to be closer to you this time. I want to touch you, and kiss you… and hold onto you." She smiled. "Remember," he said, softly, "tell me if you don't like it, or if it hurts, or you want to stop." She nodded.

He raised her, positioning her above his aching cock, then very slowly, lowered her down again.

"Stop!" she cried almost immediately and he stilled, the head of his cock only just inside her. He went to lift her off, but she shook her head. "No, don't," she said quietly. "I just need to get used to it." She looked at him, a soft smile on her lips. "I told you… you're a lot bigger than I remember."

He couldn't help but grin. "Let me know when you're ready to carry on," he whispered, kissing her neck.

"I'm ready," she said quickly and, he lowered her down a little further. "Oh… Jeez." She flinched, curling into him and he stopped again. "You're stretching me so much, Nick." She stared at him. "Are you sure it fits?"

He smirked. "Yes. I'm sure. You're wet enough; you just need to relax, baby, that's all." He held onto her. "Take a deep breath," he urged. "And let it out real slow." As she did, he lowered her a little further. "Okay?" he asked and she nodded. "Just let it happen," he said. "Trust that I won't hurt you, and let it happen."

"I know you won't hurt me," she whispered. He lowered her a lot further this time. "How much more is there to go?" she asked. "We must be nearly there by now."

He smiled again. "No… we're about half way," he replied.

"Seriously?"

"You can take it, baby. You did before."

"I know… I remember."

"Then remember how good it feels," he whispered. "You used to tell me you loved to feel so full. You said it made you feel complete."

She nodded and let out a moan as he lowered her further. "Oh, God… Yes! Like that," she breathed.

"Better?" he asked. She nodded. She seemed to be getting used to it. "Okay," he said quietly. "You take over. You've got about three or four inches left to go." He released her as she put her weight on his shoulders and lifted herself just a fraction, waiting, holding her breath and letting it out with a long deep sigh, before moving down on him, taking the remainder of his length in one go.

"Oh… Yes!" she screamed. "Right there. That's so good. So, so good."

It was. It surpassed even his wildest dreams. He'd never felt her like this before. In the past there had always been a condom between them, but as she settled onto him, he was acutely aware of her soft walls clasped tightly around him. She was like a velvet sheath over his throbbing cock and it was all he could do not to fill her. He focused, swallowing down the lump in his throat.

"Move, baby," he urged. "Take me."

She looked into his eyes and, without hesitation, she started to ride him, slowly at first, rocking against him, clearly getting used to the sensation of having him so deep inside her. Then, using his shoulders for leverage, she started to increase the pace, going faster and faster, taking him harder with every stroke, a guttural cry emitting from deep in her throat each time she slammed down onto him. He put his hands on her waist, holding her steady as she rose up and down on his thick shaft, her head rocking back in rapture. It was almost too much for him to bear.

"I'm sorry, Bex," he murmured. "I can't last much longer."

She flexed her hips into him and he felt her thighs shudder, felt that familiar ripple deep inside her. God, he'd forgotten how good that was. She was gonna come, real soon. He just had to hold on a few seconds more…

"Please wait," she urged, staring at him. "I'm so close."

"I know, baby." She stuttered out a deep breath, let her head roll back and, with an almost anguished cry, he felt her inner muscles grip him tight as she screamed out his name. That was it for him. He yelled out a long-held howl, and he let go inside her, pouring himself into her, so deep, over and over until his cock ached. And still she rode him, still she cried on him, tears pouring down her cheeks, begging for it to never end, demanding more, pleading for his love, for all of him. He held her, watching her calm, and reassuring her, whispering his love, telling her she was safe, she was his, she always had been, always would be. He wiped away her tears with his thumbs and kissed her tenderly, not letting her go until her breathing had returned to normal.

"I'm sorry," she murmured, her head resting on his shoulder.

"What for?" he asked, surprised.

"For crying. For getting so emotional."

"Hey. It's fine."

"It just all came out," she whispered. "All the lost years, all the sadness."

"Don't be sad." He leant back and cupped her face with one hand, while he continued to hold her with the other.

"I'm not. I was; but I'm not anymore."

"Good." He smiled at her and covered her lips with his own, kissing her deeply.

He broke the kiss eventually and stared into her eyes. "You said you wanted more…" he said, smiling. "Well, actually it was more of a command than a request." He grinned. "Did you mean right now?"

She squirmed. "Oh God. You're still so hard." Her eyes widened, the familiar fire returning.

"Of course I'm still hard. I'm still inside you, for one thing." He put his hand behind her head and pulled her closer, then whispered in her ear, "But I'm gonna be hard for a helluva long time yet. I've got nine years to make up for."

"In one night?" she teased.

"No, but just because we've got forever, doesn't mean we can't start right now." He flexed his hips up into her and she ground hers onto him, taking him deeper than ever and letting out a throaty giggle as she started to move again.


Nick parked his truck alongside Jake's BMW, noticing that Mark's car was there also.

"I didn't know Mark was going to be here," Becky said.

"Neither did I, but I'm not that surprised. Emma probably wants to talk weddings with Cassie." He switched off the engine. "Oh, and I forgot to mention; Jake and Cassie have a little girl. Her name's Maddie. She's four, she's completely adorable, and she's deaf."

"Oh, okay."

"Sorry. I probably should have told you that before now."

"How does she communicate?" Becky asked.

"We can all sign. Well, we can sign a little bit." He smiled at her. "Cassie's amazing, and Jake's catching up. Emma's really good too."

"And you?" she asked.

"I get by, but don't worry about it. We'll help you out." Becky nodded. "Ready?" he asked.

She nodded and he got out and came around to her side, opening the door and helping her down. He put his hands on her waist. "Did I thank you for last night?" he asked, leaning in and kissing her gently.

She smiled. "Yes, you did… and this morning. Several times."

"I'm sorry we didn't get much sleep."

"Don't be," she murmured. "I'm not."

He took her hand and led her along the path and up the steps onto the porch of the beach house.

"This is a beautiful place," Becky said, looking around at the ocean view.

"Yeah. It was Cassie's mom's, until she died, last spring," Nick explained, pulling the screen door open and putting his hand on the door handle.

"Shouldn't we knock?" Becky whispered, pulling him back.

"No-one knocks here." Nick grinned at her and pushed the door open. "Hi guys," he called out. Everyone moved toward them at the same time and they all greeted Becky like they'd known her forever. Mark gave him a look over the top of Emma's head – a kind of knowing smirk that he didn't really understand.

Maddie was standing by Cassie, who leant down, ready introduce her, just as Becky knelt in front of the little girl and started to sign. Nick stared at her, not following anything of what was being said, before he glanced up at Cassie. Maddie grinned and signed something back, and Becky laughed, before getting up. She looked around, seemingly surprised to find everyone staring at her.

"What was that about?" Nick asked.

Becky looked embarrassed, moving closer to him again, and Cassie stepped forward, taking her arm. "Your girlfriend was just telling my daughter that she's wearing a beautiful dress, and how much she loves her hair, and Maddie offered to let her play with her dolls later on." She looked at Becky. "You sign better than I do," she said, pulling Becky away from him and into the kitchen.

"I've got a cousin," she explained, glancing back at Nick, who thought she looked a little worried. "He's a lot older than me and he and his wife had a son twelve years ago. He was born deaf and the whole family learned to sign."

"I didn't know," Nick said, coming and standing beside her.

"Why would you?" she asked, leaning into him.

"I feel such an idiot for saying we'd help you out."

"Well, Becky can help us instead," Mark suggested, as they all sat down around the table.

Maddie came and sat beside Becky, bringing a doll with her, and offering it to Becky.

"That's her favorite," Jake said, smiling. "You are honored."

Becky smiled down at Maddie, then lifted her onto her lap and started playing. Nick took a seat beside her, his heart more full of love than ever.

Over lunch, Mark produced a bottle of champagne, and everyone toasted Emma, who was now the proud owner of the coffee shop. Nick noticed her blushing, but felt proud of her for finally achieving her ambition, even if she was very quick to praise Mark for his support and Nick for all his legal help. Afterwards, Jake took Nick up to his office in the converted attic, and Mark followed, saying he was intrigued by Nick's plans for his house, leaving the women downstairs with Maddie. Becky seemed more comfortable now and Nick was less concerned about leaving her.

"So?" Mark said once they were upstairs.

"So what?" Nick asked.

"Care to explain why my new hotel manager called me during the week and told me that my business manager had moved out of her room at the hotel on his first day, and was last seen leaving the premises... with you?" He smirked again.

Nick shook his head. "Christ, I hate this place sometimes," he said. "Can't a guy have any secrets?"

"No," Jake replied, a smile forming on his lips.

Nick let out a sigh. "Okay. Becky's moved in with me."

"Already?" Mark feigned surprise.

"Yeah, already."

"You don't think you're rushing things?" Mark was struggling not to laugh.

"No," he replied. "Nine years is not rushing things."

Jake shrugged. "He's got a point, you know." He leant in closer, lowering his voice. "The thing is, was it worth the wait?"

Nick couldn't help the smile that tweaked his lips. "No comment," he replied.

Mark laughed. "I think we'll take that as a yes. I can't see why else the two of you look so damn tired."

Nick held his hands up in surrender. "I'm saying nothing."

"I think we gathered that," Mark replied. "But I'm real pleased for both of you."

They sat down around the large desk where Jake had laid out some plans.

"And," Mark added, "remember where I am if you need any help with that shit of a husband of hers."

Following a productive hour upstairs, the result of which was that Jake was going to finalize the plans and come up with estimates for building Nick's house, they all went for a walk along the beach and, on their return, Cassie made them coffee. As they walked through into the living room, Maddie came running from her bedroom, straight into Nick, knocking hot coffee all over him.

"Shit!"

Cassie and Becky went over to him, while Jake grabbed Maddie.

"Is she okay?" Nick asked, more concerned for Maddie than himself.

"Yeah, she's fine," Jake replied.

"I think you should take your shirt off," Cassie said.

"It's not that bad." Nick didn't want any fuss.

"She's right, Nick," Becky agreed. "Take it off before it really burns." She pulled his waistcoat off, and yanked his shirt from his jeans before pulling it over his head.

Nick stood there, topless, and feeling embarrassed.

"Your skin's already red," Becky said, studying his chest. "Come into the kitchen."

She took his hand in hers and dragged him through to the kitchen, where Cassie was running a bowl of cold water and adding ice cubes from the deep freeze.

"Here," Cassie was dowsing a towel in the icy water, "use this."

Becky took the towel and held it over Nick's chest. It felt soothing, he had to admit, and he let out a long sigh.

"Thanks," he murmured.

"I'll leave you to it," Cassie said.

"You're sure Maddie's okay?" Nick asked, turning.

"Yes, I'm sure. She should have been more careful."

"It wasn't her fault," Nick said, turning back to Becky and looking down at her. "Will I survive?" he asked, smiling.

"I think so." She grinned up at him. "I just need to hold the towel there for a bit longer."

"I like having your hands on me, although I'm not sure I like standing here like this," he whispered.

"Why?"

"I feel exposed," he admitted.

"Seriously?" Becky smiled, clearly surprised by his discomfort. "I'd have thought you'd be used to admiring glances."

He shrugged and moved a little closer. "Even if I was, there's only one person whose admiration matters to me."

"Good," she murmured.

He leant into her and kissed her gently, just as they heard a cough behind them.

"I brought you a shirt to put on," Jake said, smirking. "It's probably not your style," he added, "but it's better than nothing."

"Sure is," Nick replied. "Thanks."

Once Becky was sure no lasting damage would be done, she helped Nick into the shirt and slowly did up the buttons, not taking her eyes from his.

"You're enjoying this a bit too much," Nick whispered.

"I can't help it if I like looking after you," she replied.

"And there was me thinking you were just enjoying looking *at* me."

"I didn't say I wasn't."

He leant down again and kissed her cheek. "I think we'll continue this later…"

She nodded, looking up into his eyes, and he took her hand, leading her back into the living room.

Emma looked up at him as he and Becky sat down opposite her and Mark. "You kept that hidden well," she said, smiling.

"What?" he asked, pretending innocence, even though he knew precisely what she meant.

"The ink," she explained. "I've never seen it before."

"Neither have I," Jake added.

"Nor me." Cassie joined in.

"Yeah, well…" He didn't really know what to say.

"Why has no-one seen it?" Becky asked. "You've had it for nearly nine years…"

"Nine years?" Emma couldn't hide her surprise. "And none of us have ever seen it, even though you stayed with me… twice?"

"No. I've made a point of never taking my shirt off in front of anyone," Nick explained. "I didn't want anyone to see it."

"Why?" From the tone of Becky's voice, he wondered if she thought that meant he'd been ashamed of it… or, worse still, her.

He pulled her into his arms. "Only because I didn't want to answer questions about us, or you, or our relationship, and more particularly, how I fucked up. Keeping it hidden had nothing to do with anything, other than wanting to bury my feelings, that's all." He looked into her eyes, ignoring everyone else in the room. "It was about me, Bex, not you."

She nodded her head and nestled into him.

"So," Emma said, looking at him, "the 'B' is for 'Becky'?"

"Of course."

"And the roses?"

"Everyone knows roses are the flowers of love." Mark put in, winking at Nick.

"And you told me you weren't interested in flowers," Emma teased.

Mark leant over. "Leave your brother alone," he whispered, kissing the top of her head affectionately, and Emma smiled across at Nick. He got the feeling he hadn't heard the last of that one.

Later on, Emma, Cassie, and Becky cooked a roast beef dinner, and Nick kept a watchful eye, relieved to see and hear Becky laughing a lot. Despite her earlier nerves, she'd settled in well with his friends, which didn't surprise him in the least. They sat around the table eating together, and then Maddie insisted Becky put her to bed and she signed her a story, which impressed everyone, but probably Nick more than anyone else.

When they were leaving, Becky reminded Mark that she was going to need Monday morning off to go and see Tom Allen about her divorce.

"I haven't forgotten," Mark replied. "Take the day, if you need to. Kyle seems to have things under control at the hotel, and there's nothing else that can't wait for a day."

"I won't need the whole day. I'm sure it'll be fine."

They all said goodbye and Nick drove them back to the trailer.

Even in the darkness, he noticed Becky's eyes closing on the short journey. He wasn't that surprised. It had been a long day, and they'd had almost no sleep the night before. Although he'd said they didn't need to make up for the nine lost years in one night, they'd done a fine job of trying to.

When he pulled up outside the trailer, Becky didn't stir at all. He turned off the engine and got out, going around to her side and lifting her into his arms.

"Hello," she murmured, resting her head on his shoulder and nuzzling into him.

"You're meant to be asleep," he replied.

"I am..."

He smiled and, locking the car, carried her into the trailer.

# Chapter Thirteen

## *Becky*

"What's bothering you?" Nick asked.

After he'd undressed her the previous night, she'd fallen asleep on him, cradled in his arms, feeling safe and loved. Then this morning, they'd woken, their bodies entwined, and he'd made love to her for an hour or so, before they'd taken a shower together.

Now, they were sitting eating brunch. Well, Nick was eating; Becky was pushing her food around the plate.

She looked up at him, but didn't reply.

"Is it tomorrow?" he asked.

She nodded, finding it hard to speak.

"You're nervous?" Nick's voice was filled with concern.

"Yes."

"Why?"

"Because I'm gonna have to tell him everything, aren't I?" The thought of telling a stranger what Tyler had done to her filled her with dread.

"Yeah, you are."

She put her fork down on the side of her plate, her food barely touched.

"Do you want me to be there with you?" he offered. It wasn't something they'd discussed before.

She looked up, a smile touching her lips.

"Would you?"

"Of course. If it's what you want."

"It won't…" She paused. "It probably won't be easy for you."

"I'm sure it won't," he agreed. "But it won't be easy for you either. It'll be better for both of us, if we're together. I'll only sit in my office worrying about you."

"You will?"

"Of course I'll worry about you. I hate the idea of you going through that alone." He sighed. "You need to get used to the idea that I care about you, Bex. I care about you a lot."

She stared at him for a moment. "I care about you too."

"I know." He got up, came around to her side of the table and pulled her to her feet and into his arms. "I know you do," he whispered.

She looked up into his eyes. "Are you sure though, Nick? I mean, about coming with me tomorrow. You're going to have to hear details about Tyler and me – and our marriage."

"I get how this works, Bex. I've done it before."

"But not when it's someone you're involved with."

"Obviously not," he admitted. "But I can take it. If you need me, I'll be there."

She leant into him, resting her head on his chest and welcoming the feeling of his strong arms around her, his hand on her head, stroking her hair.

"There's one thing though," he said softly. She looked up at him. "I think, as far as Tom's concerned, we should pretend we're just friends, not lovers. It might not help your case."

She smiled. "You called me your lover," she whispered. "That's what you used to call me."

"That's the thing about lawyers… we're sticklers for accuracy. You are my lover, Bex."

She nodded. "Yes, I am."

He bent forward, his lips poised over hers. "Wanna prove it?" he whispered.

"Again?"

"Yeah… again." He captured her mouth, claiming her and walking her backwards to the couch, where he lowered her onto the soft cushions. Lying her down, he leant over and, undoing her jeans, he yanked them and her panties off, dropping them to the floor and standing again to admire her. She couldn't help but notice the outline of his hard erection through his jeans and she wanted to touch him. He was just about to move between her legs, when she sat up and held him still, shifting and grabbing his hips. "What's wrong?" he asked, looking down at her, concern etched on his face. "I thought—"

"I know, but…" She still wasn't her old self. She couldn't yet say what was going through her mind, so she let her actions do the talking and reached up, her fingers fumbling with his belt.

"Do you need a hand with that?" he asked, a smile forming on his lips, but she shook her head.

"I'll manage." She tried again, her fingers shaking less this time as she released the buckle and undid the button behind it, then lowered his zipper. She tugged down his jeans, freeing him, and he stepped out of them and quickly pulled off his shirt before she took him in her hand, circling him gently, her fingers and thumb barely meeting.

"Oh, God…" Nick hissed between his clenched teeth, "that's so good."

She glanced up and saw his steely gray eyes piercing hers as she moved her hand slowly up and down the whole length of his shaft, building a steady rhythm.

She stared at his cock in her hand and licked her lips slowly, wondering what it would be like to taste him again, and whether she could.

"You don't have to do anything you don't want to, you know that, don't you?" His words interrupted her train of thought.

"Of course." She started moving her hands again. "I know you're not Tyler."

She saw his expression change, his eyes darken and his lips form into a thin line, just before he grabbed her hand.

"Can we talk?" he asked.

"Um… sure. Did I do something wrong?"

He crouched down in front of her, still holding her hand in his, looking deep into her eyes.

"No, baby. You didn't do anything wrong. It's just, well… I find it kinda hard…"

"What?"

"Him."

"Tyler, you mean?"

He nodded slowly. "I know he's a fact in your life and there's nothing we can do about that, apart from what we're already doing, but I really don't wanna think about him when we're together." He swallowed hard and she could see the emotion in his face. "I'll be here for you. If you wanna talk, I'll listen to anything you need to tell me, and I'll come with you when you see Tom, please don't doubt any of that. But I can't think about him when we're making love. I can't have him in my head, Bex. I can't think about him being with you, or what he did to you."

"It's okay," she whispered, leaning forward.

"No, it's not. What he did to you will never be okay."

"You're right, it's not okay. But I'm sorry. I shouldn't have said his name."

"It's not just saying his name…" He paused. "It's knowing you're thinking about him."

"I'm not." She leant back, pulling away from him, closing her legs and curling in on herself. "I'm not," she repeated.

He huffed out a sigh, sat down beside her and leant in closer, pulling her into him. "Yeah, you are… just not in the way that you think I mean," he whispered. "I'm not saying you're thinking about him romantically. I know you're not. But, just now," he continued, "you were thinking about something you used to do to me, weren't you?" He waited, and eventually she nodded her head, just once. "You used to take me in your mouth. What you could do to me was mind-blowing, and that memory has fed so many of my dreams about you over the years. But I know, just now, you were thinking about the times he made you do that, and you were wondering if you'd be able to do it with me again."

She looked up at him and her mouth dropped open. "How did you know?"

"I told you, I can read your body."

"And my mind?" she queried.

"Well, no. But I saw the way you were looking at me. You were licking your lips, staring at me. It wasn't hard to work out what you had in mind. But the look in your eyes was… well, it was pure fear."

"I'm sorry." She curled up a little more.

"I don't want you to be sorry, Bex. I want you to feel safe with me."

"I do."

It was like he hadn't heard her. "I want you to realize you don't have to do anything – not one damn thing – that you're not comfortable with, and I want you to understand, if what he did to you has changed how you feel about doing certain things with me, then that's okay… well it isn't, but you get what I mean. I'm happy… I'm absolutely ecstatic, that you're back in my life, that I get to hold you and kiss you and wake up next to you, that I get to make love to you. If what we have now is all we ever get, then I'm more than okay with that, and how I feel about you isn't gonna change. Not ever."

"I know," she whispered, snuggling into him. "And I do feel safe with you." She kissed his neck, just gently.

"Good," he replied, his fingers gliding down her back.

She shuddered. "The thing is," she murmured, "I would like to try that again."

"You wanna take me in your mouth?" he asked and she nodded her head. "You're sure?" He raised her face to his, looking into her eyes.

"Yes. I want to taste you again."

She didn't wait for him to respond but moved down his body. She hoped he wouldn't touch her head, or force himself into her mouth, like Tyler had done. Nick would be gentle, she knew that, but even so…

He settled down into the corner of the couch and she quickly took off her sweater and bra, then rested between his legs, holding him in her hands, as she ran her tongue gently over and around the tip of his cock.

"How far do you want this to go, Bex?" he asked, just as she opened her mouth.

She looked up at him and smiled. "As far as you like."

He grinned and put his hands behind his head, his eyes not leaving hers. She understood what he was doing, without him saying a word.

He got that he couldn't touch her, and he was letting her know he wouldn't. She had control. "Sounds good to me, babe," he murmured, and let out a long, deep groan as her lips closed around him.

"Oh, God… That's so deep," she whispered, barely able to speak. After Nick had climaxed in her mouth, they'd held each other in contented silence while he caught his breath, and then she'd screamed herself hoarse through three orgasms during the course of the afternoon. Now, they'd eaten the Moroccan lamb and vegetables Nick had prepared and cooked while she'd snoozed away the early evening. They'd drawn the curtains, turned up the heating just a fraction, lit some candles, and were more than halfway through a bottle of red wine.

"Is it too much?" he asked, stilling. He was standing, looking down at her, while she lay on her back, on the edge of the cleared dining table, looking up at him as he held her ankles wide apart, his cock buried deep inside her.

"No." She shook her head. "It's never too much."

He smiled. "Touch yourself," he said, "like you did in the hotel room, when I guided you. I wanna watch you this time."

She didn't hesitate, but reached down between her legs and started to rub herself, slowly to start with, but then faster and faster, her back arching off the table as she soon felt the familiar shiver run through her body. He moved her ankles a little further apart, spreading her legs still wider and giving her even easier access to her hard clitoris.

"God, if I'd known I could do this…" she muttered almost to herself.

She heard him chuckle and looked up at him. He mouthed 'I love you', gazing down at her, then let his eyes drop to her hand, watching her pleasure herself as he increased the speed of his strokes, taking her even deeper.

"Oh, Nick," she groaned, "you're gonna make me…"

And with that, she let out a loud scream, her body contracting into her orgasm, and she felt him plunge into her one last time, heard his loud howl, that seemed to start in his stomach and fill the whole trailer, maybe even the whole forest, as he let go inside her.

"Please take a seat," Tom said, standing behind his desk and offering Becky a chair opposite him. Neither she nor Nick had slept very well, and at around four that morning, they'd both admitted defeat and he'd just held her in his arms until it was time to get up. She glanced around Tom's office. There was only one chair and she looked quickly at Nick, feeling suddenly afraid that he'd be forced to leave her alone. "You really shouldn't be in here," Tom added, looking at Nick.

"I'm staying," Nick replied, his voice firm. It was the first time she'd seen him in his professional environment and, although he still looked like her Nick – his eyes still soft, his smile still loving – there was a hardness to his voice when he spoke to Tom that she didn't recognize, and she knew the older man wouldn't argue with him.

Tom looked from one of them to the other and shrugged.

Nick went outside, returning moments later with another chair, and placed it beside Becky's, before sitting down. They looked across the desk at Tom. He was very different to Nick, and not just in the fact that he wore an absolutely pristine suit and looked immaculate. Judging from the way he fiddled with just about everything on his desk, he seemed nervous and high-strung, while Nick sat back in his chair, his legs crossed, his arms folded across his chest, a picture of calm relaxation. She wondered how Tom and Nick got along in their professional relationship; she could imagine there were arguments between them.

Tom looked up, making eye contact with her, and ignoring Nick. "Now," he said, his voice quiet. "I need you to tell me how you met your husband."

"How I met him?" Becky was surprised and confused. "Why is that relevant?"

"I'm just looking for background information, that's all."

"But, surely, this is about how the marriage broke down, not how it started."

He stared at her for a long moment. "Why do you want a divorce, Mrs Howell?" he asked, out of the blue. "What is it you feel your husband has done wrong?"

She could sense the tension in Nick, even though they weren't sitting that close together, and replied quickly before he could say anything. "He's had at least one affair, to my knowledge," she said.

"Well, I don't know if you're aware," Tom replied, looking smug, "adultery isn't always admissable as grounds for divorce. Not in Massachusetts, which is where you'd be filing."

"He told me that," she whispered.

"Then maybe you should've listened to him, my dear."

"Stop being a patronizing ass," Nick cut in, getting to his feet. Becky reached out and grabbed for his hand, but he pulled away from her. "You and I both know that's bullshit, Tom. His adultery *is* admissable as grounds. But she doesn't have to use it if she doesn't want to; she can go for a no fault divorce." Nick was breathing heavily.

Tom was very red in the face, staring up at Nick. "This has nothing to do you with you," he hissed.

"It has everything to do with me, if you're going to bullshit a client our firm is representing."

"I wasn't aware Mrs Howell was a client – yet," Tom replied.

"Are you refusing to take her case?" Nick asked.

"No. But I'm not convinced she has grounds…" He paused. "And, if I'm being honest, I'm not even convinced she actually wants a divorce."

## Nick

Before he could even form a response to Tom's statement, Becky was standing beside him.

"Of course I want a divorce. I hate him. He was unfaithful to me, and he beat me. He tried to rape me, on more than one occasion. I don't just *want* a divorce, Mr Allen, I *need* one."

Tom was staring at Becky, his face almost white. He was clearly shocked. *Good.*

"What the hell are you doing?" Nick asked him. "Mrs Howell has already told you what she wants and it's not your place, or your job, to query that. You're here to listen to her story – all of it, not just the bits you want to hear – and to give her legal advice, not marital counseling. Besides which, the time for any kind of reconciliation has long since passed."

"Divorce is messy." Tom seemed to be ignoring Nick and kept his eyes fixed on Becky. "It's not always the best solution. Sometimes even a bad marriage can be saved."

"Are you fucking serious?" Nick said, raising his voice. "She's already told you, he beats her, he abuses her, and he's having at least one affair. He's the one who gave up on the marriage, not her. Why the hell should she try and reconcile anything? Why should she try and make it work, when he clearly doesn't give a damn? In reality, he should be behind bars, but Mrs Howell doesn't want to have to go through the ordeal of going to court over what he's done to her. All she wants is to be free of him."

Tom was staring at Nick now, his mouth slightly open, clearly taken aback. *Damn.* He'd been trying to remain impartial, but clearly that hadn't worked. He needed to rein in his emotions, so Tom couldn't guess that there was anything going on between him and Becky. He heaved in a long breath and stepped back, resuming his seat and crossing his legs again.

Becky sat back down too and he stole a glance at her, but she was staring at Tom. He longed to reach over and take her hands in his, offer her some reassurance, but there was nothing he could do – not yet.

"I think, Mrs Howell," Tom began, his voice more subdued, "the best route would be for you to try and speak with your husband."

Nick looked up at Tom. His face was still pale. He was looking at the file on his desk now, not making eye contact with either of them.

"Speak to him?" Becky said. "I can't do that."

"You don't have to," Nick replied. He got up and offered her his hand. She took it and let him pull her to her feet. He wanted to go one step further and take her in his arms, but he held back. "We're leaving," he continued. "I'll find you another lawyer, being as my partner clearly isn't interested in dealing with your case." He pushed his chair to one side and guided her toward the door. "Or, I'll represent you myself, if I have to…"

Becky turned as he opened the door, looking back at Tom. "How much do I owe you?" she asked.

"There's no charge," Nick replied. There had better not be, anyway. If Tom even thought about trying to charge her…

"It's all been taken care of," Tom replied, looking up at them both.

"It has?" Nick said, turning back to face him. "By whom?"

"I had a call this morning, from Mark Gardner. He said he'd cover all of Mrs Howell's legal fees. No limits."

From behind him, he heard Becky let out a sob. Coming on top of the disappointment of the meeting, Mark's kindness was too much for her. "I'm just gonna make sure Mrs Howell is okay," he said to Tom. "And then I'm coming back to talk to you. Don't even think about leaving." Tom's mouth dropped open, but Nick didn't give him a chance to reply before slamming the door closed.

Without saying a word to Tina, their secretary and receptionist, he led Becky through the door, onto Main Street and out of sight of the office, before he pulled her into his arms, holding onto her as she sobbed into him.

"I'm sorry," he whispered into her hair. "If I'd known…"

"It's not your fault," she murmured.

He leant back a little, holding her face in his hands and looking into her eyes. "I'll work it out," he vowed. "I promise. I'll find someone who'll help you. And if I can't, I'll do it myself."

"I don't want you to get into trouble."

"I won't."

He held her again until her sobs subsided, then took her hand in his. "I've gotta see if I can find out what's behind this," he said. "I'm gonna take you to the coffee shop. You can sit with Emma for a while, until I've spoken to Tom." He guided her along the sidewalk. "You'll be safe with Emma, and I won't be long."

"Don't…"

"Don't what?"

"You're not going to hit him, are you?"

He shook his head. "I'm tempted, but no."

He opened the door to the coffee shop, which was quiet, and saw Emma standing behind the counter. He led Becky over and explained the situation. Emma came around the counter and brought them both over to a booth, sitting Becky down.

"I'll make you a coffee and we'll sit together until Nick gets back," she said softly.

"Thank you," Becky's eyes filled with tears again. "I'm sorry. I'm being silly."

"No you're not," Nick said. He turned to Emma, putting his hand on her shoulder. "I won't be long. Call me if you need me."

She nodded and went back behind the counter to make Becky a coffee, while Nick leant over and kissed her gently. "I'll be back before you know it," he said.

"Please be careful," she whispered.

"I'm always careful." He smiled down at her, trying to sound reassuring. "Don't worry. Emma will look after you. I really won't be very long at all, and then I'll take you home." He kissed her again.


"He's on the phone," Tina said, as Nick walked straight toward Tom's office.

"I don't care," Nick replied and opened the door, closing it behind him.

Sure enough, Tom was talking into the phone, but stopped as soon as he saw Nick and said, "I'll have to get back to you," before hanging up the call.

Nick stepped forward and put his hands on the edge of Tom's desk, leaning over toward him. "What the hell is wrong with you?" he asked, keeping his voice as quiet as he could manage.

"There's nothing wrong with me," Tom replied.

"Really? Then why are you being like this? It can't be the money, not if Mark Gardner's offered to cover her fee."

"I'm just not convinced she really wants a divorce."

"And what's that got to do with you?" Nick raised his voice a little. "She's made up her mind. She's come to you for legal advice. It's not for you to say whether she's right or wrong."

"I can't advise her if I don't think she believes in what she's doing."

"Why the fuck not?" Nick shouted. "You've advised and represented countless other people you knew damn well didn't believe in what they were doing. What's different this time?"

Tom didn't reply.

"There's something going on here," Nick said, coming around to Tom's side of the desk. "I know there is." He spun Tom's chair, so they were facing each other, but standing too close for him to get up. "And I'm gonna get to the bottom of it. But first I'm gonna take Becky – Mrs Howell – home. I don't know when I'll be back." He turned to leave.

"Wait," Tom said and Nick stopped. "Nick, please."

Nick paused then turned back. "What?"

"I've known you for a long time," Tom said. "I'm speaking as your friend now, not your partner." There was a long pause and Nick saw a vein pulse on Tom's forehead. "Be careful," he whispered. "Messing with Mrs Howell and her husband could prove a lot more costly than you think."

Nick smiled slowly. "If you think for one second that I'm scared of Tyler Howell, you seriously need to think again."

# Chapter Fourteen

*Becky*

Becky clasped her hands around the coffee cup so Emma couldn't see them shaking. She wanted to go somewhere quiet and curl up by herself. No, that wasn't true. She wanted Nick to hold her, while she curled up. She wanted him to tell her could still make it alright. Except she didn't think he could.

She'd honestly thought things were finally turning around. All she'd needed was a divorce from Tyler and she could move on and be with Nick, but now it seemed she couldn't even do that.

"It'll be okay," Emma said.

Becky looked up. Emma was sitting opposite her in the booth.

"Nick will deal with everything. He's good at what he does, Becky."

"I know," she whispered. "I know he is. I'm just not sure a good lawyer is what I need."

Emma tilted her head to one side. "What do you mean?" she asked.

Becky shook her head slowly. "I think I might need a crooked one."

Emma leant forward. "Why?"

"Because there's something going on here," Becky replied. "I imagine Tyler's behind it somehow, and he's not averse to bending the rules."

"Well," Emma said, smiling, "Nick's as straight as they come. He always obeys the rules. But he knows a few tricks too."

"He sure does."

Becky twisted round at the sound of Nick's voice and moved over so he could sit beside her. He put his arm around her and pulled her close.

"You okay?" he asked.

She shrugged. "Not really."

"Becky thinks Tyler's behind this," Emma explained.

Nick looked at her for a moment. "Well, someone's got Tom scared," he replied. "Whether it's Tyler or not, I don't know."

"Who else could it be?" Becky asked, looking up at him. "Who else would even be interested in me divorcing him?"

"I don't know. The question is, how did Tyler know you were going to see Tom? You didn't tell him."

"I haven't even contacted him." Becky heard the panic in her own voice.

"I know, baby," Nick reassured her. "I'm not doubting you."

"Do you want a coffee," Emma offered, clearly trying to break the tension.

"No, thanks," Nick said. "I think the best thing we can do is to go back to my place." He turned to Becky. "Unless you need to go into work?"

She shook her head. "I couldn't concentrate even if I did. And Mark said I could take the day off, so…"

"Mark will be fine," Emma said. "Go home. Get some rest."

"Thanks for looking after her," Nick replied, getting to his feet and pulling Becky with him.

"You're welcome. I didn't do much." He leant down and kissed Emma's cheek. "Call me later,".

Nick nodded then turned to Becky. "Come on," he said. "Let's get out of here."


"Is it going to be impossible now?" Becky asked.

They'd been home for over an hour and had spent all of that time lying on the couch, side by side, with Nick's arms close around her.

"No," he replied. "It just means we've gotta find another lawyer." He hesitated. "I could represent you, but I'd rather try and find someone else first, if we can. If Tyler found out we're together, and I was representing you, he could make things real difficult."

She nodded. "I don't want to do anything to harm your career."

"Fuck my career. That's not what I meant. He could make things difficult for you, Bex. I don't want that to happen. I care about you." He kissed her gently and let out a sigh. "Sorry," he said, releasing her and sitting up. "I can't handle this."

"Can't handle what?" Her voice was filled with fear, her eyes with tears. "What are you saying, Nick?"

"Hey," he said, putting his arms around her again. "I just mean I feel so powerless sitting here doing nothing. I know there's something behind what Tom did. I've gotta try and work out what. But first, we need to find you another lawyer."

"Can't we just go on the Internet and look for one?"

"We could," he said, getting up and holding out his hand, "but I'd rather use someone we know is on your side, and we both know a man who wants to help, and who might be able to pull some strings for us."

She took his hand and let him pull her to her feet. "Who?"

"Mark," he said. "He's working from home today. And we're gonna go see him."

Mark sat staring at them across his desk, his mouth slightly open.

"He really suggested you should talk to the asshole?" Becky nodded her head. "Even after you'd explained that he used to beat you?"

"Well, he actually suggested it after I'd explained that Tyler had tried to rape me."

She heard Mark gasp, then he suddenly got to his feet and moved away toward the window that overlooked the rear garden and the ocean beyond. Silence descended, and dragged on for several minutes before he came back to his desk, picked up his phone and tapped the screen a few times.

"This is Mark Gardner," he said. "Put me through to Jeremy."

There was a pause, during which Becky stole a glance at Nick, who shrugged, and turned to look at Mark.

"Jeremy," he said. "I'm well, thanks. I need a favor." There was a pause. "No, I haven't burned down any more hotels. I didn't burn down that one, if you remember rightly. This is a little more personal than that." They all waited again, while Mark listened. "I need you to see a friend of mine. Her name's Rebecca Howell. She needs a lawyer to handle her divorce." Again there was a moment's hesitation. "Yeah, I know you don't normally deal with this kind of thing, but I'm asking you to make an exception. That's the favor. I'm not asking you to do it for nothing. I'll cover all expenses, and I want you to make sure I'm billed personally. I don't want this to go through the company." Mark turned away from them and leant against the edge of his desk. "No, it's nothing like that. We're not involved at all. Becky works for me. If you bill the company, the guys in the finance department will see, and the last thing she needs is to become the subject of office gossip…" He paused. "Don't worry, it's fine. I'm not offended; it was a natural misunderstanding. There is one other thing though… I need you to see her tomorrow." Becky looked up and saw Mark's shoulders slump just slightly. It looked like his lawyer couldn't fit her in. "I don't care," Mark said all of a sudden. "Then make the fucking time, Jeremy." He listened for a while, then said, "Thank you," and hung up. Taking a deep breath, he turned around.

His eyes met Becky's and she sucked in a breath at the compassion she saw. "I know you've never actually met him," Mark said, his voice really soft, "but Jeremy's okay. He'll help you." He turned to Nick. "And you're going with her, just to make sure he does." He opened his laptop and starting typing.

"Naturally," Nick replied. "Where are we going?"

"Boston. Your appointment is at eight-thirty in the morning, so you're gonna have to drive down there this evening and stay overnight. Emma and I haven't gotten around to finding an apartment in the city yet, but you can go to the Gardner Central," he said, looking back to Becky. It was their premier hotel in Boston. "I've just booked you into the Riverside Suite."

"Is that good?" Nick asked, and Becky let out a slight laugh.

"It's one of the best," she replied. "Even you'll like it. There's a view of the river."

Nick nodded and she felt him relax a little.

Mark looked at them again. "Is there something I should know?" he asked.

"Nick doesn't like hotels," Becky replied.

"Oh… doesn't he?" Mark stared at him, but Becky could tell he was struggling to keep a straight face.

"So what if I don't?" Nick said. "As I tried to explain to Bex, I didn't buy a plot of land in the middle of the forest, so I could be cooped up, staring at four walls."

"To be honest," Mark replied. "I don't like hotels that much either."

"You don't?" Nick was clearly confused.

"I usually stay at the Central when I'm in Boston, but I never really enjoy the experience."

"And this is where we're gonna be staying?" Nick queried.

"Yeah – for one night. I'm sure you'll cope."

"What don't you like about it?" Becky asked. She was interested, and it was a good diversion from her own problems.

"Well, it's probably just that I'd rather be here with Emma, but it's kinda impersonal, that's all."

"Well, maybe we should learn something from that?" Becky said, raising her eyebrows at him.

"Perhaps we should," he replied. "But can we deal with one thing at a time?"

She nodded and watched him writing down some notes on a piece of paper, before pushing it across the desk.

"That's Jeremy's address, and contact number. Like I say, he's expecting you at eight-thirty and he'll give you an hour."

"Thank you, Mark."

"Don't thank me," he replied, staring at her. "I just wish you'd told me sooner."

"I couldn't. I couldn't tell anyone."

"Becky doesn't find it easy to talk about," Nick explained.

"No. I guess that's understandable."

"Can I ask," Nick said, his voice sounding a little distant and businesslike. "what's the name of Jeremy's company?"

"Slater Wilson," Mark replied. "Jeremy is the Slater part of that. Why do you ask?"

"Because Tyler works for a Boston firm," Nick explained. "I just wanted to make sure they're not connected."

"And are they?" Becky asked.

"No, not to my knowledge. I know of Slater Wilson. I interviewed with them, but I don't know of any connection with Tyler's firm."

"What if this man won't help us?" Becky asked, suddenly feeling afraid.

"He will," Mark said, getting up and coming around to their side of the desk. "I've known him all my life. He went to college with my father and Slater Wilson have been working for the company and my family since before I was born. Even if Tyler can manage to somehow influence Tom Allen, those tactics won't work on Jeremy, believe me."

"What I can't work out is how Tyler even knew I'd be seeing a lawyer," Becky said.

"I know. That is weird," Mark replied.

"Well, whatever's going on, let's just forget about it until we get back from Boston," Nick said. "Then I'll do some digging."

Becky turned to him. "You will be careful, won't you?"

"Of course. I already told you. I'm always careful."

## Nick

"Better?" he asked as Becky nestled back into the hot bath, filled with luxurious bubbles.

"Hmm… thanks." She looked up at him and smiled. It didn't reach her eyes, but it was better than the tears she'd been crying most of the way into the city.

"I'll leave you in peace," he said. "And when you've finished in here, we'll order some dinner and get to bed."

"Are you okay?" she asked, sitting up a little, a worried expression crossing her face.

"I'm fine," he lied. He felt anything but fine. He hated being here; and not just in this deluxe and sumptuous hotel suite. He hated being in Boston. All it did was remind him of his time at college; of losing Becky the first time around. Still, this wasn't about him. It was about Becky.

He went over, leant down, and kissed her gently on the forehead, then turned and left the bathroom, returning to the opulent bedroom, where he lay down on the bed and stared at the ceiling, his hands resting behind his head.

A couple of days ago, everything had seemed so straightforward, and now it felt like it was all such a mess. He wanted to try and work out why Tom had done what he did. He was a family man, and Nick had known him come down heavy on abusive husbands in the past. It didn't add up, unless Tyler had got to him, but as he'd said to Becky, how could Tyler even have known she was seeing a lawyer?

He tried to think straight. Tom hadn't been the same since he'd taken on the contract from GHC, which was hardly surprising since the workload had doubled overnight. That wasn't really a good enough reason for his responses to Becky though. He could've just turned her down; he didn't need to give her such dumb advice into the bargain. No, there was something else behind this. He wondered if everything was alright at home? Tom's wife had been sick a few years back. She'd had breast cancer, but she'd caught it early and been treated. As far as Nick knew, she was fine. Unless… unless she wasn't alright. What if it had come back? That's what happened to Jake's mom all those years ago, and the cancer had spread real fast, claiming her in just a few months. It would make sense of Tom's tiredness, his irrational behaviour, his need for more money. God, what must he be going through? Nick resolved to make sure and find out when they got back to Somers Cove, and to be more supportive.

"Are you sure you're okay?" Becky's voice pulled him back from his thoughts and he looked over toward the bathroom.

"I am now." He smiled at her. She'd tied her hair up before getting in the bath, and now she'd wrapped a towel around her. "You're so beautiful," he said.

"Well, I don't know about that, but I do feel much better for that bath," she murmured.

"You weren't in there for very long."

She walked slowly over to him. "No. I was missing you. But it was very relaxing… And now, I think it's your turn," she said.

"What for?" he asked. "I'm not in the mood for a bath, if that's—"

"I wasn't talking about a bath," she replied. "But you're on edge, and I can think of far more effective ways of getting you to relax than a bath."

He smiled. "You can?"

She nodded and released the towel, letting it fall to the floor.

"That works for me," he said, looking her up and down.

"Oh, there's more," she whispered, just before she clambered onto the bed, crawling over to him, a fiery glint in her eye. She ran her hands across his chest, leaning down and kissing him deeply. Then she sat up and turned, straddling him so she was facing his feet, and started moving backwards up his body.

"That's one fucking amazing view," he said, reaching out and grabbing her ass, squeezing gently. She squirmed and moved back further still, until she was poised over his face. He leant up and licked along her soft glistening folds, parting them and flicking around her swollen clitoris. She groaned and shuddered, grinding herself down onto his face. She shifted forward a little and then he felt her fingers fumbling with his belt, undoing it and the button, then lowering the zipper. His cock sprang free and he felt her hands wrap around him, moving slowly up and down his length, before settling at the base. She leant down and, as he sucked and licked her hardened nub, he felt her mouth close around him.

The man sitting across the wide walnut desk was exactly what Nick had imagined. An old-school lawyer, suited and smart. Jeremy was probably in his mid to late fifties, but had worn well, his hair graying at the temples, but otherwise still dark brown. He wore rimless reading glasses and had a tanned complexion. His dark navy suit was tailored, and looked expensive.

"You're a lawyer?" he said to Nick, looking him up and down over the top of his glasses.

Nick was used to this reaction and just nodded.

Jeremy turned to Becky. "You want Mr Woods to stay?" he asked.

"Yes, I do." Becky's voice was almost inaudible.

"Very well," he replied, giving Nick a look that told him he knew exactly what was going on between the two of them. "I'm going to ask you a lot of questions," he said to Becky. "I'd like you to answer them honestly, giving me as much detail as possible." He turned back to Nick again. "And I'd like you to keep quiet, unless I ask you not to."

Nick held up his hands. "Okay," he said.

Becky sat back a little further in her seat as the interrogation began. When prompted, she detailed everything that had gone on between her and Tyler. Jeremy wrote down the odd sentence, but mainly studied her as she replied. She took frequent breaks and broke down a couple of times, when describing the worst of Tyler's assaults, so Nick moved his chair closer and held her hand. He figured that if Jeremy had already worked out that he and Becky were together, it didn't matter much what he did, and he wanted to support her.

After nearly forty-five minutes, Jeremy finally leant forward, looking down at his notes.

"You've got more than adequate grounds to file for divorce, Mrs Howell," he began. "And you could easily cite Mr Howell's adultery, or his cruelty toward you." Nick glanced at Becky. She was nodding her head, but she looked a little confused and he squeezed her hand tightly. "However," Jeremy continued, "being as I'm guessing your husband is unlikely to make things easy on you, I'd suggest you file instead for what's called a contested no fault divorce. It will probably be quicker and will definitely be less complicated than using his misdemeanors against him."

Becky turned to Nick. "Is that the same thing you were talking about?" she asked.

"Yeah, it is," he confirmed, giving her a reassuring smile.

Jeremy coughed and stared at Nick. "Let me explain," he said. "Going down the route I've suggested, you'll probably be divorced in around fourteen months—"

"Fourteen months?" Becky was shocked. "That long?"

"Yes. You have to wait a minimum of six months before you can have a hearing, but your husband can drag that out – and he probably will. Once we can get in front of a judge, things speed up and then it's just down to waiting for the divorce to go through it's natural process. When filing in the state of Massachusetts, we usually say to allow fourteen months for this kind of divorce."

"And there's no way to speed it up?"

"Well…" Jeremy looked dubious. "There is one way. You'd have to convince Mr Howell not to contest the divorce at some point within those first six months. If you can do that, then the petition can be converted to uncontested, the judge sets a hearing date and things progress much more quickly. In that instance, you'd probably be divorced within around seven to ten months – depending on how long it takes to persuade Mr Howell and how quickly you get a hearing date."

"That sounds better, although it's still such a long time." She looked at Nick again. "But what's the point? Tyler's never going to agree."

Nick leant toward her. "Bex," he said, "what does it matter how long it takes? You've been married to him for years. As long as you get free of him in the end, who cares if you have to wait?"

She gave him a slight smile and nodded her head.

"Mr Woods is right," Jeremy conceded. "You can't think of it in terms of taking a long time, just in terms of doing what's best for you."

"And you'd definitely advise doing this no fault thing?" Becky asked him.

"Yes."

"And you, Nick?" She turned toward him again.

"I'm not here to give you legal advice. But you don't have to decide today. If you want to take some time and think it through…"

"No. I want to get this over with," she said, her voice much stronger again. "I just want to make sure I'm doing the right thing." She hesitated, just for a moment, then looked back at Jeremy. "I'd like you to go ahead," she said, firmly.

"Okay," he replied, nodding his head, and coughing, seemingly embarrassed. "It's… it's fairly obvious to me that you and Mr Woods are in a relationship," he said.

"And?" Nick replied, before Becky could say anything.

"And nothing," Jeremy said. "But it would be best if Mr Howell didn't find out about that."

"Yeah… we know." Nick wanted to point out that he wasn't stupid, but he didn't.

Jeremy turned back to Becky. "I'll get the paperwork drawn up." His voice was more normal now. "Where would you like me to have it sent?"

"Can you send it to me at the Gardner Oceanic Hotel?" she said immediately. Nick looked across at her but her eyes were still fixed on Jeremy. Why wasn't she having it sent to his address? Jeremy knew they were together, so what did it matter? She gave him the full address of the hotel. "Mark it private, for my attention," she added.

"Very well," he replied, getting to his feet and holding out his hand.

Becky rose before Nick. He was still feeling a little confused. Was Becky going to move back to the hotel? Did she think she had to do that to help with the divorce? Surely not. She'd have discussed it with him. Wouldn't she?

They were an hour into the drive home before either of them said anything.

"Are you going to talk to me at all?" Becky asked. "Even if it's only to tell me why you're not talking to me?" He heard what sounded like fear in her voice. He didn't like that – besides, he needed answers himself.

He glanced up ahead and saw there was a gas station.

"Yeah," he said and indicated right. "I will in a minute." She gasped and he heard a sob. "Please... don't, baby," he said, as he by-passed the fuel pumps and pulled up outside the convenience store, turning off the engine.

"W—what's wrong?" she asked.

He twisted in the seat and his heart broke as he saw tears streaming down her cheeks, knowing he was responsible for the fact that she was hurting.

"Don't cry," he said softly.

"How can I not cry," she sobbed. "I feel like you're mad at me."

"I'm not. Remember? I said I'm unlikely to ever get mad at you. I meant it."

"Then what..." She seemed unable to finish her sentence.

"I'm confused. I don't understand why you told Jeremy to send the papers to the hotel. Are you leaving me?" He heard his voice crack as he admitted his own insecurities and the direction his thoughts had been taking during the last hour of silence.

"Of course I'm not leaving you."

He sighed out his relief. "Then are you thinking you have to move back there so Tyler doesn't find out about us? Because if you are... well, you know that's completely pointless. I'll just follow you, and our relationship will be even more public than it is now. I'll hate living in a hotel, but I'll follow you no matter where you go. I love you and I'm not letting you go, Bex. Never again."

# Chapter Fifteen

*Becky*

She stared at him for a moment, startled by his uncharacteristic moment of insecurity, but also by the fact that he'd be prepared to sacrifice his independence and his freedom, for her. She knew how much that meant to him. She smiled. "I love you too, Nick. So much. And I wasn't thinking I had to move anywhere," she said.

"Then why have the papers delivered to the hotel?"

"Because I was trying to be considerate. I know you hate all the reminders of Tyler. Let's face it, you struggle with saying his name, so I just wanted to try and keep my divorce at arm's length."

He started to smile. "I don't think that's gonna be possible," he whispered.

"Maybe not, but I thought, being as I go into the hotel to work, I could just pick up the paperwork while I'm there, and you wouldn't have to look at it, or be reminded of him."

"Yeah… except I've got every intention of helping you go through the damn paperwork," he replied. "I wanna make sure there are no slip ups. You're not on your own, Bex. I'm with you every step of the way." He leant over and kissed her just gently and, as he broke the kiss, she clambered across and sat on his lap. "Thank you for being so considerate," he whispered, putting his arms around her, "but I can take it."

"Really?" she asked. "After the way you've been since we got back to Boston?"

He held her closer. "I know I've been quiet, and I'm sorry. But that had nothing to do with him. That's just being back there. It reminded me of losing you. That's all." There was that chink of insecurity again. It was being back in the city that did it. She could see that Nick needed to be in his forest, in the wide open space.

"Well, you're not gonna lose me again."

"Good."

She caressed his face gently. "Thank you for everything, Nick."

"Don't thank me," he whispered. "Never thank me."

"But I owe you so much. You saved me."

"You owe me nothing. And I didn't save you." He twisted her around so they were facing each other. "You forget how strong you really are," he told her.

"Well, I don't feel very strong right now. I feel like I could use a good long hug. Please take me home."

He smiled. "Home?"

"Well, yes. Your place. Where you belong. Do you mind if I call it home?"

"Mind?" He kissed her, his tongue delving deep into her mouth. "Hell no," he murmured as he broke the kiss. "You're gonna have to get off my lap, unfortunately." He smirked. "And I'll take you home... and then I'd really like to take you bed. Our bed."

"I like the sound of that."

"Hmm. I thought you might."


Her fingers knotted into his hair as she ground down onto him, feeling him deep inside her, her breasts hard against his chest.

"Take me harder, baby," he muttered into her neck, nipping at her skin with his teeth, and she moved a little faster.

Their clothing was scattered between the front door of the trailer and the bedroom. They'd torn it off, throwing or dropping each garment as they'd frantically undressed each other, between kisses, until they'd reached the bed, where Nick was now sitting, holding her as she straddled him, riding him, their breathing ragged and desperate.

"That's so good," she whispered. She was getting close now.

"Come for me," Nick urged. "I need to feel you come, Bex."

His words pushed her over the edge and she closed her eyes, throwing back her head and screaming out his name as he groaned out his pleasure, pulled her down hard onto his swollen cock and exploded deep inside her.

As she started to calm, he lowered them both down onto the bed, so she was lying on top of him, and looked up into her eyes.

"You're incredible," he said, kissing her gently.

"I think you'll find that's you," she murmured back, snuggling into him.

Keeping them connected, he held her in his arms, running his fingers up and down her back and planting soft kisses on her neck and shoulders.

"I've had an idea," he whispered.

"What's that?"

"Wanna try something new?"

She raised herself up slightly, looking down at him.

"Something new?" She bit her bottom lip. "Is there anything we haven't done yet?"

He smirked. "Oh yeah, baby," he said, his voice dropping. "There are all kinds of things we haven't done yet… But I'm not talking about that."

"Then I don't…?" She was confused.

"I'm talking about us doing something together that we've never even considered attempting," he explained. "Something, a little more adventurous."

"Such as?" She was intrigued now.

"Such as cooking dinner together."

She stared at him for a second, then burst out laughing. "I wondered what you had in mind then," she said.

"I've got all kinds of things in mind," he replied. "But we can do those after dinner." He leant up and kissed her. "I'm hungry, and we've never cooked a meal together."

"No, we haven't, have we?"

"So… let's give it a try."

Sitting in her office on the third floor of the hotel the next morning, Becky couldn't stop smiling. Cooking dinner the previous evening had been more adventurous than she'd anticipated. It might have been less interesting if they'd put some clothes on first; but they hadn't. She'd only just put the pasta bake into the oven, when Nick had spun her around and lifted her into his arms. She'd wrapped her legs around his waist and grabbed his shoulders just as he'd entered her – real hard. She felt herself blushing, recalling how loudly they'd both climaxed, and picked up her pen, trying to concentrate on the correspondence in front of her.

It was tough. Her mind was filled with the memory of the power in his arms as he'd held onto her, controlling their movements, how deep he'd plunged inside her, his voice as he'd whispered in her ear, telling her how good she felt, describing the sensations on his cock as he'd moved her up and down his length… it was impossible to even think straight.

The knocking on her door made her jump and she sat up, a little breathless, straightening her clothes, as though she'd actually been doing all the things she'd been thinking about.

"Come in," she called.

"It's just me, Mrs Howell." Kyle came into the room, carrying a large envelope. "This arrived for you. Somebody put it on my desk by mistake. God knows why. It's clearly addressed to you."

He stood in front of her and handed the envelope across.

"Thanks, Kyle," she said, taking it from him. "You must call me Becky," she said. "At least when we're in private."

"Okay," he replied, smiling. He was a good looking young man. Becky knew from his resumé that he was twenty-six, and he was well-built, with short blond hair and piercing blue eyes. He'd been an instant hit with all the staff, which wasn't surprising, considering how agreeable he was. But he also knew how to get things done. All in all, he was a great choice for a manager.

"We'll stick to Mrs Howell and Mr Langton when we're around the guests though," Becky said. "It wouldn't do to appear too informal."

"Absolutely," he said, just as his phone rang. He pulled it from his pocket and answered it, "Langton," sounding very businesslike. He listened for a moment or two, and then said, "Well, I'm not surprised. She specifically requested no flowers in the room." He waited again. "I know it's the honeymoon suite, but she has severe hay fever. Did no-one read the note I left on the file?" He let out a sigh. "Okay, I'm coming back down now." He hung up, rolling his eyes.

"Trouble?" Becky asked.

"Nothing a complimentary meal won't solve," Kyle replied. "I'm just going to find out who's responsible…" He walked toward the door.

"Have fun," Becky said as he left, closing the door quietly behind him.

She stared at the envelope in front of her. She didn't need to open it to know what was inside. Picking up her phone from the desk, she typed out a message to Nick.

*— Just got the papers from Jeremy. Too nervous to even open the envelope. Does that make me pathetic? B xxx*

His reply was immediate.

*— No. Don't bother opening it. Bring it home tonight and we'll look at it together. What time will you finish work? N xxx*

*— About six-thirty. Why? xxx*

*— I'll make sure I get home before you. I don't want you sitting at home worrying by yourself. I love you. N xxx*

She smiled and tapped out 'I love you too', adding a long row of kisses before pressing send.

"I intend to collect on those kisses," Nick said as soon as she walked in the door. He was in the kitchen, chopping up an onion and, as she dropped her purse on the couch and shrugged off her jacket, he poured her a glass of chilled white wine and brought it over to her. "I think you need this," he murmured, kissing her cheek.

"Oh God, yes. Thank you." She took a large gulp of wine and closed her eyes. "That's really good," she said.

"I know." He nodded toward the envelope she was clutching. "Wanna take over the cooking?" he suggested. "And I'll take a look at that for you?"

"Would you mind?"

"No. Of course not."

He took the envelope from her and held her hand, walking her to the kitchen. He sat down at the breakfast bar, while Becky went around the other side and continued preparing the dinner.

"We'll look at this after we've eaten," Nick murmured, thumbing through the document, almost as though he was talking to himself. "It won't take long. Then I'll send it back to Jeremy tomorrow and you can forget about it for a while. He'll deal with everything from now on."

"When will I hear from him?" she asked.

"That kinda depends on how Tyler reacts, but Jeremy will contact you if he needs to." He sounded reassuring and she threw the onions into the pan of oil and took another sip of wine.

"I've got no idea what I'm cooking here," she said. "I'm just chopping onions, peppers and mushrooms." She looked down at the vegetables laid out in front of her.

"I was making sauce to go with some pasta," he replied, getting up and coming around to her. "I thought we'd keep it quick and simple tonight."

"So we've got time for that?" She nodded at the form.

"No… so I can take you to bed and distract the hell out of you," he whispered in her ear.

The last couple of days had been magical.

Every morning, she'd wake in Nick's arms and he'd kiss her tenderly and make love to her with such gentleness it was breathtaking. While she showered, he'd make breakfast, so she could leave in time to get to work, being as she had the longer journey.

Then, in the evenings, they'd cook together and, afterwards, they'd go for walks in his forest, or snuggle up on the couch and watch a movie, or just lie in each others arms and talk, or read, until it was time for bed.

At night, they made love with more intensity, more fire, and she would fall asleep, breathless and satisfied, cradled in his arms.

Work had become much more busy though and that meant life at home was about to change. She was dreading breaking the news to Nick and drove home that Friday night, filled with trepidation.

"Wanna tell me about it?" Nick asked over dinner.

"About what?"

"Whatever it is that's bothering you. You've been nervous all evening. Tell me what's wrong."

She put down her fork. "I've got some bad news," she said.

"Have you heard from Jeremy?" Nick asked, leaning forward and taking her hand in his.

"No." She shook her head. "This is to do with work."

"Okay," Nick said, seemingly relieved.

"Do you remember I told you my job involved me having to travel around?" Becky said quietly, and Nick nodded. "Well, that's gotta start again next week. Kyle's settled in, and I've caught up with the backlog of my own paperwork…"

"Okay. So you're going away?" He sounded wary, bordering on scared.

"Yes. Just for a couple of days," she said.

"A couple of days…?"

"Yeah. This is just routine for me. I have to go and spot check hotels every so often. Next week, I'm doing four in Vermont. I'll leave on Tuesday and be back on Thursday."

"So you'll be here for the wedding?" Mark and Emma's wedding was due to take place the following weekend.

"Of course." She stared into his eyes. "Are you sure you're alright with this?" she asked.

"Well, obviously I'd rather you didn't have to go," Nick said. "I like having you here. But we knew this would happen. I get that it's your job, and you love what you do."

She let out a long sigh. "This is the part of my job I used to love the most," she said quietly. "It meant I could be away from him."

"I can understand that," Nick replied.

"But now, I'm not so sure."

"Hey," he said, getting up and pulling her to her feet. "It's fine. I'll miss you, but we can talk on the phone, and I'll be here waiting for you when you get back."

She leant into him and he held her close. "I'm so lucky," she whispered into his chest.

"No, Bex. I'm the lucky one."


She opened her eyes as her alarm went off at seven on Wednesday morning and turned to find an empty bed.

"Oh," she said out loud. How could she have forgotten he wouldn't be there? She turned back and grabbed her phone from the nightstand.

There was a message waiting for her already, timed at five-thirty, and she smiled as she read it.

*— Good morning, beautiful. Slept really badly, so got up and did some work. The bed was too empty without you. Tomorrow night can't come soon enough. Love you, N xxx*

She didn't bother to reply, but called him instead.

"Hello." He answered on the first ring.

"I missed you too," she replied. "It took me hours to get off to sleep. It wasn't the same without your arms."

"I know. I couldn't handle not having you beside me," he admitted and coughed. "Still," he said, clearly trying to sound more cheerful, "just one more night and you'll be home."

"I can't wait."

"Neither can I." She heard the smile in his voice.

"Any news?" she asked.

"Just that I heard from Jake late last night," he replied. "He sent through the estimate for the build on the house."

"And?"

"And I don't have enough money saved up."

"Oh." She couldn't hide her disappointment. The trailer was comfortable and she already felt like it was home, but she knew how much Nick wanted to build the house, for both of them. Now, she wished, more than anything, that she could help out herself. If only…

"Don't sound so worried," he said. "I'm gonna go and see the bank today. I'll borrow the rest of the money."

"Should you do that?" she asked.

"Of course. It'll be fine. I want us to have a proper home together." His voice dropped to a whisper. "I'll do whatever I have to do to make that happen." There was a moment's pause but, as there was a lump in her throat, she couldn't fill it. "What time do you think you'll be home tomorrow?" he asked.

"Probably around six," she replied, clearing her throat. "I'll call, or text you, if I'm gonna be much later than that."

"Okay. I'll make sure I'm home before then. I don't want to miss a single minute with you."

She smiled.

"Do you think this will get any easier?" she asked.

"No. But don't worry about it."

She'd never liked her job less. "I miss you, Nick."

"I miss you too, baby."

The following day dragged by, probably because, by around three o'clock, Becky was almost breathless with the anticipation of seeing Nick again. It was hard to believe it had only been a couple of days since she'd been in his arms – it felt more like months. As she drove back to Somers Cove, she wondered how on earth they'd managed to live apart for nine years.

It was around ten after six by the time she pulled up beside Nick's truck and, as she switched off the engine, her car door suddenly opened and she looked up. He was standing there, gazing down at her, holding out his hand. She took it and let him pull her to her feet and into his arms. It felt good to be held.

One of his hands roamed down her back while the other cupped her chin and raised her face. His kiss was intense, his tongue darting into her open mouth. His groan was loud as he stepped closer, flexing his hips into her. God, he was so hard already.

Then everything happened really fast. One minute they were kissing, and the next, he'd turned them and walked her backwards, pushing her up against the door of his truck, using his feet to move her legs apart. He yanked up her skirt around her waist and she felt his hand delve inside her panties, discovering her drenched core.

"Yes," she hissed between her teeth, as he pushed two fingers inside her. "Oh, please, yes…"

He twisted and circled his fingers inside her until she was on the brink of coming, then he stopped and knelt down, removing his fingers and pulling down her panties until they were around her ankles. She stepped out of them and gasped as he lifted her left leg, supporting her, while he traced a line along her soft wet folds with his tongue. Just as she felt the beginnings of her orgasm again, he stood, her leg now raised even higher, draped over his bent arm. She was so exposed, and the chill air against her naked skin felt gloriously liberating. He entered her, groaning loudly as she took his whole length. Exactly when he'd undone his jeans, she had no idea, but he felt huge, pounding into her. She forced her hips forward, desperately trying to get more of him, and they were both on the edge within moments.

"Come for me," he murmured into her mouth. "Now."

He bit her bottom lip, then sucked it into his mouth, just as the first wave of pleasure washed over her and she screamed out his name into the dark night sky. He thrusted into her hard, once… twice more, then, with an almost wild, howling cry, he exploded deep inside her.

Slowly, her breathing returned to normal and she opened her eyes to find him staring down at her.

"Hello," he murmured, pulling out of her and lowering her leg to the ground. "I'm sorry."

"Oh, please don't apologize." She smiled up at him. "That was just what I needed."

"Me too." He leant down and kissed her gently. "God, I've missed you."

"I've missed you too. But I've gotta say, it's almost worth it, if you're gonna do that to me every time I come home."

He smirked. "Oh, we're nowhere near done yet," he said.

"Good." She shuddered at the thought of whatever he had in mind.

He pulled back, his concern obvious. "Sorry if I was a little rough. I didn't hurt you, did I?" He started to straighten her clothes, and pulled up his jeans, fastening them.

"No, you didn't."

"It was nothing like…" She knew what he was thinking, and hastened to reassure him.

"No, Nick. You could never be anything like him." She reached up and touched his cheek with her fingertips. "I meant what I said. I needed that. You always give me what I need. It felt wonderful."

He looked down at her. "Which bit?" he asked, smiling a slow, sexy smile.

"All of it,." She felt herself blush. "Weren't you worried someone might see us?"

"No. Do you honestly think I would have done that if there was even the slightest chance of someone seeing us?"

"But we're outside…" She looked around.

"Yeah, on private land. Private land which I own. The only way to get here is the same way you just drove in. I think we'd have noticed another car. And no-one can come at us through the woods. Although you can't see it from here, it's all fenced off. And there isn't another property for three miles."

"So we're totally secluded?" She looked up into his eyes.

"Yes, of course."

"Then do you think, we could…?"

"What?" he asked, looking confused.

"Do you think we could do that again? Maybe on a blanket next time? Perhaps when it's a little warmer?" Her cheeks flushed with embarrassment.

"You liked being outside then?" He moved closer, holding her in his arms.

She nodded, but was too shy to tell him just how much she'd enjoyed it.

He kissed her deeply. "Then I'll work something out," he whispered. "But right now, it's getting kinda cold out here and I need to take you to bed." And, without saying another word, he bent down and, picking up her panties with one hand, lifted her into his arms and, kicking her car door shut, carried her into the trailer.

∽

## Nick

"Are you absolutely sure we have to adhere to this tradition?" Mark asked, standing on the doorstep of his and Emma's house and looking down at his soon-to-be wife.

"Yes!" Everyone answered in unison. Mark looked around the gathered faces and shrugged his shoulders.

"I don't see why I'm not allowed to sleep with my own fiancée the night before our wedding."

"Because it's bad luck for you to see her in the morning," Cassie told him, shooing him away, toward Jake's car.

Nick smiled and put his arm around Becky. He was going to be the fox in the hen house for the evening, but no-one seemed to mind, except maybe Mark, who clearly wanted to stay home with Emma himself.

"C'mon," Jake called from the car. "I'm sure you can live without her for one night. You've got the rest of your lives to be together." Nick caught the wink Jake gave Cassie. It would be their turn next; their wedding was planned for just a couple of months' time.

"Okay," Mark said, and pulled Emma toward him, giving her a long, deep kiss, regardless of their gathered friends. Becky leant into Nick and he held her closer.

"Now, go," Cassie joked, as Mark finally broke the kiss.

Reluctantly, Mark went over to Jake's car, throwing his bag and suit carrier into the trunk. Before he'd even got there, Nick gave Becky a squeeze and whispered, "Just give me a minute." She nodded and he let her go, walking over to Emma and putting his arm around her shoulders.

He looked down at her. "You okay?" he asked quietly. He could see her eyes glistening as she looked up at him, but she didn't reply.

Mark turned and Nick just gave him a slight nod, which Mark returned, then he blew Emma a kiss and climbed into Jake's car, giving her a wave as they drove off.

"It's just one night," Nick whispered.

"I know."

"And we're all here."

Emma sighed. "I know."

"And it's not the same, is it?"

She shook her head and he turned her, holding her close.

"Thank you for being here," she murmured. "I know I've got Cassie and Maddie, and Becky. But having you here makes all the difference."

"Where else would I be?" he asked.

"With Jake and Mark?" she suggested. "Down at the beach house."

"I'd far rather be here," he replied.

She looked up at him. "You would?" A smile formed on her lips.

"Yeah, I would."

"Do you have any idea what you're letting yourself in for?"

He shook his head slowly. "None whatsoever."

She laughed. "Oh dear." She patted his shoulder. "Poor Nick."

He shrugged. "I'm sure it won't be that bad."

Two hours later, he revised his perspective. He was worried he might be permanently scarred, having seen his sister, Cassie, and Becky in face masks, but what was worse was that Maddie had insisted Nick should join in, and had plastered the gloopy green paste all over his cheeks. He'd then chased her around the house, pretending to be a monster, but she'd got her own back by demanding that he sit quietly while she painted his nails – bright pink. Becky was clearly enjoying herself – and his humiliation – and she now had the photographs to prove it. As far as Nick was concerned it was worth it. He didn't think he'd ever seen Becky laugh so much.

Once the face mask was removed – and Nick did have to admit, his skin felt all the better for it – they sat down to eat in the kitchen. Emma had made a mild chicken curry, which tasted incredible, and afterwards, Cassie took Maddie up to bed, while Becky sat beside Nick on the couch and set about removing the nail polish.

"You sure you want this taken off?" she asked, trying to stifle a laugh.

"Absolutely sure," he replied. "I only agreed because you promised it'd come off."

Emma chuckled from the couch on the other side of the room. "At least Becky's got the evidence on her phone," she said.

"Yeah. And if that 'evidence' ever sees the light of day…" he threatened.

"Then what?" Becky teased. "What will you do to me?" Her eyes had widened and, as she opened her mouth, he could see her tongue. He was hard in an instant.

"I'll think of something," he whispered and Becky sucked in a breath, her eyes boring into his. Now all he wanted to do was to take her to bed.

He glanced across at Emma and she gave him the sweetest smile. He knew she was pleased to see him happy and the feeling was entirely mutual.

Emma was the most beautiful bride he'd ever seen. Her dress was vintage, peach-colored lace in a column style, with a low-cut back. She had the tiniest baby bump, but unless you knew she was pregnant, it was real hard to tell. Her hair was piled up on top of her head, with a few loose strands hanging down by her face, and seemed to be dotted with tiny flowers and diamonds. When she appeared at the top of the stairs, she took his breath away.

"You look more beautiful today than you ever have," he whispered to her, as he took her hand.

The weather had done them a good turn, and it was warm enough to hold the ceremony outside. Chairs had been set out in the garden, and Mark and Emma would say their vows overlooking the ocean, just as she'd planned.

"Is everything ready?" she asked, sounding nervous.

"If you're asking whether your future husband is here, the answer is yes. He's been pacing up and down out there for the last ten minutes waiting for you." Nick smiled. "I guess we'd better put him out of his misery."

She smiled up at him and he knew the glow in her eyes and on her face wasn't just because she was pregnant.

He linked arms with her and went to move, but she pulled him back.

"What's wrong?" he asked.

"Nothing. I just wanted to say…" She paused, clearly struggling with her emotions. "I just wanted to say thank you for being here for me. And I don't just mean today."

"I'll always be here for you, Em. Even after today. You getting married doesn't change that."

She looked up into his eyes. "He'll never hurt me again, you know that. I mean, you do trust him, don't you?"

"Of course. I didn't to start with, but I do now. I know he'll look after you." He smiled. "I'm just the back-up. And I'm not going anywhere. Now, are you ready?"

She nodded, but as he moved forward, she pulled him back again.

"Just one more thing," she said.

"What's that?"

"I'm really pleased for you."

"For me?" He was confused.

"Seeing you with Becky last night," she explained. "You're so happy – both of you. I'm glad you found each other again."

"So am I." He chuckled. "So am I."

She sighed contentedly. "We both got lucky, didn't we?"

"Oh, I don't know about that," he said. "I think it's Mark and I who got lucky, and I'm pretty damn sure he'd agree with me." She blushed and he leaned closer. "Now, before he comes looking for you, let's get out there."

Taking the walk down the aisle quite slowly, Nick looked at the gathered faces, all of which were focused on Emma. As they passed by Mark's sister, Sarah, who was sitting beside Maggie, Mark's housekeeper from his property in Boston, he felt Emma flinch and he gripped her a little tighter. Although he knew Emma was trying her best to reconcile Mark and Sarah, he also knew she was struggling with the damage Mark's sister had done to them both. He wasn't entirely sure she would ever come to terms with that. He nodded and smiled to friends and acquaintances, which accounted for pretty much everyone there, being as most of the town had been invited, and very few had declined. The only real notable absentees were Tom Allen and his wife. After several attempts over previous days, Nick had finally sat Tom down and talked through his problems. He'd discovered that, sure enough, Cathy had found another lump. She was having tests and they were both worried the cancer had returned. Nick had apologized for not understanding sooner, and had said he'd do whatever he could to help. He'd offered to take on some of the work from GHC, but Tom had refused, which struck Nick as odd, although he didn't query it at the time. He didn't think Tom could handle another argument.

He and Emma were nearly at the front now and, as they passed by Becky, he gave her a wink and a smile. She nodded and smiled back, looking a little shy. He'd meant every word he'd said to Emma earlier. No matter that it was Mark's wedding day, Nick knew he was the luckiest man in the world to have found Becky again.

"It's a beautiful wedding," Becky whispered. "Everyone's so relaxed." It had cooled off a little, so the guests had moved inside, filling the downstairs of Marks and Emma's home. Becky was sitting in the corner of the one of the couches with Nick perched on the arm beside her.

"Yeah. I think that's what Emma was hoping for. She just wanted everyone to have a good time." He leant down and kissed her, then continued, "And I'm mighty grateful for that, because I don't have to make a long speech. I'm already making enough of a sacrifice putting this damn tux on again…" His voice faded.

Becky chuckled. "You don't look very comfortable," she said. "Even if you do look really sexy."

He smiled, looking down into her eyes. "Nowhere near as sexy as you." She hadn't brought anything with her suitable for the wedding. She'd expected to go home again a week or so after the opening, and travel back up for the wedding. So Nick had surprised her by ordering the pale blue and yellow floral patterned dress she was wearing. He'd bought it while she was in Vermont and she'd burst into tears when he'd given it to her.

Nick leant back a little and looked around at the gathered faces. Across the other side of the room, he spotted Jake and Cassie, with Jake's dad, Ben, talking to Maggie. Both Ben and Maggie seemed very taken with each other and, judging from the expressions on Jake and Cassie's faces, they were finding the situation amusing.

"What are you smiling about?" Becky asked, staring up at him.

"That." He nodded across the room.

"That's Jake's dad, isn't it?"

"Yeah, that's Ben." Nick's smile broadened as Maggie laughed at something Ben had said. Her eyes lit up and she placed a hand on his arm, which Ben promptly covered with his own.

"Do they know each other?" Becky asked.

"No. As far as I know, they just met today," Nick replied.

"Well, they seem to be getting along really well." She smirked.

"Yeah… don't they…"

Becky looked up at him. "Is that a problem? Neither of them seems to be attached to anyone. I mean, Jake's mom died years ago, didn't she?"

"Yeah, she died when Jake was nine."

"Then why are you – and evidently Jake and Cassie – looking so amused by the whole thing?"

Nick leant down closer and lowered his voice to a whisper. "Because Cassie's mom, Kate, and Ben were together for a few years, before Kate died."

"Oh." Becky nodded. "And she died last year?"

"Yeah, last spring."

"And how long were they together?"

"About four years, I think. I'm not even supposed to know about it," he murmured into her ear. "I only found out because I was on my way home from work and Ben was falling out of Mac's Bar, so drunk he could hardly stand. He's not normally a drinker, but he was in a bad way, and I took him home and sat with him, while he talked. It was right after Jake and Cassie left to go live in Portland at the end of last summer and I think it had suddenly hit him that he was gonna be on his own for a lot of the time. He told me all about him and Kate…"

"I assume Jake and Cassie know?" Becky asked, her voice as low as his.

"About him and Kate? Yeah."

"No, I mean that he was so upset about them leaving."

"Oh. No. He came and saw me the next day and swore me to secrecy, and we've never spoken about that night since. I made a point of keeping an eye on him for a while, but with Jake and Cassie coming back every weekend, and him visiting them in Portland, they don't give him time to be as lonely as he feared."

Becky leant up and kissed his cheek.

"What was that for?" he asked.

"It was for you… just for being you."

He shrugged and was just about to kiss her back when he felt his phone vibrate in his inside pocket.

"Hang on," he said and pulled it out, checking the screen. Mark had given him Kyle's number, and he'd stored it into his phone. "That's weird," he said and put it to his ear. "Hi, Kyle."

He saw Becky's eyebrows rise and her mouth open. She'd obviously forgotten that there was only one reason Kyle was likely to be calling him, and he could already feel his muscles tightening.

"Sorry, to disturb you," Kyle said. "Mr Gardner asked me to call if Mr Howell turned up. And I know Mrs Howell isn't here, so she's perfectly safe, but…"

"But what?" Nick asked, sensing there was something wrong.

"The guy's here, and he's drunk. Noisy drunk. I'd say bordering on violent drunk."

"Can you call the cops?" Nick asked, and Becky clasped his arm, looking even more confused and inquisitive. She offered to take the phone from him, but he shook his head.

"I'd rather not," Kyle replied. "I don't think Mr Gardner would appreciate the bad publicity that might follow."

"Yeah. I see what you mean," Nick said. He sighed. "Okay, I'll come down there."

"Thanks, Mr Woods."

"No problem. It'll take me about a half hour, I guess."

"Okay."

"Don't let him near any women," Nick added.

"I kinda got that message from Mr Gardner." Kyle lowered his voice.

Nick hung up the phone and put it back in his pocket, then stood and held out his hand to Becky. She took it and he pulled her to her feet.

"What's wrong?" Becky asked him. "Who were you talking about, and why was Kyle calling you and not me, or Mark?"

"I'll explain in a minute," he replied. "I just need to find Mark." Nick looked around and spotted him easily, near the entrance to the kitchen, talking to Doc Collins. Luckily, Emma wasn't anywhere close by. "Come with me," he said and, keeping a firm grip on her hand, he led her over to where Mark was.

"Sorry to intrude," he said, "I need to borrow Mark."

"Certainly," Doc Collins replied. "I should probably go and rescue my wife." He nodded toward a gaggle of women, who were standing in the kitchen, arms folded and chins wagging. "She hates those gossiping hens, and I promised not to leave her alone with them for too long." He walked away and Mark turned to face them.

"What's wrong?" he asked. "You've got that look on your face."

"We need to go outside," Nick said.

"Again?" Mark said, smirking. "Seriously? How often are you gonna do this to me?"

"I'm serious," Nick told him. "I've had a call from Kyle." He glanced briefly at Becky, hoping Mark would understand.

"Okay. Let's go out front," Mark replied, clearly sensing the urgency now, and leading them through the crowded living room to the front door.

Once outside, he turned. "Tell me," he said bluntly.

Nick pulled Becky into his arms, holding her close. "Becky's husband is at your hotel." He felt her recoil and tightened his grip on her.

"And?" Mark said. "There's more to it than that, or Kyle could handle it himself."

"He's drunk," Nick continued. "Very drunk and getting louder by the minute. Kyle's worried he's gonna turn nasty. He doesn't wanna call the cops, in case any bad publicity comes out of it, so I've said I'll go over there and deal with it."

"You can't," Becky whispered, looking up at him.

"I'll be fine," Nick replied, kissing her gently.

"I'll come with you," Mark said.

"Like hell you will." Nick wasn't about to let that happen. "It's your wedding day. Your place is here – with Emma. In any case, you're the one he's paranoid about. I really don't think that seeing you is gonna help. And I want you to take care of Becky for me while I'm gone."

"No!" Becky raised her voice. "You're not going without me."

"I am, babe." He remained calm and quiet, despite the turmoil of emotions he was experiencing. "I don't want you anywhere near him."

"But… I need to face him, Nick. I'm gonna have to do it sometime." Despite her words, she sounded scared. "I need to show him I'm not frightened of him anymore."

"Even if you are?" He looked into her eyes.

"I won't be if you're there," she whispered.

He thought for a moment. He knew she wanted to do this, to prove a point to herself, as well as to Tyler. Sure, he could try and insist she stay with Mark, but he didn't think she'd thank him. And besides, he wasn't really the insisting type.

"Okay," he said reluctantly. "I'll take you with me."

"Thank you," she murmured.

"If anything happens," Mark said, "screw the publicity and call the cops. Kyle will help out if you need him. He's a good guy."

Nick nodded. "Don't tell Emma where we've gone," he said. "I don't want her to worry."

"Okay," Mark replied, as they headed toward Nick's car. "Don't take any shit from the guy."

"I won't," Nick called over his shoulder.

# Chapter Sixteen

*Becky*

Before they'd even driven onto the main road, Becky was starting to regret her decision. Her palms were damp with sweat and her stomach was churning. Her eyes darted everywhere, although quite what she expected to see, she wasn't sure.

"I can take you back," Nick said, lifting his foot off the gas.

She shook her head. "No. I have to do this." Her voice carried a lot more conviction than she felt.

"You really don't, you know."

She turned to him. "I do, Nick. I can't spend the rest of my life living in fear of him."

"You don't have to. I told you, I'll look after you."

She reached over and put her hand on his thigh. "I know you will, but I want to be able to look after myself too."

He nodded and speeded up again.

"What do you think he'll do?" Becky asked, sounding scared.

"I don't know. To be honest, I'm surprised you haven't heard from him before now. He didn't hold back in calling you and demanding you return home, when you went up to Manchester, did he?"

"No," she whispered. It had occurred to her that Tyler had been uncharacteristically quiet during her absence, but she hadn't wanted to tempt fate by dwelling on it.

Nick cleared his throat. "Whatever he does, whatever happens when we get there, Bex, you've gotta act calm. And, more important than that, you've gotta act like we're not together. We can't afford to give him that ammunition – not now."

"Then how are we gonna explain the fact that we've just arrived at the hotel together?" she asked, feeling the panic rise inside again.

"It's pure coincidence," Nick replied calmly. "It makes sense that we'd both be at Mark and Emma's wedding. We can just tell him that I offered to drive you over."

"Do you think he'll fall for that, bearing in mind I used your name to stop him from raping me?"

Nick shrugged. "I don't know. It's a chance we're gonna have to take." He paused for a moment. "Please remember, Bex, my heart was always yours, it still is, and it always will be and, no matter what I say or do when we're with him, you need to remember that I'm only trying to keep you safe."

"You're scaring me," she murmured. "What are you planning?"

"I'm not planning anything," he replied. "I just want you to ignore everything I say and do, that's all. None of it will be for real – it's just for his benefit."

"Okay," she whispered.


"Jeez," Nick said quietly as he helped her from the car, "you can hear him from out here."

"Yep… that's Tyler." Becky could feel herself shaking.

"I know you're nervous," Nick whispered. "But I can't hold you. He'll be able to see. I can't even hold your hand, so just try and be strong. Remember, I love you."

She nodded her head and tried her best to feel as strong as Nick seemed to think she was.

They walked together into the hotel, careful not to touch in any way.

Tyler was standing by the reception desk, shouting at Kyle, demanding to see Becky. As they approached, he turned, a sly smile forming on his face.

"Here she is," he said, waving his arm expansively. "I knew she couldn't stay away." He wobbled slightly, then looked at Nick and frowned. "What are you doing here?" he asked.

Nick looked down at him. "Let's go sit somewhere quiet," he said, taking Tyler's arm.

Tyler shook himself free. "Not until you explain why the fuck you've just walked in the door with my wife."

"That's real simple," Nick said, still keeping his voice deliberately placid. "We were both at Mark and Emma's wedding. Becky's car was blocked in, so I offered to drive her over."

Tyler nodded slowly, then turned to Becky, who was standing slightly behind Nick. "Gardner's wedding?" He'd raised his voice again. "Don't look so sad. Just because he's married now doesn't mean he won't still fuck you, although God knows why he'd want to…"

Becky felt herself redden as Kyle and every other member of staff within earshot focused on her.

"C'mon," Nick said, still seemingly unruffled, "let's find somewhere quieter to sit."

"No." Tyler was being belligerent. "Tell me, Nick, old buddy," he continued, "what are you doing these days?"

Nick shrugged. "Oh, nothing much. I just work for a local firm of lawyers in a little town up the coast."

"Seriously?" Tyler could barely stop himself from laughing. "Nick Woods, A-grade student, top of the class and most likely to make it big, had to settle for small-town?"

"Yeah," Nick replied, looking disappointed. "We haven't all got what it takes to make it in the city." Becky knew he was letting Tyler crow, diverting the heat from her. If she hadn't already loved him with everything she had, she did now.

"I guess not." Tyler seemed to be thinking, looking from Nick to her and back again. "You married?" he asked.

"No." Nick kept his answer short.

"No?" Tyler repeated, then turned to Becky. "Anything you wanna tell me?" His eyes had that hostile glare she knew so well.

Before she could answer, Nick intervened. "If you're gonna suggest there's anything between Becky and me," he said, "then you'd be wrong. I might not be married, but I'm living with someone, and we're very happy together, so I'm not gonna do anything to screw it up." Nick told a good tale, there was no doubt about that. She almost believed him herself.

"Anyone I know?" Tyler asked, still seemingly suspicious.

"No. It's someone from my past. We lost touch, but then met up a while back and found we couldn't live without each other." Becky knew he was talking about her and felt a glow flicker inside.

"How romantic," Tyler sneered. "But take my advice and marry her," he added. "You get so much more control." He turned back to Becky. "Isn't that right?"

She didn't reply.

Nick shook his head. "I don't need to get married," he said. "I've already got everything I want. Besides, marriage is overrated. I don't believe in it." Becky's glow fizzled out. He'd told her to ignore whatever he said, but somehow she sensed he was telling the truth on this.

"Look," Nick continued calmly, "why don't you and I go somewhere and have a drink? Something's obviously bothering you. We can talk it over."

Tyler looked at Nick. "You're damn right something's bothering me," he replied and pulled an envelope from his inside pocket, throwing it at Becky. "You can't divorce me, you dumb fucking bitch," he exploded. "How many times do I have to tell you before you get it into your stupid head? You don't have grounds. Besides, you're mine. You always will be."

"Hey, man," Nick said, stepping in front of her. "I really don't think you should be discussing this while you're drunk. You need your wits about you for a conversation like that." To Becky's surprise, Tyler nodded his head. "And this isn't really the right place."

Nick quickly grabbed the envelope from Becky and shoved it into his pocket, before turning and putting his arm around Tyler's shoulders. "C'mon," he murmured, "I'll take you somewhere for a drink and we'll talk it through." He started to push Tyler toward the door, looking back to Becky and mouthing 'stay here' to her.

As he got to the door, he turned again and she saw him catch Kyle's eye and nod toward her. And then he was gone.

Before she'd even had the chance to consider what was going on, Kyle was by her side, steering her into his office and out of sight.

"Sit down," he said quietly. "I'll get us both a drink from the bar. I think we could use one after that."

She hadn't sat down on the couch before the tears started to fall. Nick had been right. She shouldn't have come. She wasn't strong enough for this, and now she was alone, her fears were overwhelming her. What was Nick going to do? What was Tyler going to say? And once Nick came back, would anything ever be the same again?

∞

## Nick

Nick looked around the bar of the small hotel, a few miles down the coast. He'd been here before a couple of times with clients, but it wasn't somewhere he'd consider himself a 'regular'. It was quiet, but then that wasn't surprising, given it was the middle of a Saturday afternoon in late March. He'd chosen this place precisely because he knew it would be quiet, and because he was unlikely to see anyone he knew.

He was sitting opposite Tyler at a small table.

"She's never been there for me," Tyler slurred, taking another gulp of the second double scotch Nick had bought him. "I've given her everything and she's never helped me, never once supported me." He leant back, rubbing his hands across his chest. "And she's boring as fuck in bed," he said loudly. "It was never great with her. She was always a real let-down, you know… like banging a plank of wood… a real dry, worn out, shabby plank of washed-up wood, if you get my meaning." He gave Nick an exaggerated wink, then reached for his glass and swallowed down the rest of his drink. "I mean, I still fuck her whenever I want," he added, slamming the glass back down on the table and leaning in toward Nick. "I just don't want to all that often, not with Rebecca, anyway." He sniggered.

Nick clenched his fists underneath the table, seething quietly.

"I'm gonna fight her," Tyler continued, contemplating his glass.

"Want another?" Nick asked, getting up from the table. He needed a break and he also intended getting Tyler as drunk as possible.

"Sure."

Nick went to the bar, taking his time over ordering the drinks. He was in no rush to get back.

When he returned, Tyler looked up at him as though he'd forgotten Nick was even with him. "Where was I?" Tyler asked.

"I can't remember." Nick hoped Tyler wouldn't either.

Tyler seemed to be thinking. "Oh, yeah. I'm gonna fight her," he said. "If she thinks she can try and divorce me, I'm gonna make it real hard on her. I'm sure as hell not gonna be made to look like the bad guy in this." He took a long sip of his scotch. "I'm gonna be the victim," he said, grinning inanely.

The temptation to wipe the smile from his face was almost too much and Nick sat on his hands, taking deep breaths.

"I'm on the verge of being made partner," Tyler continued, waving his glass around. "The way they are at my firm, I won't stand a chance at a partnership if she divorces me. She's always known that and she's trying to ruin everything for me, just like she's always done. She's a vindictive bitch." He added the last sentence as a kind of afterthought, before leaning back and staring at Nick vacantly.

Nick thought about suggesting they call it a day. He wasn't sure how much more of this he could take. He went to open his mouth, but Tyler got there first.

"You know what really gets to me?" he said, sounding somehow offended. "She could've divorced me any time. I mean, I've been screwing around since before we got married, so she's had plenty of chances to leave. But no… she had to wait until it really matters to me." He swallowed down some more scotch. "Do you know? When she found out I was banging someone at the office, she insisted I end it." Tyler swayed in his chair. "Why the fuck would I wanna do that? I mean, why would I give up great sex for Mrs Boring As Shit between the sheets…" He swayed a little more. "And why the fuck Mark

Gardner keeps banging her is anyone's guess." Nick tried to keep his face expressionless. "Don't look so shocked." He'd obviously failed. "They've been at it for years. Rebecca slept her way into the job. That's obvious. Whoever heard of a guy like Gardner taking on a rookie like Rebecca at her age? He had to be screwing her." He chuckled. "Well, I guess he's not as choosy as some of us." He finished his drink and tried to put his glass down on the table, missed and let it fall to the floor. "If this divorce is her idea of revenge for whatever it is she imagines I've done," he slurred, "she's gonna find out that I don't lose. Ever." He waved a finger at Nick, and fell forward onto the table, hitting his head hard.

"I seriously hope that hurt," Nick whispered to himself.

He took a clump of Tyler's hair in his fist, raised his head and let it drop again, banging heavily onto the wooden surface of the table. He was unconscious.

Nick got up and went over to the bar. The barman was staring at Tyler.

"I hope you're gonna deal with that," he said.

"I need a room," Nick said by way of an answer.

The man looked at Nick. "For him?"

Nick nodded. "I'll pay you twice the going rate, plus an extra two hundred for any mess he might make."

The man thought for a moment. "Deal," he said. He quickly worked out the amount and Nick handed over his credit card in return for a room key. "It's a ground floor room." He nodded toward some double doors. "Through there, down the corridor, second on the left."

Nick nodded and went back to Tyler, turning him in his chair and lifting him over his shoulder. He groaned, but Nick ignored him and headed through the door, following the barman's instructions.

The room was basic. There was a bed, a nightstand and a closet, with a small bathroom just inside the door. Nick dropped Tyler onto the bed, none too carefully, and opened the window.

He reached into his pocket and pulled out the envelope Tyler had thrown at Becky earlier, putting it beside him on the bed. He was about to turn away when Tyler stirred and opened his eyes.

"I won't let her get away with this," he said. It was suddenly as though he was completely sober. His voice had a menacing tone that made Nick stand still and listen. "I'll take everything she's got. And I mean *everything*. And I'll destroy anyone who tries to help her." Tyler was staring up at him, his eyes penetrating Nick's. "And then I'll go after Gardner and I won't stop until I've ruined him – professionally, and personally. No-one fucks around with my wife and gets away with it. I'll make him wish he'd never set eyes on her."

# Chapter Seventeen

*Becky*

For around half an hour or so, Kyle tried to make small talk. But then he gave up and went back to working at his desk, while Becky sat, nursing the large brandy he'd brought her in from the bar. She wasn't used to strong liquor and the first sip had felt like it was burning a trail all the way down to her stomach. Even so, it was nice to have something to do with her hands, just to stop them from shaking so much.

"You do know there's nothing between me and Mark, don't you?" she said, all of a sudden, worried that Kyle would think Tyler had been telling the truth.

Kyle looked across at her and smiled. "Yeah," he said. "I wouldn't have believed it anyway, but Mr Gardner explained what your... your husband's like when he asked me to look out for him."

"Oh." Now Becky felt embarrassed and sat back, looking away from Kyle.

The time seemed to drag on, although that was probably because she checked her watch every five minutes, wondering why Nick had been gone for so long. What on earth could he and Tyler be talking about – well, her obviously – but what was Tyler saying? And how was Nick reacting?

After almost two hours, the door to the office opened abruptly and Nick walked in. She looked at him and saw an expression she'd never seen on his face before. It was pure rage. He was doing his best to hold it in check, but she could see such anger in his eyes, she cowered back into the couch.

He turned to Kyle. "Thanks for taking care of Becky," he said, his voice a little more curt than usual.

"No problem," Kyle replied. He looked like he expected Nick to say something else, but Nick turned to Becky instead.

"C'mon," he said, his voice much softer now. He held out his hand to her.

"Where are we going?" she asked, unable to hide the fear in her voice.

He walked over and crouched down in front of her. "Back to the wedding," he said.

"Is everything alright?" she asked.

"I'll tell you all about it later," he replied.

Was that supposed to make her feel better? If so, it didn't work.

Nick got up again and lifted her to her feet, taking her hand in his and leading her across to the door. "Thanks again," he said to Kyle as he let Becky out first. "I'll get Mark to call you."

"Fine," Becky heard Kyle say as the door closed behind them.

All the way back to Mark and Emma's house, Becky's nerves played havoc with her. She couldn't sit still; she found it hard to breathe and her stomach was turning somersaults. Even so, she couldn't bring herself to ask Nick what had happened.

Nick had the security code for the gates and let them in and, as he parked up at the front of the house, she turned to him and grabbed his arm. He looked across at her.

"Don't worry," he said quietly.

"How can I not?"

He ran the backs of his fingers down her cheek. "It'll be fine," he said, "but we need to find Mark."

He didn't wait for an answer, but climbed out of the car and came around to her side, opening the door and helping her down. Then he took her hand and led her around the back of the house.

Mark was in the kitchen and they found him easily. He glanced up, seeming to know they were there and excused himself from the conversation he was having with Mrs Adams, who'd owned the coffee shop, until Emma recently bought it.

"You've been gone ages," he said.

"Yeah," Nick replied abruptly. "We need to go somewhere quiet. Just the three of us."

"Okay. My office." Mark led them through to the entrance hall and unlocked the door to his office, closing it behind them. "Whatever that asshole said about me and Becky, it's not true," Mark said, before Nick could even open his mouth. "I love Emma. Surely you know that by now. I'd never—"

"I know," Nick interrupted, raising his voice a little. "I know your relationship with Bex is professional and I trust you both. This has got nothing to do with that."

Mark seemed to pale a little. "Then what's it about? Why do you need to see me?" He looked from Nick to Becky and back again. "Surely anything that piece of shit had to say concerns the two of you, not me."

Nick sighed deeply and Becky's heart ached for him. What must he have gone through? "I'm not gonna tell you everything he said," Nick told Mark. "A lot of it was real personal and related to him and Becky." He gripped her hand a little tighter as he spoke.

"Okay," Mark replied. "Tell me what you can, and what it's got to do with me."

"When we got there, he was being real loud, and real obnoxious," Nick began. "I wanted to get him away from the hotel, and – more importantly – away from Bex. So, I suggested he and I should go for a drink."

"Jeez," Mark said. "That had to be hard."

"Tell me about it," Nick replied. "I took him to a small hotel down the coast and he laid into Becky a little; he talked about the divorce." He heaved out a long breath. "It wasn't pretty." A short silence followed, during which neither Becky nor Mark seemed to be able to think of anything to say. "Then he passed out – I'd given him a few really large scotches, and that was kinda the plan. I took him to a room, and threw him on the bed. But, I guess he wasn't as far gone as I thought he was…" Nick paused.

"What happened?" Mark asked.

"He made a few threats," Nick replied. "And he sounded real sober when he did it."

"Threats against whom?" Mark's voice was colder than Becky had ever heard it.

"Becky for a start," Nick said. "He said if she tries to go ahead with the divorce, he's gonna take everything she's got." He turned to Becky. "I expected all of that, and I won't let him hurt you. He won't touch you ever again." She leant into him and he put his arm around her.

"And?" Mark stared at Nick. "I'm sensing there's more."

"And he said he'll destroy anyone who tries to help her, which I think might have been a veiled threat against me – to warn me off. He didn't seem to realize the connection between Becky and me, so it can't have been anything more than a guess on his part." He paused. "And then he said he's gonna go after you."

"Let him." Mark smiled slowly. "Just let him. I've always wanted to spend a few minutes alone with that fucker."

"That wasn't all," Nick added. "His exact words were that he wants to ruin you professionally – and personally. I think he was talking about Emma."

Becky pulled away from Nick and turned to face Mark. "Oh God," she said. "What have I done?"

"You haven't done anything," Nick told her.

"But…"

"But nothing." Mark's voice cut through her. "I'm not scared of him."

"And what about Emma?"

"Stop worrying. I can protect Emma." Mark turned to Nick. "Do you think he meant it, or was it the drink talking?" he asked.

"I don't know. He sounded sober, but he'd put away a helluva lot of booze. I deliberately didn't react to the threats, just in case. If it was the drink talking, he probably won't remember it in the morning and me reacting would just have made it more memorable."

"Sounds sensible."

"Even so, I think we need to take precautions," Nick added. "We know how dangerous he is, especially with women."

"You left him at this hotel?" Mark asked.

"Yeah. He'll wake up tomorrow with a hangover – hopefully – and the divorce papers for company.

"You gave them back to him?" Becky whispered.

"I think 'gave' would be putting it a little strong." He smiled at her, just briefly, then looked back at Mark. "I don't think we should tell Emma about this. Not today anyway."

"She'll have to know at some point," Mark said. "I can't keep it from her."

"I know. But I think she has the right to enjoy her wedding day, don't you?"

Mark nodded.

"Besides," Nick added, "I think it's wise to wait until we know for sure that the threat is real. Tyler might not remember a damn thing in the morning. There's no point in scaring Emma when there's no cause."

Mark glanced at Becky. "And what about Becky?" he asked. "She's scared too."

"I know that, for fucks sake." Nick raised his voice, then stopped. "Sorry," he said.

"It's okay," Mark replied.

Nick turned to Becky. "I know you hate anyone interfering, but I'm gonna ask you and Mark if you can stop travelling around for the time being. I can't take care of you if you're not here, baby." He cupped her face in his hand, searching her eyes. "I'm sorry. I hate coming across all dictatorial, but I won't be able to do much if you're in New Hampshire or Vermont."

She felt herself fall into him, grateful that he even wanted to look after her, considering what he must've been through that afternoon.

"That's fine with me," Mark said.

"Me too," Becky whispered. "Thank you."

"Don't thank me, baby," Nick said. "I really hate having to sound so controlling."

Becky sighed. "You can be as controlling as you like, as long as I'm safe from him."

"You'll be safe. I promise."

"At the risk of sounding just like Nick," Mark added, "I think it's best if you work from here for now." Becky turned to face him. "Nick has to go into his office and today has shown that Tyler can get into the hotel – even if Kyle did stop him. If you're here with me, Nick will know you're safe."

"And Emma?" Becky said. "What about when she's at work? Who's going to keep her safe?"

"My office is two minutes from her," Nick replied.

"Then we'll have to warn her about Tyler," Mark said sounding relieved. "If you expect her to call you if he shows up, she's gonna have to know."

"Maybe, but she doesn't have to know he's threatened her, does she? We can tell her he's a threat to Becky and that he might just show up in town."

"I don't like lying to her," Mark confessed. "It got me in trouble before. I'm not sure she'd forgive me for doing it again."

"I'll lie to her then," Nick replied. "At least until we know for sure whether she's really in danger." An uneasy silence followed. "I don't suppose you can bring your honeymoon forward?" Nick suggested. "You'd both be safer still if you weren't even here."

"No, not really," Mark replied. "We're going while they do the refurbishments on the coffee shop. Emma can't really be away while the place is open for business."

Nick nodded.

"Okay. Well, we'll work something out. In the meantime, we won't tell Emma anything at all for today and, sometime tomorrow, we'll come over here and sit down together, and explain to her what's happened, and that Tyler is threatening Becky and she'll be working from here and, if he turns up at the coffee shop, she's to call me immediately."

Mark sighed, ran his fingers through his hair and glared at Nick, then slowly nodded his head.

Becky had surprised herself by keeping it together for the rest of the wedding, knowing that Nick wanted Emma to enjoy the remainder of her day. Even during the short journey back home, she stayed strong, but as he parked up in front of the trailer, she found it impossible to hold her emotions in check any longer and let out a sob, covering her face with her hands as tears streamed from her eyes. Nick didn't say a word. Instead, he got out of the car, came around to her side and lifted her gently into his arms, carrying her into the trailer and straight through to the bedroom. He laid her down in the middle of the bed, then took off his jacket, and dropped it on the floor, before lying down beside her, pulling her close and holding on to her.

For a long while, the only sound that filled the room, was Becky's soft weeping, but eventually, she calmed, the tears slowed, and she looked up at Nick in the moonlight.

"What did he say?" she asked, fearing his answer.

"Nothing good," he replied.

"Can you tell me?"

She felt Nick's chest heave as he sighed. "Sure," he said. "He was very uncomplimentary about you… about how you are in bed. He also said he was still sleeping with you, although those weren't his exact words. He was a lot more blunt than that."

Becky clasped his arms. "You didn't believe him, did you?"

He looked down at her. "No, of course not, Bex. I know it's not true. Any of it."

"Something's bothering you," she said. "Is it the threats?"

"I'm less worried about that," he said, surprising her. "I know, between Mark and I, we can keep you and Emma safe." He shrugged. "Let's face it, I'm not even sure he meant it. He was really drunk."

"So what's eating at you, Nick?"

He pulled her closer still, so she was pressed tight against him. "I hated the way he talked about you; like he owned you, like he had rights over you and wasn't ever gonna give them up."

"It was always about ownership with him. But I never belonged to him, Nick. I've always been yours."

"And I'm yours."

"Was it really that hard? Talking to him, I mean?" she asked, after a moment's pause.

He leant back a little, staring into her eyes. "Apart from losing you nine years ago, it was the hardest thing I've ever done."

## *Nick*

Nick woke early, his body wrapped around Becky's. She felt soft and he pulled her closer, and she let out a gentle moan, snuggling into him. The night before, they'd eventually undressed and climbed into bed, bone tired. They didn't make love, but he'd held her until she'd fallen asleep.

"Good morning," she murmured, all sleepy.

"Hello," he replied, kissing her neck and shoulders.

"Hmm… that's nice," she whispered.

He moved lower, tracing delicate kisses over her breasts, capturing her nipples in his mouth, one at a time. He heard her sigh out her pleasure, then felt her hands on the side of his face, raising him back up toward her.

"Make love to me, Nick," she murmured. "Please." Her eyes implored him to give her what she needed.

Without saying a word, he rolled her onto her back and knelt between her legs, spreading them wide apart with his own, then placed the head of his cock at her entrance and pushed inside her. She gasped, and moved her hips up to meet him, matching his rhythm, stroke for stroke. Their eyes and bodies were locked as he poured his love into her, showing her with every move that he was hers. It didn't take long for Becky's breathing to change, for him to feel the tightening inside, and for her to finally cry out his name. Hearing that pushed him over the edge and, with one final thrust deep inside her, he filled her, whispering his love.

Turning them onto their sides, facing each other, Nick held her in his arms. "I know you don't feel safe right now," he murmured. "I know he intruded into your sanctuary – well, our sanctuary – but I promise you, I will not let him hurt you ever again. Do you understand?"

She nodded. "But you're wrong about one thing," she whispered. "I do feel safe, as long as you're with me."

Monday morning came around far too soon. They'd spent part of Sunday with Mark and Emma, explaining about Tyler and what had happened the previous day. Mark still wanted to tell Emma the full story, but Nick was adamant there was no need to worry her until they knew there was a definite threat to her. They showed Emma a picture of Tyler from the Internet and told her that, if he came into the coffee shop, or she saw him around town, she had to call Nick and he'd be with her in two minutes. Nick felt justified in his decision the moment he saw the way her face paled on hearing that.

Sitting at his desk, he was finding it hard to concentrate. He'd already gone over to the coffee shop twice, using the pretext of buying muffins and drinks as an excuse. Emma seemed to jump every time someone came in the door and he tried to reassure her that Tyler had probably already headed back to Boston, hungover and feeling sorry for himself. He had a job in the city, after all. She'd seemed to be placated by that.

The knock on his door made Nick start and he kicked himself mentally. Even he was getting jumpy. "Come in," he called and looked up. "What the…?" He got up from his desk and made it to the door before Mark had even closed it behind him. Becky released herself from Mark's grip and fell into Nick's arms.

"Your receptionist said it was okay to come straight in," Mark explained.

Nick nodded. "What's going on?" he said to Becky, but she seemed incapable of speech. He looked up at Mark, who was running his hands down his face. "Mark?" he asked.

"I was gonna call you and get you to come to our place," Mark began, "but then I remembered you can't really leave town while Emma's here, so I brought Becky to you."

"Okay, but what's happened?" He guided Becky round to his side of the desk, sat down in his chair and pulled her onto his lap. She sobbed into his shoulder uncontrollably, while he gently stroked her hair. Mark sat opposite, staring at them.

"We were working at the house," he said quietly, "when Becky got an email from Jeremy and she just kinda broke down." He looked at Nick, a little embarrassed. "Let's just say, it was obviously you she needed, and not me."

Nick nodded and pulled Becky closer. "What did Jeremy say?" What on earth had happened?

"Just that he couldn't represent her anymore. His message was quite blunt."

*What?* "He didn't say why?" Nick asked, feeling the rage boiling instantly inside him.

"No." Mark shook his head. "I wondered if there was something difficult about Becky's divorce… some reason why lawyers seem to keep turning her away?"

"There's nothing like that," Nick said. "As divorces go, it's quite straightforward."

Mark nodded now, seemingly confused.

Nick leant back a little, looking at Becky. "Is the email on your phone?" he asked her. She gave a slight incline of her head. "May I see it?"

She nudged her purse in his direction, then buried her head again. Nick unzipped her purse and delved inside until he found her phone, and the email she'd received. Mark was right, it was blunt. Not rude, but blunt.

"Right," Nick said. He wasn't about to take this lying down. At the bottom of the e-mail was the contact number for Jeremy's firm. Nick dialed it up on his landline. "Put me through to Jeremy Slater," he said as soon as the call was connected. He noticed Mark's raised eyebrows. After a few moments, he heard Jeremy's voice.

"Hello."

"This is Nick Woods," he said. "I'm Mrs Howell's—"

"I know who you are," Jeremy cut in. "And, being a lawyer yourself, you must be aware, I can't speak with you. You're not my client."

"Well, according to the email you sent this morning, neither is Mrs Howell any more."

There was a short silence. "No."

"In which case, you can speak to me, and you can explain to me, lawyer-to-lawyer, why exactly you're doing this. Because I'm finding it hard to believe that a simple contested no fault divorce is too complex for a firm like yours…" Nick filled his voice with as much disdain as he could muster.

"Of course it isn't."

"Then explain it to me, because I really don't understand."

"I can't tell you my reasons," Jeremy said, his voice quiet – almost fearful. "But I can tell you that Mr Howell knows some really powerful people. I know you and Mrs Howell are more than just friends," he continued, "and I feel I should warn you to stay away from her."

"Stay away from her?" Nick felt Becky tense in his arms. "Are you saying Mr Howell is threatening me?"

"I'm not saying anything," Jeremy replied, "other than that you should be careful who you side with in this…" His voice faded to a whisper.

"It's not a matter of sides," Nick shouted. "This is about basic right and wrong. If you're bending to pressure from Mr Howell, then you've clearly forgotten which is which."

Mark got to his feet. "Give me the phone," he said to Nick, holding out his hand. Nick looked up, saw the fury in Mark's eyes, and offered him the handset.

"Slater," Mark said abruptly. "Gardner here." Nick noted Mark had dropped their previous first-name terms. "Wanna tell me what the fuck is going on?"

Nick watched as Mark paced his office floor a couple of times, then stopped and looked at him and Becky. "Seriously?" he said. "You're seriously gonna drop Becky's divorce because that asshole has friends in high places and he's putting a little bit of pressure on you?" Mark listened again. "I asked you to do this as a personal favor." He fell silent, waiting. "What do you mean, you've got too much to lose?" Nick noted the cynical tone in Mark's voice. "Are you serious?" Mark sat down, his eyes fixed on Becky. "You told me when we met for lunch a couple of months ago that Gardners are now your biggest client," he said quietly and calmly. "Well, we're not any more. You're fired…" He stopped talking for a moment, then sat forward, his face reddening a little, his eyes dark with anger. "Don't you dare bring my father and your friendship with him into this. You just fucked over that friendship. Whatever happens now is entirely of your own doing." He fell silent again. "I'm not interested, Jeremy. It's too late for that. I want all of our files delivered to my office in Boston by the end of the day… I don't care. I don't want excuses. Just do it." He stopped, waiting again. "Well, maybe you should've thought about that before you sent your email to Mrs Howell," he said. "When you look back on this, I really hope you'll think it was worth it." He hung up the call and put the handset down on Nick's desk.

Nick stared at him. "What?" Mark said.

"Nothing," Nick replied. "I've just never seen you like that before."

"It doesn't happen very often." Mark let out a long breath, seeming to calm down.

"You can be a mean son-of-a-bitch when you have to be."

"Yeah, but only when I really have to be." Mark smiled, although it faded quickly. "The question is, what are we going to do about Becky's divorce?"

"Oh, that's simple. I'm not fucking around anymore. I'll represent her," Nick replied. Becky leant away from him, staring.

"You can't," she said.

"Yeah, I can. Believe it or not, I'm actually a qualified lawyer."

"But we're together," she said, not feeling the humor.

"So? No-one really knows about that, and as long as we keep it that way, it'll be fine. Anyway, it's not unheard of for lawyers to have affairs with, or even fall in love with clients during divorce cases. We just got there a bit ahead of time…" He smiled at her, trying to cheer her up.

"Except you didn't," Mark put in. "Becky's been trying to divorce Tyler for years."

"Yeah... I meant that we were originally together nine years ago," Nick replied.

"Oh, I see."

"You're sure you won't get into trouble?" Becky said.

"I'm sure." He hugged her tighter. "Besides, there's no-one I'd rather get into trouble for – or with." He kissed her.

"I can always go visit Emma, if I'm in the way," Mark said, grinning.

Nick chuckled and broke the kiss, glancing at Becky. She was blushing and buried her face in his shoulder. "Well you kinda are," he said, smiling at Mark. "But as much as I'd like to take Bex back to the trailer for the afternoon, I need to get on. I wanna try doing some digging. I wanna know how the hell Tyler has managed to exert so much power over two separate lawyers in different states. I was gonna start looking into it when Tom turned Becky away, but then we got wrapped up in dealing with Jeremy, and the wedding, and then I found out Tom's wife is sick... and that means I've been busier here, so I haven't had the time. But I'll make the time now. We need to know what we're up against."

"Yeah. That sounds like a good idea," Mark said. "If you need any help, let me know."

Becky twisted, looking up at Mark. "I'm sorry," she murmured.

"What the hell for?" he asked.

"Your lawyer. You've known him since you were born. He's represented the company for years, and now... It's all my fault." She started to cry again, and Nick held her close.

"Bullshit," Mark said simply. "I don't need people working for me who aren't one hundred percent on my team. If Jeremy can be so easily swayed, then I'm better off without him." He glanced at Nick. "Besides, I think I know a much better lawyer anyway."

# Chapter Eighteen

## *Becky*

Once Becky had calmed down, which took a while, they all went over to the coffee shop for an early lunch. Emma was surprised to see them, and they explained to her what had happened with Jeremy. She gave Becky a hug, which almost started her crying again, and made them all coffee while they chose what they wanted from the menu.

"Being as Becky's working at our place," she said to Nick, joining them for a few minutes while they waited for their order to be cooked, "why don't you come over later and I'll make us all dinner?"

Nick glanced at Becky and she knew he was looking for her approval. As much as she wanted to just go home and curl up with him, she appreciated everything Mark and Emma were doing for them, and she gave Nick a quick nod of her head.

"Sure," he said. "Sounds great."

"Do you think you'll have any news by then?" Mark asked him.

"I doubt it," Nick replied. "I've already got a stack of work to do first. If I get time, I'll start looking into what Tyler Howell has that we don't." He looked at Becky and gave her a reassuring smile.

After lunch, the three of them walked back to Nick's office where Mark had parked earlier. Nick gave Becky a long, intimate kiss while Mark leant against the door of the car.

"I'll see you later," Nick whispered. "And call me if you need to talk. Okay?"

She nodded and let him lead her around to the passenger side of the car, lowering her into the seat.

"I love you," he murmured, leaning down and kissing her again.

"I love you too."

He closed the door and went around to Mark. They spoke for a few minutes, then Nick went into his office, giving her a wave and a wink, while Mark got into the car and reversed out of the parking bay.

"What was that about?" Becky asked as he selected drive and headed off down Main Street.

"What?"

"You and Nick. What were you talking about?"

He glanced at her. "You," he replied. "Nick was just asking me to keep a close eye on you this afternoon; make sure you're okay. That's all. The guy's in love with you, Becky; he's bound to be concerned."

"He's not the only one," she said quietly.

It was a tough afternoon. Almost everything she did went wrong. Even making coffee proved challenging, and when she spilt the milk the second time, she burst into tears.

"Pull yourself together," she chided herself out loud.

"You don't have to," Nick replied from the doorway. She jumped out of her skin.

"You're here?" she said, checking the time. It was only just after five-thirty.

"Yeah. Mark just let me in and told me where to find you. I couldn't concentrate. I decided I might as well come here and not concentrate with you."

She ran over to him and threw herself into his arms.

"God, you feel good," he whispered into her hair.

"So do you."

"Are we abandoning work *and* coffee?" Mark said from behind them, a broad smile on his face.

"Looks like it," Nick replied.

"Okay, I'll open the wine instead," Mark said.

"It's not even six o'clock yet," Becky reasoned.

"It is somewhere in the world."

They sat around the kitchen island. Becky and Mark drank wine, while Nick had a beer and explained he hadn't had time to do any digging into Tyler's influence over Tom and Jeremy, but he hoped to get around to it the following day.

"I want to tell Emma about the threat," Mark said, out of the blue.

"I thought we went through this already," Nick replied.

"We did. But you don't seem to understand. I'm in love with your sister. She's my wife and my world, and I can't lie to her. You know what happened when we first got together; you know what it nearly cost us. And that was just a white lie… This is so much more than that." He let out a long breath. "I'm not asking, Nick."

Nick sighed. "Okay. We'll tell her when she gets home." He glared at Mark. "But you need to be prepared for the consequences."

"Of having lied to her, or of the threat?"

"Both."

They let Emma get into cooking the meal before Mark explained what had really happened when Nick spoke with Tyler. She was de-seeding peppers at the time and looked up to face them, all sitting opposite her at the huge kitchen island.

"You lied to me?" she said, and Becky noticed tears welling in her eyes. "Mark?"

He was by her side in moments and Becky wondered if she and Nick should leave the room and let Mark and Emma have some privacy. She went to get up, but Nick held her firm in her seat and when she looked up at him, he shook his head, just once.

"I'm sorry," Mark replied.

"How could you?" she said. "After—"

"Don't blame him," Nick cut in. "Em, this was one hundred per cent down to me. I convinced Mark that we shouldn't tell you until we knew for sure that Tyler's threat was for real. We still don't know that, but Mark said he hated lying to you, and keeping secrets from you. He told me he was gonna tell you anyway. He wanted to be straight with you from the start, so if you're gonna get mad at anyone, get mad at me. Okay?"

Emma turned from Mark and glared hard at Nick. "Don't you trust me at all?" she said.

"Yes." His voice was so soft, it took Becky's breath away. "You know I do. But I care about you, Em. You're my sister, and I love you. I just thought my way was best. If I was wrong, I apologize."

"Well, you were wrong," Emma said. "I'm not that weak, Nick."

He leant forward, putting his hand out for her to take. She ignored it. "I know you're not," he said, leaving his hand where it was. Becky felt for him. He was trying to look out for Emma, just like he'd always done. "You're not weak at all. You're an incredibly strong person, Em." She stared at him and shook her head, seemingly in disbelief. "You are," Nick reiterated.

"If I'm so strong," Emma said, tears welling in her eyes, "why did you lie to me?"

"Maybe I was being over-protective," he replied. "I'm sorry."

"I'm sorry too," Mark added. "Say you forgive us?"

"I forgive *you*." Emma leant into him, making it clear her forgiveness was limited to her husband.

"Don't be too hard on Nick," Mark said, putting his arms around Emma and holding her. "You're blaming him for caring – because that's the only reason he did this."

"Em?" Nick said. "I'm sorry."

"Hmm." Emma stared at Nick again. She was clearly finding it hard to accept his actions.

"There's another reason that Nick's being so wary," Becky said, taking a deep breath. "He knows what Tyler's capable of. Mark does too... but not in as much detail."

She felt Nick's grip tighten on her hand.

"So do I. I know he beat you, Becky," Emma said, her voice much more gentle.

"He did a lot more than that," Becky replied.

"You don't have to say anything," Nick interrupted.

"Yeah, I do. I think Emma has a right to understand exactly why you're being so protective. Besides, if he's threatening her too, she needs to know the truth." Becky kept her eyes fixed on Emma. "He tried to rape me," she said quietly. "Three times. And it was only really by luck on all three occasions, that he didn't succeed."

Nick sighed loudly. "I'm sorry, Bex," he said. "But if you want to tell Emma the truth, then that's not what happened. That's not how it was, is it?"

She turned and stared at him, tears already forming. "What do you mean?" She'd told him about what Tyler had done. Was he saying he didn't believe her after all?

"You described all three assaults to me," he said, "in great detail. You can't call the first time an *attempted* rape."

"I know," she murmured through her tears.

"Come here." He got up and stood beside her, pulling her into his arms. She rested her head on his chest and he stroked her hair. "I'm so sorry," he murmured. She buried her head and sobbed. "What you described to me was rape, Bex. You didn't consent to what he did to you… and it wasn't luck that he failed that first time, was it?" Becky shook her head, swallowing down her tears. "Neither was it very lucky that he took his inabilities out on you, and broke two of your ribs…" His arms tightened around her. "I'm sorry, baby, but you can't make excuses for him. He raped you."

"I know," she whimpered into him. "I've always known. I just didn't want to admit it."

"Then I'm sorry I've made you." He placed a finger under her chin and raised her face to his, then leant down and kissed her gently.

"You're right," she said, leaning back a little and looking up into his soft gray eyes. "He's a rapist. He doesn't deserve for me to diminish that, just because I don't want to face up to it."

She leant into him and let him hold her again, relishing his strong arms around her. After a short while she looked up. Emma had turned white and was clinging to Mark.

"You're safe," Mark told her, although he looked pretty shocked himself. "We'll make sure you're safe. He's not gonna hurt you."

Emma looked up at him. "I'm not thinking about that," she said. "I'm thinking about what Becky's been through." She reached across the island and Becky mirrored her movement and joined their hands, feeling Emma's grip hers firmly. "I know Nick's there for you," she said. "And I know he always will be, but if you ever want to talk, you know where I am."

Becky's vision blurred as her eyes filled with tears again.

"Thank you," she murmured.

With a squeeze, Emma removed her hand and held onto Mark again, although her eyes were now fixed on Nick. "And as for you," she said, pausing for a moment, while they all held their breath, "you just go on being as over-protective as you damn well please." They all heaved out a collective sigh of relief. "Only don't ever lie to me again."

"I won't," Nick replied.

While the dinner cooked, they all sat around the island unit and Emma asked Nick to tell her exactly what Tyler had said. He wouldn't give her details about anything that related to Becky, but told her everything he'd told Mark.

"And your lawyer is now refusing to act for Becky?" She turned to Mark.

"Yeah," Mark replied.

"So I'm gonna take the case," Nick said.

"Is that wise?" Emma asked.

"My thoughts exactly," Becky added.

Mark and Nick looked at each other and smiled. "Now who's being over-protective?" Nick said. "I told you, it'll be fine."

Becky sat on Nick's lap now, nestling into his strong arms. "I've been thinking this afternoon," she said. "I've been incapable of doing much else."

"And?" Nick prompted.

"And, it seems to me that Tom and Jeremy must have had skeletons in their closets. And that Tyler must have discovered what those skeletons are, and have blackmailed them into dropping my case."

"I've been thinking the same thing myself," Nick admitted.

"So, what if he manages to find out something about you?" she asked, staring into his eyes.

"I don't have any skeletons," Nick said.

"None?"

Nick looked confused. "No," he said. "You know me, Bex. I've not hidden anything from you."

"I know." She wasn't sure how she was going to say this. "But there are aspects of your life that I'm sure you don't want anyone to know about."

He shifted in the seat, moving her forward a little so he could look at her properly.

"What are you talking about?" he asked.

She took a deep breath. "Emma," she said.

"What about her?"

"The tablets," she whispered.

"You told her?" It was Mark who spoke first.

Nick looked up. "I had to," he explained, his eyes fixed on Emma, not Mark. "I'm sorry."

"Why?" Emma asked. She wasn't upset, she was just asking the question. "Why did you tell?"

"Because Becky was concerned—"

"No, I was jealous," Becky put in. "We're doing the truth thing, aren't we? So, be honest." She turned to Emma. "I was jealous," she repeated. "When Nick and I first got back together, he seemed to spend a lot of time either worrying about you, talking about you, or being with you. I felt a little left out, I guess." She shrugged. "It was stupid of me, but after Tyler…"

Emma nodded and smiled. "It's okay," she said. "That makes sense. And I'm glad you know."

"I understand it's a secret," Becky added. "Nick explained that no-one else knows except him, you and Mark, and I'll never tell anyone. I promise."

"It's fine," Emma said quietly. "I know I can trust you."

They all sat in silence for a moment before Nick spoke.

"What makes you think Tyler could use Emma's secret against me?" he said quietly, holding Becky close.

"Just the fact that she's your sister, and that it's a secret," Becky replied.

"How on earth would he even find out?" Emma asked.

"I don't know. Maybe he'd manage to get access to your medical records?"

There was another pause. Again, it was Nick who broke it. "Even if he did, what do you think we'd do?" he asked.

"Well, if he was saying you had to stop representing me, or he'd go public with Emma's secret, then I guess…" She didn't want to say the words.

"You think I'd throw you under the bus?" Nick turned her on his lap, so they were facing each other. "You really think I'd do that?"

"I wouldn't expect you to throw Emma under the bus either. She's your sister. I understand how you feel about her."

"And yet you don't seem to have a damn clue how I feel about you," he said. He closed his eyes, just for a moment and, when he opened them again, they were glistening. "Let's say, just for the sake of argument, that Tyler somehow managed to find out Emma's secret," he said. "And let's say he contacted me and threatened to use it against me, if I refused to stop representing you." Becky nodded, showing she understood. "I'll tell you exactly what would happen," he continued. "I'd come see Emma, and she'd tell me…"

"To tell Tyler to go to hell," Emma finished his sentence. "And then I'd tell everyone the secret anyway, so he had no power over Nick."

Becky shook her head this time. "I couldn't ask that of you," she said.

"You wouldn't be," Nick replied. "Emma may be vulnerable sometimes, but I know her well enough to know that she'd never let a guy like Tyler get away with something like that."

"No, I wouldn't," Emma said.

Becky looked from Nick to Emma and then to Mark, who was staring at her.

"I've known you for a long time, and I know what you're used to with Tyler," Mark said gently. "But you need to remember, that part of your life is over. No-one is gonna treat you badly anymore. We care about you, Becky. All of us. We just wanna help."

"I know," she whimpered, tears starting to fall.

Nick held her close. "I know it's hard for you," he said softly. "I get that he ground you down, but you're so safe, baby. I love you more than I'll ever be able to tell you. Please don't ever doubt that."

"I don't. I honestly don't"

"Then trust me. I will always put you first. I will always do what's right for you. I'd give my life for you, Bex… so please, just trust me."

## Nick

Becky cried herself to sleep that night, holding on to Nick and whispering over and over that she did trust him, begging him to believe her. He reassured her repeatedly that he did, that he loved her and would never do anything to hurt her and, eventually, she calmed, her breathing altered and he knew she'd cried herself out.

He, however, was wide awake, and after an hour or so lying in bed, staring at the ceiling, listening to Becky's even breathing, he knew he had to do something. He unfurled her arms from around him and slid out of bed. She moaned softly, but then turned over and continued sleeping, and he put on some shorts and went through into the living room, sitting down at his desk and firing up his laptop.

To start with, he searched simply for Tyler Howell. The first page of results centered around his law firm's website, which was of no interest to Nick, so he moved onto page two, and started scrolling through the listing, stopping dead halfway down the page, when the name Garrett Howell leapt off the screen at him. Garrett Howell was Tyler's father. 'Garrett' wasn't the most common name in the world. Surely…

He opened another window and searched for Garrett Howell, holding his breath while the results displayed, then sitting back as the truth slowly dawned on him. Sure enough, Garrett Howell was the CEO of GHC Engineering. He got up and fixed himself a coffee, then came back and thought through what he'd discovered. If Garrett was an old friend of Tom's, it made sense that he'd maybe put pressure on Tom not to represent Becky in his son's divorce, but that didn't account for Jeremy's withdrawal from the case. He took a large gulp of coffee. He was going to have to confront Tom in the morning, regardless of how sick Cathy was. He needed to know what had gone on, if he was ever going to make sense of it all.

"Please, Nick," Becky's nails dug into his shoulders as he ground into her. "I'm so close." He knew she needed this more than ever and swiveled his hips, plunging harder and harder, taking her deeper. "Oh God, yes," she hissed, throwing her head back into the pillow and screaming her pleasure. "I love you."

"I love you." He thrust into her again, just once, and let go, deep inside, feeling the joy of his release, before he collapsed down onto her.

"You… you disappeared in the night," she murmured, breathlessly.

"Yeah. I didn't think you noticed." He raised himself up on his elbows.

"Of course I noticed. I was just too exhausted to come find you."

He smiled. "I just went and did a little work, that's all."

She nodded and leant up to kiss him. He decided not to tell her what he'd found out until he'd spoken to Tom. In the cold light of morning, he'd realized it might be a coincidence and he didn't want to worry Becky until he knew for certain.

"How's Cathy?" Nick asked, closing the door to Tom's office behind him. He walked over to the desk and sat down, uninvited.

Tom looked up. "It wasn't the cancer," Tom said, his relief obvious. "Just some benign cysts."

"So, she's okay?" Nick asked, just to make sure.

"Yes. Thanks for asking," Tom said. "And thanks for covering here. I know I've been preoccupied."

"That's okay." Nick crossed one leg over the other. "Now, I've got a favor to ask in return." Tom raised an eyebrow inquisitively. "I need some honest answers from you… and no bullshit." Tom went to speak, but Nick raised a hand, cutting him off. "Why didn't you tell me you had a conflict over representing Becky, because her husband is Garrett Howell's son?" He saw Tom's face pale and knew he'd hit home.

"How much do you know?" Tom whispered, looking quickly at the door behind Nick.

Nick didn't really know very much at all, but decided to bluff. "I know everything," he said.

To his surprise, Tom crumpled in front of him, covering his face with his hands, his shoulders shaking. He was clearly crying and Nick felt embarrassed for both of them.

He waited in silence until Tom had quietened. "It wasn't even really an affair," Tom muttered, lowering his hands. He reached forward, pulled a Kleenex from the box on his desk and wiped his face. He didn't make eye contact with Nick, but continued, "It was just a one off." He sniffed loudly. "It was years ago, when Cathy was pregnant with Ethan." He shook his head. "That's why we stopped seeing them. Shelley – that's Garrett's wife – she and I both regretted it and we didn't want to meet up again, but I guess Garrett found out. He blackmailed me into taking on his work, and then into refusing to represent Mrs Howell."

"And why exactly did he need you to represent his company?"

"I can't tell you."

"Can't, or won't?"

Tom said nothing.

"Okay," Nick said. "If you won't tell me that, then explain how you even knew about Becky?"

"I didn't, not to start off with," Tom replied. "We were sitting in his home office that weekend when I went to visit him, and he'd just finished telling me, in no uncertain terms that if I didn't handle his company's legal affairs in relation to this highway contract, he'd tell

Cathy what had gone on between me and Shelley, when he got a call from his son. Tyler said his wife had gone off on a business trip a couple of days before – but only after he'd assaulted her…"

"He'd damn near raped her, Tom," Nick interrupted and noticed Tom flush. "Assault doesn't really cover what he'd done to her. And it wasn't the first time."

"I know," Tom whispered. "Tyler had calmed down and sobered up by the time he called his dad and was worried she might press charges against him, or sue him for divorce – or probably both."

"Why was he so worried? He'd never been concerned before?"

"Because this time was different. He said he'd always been able to threaten her into doing what he wanted, but this time she wasn't scared of him. He was worried that she might actually take action."

"So what happened?" Nick inquired.

"Garrett flew into a rage at Tyler, and then asked my advice. Having just got the contract, he didn't want his son involved in a messy, high profile divorce, or being arrested on a sexual assault charge. He was worried about the publicity." He looked up at Nick. "What was I supposed to do?"

"Well, I guess you could've tried not sleeping with the guy's wife in the first place, and maybe being faithful to your wife… your pregnant wife? They sound like reasonable suggestions to me." Nick couldn't hide his sarcasm.

"Don't you think I regret that enough?" Tom shouted.

Nick took a deep breath. "So, what did you advise him?" he asked.

Tom shrugged. "I told him the best thing was to do nothing. I suggested he avoid contacting her at all, keep his head down and hope it all blew over. His father drilled that into him." That made sense of why Tyler hadn't contacted Becky – at least not until he'd received the divorce papers, anyway. He was following daddy's orders.

"That was your best advice?" Nick said.

"That was what I told him. It wasn't good legal advice, but I didn't want to get involved. It was only when you came in here the following week and mentioned Mrs Howell's name that I realized the connection between you and her and Tyler. I didn't want to take the case because of the conflict of interests, but I couldn't tell you that at the time, so I tried to put you off."

"Without much success," Nick admitted.

"Once we'd set up the appointment and you'd left, I called Garrett," Tom said, sheepishly, his voice barely audible.

"You did what?" Nick sat forward.

"I called Garrett," Tom repeated. "I didn't mention you. I told him Mrs Howell was in the area on business and had come to me for legal advice. I asked him what he wanted me to do."

"You son-of-a-bitch," Nick growled.

"I knew if I just dealt with her properly, then Garrett would expose my fling with Shelley to Cathy."

"What did he tell you?" Nick asked.

"He told me to do exactly what I did… to advise her she had no grounds for anything."

Nick stood quickly, his fists clenched, and noticed Tom flinch back into his seat, fear filling his eyes.

"Tell your puppet master this…" he growled. "I'm gonna represent Becky, and there's not a damn thing he can do to stop me." He turned toward the door. "We're through, Tom," he said quietly. "I'll keep my office here for the time being, until I can find somewhere else, but our partnership is over."

When he got to the door, he opened it and glanced back at Tom, who was sitting at his desk with his head in his hands.

Tina went to hand Nick his messages, but he waved them aside, going into his office and grabbing his laptop.

"I'm going out for the rest of the day," he told Tina, as he came back out again. "Call me if anything urgent comes up."

He didn't wait to hear her response, but went out of the office, across the road and into the coffee shop.

"What's wrong?" Emma asked, as soon as he walked through the door.

"It's a long story," Nick replied. "I need to sit and think for a while. Can I do that here?"

"Sure." She nodded toward one of the booths at the back. "Take a seat. I'll bring you a coffee."

"Thanks, sis."

Nick sat quietly, thoughts running round and round in his head. He worked out quickly that Garrett Howell probably wasn't overly worried about publicity when it came to anything Tyler did. However, he might well be worried about the press, or the authorities looking too closely at his business dealings. And his most recent business dealing was the awarding of the highway contract, which meant there had to be something illegal, or at least immoral in that deal, and that could easily mean that senator was involved as well. It was the only reason Nick could think of that Garrett would need a malleable lawyer – to hush everything up. The question was, what needed hushing up? Nick wasn't sure where to begin with looking into that and, at the moment, he was still too mad with Tom to think straight.

His phone rang and, without checking the screen, he picked up.

"Hello?" he said.

"Nick." The male voice on the end of the line was unfamiliar.

"Who is this?" he asked.

"You mean you spent most of Saturday afternoon with me, and you can't even recognize my voice? I'm offended." Nick felt the hairs on the back of his neck stand on end.

"Tyler," he said quietly.

"I hear you've been talking to an old friend of my dad's," Tyler said. It sounded to Nick like he was smiling, the kind of smile Nick wanted to wipe off his face.

*News travels fast,* Nick thought. Tom must've called Garrett the moment Nick left the office, and Garrett must've called his son straight away.

"And?" Nick didn't want to give anything away.

"And I'm just calling with a piece of friendly advice."

"Since when were we friends, Tyler?" Nick asked, hardening his voice.

"We were… once," Tyler persisted.

"If you believe that, you have a very different recollection to me," Nick replied.

"I'm trying to be nice here," Tyler said, and Nick heard him take a deep breath. "I hear you're going to represent Rebecca."

"Yes. What about it?"

"I'm advising you to think again – as a friend, that is."

"Like I said, Tyler, we were never friends."

There was a moment's silence. "I warned you I would destroy anyone who helped her… You need to forget about representing her."

"Or what?" Nick asked.

"Or I'll forget about Rebecca *and* Gardner for now and I'll put you at the top of my shit list. It's not a comfortable place to find yourself, Nick."

"Put me anywhere you like on your fucking list. You may be able to scare off Tom and Jeremy Slater, but it's not gonna work on me."

"We'll see… Watch your back, Nick."

The line went dead.

Nick sat staring at his phone for a while. Hearing Tyler's voice threatening him directly was unnerving, but it didn't really change anything. He didn't want to overreact and scare Emma – not when Mark wasn't with her. The best thing to do was to just tell everyone what had happened when they were all together, when he took Emma home that night, rather than making a big deal out of it now. Except, maybe he'd just warn Mark – make sure he was on the alert. He sent a quick text.

— *Just heard from T. Don't let Bex out of your sight. N.*

Mark's reply was immediate.

— *What about Emma?*

— *I'm with her. Don't worry. It's me he wants now.*

"Are you okay?" Emma asked as he helped her into his truck.

"Sure," Nick replied. He was going to tell her about Tyler's call, but he wanted to wait until they got back to her place. He didn't want to have to repeat their conversation more than once. The more he'd thought about it, the more melodramatic it all seemed. What could

Tyler do to him, or anyone else, for that matter? None of them had anything Tyler could use against them anyway…

"Earth to Nick," Emma said, waving her hand in front of his face. "Are we going home?"

"Yeah." He smiled across at her, starting the engine.

"I know there's something on your mind," she said. "But I also know when you're not about to tell me. So, why don't I tell you my news instead?"

"Your news?" he replied, reversing out of the parking space.

"Yeah. I've had a good day," she said and he noticed her smiling.

"Go on then, tell me about it."

"Well," she began, "I don't think Mark or I told you about the conversation we had with Sarah at the wedding."

"No."

"Hmm, I guess we have been a little preoccupied," she said, "but Sarah asked to see us right at the end of the day – just before everyone left – and she told us she's got a boyfriend."

"Seriously?" Nick looked across at Emma, who was smiling at him. "She's not unattractive."

"I know. But she's also trouble." He smirked. "Did Mark go into protective brother mode?"

"No." Emma seemed thoughtful. "He just shrugged."

"He's not ready to forgive her yet, is he?"

"No. I'm not sure he ever will be." She shook her head. "The point is that she finally wants to move out of the Boston house. She and her boyfriend are at the stage where they're talking about spending the night together, but he's sharing a house with a few other guys, and she's thinking it'd be nice to have somewhere they can be together that's a little more intimate and cosy than a six bedroom house, with staff. Those were her words, not mine."

Nick nodded. "Yeah, I kinda worked that out."

"The thing is," Emma continued, "if she's gonna move, she needs Mark to fund it for her. She doesn't inherit until she's twenty-one, so he'd have to pay for it."

"I see. Well, I guess if he sells the house in Boston, he'll have plenty of spare cash."

Emma chuckled. "That's not how it works in Mark's world," she said. "He told Sarah she could start looking for somewhere to live, and he's given her a budget. Then, once she's moved out, he'll sell the Boston house."

"It's a whole other way of life, isn't it, sis?"

"Yeah, it is." She sighed and he sensed her discomfort. "What hadn't dawned on Sarah until Mark pointed it out, was that, once the house is sold, Maggie will be unemployed and homeless…"

"Of course," Nick said. "That seems a bit unfair."

"Well, it would be, but Mark's suggested she move in with us."

He glanced at her. "And how do you feel about that?" he asked.

"Oh, I'm fine with it. Mark and I talked it over, and he called Maggie the following evening. She's really excited." He heard the enthusiasm in her voice and relaxed. "Maggie's so lovely. We get along ever so well, and – to be honest – she'll be good company for me when Mark's away. I can't keep relying on you…"

"Yeah, you can."

"I know, but you've got Becky now."

"And she understands."

Emma coughed and he wondered whether she was getting emotional. He waited.

"Mark still wants to get an apartment in the city," she said. "But only because he doesn't really like staying at the hotel. He'd prefer to have a base there that's his – well, he says it's ours, but…" Her voice faded to a whisper.

"It is yours, Em. You're married, and I seem to remember the guy standing beside you and vowing to share everything that he has with you. So, let him."

"I'm trying."

He looked across at her briefly, and smiled.

"Mark's been looking into converting the space above the garage into an apartment for Maggie," Emma continued.

"Sounds like a good idea."

"He's gonna get Jake to have a look at it." She stopped for a moment. "But that's not the really good news."

"There's more?" he said, expectantly.

"I was talking to Josh today," she replied. "I was telling him that I don't know how I'm gonna cope when he goes to college, and he told me he's not going."

"He's not?"

"No. You know his story, Nick…" He did. Josh had been raised by his grandmother after his parents had both died tragically within a year of each other, when he was about four or five years old. His grandmother had suffered a stroke about nine or ten months ago now, and Josh had become as much her carer as anything else.

"He's staying for Dorothy?"

"Yeah."

Nick sighed. "That's a shame."

"I know." Emma paused. "We got talking and… well, I offered him the job of manager."

"You did?"

"Yeah. He's good at what he does, and he's great with the customers."

"I know he is."

"And I'm gonna see about sending him on some part-time courses too, or maybe looking at some online ones, so he can still get some formal business qualifications. We talked it through for an hour or so today and he's really enthusiastic."

"But that's great, Em," Nick said. "It solves your problems about what to do when the baby's born, and it probably made him feel valued too."

"He is valued. I made a point of telling him that… He's not the most confident kid on the block, and I know how that feels. I had you and then Mark to help me. I…" Her voice faded again.

"You thought you'd help a kindred spirit?" he offered.

"Something like that."

"Good for you, Em."

"Obviously he can't start until he finishes high school in June, and I've told him I'm still gonna go in every day until the baby's born, but then we'll have to see what happens… And, of course, I'll have Maggie to help out with the baby, if I do decide I want to work."

"Well, the good thing is, you've got options," Nick said. "You can see how you feel when you get there. You know we'll all support you."

She leant across and rested her head on his shoulder. "You always have."

By the time he parked outside Mark and Emma's house, he'd almost forgotten about Tyler's call, but Emma hadn't.

"Now we're here, are you gonna tell us what's troubling you?" she asked as soon as they were inside, in the kitchen. Becky and Mark stared at him and Nick quickly explained about Tyler's call, making light of the threat.

"You really don't think he meant it?" Emma asked, swallowing hard.

Nick shook his head, although he noticed Becky was pale and quiet, and he hugged her close, then went on to explain his conversation with Tom from that morning, which had diminished in significance after Tyler's call.

"So," Mark said when Nick had finished talking, "this was all to do with Tom screwing Tyler's mom?"

"Yeah. Garrett Howell blackmailed Tom into taking his work, and then blackmailed him again to decline Becky's case."

"And Jeremy?" Emma asked.

Nick shrugged. "I guess Becky was right. Jeremy must have a skeleton too. Garrett, or Tyler must've found out what it was and used that to get him to drop Becky's case."

"So how did Tyler find out about you representing me?" Becky asked.

"That was Tom," Nick replied. "I told him our partnership's over, and suggested he let his puppet master know that I'm not scared of him."

"Was that wise?" Mark asked.

Nick shrugged. "I don't know, but on the whole, I'd rather have things out in the open. At least we all know where we stand."

"Does he know about us?" Becky sounded scared.

"He didn't mention it, and I think he would've done."

Mark nodded. "I think you can be damn sure about that."

"Well, I guess that's something." Becky didn't sound convinced.

Sitting in the coffee shop the following morning, with his laptop set up in front of him, Nick felt exhausted. He'd struggled to sleep the previous night and now he found himself drifting into a daydream every so often. His phone rang and he jumped, wondering if it was Tyler, calling to issue more threats. He checked the screen. It wasn't – Nick had programmed Tyler's number into his contacts list so he could be forewarned. This was an unknown number and, normally, Nick would have declined the call, but with everything that had been going on lately, he decided to take it.

"Hello?" he said, cautiously.

"Hello." The female voice on the end of the line wasn't one he knew. "Is that Nick Woods?"

"It is."

"I don't know if you remember me," the woman said. "My name's Kelly Young. We knew each other at college."

Kelly? What the hell did she want? "Yeah, I remember you," Nick replied, unable to hide his suspicion.

"I…" she faltered. "I need to see you," she said.

"Why?"

"Because I have information about Tyler Howell." Her voice had dropped to a whisper. "I can't talk on the phone," she continued. "Can we meet somewhere?"

Nick thought for a moment. "I guess," he said. "Where?"

"Can you come to Boston?" she asked. Nick thought for a moment. He knew Emma was taking the next day off work to go over the refurbishment plans. The timing was perfect.

"Okay," he said. "But I choose where."

There was a second's hesitation. "Alright."

"I'll meet you at the Gardner Central hotel," he said. "Noon tomorrow."

"I can't make noon," she whispered. "It's gonna have to be later – say around three in the afternoon. And I can't see you in public."

"Fine, I'll book a room." He paused, just for a moment. "I'm warning you… try anything with me Kelly, and I'll walk, okay?"

"Okay."

He hung up.

# Chapter Nineteen

## *Becky*

As soon as Nick and Emma walked into Mark's house that evening, Becky knew something was wrong.

"What's happened now?" she asked as he came toward her.

"What makes you think something's happened?"

She looked up at him. "You're always telling me you can read my body... Well, I can read your face. You look pre-occupied."

He sighed and took her hand, following Mark and Emma into the kitchen.

"I'll have to perfect my poker face," he said.

"Or you could just tell me what's happened," Becky replied.

"I don't know that it's anything bad." He sat down at the island unit and pulled her onto his lap. "It's just a bit weird."

"Tell me," she urged.

"I had a call today," he began.

"Not from Tyler again?" Becky felt her stomach churning.

"No, not from Tyler. It was from Kelly."

"Kelly Young?" Becky was stunned and she was sure it showed on her face. "Seriously?"

"Yeah. Seriously."

"Care to enlighten us?" Emma said, getting salad ingredients from the refrigerator. They'd decided that, for the time being, Nick would drop Becky with Mark in the mornings and drive Emma to work, staying with her for the day, being as he didn't want to use his office anymore. Then in the evenings, they'd make the return journey. Tonight, Emma had said she'd cook again, because Nick was so tired.

Nick looked at Becky. "You tell them," she said.

"Okay." He took a breath. "When we were at college, Kelly shared an apartment with Bex," he explained, then lowered his eyes. "For a while, I kinda liked her."

"You asked her out," Becky said.

"Yeah, I did. And she turned me down flat."

"Ouch," Mark said, smiling.

"No, not at all," Nick said. "It turned out to be a blessing in disguise. I was licking my wounds in a coffee shop, when Becky appeared. She was a waitress there, and… well, we got together."

"You didn't know they shared an apartment?" Emma asked.

"Not to start with, no." He leant into Becky. "Then we went to a party at the end of our third year, and I was an idiot."

"What did you do?" Emma asked, disapprovingly.

"I spent a bit too much time talking with Kelly about some college stuff. And that gave Tyler the opportunity to make a move on Becky. She thought I was still interested in Kelly and when Tyler told her I was fooling around behind her back – which I wasn't – she believed him, and they ended up kissing. I saw them, and in some kind of dumb revenge, I kissed Kelly."

"You really are an idiot," Emma said.

"I know."

"Um, excuse me," Becky interrupted. "I think we were both idiots. I was the one who believed Tyler's lies, remember? I was the one who let him kiss me…'

"Yeah, but only because I ignored you. I gave you a reason to believe him."

"I still should've had more faith. I shouldn't—"

Nick put his finger on her lips. "We agreed, remember? We weren't gonna play the blame game anymore. It's in the past. It stays there."

Becky nodded.

"Okay," Mark said, clearing the air. "We've established who Kelly is. Why does she want to see you?"

"She says she's got information about Tyler."

Becky sat up and looked at him. "What kind of information?"

"I don't know," Nick replied. "She said she couldn't tell me on the phone. She was very secretive about it. She asked me if I'll go to Boston tomorrow to meet with her. I said I'd only meet in a place of my choosing," Nick continued, looking across at Mark. "I chose the Gardner Central."

"A man of good taste," Mark said, smiling.

"The thing was, she then said she wouldn't see me anywhere public, so I had to say I'd book a room."

Becky pulled away from him. "You did what?"

"I said I'd book a room."

"You're gonna be on your own, in a bedroom, with Kelly Young?"

"Yeah." Becky went to get up, but he pulled her back down onto his lap, holding her in place. "And you've got nothing to worry about," he said. "Nothing's gonna happen. I promise."

"I'll book you a suite," Mark offered, going into his office and returning with his laptop. "That way, you'll have a separate lounge area to talk in."

"She's *not* gonna get me into bed," Nick said.

"I know," Mark replied. "I'm just trying to keep it more businesslike."


They drove home in silence, and when they reached the trailer, Nick helped Becky out of the car and held her hand as they walked over to the door, letting her inside ahead of him. Before he switched on the light, he turned to her and pulled her close.

"Please stop worrying about tomorrow," he said. "I promise you, nothing will happen between Kelly and me."

"I don't trust her, Nick."

"I know you don't, but do you trust me?"

"Yes." She didn't hesitate, not for a second, and he smiled.

"Then you've got nothing to worry about. Whatever deluded ideas I had about her in the past, that's all ancient history. I worked out a long time ago that you're the only woman I want." He held her closer, so she could feel his arousal against her hip. "Back then, when I was trying to pluck up the courage to ask her out," he said quietly, "I slept around with a few other girls. I may have been interested in her, but she wasn't my sole focus – not by any means. But… when I lost you, I waited nine very celibate years for you to come back to me. I'd have waited another nine, if I'd had to. I'd have waited my whole damn life for you, Bex. Do you honestly think I'd throw away what we've got for someone like Kelly?"

Becky looked into his eyes. There was so much love in them, she shook her head, and leaned up, kissing him softly.

## Nick

Nick looked around. It wasn't the same suite he'd shared with Becky when they'd come to Boston to meet with Jeremy. He was glad of that. This was about business and he needed to focus on that.

The knock on the door made him jump, and he walked over and opened it.

Kelly had hardly changed at all. She wafted into the room on a wave of expensive perfume. She still had that hour-glass figure, shown off in a bright red, low-cut dress that accentuated her curves. She wore her hair long and looked him up and down, pouting slightly, just like she used to.

"Nick," she purred.

"Hello, Kelly." He kept his voice neutral, closing the door.

"Did you used to look this good when we were at college?" she said, coming closer and resting her hand on his chest. "You know, I've always thought of you as the one that got away."

He grabbed her wrist. "I told you Kelly." His voice held a warning note. "I'm out of here if you try anything with me. You asked for this meeting. You wanted to talk… so talk."

She pulled back, looking up into his eyes.

"Okay," she said, and walked across to the couch, sitting back into the soft leather seat. Nick took the chair opposite, leaning forward.

"What do you want?" he asked.

"Ideally, I'd like to see Tyler Howell and his father behind bars," she said.

Nick tried not to register any emotion on his face.

"Have you got a reason for that, or are you just being vindictive?" he asked.

"Oh, I've got a reason. I've got a damn good reason," she replied.

"So, you're still in touch with him then?"

Kelly laughed, but there was no humor to it. "Yeah," she said. "You could say that… I believe you're representing his wife?"

Nick nodded.

"Then, to start with, you might be interested to know that I'm the woman he's been having the affair with. We've been seeing each other for years. We were together even before he and Becky got married." She spoke without emotion.

"You?"

"Yes, me." She paused. "To be honest, Nick, we even fucked occasionally when we were at college. The whole thing at that party was a set-up."

"I know. I'm not a complete idiot."

She blushed. "Tyler planned it all out. He wanted Becky and he used me to get her."

"And you let him talk you into that? You offered to sleep with me…"

"Yeah…"

"Would you have gone through with it? If I'd accepted your offer?"

"Probably. It all depended on how far he'd got with Becky as to what I was meant to do with you. In the end, it wasn't necessary…" her voice trailed off to a whisper.

"You really think that little of yourself?"

"I wasn't looking to marry the guy. He showed me a good time whenever I wanted it. He just asked me to do that favor for him. And Tyler isn't the kind of guy you say no to."

"Did he threaten you?" Nick asked.

"No. He made it worth my while."

"Financially?"

She laughed. "No, Nick. Physically. Let's just say he and I had similar tastes. He knew what I liked, and he gave it to me."

Nick let that thought settle for a moment.

"If you're with Tyler, why is it you want to see him behind bars?" Nick asked.

"Because everything's changed," she replied, staring out the window. "I'm not always proud of who I am, or a lot of the things I've done," she murmured, her demeanor changing, "but I have limits." Nick felt like querying that statement, but didn't. She looked back at him. "A couple of nights ago, he called me," she explained. "He said Becky was still out of town and he wanted to meet up. He asked me to go over to his place. I agreed and drove over there. He met me at the door, wearing just a bathrobe and we went straight upstairs." She blinked a couple of times. "That wasn't unusual for Tyler, but when we got into his bedroom, things were very different to normal." She paused and then continued, "On the bed, was a girl. She was just lying there, naked. Tyler stood beside her and explained he wanted to watch the two of us together for a while, then join in…" Her voice faded.

"And you're not into that kind of thing?" Nick asked.

She gave Nick a look, like he was being naive. "No," she said, "that wasn't the problem. I've done all kinds of things with Tyler over the years. That's what I meant about us having the same tastes. We've had threesomes before lots of times, with both men and women. Tyler's thing is always that he likes to watch to begin with and then get involved himself."

"Okay…" Nick didn't register any emotion at all. He really didn't care what Tyler and Kelly got up to. "So what was the problem this time then?"

"*She* was," Kelly replied, staring him in the eye. "I could tell just from her face that she was too young, but her body really gave it away."

"How young is too young?" Nick asked.

"I don't know, not exactly. I didn't hang around to ask," Kelly said. "I told Tyler I wasn't into that and left. In the hall by the front door, I noticed her school bag."

"School bag?"

"Yeah. I said she was young."

"Christ," Nick hissed under his breath.

"Her name was printed on the outside of the bag. I wrote it down." She delved into her purse and pulled out a piece of paper. "Here," she said, handing it to Nick.

Nick looked down. "Linda Forsyth," he said out loud. "That was her name?"

Kelly nodded.

He stared at her. "You left a schoolgirl there… with *him?*" He got up and leant over her. "You know what he's like, Kelly. How could you do that?"

She shot to her feet. "I'm not responsible for what he does," she said.

Nick took a deep breath. "Why have you brought this to me and not gone to the cops with it?" he asked.

"What would be the point? Tyler and his father… their influence is far beyond anything you can imagine. You wouldn't believe the things they've done. They've got half of Boston PD in their pockets." She reached out and touched his arm. "But I know you'll do the right thing," she said.

"How did you even find me?" He pulled away from her.

"Through Tyler, believe it or not. He told me that he'd been to see Becky at her boss's new hotel to try and persuade her to drop the divorce, and that he'd seen you. He was gloating about how you'd never made it as a lawyer and that you just worked for some small town outfit."

"Yeah. I let him believe that," Nick said.

"So I gathered when I looked you up. You didn't tell him you're a partner."

"No. I wanted him to feel superior over me."

Kelly looked confused about that, but didn't say anything. "So, can you use it?" she said, nodding at the piece of paper he was still holding.

298

"I can probably use it against Tyler, depending on how old the girl is. If she's over sixteen, it's gonna depend on what he did to her after you left and whether she's willing to press charges. But if Garrett Howell is as influential as you say he is, I'm not sure that will get us anywhere. He'll probably just pay her off, or bribe someone along the way and it'll all just disappear."

Kelly sat down again, right on the edge of the couch. "How about if I could give you evidence that Tyler and his father were involved in a corruption," she said, looking up at him.

Nick felt his stomach flip. "What kind of corruption?"

"You'd have to guarantee to use it and follow it through," she said. "Once this goes public, they're gonna know it came from me. My life won't be worth living…"

"I'll use it," Nick said. "And I'll follow it through. You've got my word."

She swallowed hard. "About two years ago," she said, "Tyler handled Senator Anderson's divorce, during which he discovered that the dear sweet old senator had been having an affair with a sixteen year old girl – who may not have been sixteen when the affair started. Tyler handed that information to his dad, who used it to bribe the senator into giving GHC the construction contract."

"You've got evidence of this?" Nick asked.

Kelly nodded and reached into her purse again, pulling out an envelope. "It's all in there," she said, handing it to Nick.

"You work with Tyler, don't you?" Nick asked.

"Yes. How did you know?"

"Well, Becky's always known that his affair was with someone from his office, and you've just handed me documents that I'm guessing come from his workplace. It's not rocket science, Kelly."

"No, I guess not."

"You'll probably lose your job," he pointed out.

"I know." She got to her feet and shrugged. "I guess it was seeing that girl lying on his bed," she said quietly. "I finally realized it's gone too far. *He's* gone too damn far. And someone needs to stop him."

Nick parked up outside Mark and Emma's house. It was late and he was tired, but he felt like they were finally getting somewhere.

Becky came running out and, as he closed the car door, she leapt up into his arms, wrapping her legs around his waist.

"I've missed you," he said, clinging onto her.

"I've missed you too."

He looked up to see Mark and Emma standing in the doorway.

"Worth the trip?" Mark asked.

Nick lowered Becky to the ground and they started walking toward them.

"Yeah, I think so. I just need to work out what to do with what Kelly told me."

They all stared at him.

"I know you're gonna think I'm really annoying, but would you mind if I slept on it before I told you all anything? Kelly gave me so much information, and I really need to work it through in my own head first before I can make sense of it."

"Sure," Mark said, although Nick could sense Becky's disappointment.


"Are you sure you can't tell me what went on?" she said to him on the journey home.

"Nothing went on," he told her. "She gave me a name, and some information." The car behind was getting really close and Nick pulled over a little to let it pass, but instead it backed off, just slightly.

"A name?" Becky was intrigued.

"Yeah…" Nick checked in his mirror again. "What the fuck?"

He braced his left arm on the steering wheel and reached across Becky with his right as the impact hit. Becky screamed, lurching forward, but he held her in place as the car took a first, and then a second blow from behind.

"Nick!" Becky yelled.

"Hold on." Keeping his arm in place across her chest, Nick pressed his foot down hard on the gas, crossing over into the opposite lane, thanking God it was late and there was no traffic. The other car followed, but Nick crossed quickly back, then braked sharply. The other car shot past, and in his effort to brake, the driver lost control, spinning off the road, down onto the grass verge.

"Nick!" Becky cried again.

Nick didn't reply this time. Instead, he turned the truck around and floored the gas, heading out of town.

"Where are we going?" Becky asked, her voice revealing her terror.

Nick let his hand fall into her lap and gave her leg a reassuring squeeze. "The hotel," he said.

"Why not go home?" she said.

"Because whoever that was might not know where we live yet. I don't want them to find out."

"Okay, then why not go back to Mark's place?"

"Because that's where they picked us up. That car started following us almost as soon as we left their place, and I don't want to lead him straight back to Mark and Emma. The hotel is public. There are too many people there for whoever it is to try anything."

"This is Tyler isn't it?" she asked, her voice cracking.

"Tyler or his dad, yeah."

"So the threat was real then." It wasn't a question.

"Looks that way." Nick replied anyway.

"This is all my fault."

"It's not. None of this is your fault, Bex."

Becky checked them into a suite on the third floor and they went up in the elevator, letting themselves into the room.

"I've gotta call Mark," Nick said. "Being as Tyler originally threatened Emma and him too. I have to tell him."

Becky nodded and went through to the bathroom, switching on the light and closing the door behind her.

Mark answered on the second ring.

"What's happened?"

"Someone tried to run us off the road," Nick said, simply.

"Jesus Christ. Are you okay?"

"We're fine. Bex is kinda shaken up, but we're okay. I think my car might be a little the worse for wear."

"Are you back home now?" Mark asked.

"No. We're at your hotel." Nick explained his reasons, and Mark agreed with him.

"I'll come over in the morning," he said. "We can have a look at your car and talk through what to do about this. I'm thinking we need to get the cops involved now. This is getting serious."

"Yeah. I'd agree, if Kelly hadn't already told me today that Tyler and Garrett Howell aren't averse to a little bribery and corruption when it comes to the cops. I need to think this through, Mark. I'm only gonna get one crack at this guy. I've gotta get it right."

"Okay," Mark said. "I'll let you make the decision. Call me if you need me, and I'll see you in the morning."

Becky came out of the bathroom just as Nick was ending the call. She was in a daze and Nick walked over to her, taking her in his arms and bringing her over to the bed.

"It'll be okay," he said. She didn't argue. He didn't think she had the strength left. He helped her undress and then took off his own clothes, climbing into bed beside her and holding her until she slept.

Mark arrived early the next morning, with Emma, who took one look at Nick in his white hotel robe and burst into tears, hugging him.

Becky sat on the bed, looking embarrassed, while Nick held Emma in his arms, patting her hair. No-one spoke for a full minute, until Emma leant back and just stared up at his face.

"We're fine," he said reassuringly.

"I know," she whispered, and hugged him again. Then she pulled back and looked over at Becky. "You poor thing," she said. "It must've been awful." Emma went and sat beside her.

"It was," Becky replied. "But Nick was really calm. He was brilliant."

Emma turned to him. "Yeah... he always is." Nick felt himself blush.

"I think we should go back to our place," Mark said. "We can hunker down there behind the security gates and work out what to do."

"I don't want to put you guys in any danger…"

"You're not," Mark said. "Our house is probably about the safest place around here."

Nick couldn't disagree with that. "Okay," he agreed.

Becky looked up. "We haven't got any clean clothes," she pointed out.

"Well, we'll have to wear what we had on yesterday," Nick replied.

"I know," Emma said, getting to her feet. "Why don't you guys get dressed and we'll go back to our place. You can leave me and Becky there while you and Mark go on to the trailer and pick up some clothes for the two of you, and then you can stay with us for a few days. By the time you get back, we'll have made breakfast, and you can shower and change afterwards."

"God, you're sounding scarily organized," Mark joked.

"It must be because she's pregnant then," Nick replied. "She was never like that before."

"Ha. Ha." Emma tilted her head to one side, smiling over at them. "Does it sound like a good plan?"

"Yeah. All except the bit about us leaving you two on your own."

"We'll be perfectly safe at the house. Like Mark said, it's the most secure place here. No-one can get in."

Nick looked at Mark and they both shrugged. It was perfectly true. Mark had the best security system on the market. The two women would be safe for half an hour while they went to fetch some clothes. They agreed the plan and Emma and Mark waited downstairs in the lobby while Nick and Becky got dressed. Nick's truck was quite badly damaged and they decided to leave it at the hotel for now and arrange to have the local garage come out and collect it once they'd got back to Mark and Emma's.


"They will be okay on their own, won't they?" Nick asked as they drove back up the long driveway that led away from Mark's house.

"Sure. Stop worrying. We'll only be gone for half an hour. It'll be fine."

Nick settled back into the seat. "I can take the time to tell you about what happened in Boston yesterday."

"I'd almost forgotten about that, after everything else that's gone on," Mark replied.

"I hadn't," Nick said and filled Mark in on what had happened with Kelly.

"You've still got these documents, haven't you?" Mark asked. "You didn't leave them in your car…"

Nick patted his jacket. "They're in my inside pocket."

Mark shook his head slowly from side to side. "Schoolgirls," he said under his breath.

"Yeah. Schoolgirls." He looked at Mark as he pulled his car into the track that led to Nick's trailer. "You can see now why I've gotta tread so carefully."

"Yeah, I can." Mark slammed on the brakes. "Fucking hell," he whispered, under his breath.

Nick looked up, but he couldn't speak. He just stared. He stared at the space where his trailer had once stood, the space that was now a mass of blackened shapes, smoking ash and smoldering debris. He climbed slowly from the car and walked over, his hands loose by his sides. He felt, rather than saw Mark come and stand next to him.

"You smell that?" he said.

Mark sniffed. "Gas," he replied. "Someone did this on purpose?"

"Of course they did."

Mark stepped closer to the ruin of Nick's home. "There's nothing left," he murmured. "Not a damn thing." He turned. "Do you think they knew you weren't in there?"

Nick stared at him for a moment. "Who knows?" he said, honestly. He shuddered, thinking about what might have been, what might have happened if he hadn't decided to take Becky to the hotel last night. "Let's get back to your place," he said, suddenly needing to be with Becky. "There's nothing worth staying here for."

"Becky's car?" Mark nodded toward Becky's BMW. It was parked far enough away from the trailer, and had escaped any damage.

"I don't have the keys," Nick said. "I'll get them from Becky later and we'll come back for it."

"Okay." The two men got back into Mark's car. "I'm sorry about your home," he said.

"At least we weren't here," Nick replied. It was the only thing he had to be thankful for, so he was hanging onto it.

The security gates closed behind Mark's car and he drove down the long driveway in silence, turning the corner at the end and stopping dead.

"Where's Emma's car?" he said. He quickly got out, leaving his door open and running to the house. "Emma?" he called out as he opened the front door.

Nick was right behind him. "Becky?" he cried. "Em?"

The house was silent. Both women were nowhere to be seen.

Nick had his phone in his hand before Mark had turned around. He held it to his ear.

"Becky?" he said.

"Yes, what's wrong?" She sounded perfectly okay.

"Are you alright?" He needed to hear her say it.

"I'm fine."

"Where are you?" he asked, trying to keep calm.

"We've just arrived at the coffee shop."

"What the hell are you doing there?" he asked. He mouthed 'coffee shop' to Mark and both of them ran out the door to Mark's car.

"Patsy called Emma," Becky explained. "She cut her hand really badly and had to go to the ER, and needed Emma to come in and cover, but she was feeling sick, so I said I'd help out." They both got in and Mark set off again, speeding toward the gate.

"And it didn't occur to you to call me, or Mark, and let us know?" he said, abandoning any pretense at calmness. "You didn't fucking well think to tell us?"

"Don't talk to me like that, Nick." He heard the tears behind her voice as the line went dead.

"Shit!" he yelled. They'd reached the end of Mark's driveway. "You've got a fucking sports car," he said, turning to Mark. "Use it."

Mark got them into town in minutes. Even so, Nick was out of the car and sprinting toward the coffee shop before Mark had even parked up. He knew he'd hurt Becky, and probably scared her too, and he needed to put it right. Inside, Becky was sitting in a booth, tears falling down her cheeks. Emma was beside her, an arm around her shoulders. As Nick approached, Emma got up, blocking his path.

"What's the matter with you?" she asked. "Hasn't Becky been through enough, without you laying into her?"

"I'm sorry," Nick said, not taking his eyes from Becky. "I need to talk to Becky."

"Are you gonna upset her again?" Emma asked.

"No. I promise I won't. I screwed up. It won't happen again." Mark came into the shop behind him.

"Let them talk," Mark said to Emma. "Come over to the counter with me and I'll explain everything to you."

Emma moved to one side, taking Mark's hand and letting Nick sit down beside Becky.

"I'm sorry," he said again.

"You said you wouldn't get mad at me – ever."

"I know, but you weren't where you were supposed to be…"

She glared at him, steely-eyed. "Did you really just say that? I wasn't where I was supposed to be?" She said the words really slowly, then wiped her tears on the back of her hand and swallowed hard. "You're not meant to be like Tyler," she said. "You're meant to be different. You're not meant to try and control my every move; my every decision…"

That hurt.

"Emma needed my help," Becky continued. "I thought you'd want me to be with her, considering how concerned you always are for her. I thought I was doing the right thing… Evidently not. Evidently you want to try and dictate my life to me, just like Tyler did, even when you're not with me."

That *really* hurt.

"Christ, Bex," he muttered. "I've said I'm sorry."

"And maybe sorry isn't enough."

He felt the fear creeping up his spine. "What does that mean?" he whispered.

"It means some things can't be forgiven, or forgotten, just because you say sorry, Nick."

"Becky?" His voice cracked. "I really am——"

"I don't wanna hear it. Not right now. I need some time to myself." He heard the sadness behind her voice, even through her anger, and she went to get up. "Excuse me," she said.

He stayed still. "No. You're not going anywhere. Not until you've heard what I've got to say."

"Let me out, Nick." The fear in her voice cut through him, and he stood to one side, just as Mark and Emma appeared bedside him. Emma looked pale and Nick guessed Mark had told her about the trailer.

"Can you take me back to the hotel, please?" Becky said looking up at Mark.

He was clearly confused, and glanced at Nick, who nodded.

"Um… sure," he replied. "I don't know what you're gonna do about clothes…"

"Clothes?" Becky was bewildered now. "You've already got them, haven't you?"

"Didn't you tell her?" Mark asked Nick.

"Tell me what?"

"I didn't get the chance." They both spoke at the same time.

"Tell me what?" Becky repeated, turning to Nick.

"Sit down again," he said softly. "Please." She looked from him to Mark and Emma, then quietly resumed her seat in the booth. Nick sat beside her and she inched away fractionally, and he wondered if she knew how much that hurt. He focused on her, ignoring Mark and Emma, who'd sat down opposite.

"I know I hurt you, and I scared you," Nick said. "And I know saying sorry isn't anywhere near enough to make up for that. But you're wrong. I don't want to control you, or anything about you, whether you're with me or not. I know you're your own person – that's why I love you. But, Bex, you've gotta understand, you've gotta let me explain… I'm so damn scared right now." He sighed. "Someone burned out my trailer," he said. She gasped, one hand covering her mouth, while the other grabbed his arm as she moved close to him again and fresh tears gathered in her eyes.

"Nick, no," she whispered. "Burned it out?"

"Yeah. There's nothing left. All your stuff's gone too. I'm sorry."

"That's not all my stuff," she said. "I've still got things in Boston."

Somehow he managed a smile. "Yeah, but you're not likely to be able to get those anytime soon, are you?" he said.

"No. I guess not. But, even so… that was your home. Everything you had was in there."

"It was *our* home," Nick corrected. "And I don't care about that. I only care about you."

She stared into his eyes for a moment, then fell into him, clinging to his shoulders. "I'm sorry. I'm sorry." He heard her panic, her fear, and brought his arms close around her. "I'm sorry," she repeated.

"Stop it, Bex."

"But I was so horrible to you. I… Oh my God… I compared you to him, didn't I?"

"Yeah, you did, but it's okay. I understand."

"I'm sorry, Nick. I'm—"

"Enough. I hurt you. You lashed out. It's okay."

"It's not." She sobbed into him. "Please say you forgive me."

"As long as you're not gonna walk away from me…" He raised her face to his, looking into her tear-filled eyes.

"I'm not." She shook her head. "I was never going to walk away. I just needed some time. I was scared."

"I know. And that was my fault. Forgive me?"

"There's nothing to forgive."

"I promised to never get mad at you… I broke that promise."

She looked up into his eyes. "Why?" she asked. "Why did you get mad?"

He leant back, looking down at her. "You really don't understand?" She shook her head and he turned her to face him. "You and I nearly got run off the road last night, I'd just seen my home gone up in smoke, then Mark and I got back to the house, and you weren't there. I couldn't find you. I didn't know whether Tyler had decided to come after you. For a few horrible moments, I thought I'd lost you, baby. It was the most terrifying thing I've ever gone through."

"We should've called," Emma said. "It's my fault as much as Becky's."

"It's no-one's fault," Nick replied, not taking his eyes from Becky. "I shouldn't have yelled at you. I'm sorry."

Becky shook her head. "Not as sorry as I am."

"Don't be. I don't want you to be sorry. I just want you to be safe."

"I am. Well, I am when I'm with you." He finally let himself relax, and he grinned at her.

"Then you'd better stay with me." He leant down and kissed her gently. "Always."

Becky nodded, then nestled into him and whispered, "Can we go?"

"Of course… although I'm not sure where."

"Come back to our place," Mark offered. "We'll carry on with Emma's plan. We'll work things out."

"I'll close the shop," Emma added. "I don't care about any of this at the moment."

They got to their feet and Nick clasped hold of Becky's hand, just as a thought occurred to him. He turned back to her. "Tell me you're wearing your locket," he said.

She reached inside her sweater and pulled it out.

"Thank God for that," he said. "I thought that might have been lost too."

She put her hand gently on his arm. "At a time like this you're worried about my locket?"

"It's important to us, so yeah."

"I've worn it every day since we've been back together. It's too precious not to." He kissed her forehead and heard her sob. "You've lost so much, Nick," she said.

He pulled her into his arms, holding her close. "None of that matters, as long as I've got you."

Her voice was almost inaudible, but he just about heard her say, "You've got me."

# Chapter Twenty

*Becky*

All four of them sat together in Mark and Emma's living room, drinking coffee. Nick had already called the garage to arrange for his truck to be collected, and also the insurance company about both the truck and the trailer. Now, Becky was curled up beside him on the couch, the enormity of it all weighing heavy on her.

"This is all my fault," she whispered, almost to herself.

"Stop that," Nick said, letting her go and sitting forward, then turning and looking back down at her. "None of this is your fault. It's your husband's fault. And his father's, but it's not yours."

"But you've lost everything."

"No I haven't. I haven't lost you. There were a couple of times today when I thought I had, and trust me, losing my home and a bunch of possessions is nothing compared to that," he said. His words held such conviction, so much emotion, she felt yet more tears welling in her eyes. She had no reply.

"I've been doing some thinking," Nick said, filling the short silence. They all looked at him. "I've got a friend in Boston PD," he continued. He turned to Becky again. "Remember Eliot?" he asked.

"The guy who held that party?" she asked.

Nick nodded. "Yeah. He gave up law after a year or so and became a cop."

"So he didn't really give up law then," Mark said.

"Well, he did from a lawyer's point of view," Nick replied. "The point is, we stayed in touch. I mean, we're not best friends or anything, but I think I can trust him…"

"What do you want to do?" Mark asked.

"I think I should go to Boston and see him," Nick replied.

"Then I'm coming with you."

"No chance." Nick's reply was instant. "We're not leaving Becky and Emma by themselves again – not after what's gone on. I know he seems to be targeting me…"

"Which is all the more reason Mark should go with you," Emma interrupted.

"I can take care of myself."

"Oh, stop being so damn macho."

"I'm not, Em." Nick almost laughed. "I'm anything but macho."

"Then let Mark go with you."

"Tomorrow's Saturday," Mark said. "Why don't I give Jake a call and see if he can come over? He's been Becky's bodyguard before now. I'm sure he won't mind reprising the role."

"He's been Becky's bodyguard?" Nick asked, smiling.

"Yeah," Mark explained. "When she first got here, and the manager was being aggressive. Remember? I got Jake to step in and watch over Becky for a while."

Nick nodded, turning to Becky.

"Being your bodyguard is my job now, okay?"

"I thought you had gray eyes, not green ones." Becky looked up at him.

"Where you're concerned, they're green."

"When you two have quite finished," Mark said, interrupting them, just as Nick was leaning in for a kiss. "Shall I call Jake?"

"Yeah. If it's the only way I'm gonna get any peace, then I guess so."

Jake agreed that he'd come over, with Cassie and Maddie, the following morning and, after Mark had hung up the call, Emma and Becky went to make lunch. Nick sent a text message to Eliot, who agreed to meet him at the Gardner Central at one pm. Mark and Nick then followed Becky and Emma into the kitchen, sitting at the island unit.

"We'd better sort you out some clothes," Mark said. "You can change after lunch. I'm afraid I can't run to waistcoats, but I can do jeans and white shirts," Mark offered.

"Right now, I'll take whatever I can get."

Mark went into his office, returning with his laptop. "In the meantime, why don't you go online and order some new clothes for both of you? Have it all delivered here tomorrow." He reached into his back pocket and threw his wallet down on the island unit. "Hit up my credit cards if you need to."

Nick smiled. "Thanks," he said. "But I'll pay."

Within twenty minutes, he'd ordered enough jeans, shirts, waistcoats and socks to get him through a fortnight, as well as two pairs of boots.

"Your turn," he said to Becky, turning Mark's laptop around to her.

"I've never really bought much online," she murmured, feeling embarrassed.

"You haven't?" Everyone was looking at her.

"No." She knew her face had gone bright red and she focused on the space in front of her. Nick leant forward.

"What's wrong?" he asked.

He reached over and raised her face to his and she felt the tears pricking behind her eyes. "He had access to my bank account," she said. "I think I already told you that Mark pays me very generously. What I didn't tell you was that Tyler used to take the money from my account and transfer it to his own. He'd leave me with just enough to get by."

"Why?" Nick asked. "Surely, he's well paid himself."

"It was a his way of controlling me. If I had no money, I couldn't leave."

"Jesus Christ," Mark said. "Why the fuck didn't you tell me?"

"Because she couldn't." Nick snapped, not taking his eyes from Becky.

"He used to let me take out some cash each week from the ATM," Becky continued. "I'd tell him I needed cosmetics, or tampons, or whatever, and I'd save it up, so I could buy the things I wanted, like nice dresses and tops... I may have only been able to buy two or three things a year, and none of it was expensive, but it was all mine." She sniffed. "I couldn't even get a credit card. I tried, right back when we first got married, but he intercepted the mail and found the acceptance letter." A tear fell down her cheek and Nick got up, going around to her and pulling her into his arms.

"So he bought all your clothes?" Nick asked, his muscles tensing around her.

"Most of them." She looked up at him. "My office outfits are his choice. The things I wear when I'm with you, they're my own."

"Did I do the wrong thing, buying you a dress for the wedding?" he asked, looking doubtful.

She reached up, cupping his face in her hands. "No," she said. "That was a beautiful dress. He used to buy me the clothes he wanted me to wear. You didn't do that. You bought me something you knew *I'd* like to wear."

Nick let out a long sigh. "Sure?"

"Yes, I'm positive." She hesitated. "I wanted to be able to help with paying for the house, but I don't have any money. I felt so bad when you said you had to go to the bank, but there was nothing I could do..." Her voice faded to a whisper,

"Hey..." Nick stared deep into her eyes. "Don't worry about that. I can cover the house."

"I know, but I wanted to..."

"Stop it, Bex. The house will get built."

"Because you'll borrow the money."

"Yeah. People do it all the time. I can afford it." He held her gaze. "In the meantime, we need to work out what to do about your finances."

"Well, the first thing you've gotta do is to open a new bank account," Mark said.

"He's right," Nick added. "Tyler still has access to your old one."

Becky nodded.

"Let me have the details as soon as you can," Mark said. "I'll pass them onto the finance department and get them changed on the payroll." He paused for a moment, staring at her. "It'll take them a while to update the records, but I'll give you some cash in the meantime."

"You don't have to do that, Mark," Becky answered, sniffling.

"Yeah, I do," Mark replied.

Nick pulled her closer.

"And once we've dealt with that," he said, "we'll pick you out some clothes online."

"I can't pay," she whispered.

Nick shook his head. "You can pick out whatever you want, for work and home, and you can use my card."

"I'll pay you back," she replied.

He shook his head. "You don't have to. But I do have one thing I'd like you to do."

Becky smirked. "Oh, really?"

"Not that," Nick said, his eyes sparkling. "Well, not until later, anyway."

"What then?" She looked into his eyes.

"That dark red dress you wore when we had dinner at the hotel… I take it that was that one of your choices?"

She nodded. "Oh yes. Tyler would have hated that."

"Which probably explains why I loved it. If it's at all possible," Nick continued, "can you get another one of those dresses? You looked so damn sexy in that." She smiled into his kiss.

## *Nick*

"Are you sure they'll be okay?" It was the third time Nick had asked Mark that question and they hadn't been on the road for more than thirty minutes.

"They'll be fine. I'm not an idiot, Nick. I wouldn't leave Emma with anyone I didn't completely trust. And I trust Jake."

"I know," Nick said, turning to look out the window. "So do I."

"Then stop worrying."

If only it was that easy.

"You don't have to pretend with me." Nick turned. Mark's face was unreadable. He seemed to be focused on the road, although Nick noticed he checked the mirrors a lot more than was strictly necessary.

"What do you mean?" Nick asked.

"Cut the crap," Mark replied, looking in the rear view mirror again. "You've had a terrifying couple of days. You're right on the edge, Nick. Give yourself a break. Becky's not here and you don't have to pretend to be strong in front of me. I get it."

"I'm okay," Nick said.

"Yeah, right."

Nick sighed. "I need to stay on the edge, Mark," he explained. "I don't have a fucking clue what he's gonna do next. If I gave in to my fear, I wouldn't be much use to Becky, would I?"

"No. I know."

"I'm sorry, man. Can we change the subject?" Nick said. "I need to think about something else for a little while…"

"Sure."

"Emma told me about your conversation with your sister at the wedding," Nick said after a moment's pause.

Mark shrugged. "I was a little surprised, but I can't say I'm not relieved. I've been wanting to sell that house since mom and dad died. She's already looked at five or six places, and she's found one she really likes."

"That was quick."

"Yeah well, I guess the boyfriend is a good incentive."

"And how do you feel about that?" Nick asked.

"Not how I thought I would. I always expected to be like you were when I first met Emma."

"Yeah, I remember you saying."

"But I found I didn't really give a damn. That's one of the things that's made me realize Sarah can never be a big part of my life again."

This was news and Nick looked across at him.

"She can't?"

"No. Although it's mainly because of Emma, of course."

"So you noticed then?" Nick asked.

Mark glanced at him. "Noticed what?"

"How jumpy and tense Emma gets around Sarah."

"Yeah, I've noticed. I know she says she wants me to make up with Sarah, but deep down, she's still scared of her." He paused. "But if you knew about it, why didn't you tell me?"

"Because I didn't need to. I knew you'd work it out. You don't need me to tell you anything about Emma. Not anymore."

Mark smiled. "Thanks," he said and Nick knew, with that one word, how much it meant to Mark that Nick finally really trusted him.

The rest of the journey passed quickly. They talked about all kinds of things, from Mark's new hotel, and the apartment he was looking at buying in the city, to Nick's house. What they avoided talking about was Becky and Tyler. Nick's pretense that he was okay could only stretch so far and he knew Mark understood.

"Eliot Delaney, this is Mark Gardner." Nick made the introductions. Eliot had hardly changed at all. He'd maybe gained a few pounds, and a few gray hairs, which brought a wry smile to Nick's lips, but otherwise, he was still the cheeky-looking guy Nick remembered.

"Gardner?" Eliot queried. "As in Gardner's Hotels?" He looked around the foyer they were standing in.

"Yeah, that's me."

Eliot looked at Nick and slapped him on the shoulder. "You have moved up in the world," he said, grinning. "Shame your dress sense hasn't improved."

"These aren't my clothes," Nick replied. "They're his." He nodded at Mark. He and Mark had left too early for any deliveries to have been made, so he was still wearing Mark's jeans and one of his white shirts.

"I'll find us a room," Mark said, covering Eliot's blushes, and went across to the reception desk.

"How are you?" Eliot asked.

"I've been better." Eliot looked at him quizzically. "I'll explain in a minute," Nick added.

Mark came back. "We can use the manager's office," he said. "It's this way." He guided them past the reception desk and through a door to the left. There was a desk off to the right, but Mark directed them toward two couches at the other end of the room, which had a low coffee table set between them. "I've ordered coffee," he added as they sat down.

"How long has it been since you two last met?" Mark asked and Nick assumed he was trying to gauge whether they could trust Eliot.

Eliot looked at him. "Eight years?" he queried.

"Yeah, I guess," Nick agreed. "It was when we graduated."

"And you went into law, but then gave it up to become a cop?" Nick enquired.

"Yeah. That's how I got the gray hairs," Eliot replied, pointing to his temples. "Unlike Nick, I have to really work for a living."

"You obviously get more vacation time than I do. You've got a tan."

"That's because I've just been on my honeymoon," Eliot explained, as there was a knock on the door.

"Come in," Mark called and the door opened. A uniformed young man entered, carrying a tray of coffee things, which he set down on the table. "Thanks," Mark said, dismissing him again.

"You're married?" Nick asked, once they were alone again.

"Yeah. She's no-one you know. Her name's Hayley. We got married three weeks ago today."

"Congratulations," Nick said.

"Thanks."

Mark poured the coffee and handed around the cups.

"Are we just gonna sit and make small talk, or are you gonna tell me why you wanted to see me?" Eliot asked, staring hard at Nick.

Nick sat back in his seat beside Mark and looked across at his old friend.

"It's kinda hard to know where to start," he said.

"I find the beginning is usually the best place. It's less confusing."

Nick sighed. "Okay," he said and took a deep breath. "Do you remember Becky?"

"Becky Scott?" Eliot asked. "The girl who broke your heart?"

"Yeah."

"Of course I remember her." Eliot seemed to think for a moment. "Didn't she end up with that piece of shit, Tyler Howell?"

"Yeah. She married him…"

It took over an hour for Nick to tell the story. Eliot sat in silence throughout, listening. When Nick had finished, Eliot moved forward, sitting on the edge of the couch.

"Have you tried going to the local cops about the arson and the incident with them running you off the road?" he asked.

"I thought of that," Nick replied. "But we've got no evidence it was actually them who did anything. Besides, Garret Howell is so damn powerful, he'd just bribe his way out of it. I'm reliably informed he's got half of Boston PD in his pocket and I'm sure that influence isn't limited to one place. If we do anything now, we'll show our hand, and it's too early to do that. We need to use the information Kelly gave me, and we need to move carefully."

"Okay. What do you want me to do?"

"Firstly, I'm struggling with finding Linda Forsyth. I spent a couple of hours on it last night, but got nowhere. I need your help with that."

Eliot nodded. "That's easy enough."

Nick handed over the envelope Kelly had given him. "In there are the details of Senator Anderson's fling with the underage girl," he said. "It'd be useful if you could track her down and find out what went on."

"Sure." Eliot nodded.

"To avoid anyone getting hurt, we need to take them all down at the same time," Nick explained. "So I want all the evidence gathered before we make a move."

"I understand that," Eliot replied.

"We need to prove that Tyler and the senator are guilty of statutory rape – which means interviewing those two girls. Linda Forsyth might be over sixteen of course…"

"But we need to find out."

"Yeah, and then we need to prove that Tyler passed the information about Anderson on to his father and that Garrett Howell used it to blackmail the senator."

"How are we gonna do that?" Mark asked.

Eliot winked at him. "I think we can assume the girl Senator Anderson slept with was underage, and that he probably knew about it. He'd never have given in to the blackmail if that wasn't the case. If I've got a statutory rape charge I can hang over the him," he said, smiling, "I'm sure I can persuade him to help me out with the case against Garrett Howell."

"You mean you'll cut him a deal?"

Eliot's smile became a grin. "I might hint at it. Doesn't mean I'll actually do it." His smile dropped. "I don't have a huge amount of time for guys who have sex with underage girls."

Nick coughed. "You do realize that, once the Howells get to hear that you're investigating them, they're gonna start putting pressure on you."

Eliot nodded. "Yeah, I kinda got that."

"And you're okay with that?"

Eliot nodded and his eyes darkened. "Don't worry, Nick. I'm not gonna cave."

# Chapter Twenty-One

❦

*Becky*

"Thank God you're home." Becky ran out and threw herself into his arms before he'd even stood up out of the car. He held onto her, looking down into her face.

"What's wrong?" he asked and she could see the fear in his eyes.

"Nothing," she replied quickly. "I've just been worried about you."

"Well, we're back now," he said and bent down to kiss her. "This is new." He broke the kiss and looked down at her top. She was vaguely aware of Mark walking past them toward the house.

"Yes, our clothes arrived earlier," she explained. "Yours are upstairs."

"Okay," he replied. "I like this." Her top was deep turquoise, with frayed hems on the collars and cuffs. It was loose fitting and comfy. "It wasn't one of the ones we looked at together, was it?"

"No, but you did leave me to my own devices after a while… You don't mind, do you?"

"Of course I don't. I told you to buy whatever you wanted. That's why I left you with my card. Besides, you look real sexy," he murmured. "And I like the fact that it's loose. It means I can get my hands inside." He reached underneath and she gasped as she felt his fingers on her skin, moving upward. He leant back on Mark's car, bringing her with him, his fingers continuing on their journey until he was touching her breasts.

"No bra?" he whispered.

She shook her head. "They were all in the trailer, except the one I was wearing yesterday, which needs washing. I didn't order any new ones, because I like to try on my bras first. So, I'll have to go shopping for those."

"Or you could just go without a bra…" Nick grinned, then his eyes lit up. "What about panties?" he asked. "Please tell me you like to try them on too…"

"No, of course not," she smirked. "I ordered panties."

"Damn. That's a real shame. I was hoping you could put off buying underwear – maybe indefinitely." He started to tweak her nipples between his fingers. "Yeah, I could really get used to this," he muttered, kissing her hard. She breathed fast, pushing herself into him.

"Are you two coming?" Mark's voice broke the moment.

"Nearly," Nick whispered and Becky giggled. He gave her another quick kiss. "We'll carry on with this later," he said and took her hand, leading her into the house and closing the door behind them.

"Hmm… something smells good," Nick said. "What's Emma cooked?"

"Emma hasn't cooked anything," his sister's voice called from the living room. "Jake offered to make his lasagna, so I've had a lovely rest, all day."

Nick and Becky walked into the living room, hand in hand.

"Not all day," Becky said. "You did some baking with Maddie earlier."

"I don't look on that as working," Emma smiled. Becky thought she looked really relaxed. She was already curled up in Mark's arms on one of the couches. Cassie and Jake were sitting opposite Mark and Emma, with Maddie on Jake's lap and Cassie leaning against him.

Nick sat on the chair by the window, bringing Becky down onto his lap. "What else have you guys been up to?" he asked, holding her tight as she nestled into him.

"We've been painting," Becky said.

"Painting?" Mark turned to her.

"Not the house," Emma clarified. "We painted pictures with Maddie."

"Oh, I see."

"You've gotta get used to all this," Jake commented, smiling across at Mark. "It'll be your turn soon."

Mark hugged Emma closer. "Yeah. I can't wait," he said, kissing her. "I'm crap at painting though."

"You'll learn," Jake replied.

"And Jake and Maddie played ball outside for a while," Emma continued. "Which meant the three of us could do a little planning for Cassie's wedding."

"Okay," Mark said.

"And the rest of the time, we've just been chilling out," Cassie said.

"Sounds like a perfect day to me," Nick replied. "Except maybe the wedding planning part."

Becky looked up at him. "Why not that bit?" she asked.

"I got roped into helping Emma," Nick said, with an exaggerated shudder. "Never again."

"You call that helping? All you did was moan for an hour or so."

"Well, honestly… what did you expect?" Nick replied. "You know how I feel about weddings."

"Yes. And marriage." Emma smiled across at him.

Even though Nick was holding her, Becky felt a cold chill pass through her body. So, he hadn't been making it up for Tyler's benefit. He really didn't like the idea of marriage. She sighed and he tightened his grip, holding her closer. Did it matter that much if they weren't married? She had Nick. They were together and he loved her. That would have to be enough. She sighed.

"You okay?" Nick put a finger under her chin, raising her face. She nodded. His eyes examined hers. "Sure?" he asked.

"Yes." Her voice was barely a whisper against his chest.

It was enough.


Just before dinner, Nick went up to the guest room he and Becky were using, and had quick shower. Becky was sitting on the edge of the bed, waiting for him, when he came back into the bedroom.

"Hello," he said, smiling at her.

She smiled back. "I was sent to tell you dinner's being served."

"So we don't have time to pick up where we left off earlier?" Nick pulled the towel away to reveal his erection. Becky gazed at him and sighed.

"No. I'm afraid not."

He came over to her, leant down and kissed her gently. "I guess we'll have to wait then, won't we?" he teased, and pulled on the brand new jeans that were lying on the bed beside her.

"God, it's good not to be wearing underwear," he said, smirking.

"You were wearing underwear?" Becky asked, surprised.

"Yeah. I kinda had to. I was wearing Mark's jeans."

"But where did you get the underwear from?"

"Mark." Becky pulled a face and Nick laughed. "He gave me a pack of brand new trunks," he explained. "They were still in the packaging."

"Thank God for that."

"He insisted I should keep them." Becky tilted her head to one side. "I could hardly say 'no', but you and I both know I'll never be wearing them."

"Good," she murmured, rubbing her fingers along the length of his arousal.

"And if you keep doing that, we're never gonna make it downstairs," Nick added. Becky looked up at him and reluctantly pulled her hand away, getting to her feet and turning toward the door. "But that doesn't mean you have to leave." He pulled her back and kissed her deeply.

Jake's lasagna had a bit of a reputation in the town and it didn't fail to live up to it. While they ate, Mark and Nick took turns to explain their conversation with Eliot.

"Do you really think he'll help?" Becky asked.

"I think he'll do everything he can," Nick replied. "I can't ask for more than that."

She knew he was right, but his answer didn't exactly fill her with confidence.

They'd already decided they'll all stay at Mark and Emma's for the night, so that Jake and Cassie could drink, and Maddie was put to bed after they'd eaten.

Then they sat in the living room, on their third bottle of red wine, all feeling a lot more relaxed.

"Have you made a decision about the house yet?" Jake asked Nick.

"Yeah. I'm going ahead," Nick replied. "I've gotta talk to the bank though."

"I thought you'd already done that," Becky replied. "You said you were going to do it while I was in Vermont."

"I did," Nick explained. "And they approved my loan. I just needed to sign the final piece of paperwork…"

"And that was in the trailer?" Mark guessed.

Nick nodded his head. "I'll have to contact them and get them to send it though again. Or maybe I'll arrange to go in there and sign it, if it speeds things up." He looked across at Jake. "I know you're busy working for Mark now, but I need this done as soon as possible."

"Well, obviously. You guys are homeless right now."

That had a horrible ring to it.

"That sounds awful," Cassie said quietly, voicing Becky's thoughts.

"Where are we going to live?" she whispered, mainly to Nick.

"You can stay on here," Mark said.

Becky turned to him, unaware anyone else had even heard her. She shifted on Nick's lap. How could she explain, without sounding ungrateful, or rude, that she wasn't too keen on the idea. Mark and Emma had just got married. Emma was pregnant. The last thing they needed was two houseguests for an indefinite period of time. Besides, Mark was her boss…

Nick sighed. "I agree this place is secure," Nick replied, "but you two have just got married. You really don't need us under your feet. I know we said we'd stay here for a while, but it's gonna take months to build the house…"

"That doesn't matter—" Mark started to say.

"What about the apartment?" Emma interrupted. "The apartment above the coffee shop."

"It's not safe, Em," Nick said patiently. "These guys managed to torch the trailer. They could easily do the same to the apartment. I'm not gonna take that chance."

Emma stared at him, paling slightly. "Okay," she said. "But the risk won't last forever, will it? I mean, how long is it gonna take this cop friend of yours to find the evidence to bring in Tyler and his dad?"

Nick shrugged. "I don't know."

"Well, are we talking days, weeks, months?"

"Days or weeks, I'd have thought. Certainly not months."

"Right." Emma smiled. "So, why don't you stay on here until we know they're safely locked up, and then you can move to the apartment until your house is built."

Becky looked at Nick as a smile formed on his lips. "This pregnancy really is working wonders for your brain, Em," he said. "That's about the best plan I've heard of in ages."

## Nick

Later, Mark went out to the kitchen to make coffee and asked Nick to help him.

"What do you want to talk about?" Nick asked as soon as they were alone.

"Am I that transparent?"

"Well, I find it hard to believe you can't make six coffees by yourself, at your age."

Mark grinned. "Okay," he said. "I wanted to talk to you."

Nick felt himself deflate. They'd had a really good evening and now it seemed like all the negative stuff was about to close in on him again.

"Don't look so worried," Mark continued, "this is nothing to do with Tyler."

Nick looked up. "Okay… so what's it about?"

"I want to pay for your house to be built."

Nick choked and it took a minute before he could speak again. "I'm sorry?" he said. "Can you say that again?"

Mark smiled. "I'm offering to pay for your house to be built."

"Why? I've already got the money."

"I feel guilty I didn't pick up on what Tyler was doing with Becky's salary…"

"Well don't. She's good at hiding things. She's had to be." He paused. "I'm okay with paying for it though; I just need to sign the forms and we can get started."

"Can you afford it?" Mark asked, looking at him.

"Sure." Nick paused. "Well, I can provided I can still find work. I don't have a business at the moment, so I'm gonna have to start from scratch…" His voice faded as he realized the enormity of that task.

"Then let me pay for your house."

"No, Mark." Nick shook his head. "If I'm being honest, I wouldn't feel comfortable with that."

Mark sighed out a long breath. "Okay, then let me offer you a job. I recently fired my lawyer, if you recall?"

"I'm not looking for that kind of job. I wanna set myself up in my own business. I never wanted to be a cog in a big corporation. I always wanted to make the law work for the ordinary guy, who doesn't have a voice, or the money it takes to hire a fancy suit to speak for him. That's why I came back here – so I could really *do* something."

"Then why can't Gardner's Hotels be your first client?" Mark asked. "You're gonna have your work cut out for you. Once news breaks of what's gone on, Tom's dealings with GHC are gonna taint your name too. You'll be damned by association with some people, especially in a small town like this. It's gonna take a while to convince people that you were the innocent party; that you were the one who brought him to justice. Having a big client already on your books can only help with that. Besides anything else, it'll ensure you're earning enough money to pay that mortgage you're insisting on taking out."

Nick thought about what Mark was saying. It made perfect sense. He'd already thought about the fact that Tom's underhand dealings might prove difficult to overcome.

"I've got my own way of working," he said. "I don't do suits..."

"I'd noticed." Mark smiled, looking him up and down.

"No, I mean I don't do officialdom. If I'm gonna work for you, you're gonna have to be prepared to handle a little bit of unconventional."

"I think I can cope," Mark replied. "I've kinda gotten used to your rebellious ways." He paused for a moment, coming over to Nick and putting a hand on his shoulder. "That's one of the things I like about you. You see things differently. You're contrary. And while I'll admit you're unorthodox in a lot of ways, when it comes down to it, you're so damn straight. You always do the right thing – by everyone. Every damn time."

"What did Mark want?" Becky asked as they climbed into bed that night.

"He offered me a job."

She looked up at him. "A job? Working for him?"

"Well kind of." Nick pulled her close, running his hands down her back. Her skin felt soft and smooth beneath his fingers and she let out a slight moan. "I told him I couldn't work directly for him – not being employed, like you are. I'd find that too restrictive. But I'm gonna set up my own business and he's gonna be my first client."

"After me," Becky said, looking up at him.

He smiled. "Yeah, after you."

He rolled her onto her back and settled between her parted legs, leaning down and kissing her.

"God, I missed you today," he said.

"Do you wanna prove that?"

He smirked. "It'd be my pleasure..."

The following afternoon, Jake and Cassie still hadn't gone home. They were all having such a lovely, lazy Sunday. Maddie and Becky were doing a jigsaw together and they were all enjoying the relative peace and quiet after such a horrible week.

The silence was broken by Nick's phone ringing. He checked the screen, a sense of dread filling his stomach, but then sighed out his relief. "It's Eliot," he said to the collected faces staring at him, and connected the call.

"Hi," he said.

"Hello." He knew straight away that something was wrong.

"What's happened?" he asked. He glanced at Becky and saw her face had paled, so he got up and went over to her, putting his hand on her shoulder and giving her a light squeeze.

"I got a call real early this morning," Eliot replied, "from your friend Tyler."

"And?" Nick prompted.

"And he made a few threats."

"Fucking hell. Tell me you're not backing out on me—"

"Of course I'm not backing out on you." There was a pause. "The thing was, it wasn't me he threatened. It was Hayley."

"Your wife?" Becky stood up and put her arms around his waist. He held onto her with his free arm.

"Yeah. I've spent the day since then moving us into a safe house. After what the guy did to you, I wasn't gonna take any chances. She's not exactly pleased with me."

"I'm sorry, man."

"Don't be. I explained everything to her once I'd got her in a secure location. She's okay with it now. She understands what it's about."

"If you're in a safe house, does that mean you can't carry on with the investigation?"

"The safe house is for Hayley's benefit. I can take care of myself. Don't worry about that. Besides, being out of the office for a while might be a good thing. I'm one hundred per cent certain they found out I was looking into them through one of my colleagues. It's the only way they could've known about it so fast."

"Shit. They really do have the department in their pocket."

"Yeah. It looks that way. Anyway, I was just calling to let you know what's going on and to tell you I've found Linda Forsyth, and I'm gonna go see her at her school tomorrow. It's better for me to interview her away from her parents. She's never gonna admit to anything in front of them. I also wanted to tell you that, once this gets moving, I think it's gonna happen real fast, so the next time you hear from me might be after I've made the arrests. I don't wanna give them a chance to exert their influence."

"Okay." Nick looked up and saw that everyone was watching him. "Call me when you can. And watch your back, Eliot."

He ended the call and sat down. Becky sat with him. Cassie had taken over the jigsaw, but they were all waiting expectantly.

"I feel awful," Nick said, almost to himself.

"What's happened?" Mark asked.

Nick explained his conversation.

"He threatened your friend's wife?" Becky said.

"Yeah." Nick nodded his head slowly.

"Is she okay?" Emma asked.

"She was a bit mad to start with. They've only just got married. Eliot said she didn't appreciate being moved into a safe house. But once he'd explained the situation and what Tyler's done, she was okay with it."

"And Eliot?"

"He's okay. He's not backing down."

By Wednesday, they'd settled back into their routine. Mark and Becky worked from the house, while Nick drove Emma into the coffee shop each morning and worked from a booth. Mark had given him a few things to deal with, and he'd had to check up on Becky's divorce. Jeremy had filed the papers, but nothing more had happened since. He was also still handling a couple of local cases and needed to pick up the files from his desk.

"I'm just going over to the office," he said to Emma. It was lunchtime, so the coffee shop was busy and he knew she'd be safe. "Don't go anywhere, and if he comes in, go out the back to Noah and call me. I won't be long."

She nodded her head, trying to look calm, although he wasn't that easily fooled.

He jogged across the road, opening the door and letting himself into his office. Tina must have been at lunch, because the outer office was deserted. He could hear Tom talking on the phone, but had no intention of getting into a conversation with him. He went over to his own office, let himself in and pushed the door closed again. The files were exactly where he'd left them and he'd just picked them up when he heard the outer door open, and a man shouted, "Tom Allen?"

Nick recognized that voice. It was Eliot. He crossed the room and opened his door, to find four uniformed police officers standing in the reception, behind Eliot, who gave him a nod. At almost the same time, Tom's office door opened and his partner stood on the threshold, his face paling from gray to white.

"What do you want?" he said.

"I've got a warrant for your arrest," Eliot replied.

"On what charge?" Tom blustered.

"I think you mean *charges*." Eliot unfolded the piece of paper he held in his hand and started reading through the charges against Tom. Once he'd finished, he nodded to the policeman on his right, who moved forward and handcuffed Tom, reading him his rights. All of Tom's bravado had gone. He slumped forward and the policeman had to hold him up as he led him out onto the street.

"Jeez," Nick said under his breath. "I didn't expect that."

"What *did* you expect?" Eliot asked. "He's as guilty as the rest of them. I wasn't gonna differentiate, just because the guy's a friend of yours. If you wanted that kinda treatment, you came to the wrong cop."

"No, that's not what I mean," Nick said. "I mean, I didn't think it would be you making the arrest, or that I'd witness it."

Eliot smiled. "Oh, I made sure I was present at all of them," he said. "We arrested Tyler and Garrett Howell together last night at their family home. It was important we picked them up at the same time, so although I'd gathered the evidence by Monday evening, we waited until last night, because I found out that they always get together with a few buddies for a poker night at Garrett's place."

"And this?" Nick nodded toward the place where Tom had been standing.

"I spoke to the local police up here and they said I could come and make the arrest myself. Once I explained what had gone on, they were happy to oblige."

Nick sat down heavily in one of the visitor's chairs.

"Does this mean it's over?" he asked.

"In terms of the danger to you and yours? Yes. They can't get to you from where they're gonna be."

"But will they be able to get out of it?" Nick asked, looking up.

Eliot smiled. "Oh, I very much doubt it. Linda Forsyth was very forthcoming in the end. I took a female officer with me – one I knew I could trust. She got her to talk. It turned out that Linda was sixteen – just – when she met Tyler, but she explained that the night Kelly was there, after she'd gone, Tyler got mad that his plan hadn't worked out and he forced her to have sex with him. He was quite violent."

Nick felt sick. "Jesus. He raped her?" he whispered and Eliot nodded. "But how does that help with Garrett?"

"It doesn't. It helps with Tyler. Everything was already stacked up against Garrett anyway. The senator came across with the goods exactly as predicted. I told him we could get him a reduced sentence for the statutory rape if he swore out a statement that Garrett blackmailed him. He caved so damn fast, it was embarrassing."

"It doesn't seem fair that he's gonna get a reduced sentence."

"Who said he is?" Eliot replied, grinning. "Once I'd got his statement, I withdrew my offer. None of it was on the record and I told him it'd be his word against mine… The word of a rapist against the word of an upstanding cop. He yelled and swore and cursed at me. And I reminded him what he'd done. Of course, he might try and cut a deal with the DA…" He shook his head.

"What the fuck is wrong with these men?" Nick murmured.

"I'm not sure I'd call them men," Eliot replied. "I think that does the rest of us a disservice."

Nick nodded and got up again.

"I—I can't thank you enough," he said quietly.

"You don't have to. I'm just doing my job." He paused for a moment. "There is one thing, though…"

"What's that?"

"I'm gonna need to speak with Becky."

"You are?" Nick was shocked. "Why?"

"Because, I want to talk to her about pressing charges against Tyler herself."

"Why? You've already got Linda Forsyth. Why do you need Becky?"

"Because Linda was sixteen. It's not statutory rape – it's rape. And it was a while ago now, so we've got no physical evidence, just her word. A good lawyer, like yourself, could argue that she consented, even that they were in a relationship, maybe that she liked things a little rough. I want to show a pattern of violent behavior against women. Becky can help with that."

Everything Eliot was saying made sense, but Nick wasn't sure how Becky would feel.

"I'll ask her," he said.

"If she agrees, call me and we'll set it up. I'm gonna be here until tomorrow night."

# Chapter Twenty-Two

*Becky*

Nick waited until they'd eaten dinner and were sitting in the living room before starting his story. Mark and Emma sat together, holding hands, their mouths open, while he detailed exactly what had happened. Becky lay curled up next to Nick, with his arms around her, feeling the relief wash over her.

"Tyler's really in jail?" she said as he finished explaining about Tom's arrest.

"Yeah. And his father, and Tom… and the senator."

"Man, Eliot's good," Mark commented.

"He—He raped a schoolgirl?" Becky couldn't believe what she'd heard.

"Which one of them?" Nick asked. "They're all low-lifes."

"Tyler, I mean."

"Yeah. Linda Forsyth was only just sixteen. In the senator's case, the girl was even younger still."

"Dear God." Mark moved slightly and put his arms around Emma.

"The thing is," Nick continued, turning in his seat and looking down at Becky, "Eliot wants to talk to you."

"Me? Why?"

"Because he wants you to press charges against Tyler."

"Why on earth does he need her to do that?" Mark asked from across the room.

"Because, as he quite rightly pointed out to me, some asshole lawyer, like myself, would probably be able to argue that Linda consented, or even that she liked having rough sex with him and it was a regular thing between them."

"Seriously?" Emma was shocked.

Nick looked at them all. "It can all be twisted to make Tyler look like the innocent party."

"You're kidding me," Mark joined in

"No." He looked down at Becky again. "Eliot thinks that if you agree to press charges too, it'll make it obvious that Tyler's got a track record of violence against women."

"You really think it'll help?"

Nick seemed to think for a moment, then put his hand against her cheek. "I can't make you do this, baby," he said softly. "And I know how hard it's gonna be for you, if you do… But yeah, knowing how some lawyers operate, I really think it could help."

"Then I'll do it," she said straight away.

"You can think about it, if you want. Eliot's here until tomorrow night, but if you need longer, we can go into Boston and see him there."

"No. I'll see him in the morning." She was resolved. "I'll tell him everything."

"You're sure?"

She nodded.

"You want me to set it up?"

"Yes." He reached into his pocket for his phone. "There's just one thing," she said, grabbing his hand.

"What's that?"

"Can you be there with me?"

He smiled. "Of course I can."


Eliot came to the house. Becky barely recognized him, although he seemed to remember her, but then he'd been Nick's friend, not hers. Emma had gone into the coffee shop by herself for the first time in ages and Mark was working in his office, so Becky and Nick had the living room to themselves.

Eliot looked at her from his seat on the opposite couch.

"I know it's hard," he said to her, "but I just need you to take me through what he did to you."

"All of it?"

"Yeah. In as much detail as you can remember."

Becky took a deep breath and held tight onto Nick's hand. "I guess I'd better start with our wedding night…"

It took over three hours for her to give Eliot her statement and, at the end of it, she was exhausted, flopping down into Nick's arms. He held her and kissed her forehead.

"You okay?" he asked.

She nodded into him, incapable of saying another word.

"I may need you and Mark to give statements as well," Eliot said. "You can testify that Becky was beaten."

"I can to the one occasion," Nick replied, "but Mark saw Becky's bruises numerous times."

Eliot nodded. "Okay," he said. "Leave this with me and I'll get back to you." He looked at Becky. "You did really well," he said. "I know how tough that was, and I'm sorry I had to ask you so many personal questions."

"It's okay," she whispered. "If it helps, then it's fine." She sat up a little, looking at him. "The girl – Linda – is she okay?"

Eliot shrugged. "I don't know. I've got no idea what she was like before. She's quiet, withdrawn, scared. She's certainly scared of men, that's for sure. She backed into a corner when she saw me. If I hadn't taken a female officer with me, I'd never have gotten her to talk."

"He did that to her?"

"Well, like I say, I don't know what she was like before, but…" He didn't need to finish his sentence.

Later, as they lay in bed, and she rested her head on Nick's chest, Becky asked the question that had been troubling her since the previous day.

"Now he's been arrested," she began, "is it going to affect my divorce? Is it gonna hold things up?"

Nick turned them so they were facing each other and pulled her in close to his chest. "No," he replied. "If anything it might make it easier. If he's imprisoned, you have the right to divorce him."

"But that means we have to wait until the case goes to court. In the meantime, he's hardly likely to sign the divorce papers, is he?"

Nick shook his head. "No," he replied, feeling deflated.

She sagged into him. "Why?" she whimpered. "Why can't it just be over with?"

## Nick

Nick barely slept that night. He'd expected to feel better now the threat of imminent danger was over; Tyler was behind bars, along with his dad, and they could start to get back to normal. But Becky's comments about the divorce had made him realize they still had a long road ahead of them, and that she wasn't strong enough to travel it, not given the time it was going to take.

It was around four in the morning that he decided on his next course of action. There were a couple of risks, but he was willing to take them…

All he had to do was to break the news to Becky.

"You're going to Boston? Again?" She was incredulous. "And you'll be away for a couple of days? What on earth are you gonna be doing?"

"I need to see Eliot." That wasn't exactly a lie. He'd need to ask Eliot a favor.

"For two days?"

He sighed. "Do you trust me?" he asked.

"You know I do."

"Then let me do this. I'll be back in two days, and then I'll explain everything."

"And why can't you explain it now?"

"Because you'll try and talk me out of it."

She gasped. "Is it dangerous?"

"No."

"Is it illegal?"

Nick didn't reply.

"Nick?"

"I'll be back in two days."

Nick sat in the room that the school had allocated to him, alongside the female officer, called Naomi, who Eliot had sent with him. Eliot had been skeptical about Nick's plan, but had gone along with it.

"I'm gonna let you lead," Nick said quietly to Naomi. "You've met her before and she trusts you. You know what it is I need to find out."

Naomi nodded as the door opened and a young girl in school uniform walked in.

She took one look at Nick and her eyes widened. He didn't move. Didn't even get up. He did exactly what he'd said and let Naomi lead the conversation.

It only took fifteen minutes to get what he wanted, but another two hours to carry out the second interview.

"This is highly irregular," Eliot said the following morning, leading the way to the cells. "You're not his legal counsel. I really shouldn't let you in to see him. Not like this."

"I know that. But Bex did you a favor making that statement. This is me asking for a favor in return."

Eliot looked at him and nodded. "If he gives you any trouble, press the panic button."

"You mean I can't just hit him?" Nick asked, smiling.

"I'd rather you didn't. The paperwork would be a bitch."

Eliot opened the cell door and Nick walked past him.

Tyler was sitting on the cot alongside the wall and looked up as Nick entered the room.

"What's he doing here?" Tyler addressed Eliot. "He's not my lawyer."

"I know."

"Then he should only be seeing me in the visitor's room."

"Tough fucking shit." Eliot left and closed the door.

Tyler turned to Nick, a sneer crossing his face. "Come to gloat?" he said.

"No."

"Then what do you want? Get it over with and fuck off."

"Why? You got somewhere else to be?"

"Well, I won't be in here for long, if that's what you mean."

"Really? You honestly believe that?"

"I'm being charged with rape," Tyler said. "But it's her word against mine. I'm a respected member of the community and she's a deluded kid. She came onto me. All I did was oblige her."

Nick felt sick, but hid it well.

"And what about Amanda Pendry?" he asked.

"Who?"

"Amanda Pendry," Nick repeated.

"Who the hell is Amanda Pendry?" Tyler stared up at him.

"She's Linda's friend. You groomed her, texted her, took her out to dinner a couple of times. Surely you remember her? She thought it was all so romantic. She told Linda all about it… about how excited she was that someone as sophisticated as you had noticed her." Nick swallowed down the bile that was rising in his throat. "And then, after your third date, you convinced her to go back to your place, and you had sex with her."

"She consented," Tyler argued.

"Yeah. She did – she's admitted that."

"Then what the fuck are you talking about?" Tyler sneered.

"Amanda only turned sixteen eight days ago. When you had sex with her, she was still fifteen."

"So?" Tyler said.

"So that makes it statutory rape."

"It's not rape. She consented," Tyler repeated.

Nick moved forward again and leant down over Tyler, getting in his face. "You really are a dumb fuck, aren't you? Having sex with anyone who's under the age of sixteen is statutory rape. You can't argue consent in this case. You have no defense."

"She won't press charges," Tyler argued.

"She will," Nick replied. "I spoke with her yesterday. She may have consented, but now she knows what you did to her friend Linda, she's ready to make a statement against you."

Tyler swallowed, the realization dawning on him that he really was in trouble. "What do you want?" he said.

Nick stood again. "I want you to stop contesting Becky's divorce," he replied.

"The divorce?"

"Yeah. I can make this all go away. And all you've gotta do is sign the documents to convert the divorce to be non-contested."

"That's it? Straight-as-a-die Nick Woods is gonna bend the law to suit his own ends?"

"Looks that way, doesn't it?"

"How can you make it go away, if she's ready to make a statement?"

Nick put his hands in his pockets. "I can convince her she doesn't have a case. Remember me? I'm a fucking good lawyer, unlike you. I can point out to her what an ordeal it's gonna be for her. She'll back down…"

Tyler thought for a moment, his eyes narrowing. "You're banging my wife, aren't you?"

Nick didn't reply.

Tyler shook his head. "Not that it matters anyway. You're welcome to her. She always was a useless fuck." He paused. "I'll sign," he said.

Nick pulled a document from his pocket, unfolded it and handed it to Tyler.

"Sign on the last page," he said, handing him a pen.

Tyler did as he was told and handed the papers back. Nick checked the signature then replaced the document and pen in his pocket, moving toward the door.

"You're really gonna hush up a statutory rape, just so you can get to screw my wife?" Tyler sneered at him. "You're no better than I am…"

Nick turned. "Like I said, you are one dumb fuck." He moved back toward Tyler again. "Do you honestly think I'd let you get away with this?"

"But you said…"

"Yeah. I'm a better liar than you thought I was. That's why I asked to see you in your cell. There are no witnesses in here. You can claim I've said whatever you want and I'll deny it."

"Give me back that fucking document," Tyler shouted, getting up for the first time.

"Not a chance. And just so you know, Amanda Pendry gave her statement to a police officer yesterday afternoon. I've already given her, and Linda, and their parents legal advice and I'm gonna be in court with them. So whatever your deadbeat lawyers are thinking of trying, don't even go there." He reached out to knock on the door, but paused. "If you want my advice," he said, "I'd plead guilty. It'll save you some jail time. Guys like you don't fare well inside."

"Champagne?" Becky said.

"Yeah. I thought we should celebrate."

"Celebrate what?" They were all standing around the island unit in Mark and Emma's kitchen.

Nick put the bottle down on the countertop and pulled Becky into a hug, kissing her deeply.

"The fact that I refiled your divorce papers while I was in the city."

"You did?" She looked up at him and he could see the confusion in her eyes.

"Yeah. It's been changed from contested, to non-contested."

"You… you mean, Tyler's not gonna fight it?"

He shook his head, grinning down at her.

"How did you do that?"

He shrugged. "I bent a few rules."

Becky leant back in his arms, looking up at him. "What do you mean 'bent'?"

"Well, I kinda blackmailed him."

"Nick! That's not bending the rules. That's breaking the law."

He cupped her face with his hands, looking into her eyes. "I know. But I couldn't bear to see you so unhappy. Waiting to be free of him was tearing you apart."

"How did you do it?" Mark asked from the other side of the unit.

Nick explained what had gone on in Boston, from his interviews with Linda and Amanda, to his meeting with Tyler in his jail cell.

"He honestly thought you'd let him get away with rape?" Becky asked. "You, of all people?"

"Yeah, he did. But that's because Tyler never did bother getting to know people properly. Especially not people he didn't think could be of value to him. To Tyler I was just the small town kid, who became a small town lawyer."

"What made you think of interviewing Linda again?" Mark asked.

"Well, given that Linda was borderline legal, I guessed that there was every chance he'd probably slipped up in the past, so I asked her how she'd met him, and she told me about Amanda. It was a gamble, but it worked."

"So what happens now?" Emma asked after a brief silence.

"To Tyler, or with the divorce?"

"With the divorce... who cares about Tyler."

They all laughed. "Becky will get a court date, hopefully not too far away. Then her decree nisi will come through thirty days after that. She has to wait a further ninety days for her decree absolute. And then she's free."

"So how long is that in total?" Becky asked.

He shrugged. "It depends on the court date, but you're probably looking at six, maybe seven months."

He felt the relief wash off of her. "And I don't need to see him, or have anything to do with him?"

"No."

"Oh God... Thank you," she said, clinging onto his shoulders. "Thank you so much... for everything."

He kissed her gently. "You don't have to thank me, baby," he replied. "You know I'll do anything for you."

# Epilogue

## *Mid-October*

## *Becky*

"Here's to you... and freedom." Nick clinked his glass against hers.

"No. You made it happen." Becky leant across the table and kissed him. "I'd never have been free of him without you."

"It was entirely my pleasure," Nick said, looking into her eyes.

"Entirely?" She smiled at him.

"Okay, parts of it were far from pleasurable, but we got there in the end, and that's all that matters."

Becky's decree absolute had arrived in the morning mail. To celebrate, Mark had given her the day off and she'd cooked her and Nick a special meal. Nick was still working out of his and Becky's guest room at the moment. He wasn't comfortable working from the offices he'd shared with Tom Allen, and had spent more money than he'd anticipated on building and furnishing the house. He knew this set-up wouldn't work in the long-term, but it made sense for the time being, although on days like today, when Becky was home too, he got very little done that didn't involve removing Becky's clothes.

The house was spectacular. Jake had finally signed it off a month earlier. One wall was made entirely of glass and looked out toward the forest. The whole downstairs was open-plan and upstairs there were three bedrooms, each with their own bathroom. It was simple, functional, and understated. While it was being built, they'd lived in the apartment above the coffee shop, just as planned, moving in there a few days after Nick's meeting with Tyler in Boston.

Although Nick preferred his forest hideaway, their summer in the town had given them lots of happy memories. Quite often, Emma would come up to the apartment after work and, although she'd grown more and more pregnant, she still loved to cook for them. Mark would join them, and they'd eat together, talking until late at night.

The highlight of those months had been Jake and Cassie's wedding. In the lead-up to it, they'd all spent a lot of time at the beach house, helping get things ready. The day itself was perfect; exactly what Cassie had wanted. The ceremony was held on the beach, with Jake and Cassie standing on a spot by some rocks, which they said was special to them, although neither would explain why. Cassie wore a simple white dress, with a lace bodice and sheer skirt. She looked stunning and Jake's eyes had glistened in the sunlight as she'd walked toward him, with Maddie in front of her, dropping pink rose petals on the sand. Cassie had been given away to Jake by his father, Ben. Of course, Ben was probably the closest thing to a father Cassie had ever known, so it made perfect sense for him to take the role.

During the course of the afternoon, it had also become clear that Ben and Maggie had become more than friends during the few months since Maggie had moved into Mark and Emma's. Once his official duties were over, Ben didn't leave her side. They held hands and exchanged glances and, on a couple of occasions, they kissed. They were so clearly in love, and everyone was happy for them. They'd both known a lot of tragedy, but they'd found happiness, clearly intending to seize it – and each other – with both hands.

Everyone had enjoyed a truly spectacular day, which had gone on long into the evening. Becky's only hint of sadness was that she knew she'd never get to experience anything like that for herself, realizing as she did that Nick didn't believe in marriage. Still, she shook those thoughts from her head. She was lucky. She had Nick. He loved her and he told her that all the time. And she was safe.

She really was safe now. Everything had been resolved during their perfect summer.

As Eliot had surmised, the senator had done a deal with the DA. He'd agreed to testify against Garrett Howell, in return for a suspended sentence. He'd lost his job and his home, but he'd still got his liberty. As had Tom – but only just, and that was thanks to Nick, who'd testified on his behalf, that he'd been under extreme pressure, due to his wife's illness and also being blackmailed by Garrett Howell. Of course, Tom's affair with Garrett's wife had come to light and Cathy had initially reacted badly, threatening divorce. But, she'd relented and they were having marriage counseling. What Tom was going to do for a living was anyone's guess. He certainly wouldn't be practicing law again.

As for Garrett Howell himself, he never made it to trial. He had a heart attack while in custody and died in a police cell, despite the attempts of the duty officer to revive him. Few people attended his funeral. Tyler couldn't. The funeral was on the day of his hearing. He'd pleaded guilty to all charges against him. He'd been looking at a life sentence just for the statutory rape of Amanda Pendry, let alone the additional charges of the rape of Linda Forsyth and the rape and attempted rapes of Becky. As it was, he was sentenced to fifteen years in prison, without parole.

Nick waved his hand in front of Becky's face.

"You're a long way away," he said.

"I was just thinking about what a year it's been," she replied.

"It sure has." He smirked. "And it's not over yet."

"You think we can take any more?"

"Well, I'm gonna become an uncle any day now…" Nick looked down at his phone. He hadn't turned it off, or even let it out of his sight for a couple of weeks.

"I wish they'd found out whether it's a boy, or a girl," Becky said. "It would have made buying them gifts so much easier."

"I think after the year they've had, they were looking forward to a nice surprise for a change. It hasn't exactly been a bed of roses for them either."

"No, it hasn't." She still felt guilty that she'd brought so much trouble into everyone's lives.

"Stop it," he said.

"Stop what?"

"Feeling bad about it all."

"How do you do that?"

"You still need to ask?"

"I know… you can read my body." She looked up at him. "So, what's it telling you right now?" she asked, smiling.

He took her hand and got to his feet, pulling her with him. "It's telling me that, although we've had one hell of a difficult year, you can always handle a little more excitement in your life."

"I can, can I?"

He nodded. "Yeah, you can. Come with me." He put his phone in his back pocket and led her out through the folding doors that made up the bottom half of the glass wall.

"Where are we going?"

"It's a surprise."

"A nice surprise?"

"Of course."

A little way into the forest, was a small clearing and as they approached it, Becky gasped. Nick had laid out a large blanket, one end of which was covered with cushions, and which he'd surrounded by candles, burning in hurricane lamps.

"This is beautiful," she whispered.

"So are you." He led her forward toward the blanket. They both kicked off their shoes, leaving them on the edge, and she felt the downy softness beneath her feet. "We haven't had the chance to do this since we moved in," he said, "what with work and unpacking and getting the furniture arranged and everything… But I've been dreaming about this for months; ever since you told me you wanted us to make love outside more often."

He took hold of the hem of her top and pulled it up over her head, dropping it to the floor.

"God, I really love it when you don't wear a bra," he said, leaning down and capturing a nipple in his teeth, biting gently.

She twisted her fingers into his hair, holding him in place, and let out a soft moan. It was warm still, but the light breeze across her skin was exhilarating. She felt Nick's hands between them, undoing the button of her jeans and pushing down the zipper. He stepped back and then knelt in front of her, pulling down her jeans and panties and holding up his hand so she could take it and balance, while she stepped out of her clothes.

"Feet apart," he whispered, looking up at her.

She moved her feet and he ran his hands up the insides of her thighs until they reached the apex, then he parted her folds and slowly inserted two fingers inside her. Her head rocked back and she sucked in a breath.

"I'm gonna guess you like this," he murmured. "You're so wet."

"Hmm…" She parted her legs a little further, just as Nick's phone rang.

He stopped his movements and, with his free hand, pulled his phone from his pocket, checking the screen. "Now?" he said. "Seriously, Em? You couldn't wait?" He looked up at her. "Sorry, baby. It's Mark."

"Take it," she told him.

Nick answered the call. Listened for a few moments, smiled and said, "Okay. We'll be there as soon as we can."

"The baby?" she asked.

"Yeah. I'm sorry." He withdrew his fingers slowly from inside her and looked up into her eyes.

"Don't be. It's not your fault." She looked around. "I'd better get dressed."

He got to his feet. "Yeah. I'll blow out the candles. I don't want to be accused of starting a fire." He moved toward the edge of the blanket.

"Oh… you already did that," Becky said.

Nick stopped in his tracks, turned and came back over to her. "That's one fire I've got no intention of putting out," he murmured. "Not ever."

The waiting room was warm, and sterile. The walls were white, other than a couple of dull landscape pictures. It was four in the morning, and they'd been there for nearly seven hours. Nick was standing at the window with his back to her, staring out at the parking lot.

"Don't worry about her," Becky said, looking up at him from the uncomfortable couch.

"I'm not," he replied, without turning around. "I just hate being here. We're on a different floor, but the waiting rooms here are pretty much identical, and it reminds me of when I had to bring Emma in, after she'd taken the tablets. I spent hours staring out the window that night, not knowing if I'd ever see her alive again."

Becky got to her feet and went over to him, putting her arms around his waist and resting her head on his back. "Sorry," she said. "I didn't understand."

"It's okay." He turned and leant down to kiss her.

"I've been thinking," she said quietly, pulling him over to the couch and sitting down.

"Okay." He sounded doubtful.

"Now I'm divorced, I'm gonna go back to using my maiden name."

He stared down at her. "Is that what you want?" he asked.

She smirked. "Well, I certainly don't want to use his name anymore." Nick raised an eyebrow and went to speak just as the door swung open.

Mark stood there, his eyes red, his cheeks stained with tears. Becky had seen Mark in many situations before, but never like this and, for a moment, she didn't know what to say.

"Mark?" Nick got up and stepped forward.

"It's a boy," Mark said quietly. "I've got a son."

"And Emma?" Nick persisted.

"She's exhausted. Happy, but exhausted."

"I'm sure she wants to sleep more than anything," Becky said.

"She does. But she knows you're here. Come and see them." Mark stepped to one side.

"Okay… just for a minute, and then we'll go and leave you all in peace."

Mark led them along the corridor, opening the third door along on the right. Inside, Emma was sitting up in bed, leaning back against the pillows. She was cradling a tiny bundle, wrapped in blue blankets. She looked tired, but there was a smile on her face, the like of which Becky had never seen before.

"Em," Nick said, keeping hold of Becky's hand and going over to Emma's bedside.

"Hi," she murmured.

"How are you?" he asked. Becky looked up at his face and saw the concern etched there.

"Sore," Emma replied, grinning. "Sore and tired."

"We won't stop long," Becky said, leaning forward and peeking at the baby. "He's beautiful."

"He is, isn't he?"

"Have you chosen a name yet?" Becky asked.

Emma nodded and looked at Mark, who had come to stand on the other side of the bed, his hand resting gently on Emma's shoulder. "We're gonna name him Michael, after my father," he said, his voice filled with emotion.

Emma turned to Nick. "And we'd like his second name to be Nicholas… after you."

Becky looked at Nick. His eyes were shining and he nodded his head, although he didn't say a word for a moment. When he did, his voice cracked. "I'm honored," he said. "Thank you."

Becky squeezed his hand, smiling and feeling truly happy. "In a lot of ways, it's been an awful year for all of us," she said, "but this is just the perfect way to end it."

Nick leant down. "I told you earlier… it's not over yet."

## Nick

They stayed for around twenty minutes. Emma insisted that both Nick and Becky have a hold of baby Michael. Nick felt awkward holding him; it had never been his strong point, and he was relieved when he could hand the baby over to Mark, who seemed to have taken to fatherhood like a duck to water, which made Nick smile.

Becky, on the other hand, was a natural. She cradled the baby gently in her arms, cooing to him softly. Nick watched her closely, her eyes fixed on the baby's sleeping face. There was no mistaking that look. She may not have wanted a baby with Tyler, but that didn't mean she didn't want one at all. He looked up and saw that Mark was watching him, a slow smile forming on his face.

By the time they got home, the sun was starting to rise.

"It doesn't seem worth going to bed, does it?" Nick said.

"I'm not even tired anymore," Becky replied.

"Come with me." He took her hand and led her back out to the blanket in the clearing. Everything was still laid out, although they no longer needed the candles. The sun's first rays were casting long shadows across the ground.

"It's still beautiful," Becky said.

"It must've been a warm night." Nick bent down and felt the blanket. "It's not even damp." He turned to her. "Lie down with me for a while."

He lowered her to the ground, then joined her, resting his head against the soft cushions while Becky curled up beside him.

"Can we talk?" he asked her.

"Sure. What do you want to talk about?"

"Children." He decided this was a conversation they needed to have. And they needed to have it now.

"Children?" She twisted and looked up at him.

"Yeah. You told me ages ago, that your ex wanted to have kids and you didn't." Nick still struggled with saying Tyler's name, but at least he no longer had to call him Becky's 'husband'.

"That's right."

"Was that just with him, or in general."

"Oh, just with him. It would have been madness to have a child with him. I probably didn't make that very clear."

"No, you didn't." He hesitated for a moment. "So, you want to have kids then?"

"Well… yes."

"With me?"

"Obviously with you." She sat up suddenly. "Are you telling me you don't?" she asked. "Is that what this is about?"

He shook his head, pulling her back down into his arms. "No," he replied. "That's not it at all."

He felt her sigh. "So you want to have kids too?" she asked.

"Yeah… one day."

"One day?" He heard the doubt resurface in her voice.

"Bex," he said calmly, "like we said, it's been one helluva year. I waited nine years for you and I feel like we've been on a rollercoaster ever since we got back together. You only got your divorce through yesterday and I'd really like to spend some time with you – just the two of us. Call me selfish if you want, but I'd like to have you to myself for a while."

"You're not selfish," Becky whispered. "I don't see the need to rush either."

"Good." He let out a breath. "Besides, we've got enough to keep us busy right now anyway."

"We do?" Becky looked up at him again.

"Yeah. I need to work out what to do with the old offices – I can't just leave them empty indefinitely; Mark's new hotel opens in a couple of months, which is gonna keep you occupied; I've got three new clients to deal with, and there's the wedding to plan—"

"Wedding?" Becky interrupted. "What wedding?"

"Our wedding."

"Is this your way of proposing?" she asked, her head tilting to one side.

Nick shrugged. "Yeah, I guess it is." He sat up, pulling Becky with him and sitting her on his lap, so she was straddling him. "I know I'm not doing a very good job of it, but let's face it, I was never gonna get down on one knee, was I? Although that doesn't mean I don't love you, or that I don't want to share the rest of my life with you."

He looked into her eyes. But instead of seeing his love reflected, all his saw was confusion.

"What's wrong?" he asked.

"I don't understand why you're doing this," she said.

"I just explained. I love you. I wanna be with you. Forever."

"We don't have to get married to do that." She leant forward, resting her forehead against his. "You're not the marrying kind," she said softly. "You said so to Tyler, and to everyone, when we were at Mark and Emma's. I've understood that for some time, Nick. You don't believe in marriage, or weddings."

"And I'm not allowed to change my mind?"

"Only if you can give me a good reason."

"I can give you the best reason," Nick replied. "It'll make you happy."

"I don't need for us to be married to be happy. I've got you. I know you love me. It's fine."

"Fine isn't quite good enough, Bex." He held her close. "I know this is what you want. I watched you at Jake and Cassie's wedding. I know you were thinking that you'd never get to experience that."

"You're a mind-reader."

"Only when it comes to you." He traced her lips with his fingertip. "That was what you were thinking though, wasn't it?"

Becky nodded, just once. "But that doesn't mean we have to get married."

"If it's what's gonna make you truly happy, then it does. Haven't I always told you, I'll do anything for you."

"But it goes against what you believe in."

"I just don't believe in all the pomp, the ceremony, the show. I think if two people are in love, it should just be about them and whatever they want to do."

"And what do you want to do?" Becky asked.

"I want to marry you." He shifted her on his lap so they were as close as they could be. "Earlier when you said you were going to go back to being Becky Scott, I suddenly realized I didn't want you to."

"Well, I don't want to stay Becky Howell."

"No. I don't want that either. I want you to be Becky Woods. I want you to be mine. Say you'll be mine. Please."

She nodded. "I'll be yours. I'll always be yours."

He kissed her deeply, his tongue delving into her mouth and finding hers, then he lay back down again with Becky on top of him.

"Of course," he said, "I can't guarantee an entirely conventional wedding."

She smiled up at him. "I didn't for one minute think you would." She closed her eyes for a second. "Okay then. Shock me. What have you got in mind?"

"Well…" He rolled them over, so they were facing each other, on their sides. "Obviously it's your day, so you get to choose, but I'd really like to get married here."

"Where?"

"Right here, in our forest." He paused for a moment. "Do you remember the first time you came here, you said how beautiful it is?" Becky nodded. "And I told you how much better it looks when it snows?" She nodded again. "Well, I'd like to get married here, in the snow. Maybe at Christmas." She smiled. "And I'd like to decorate the forest with fairy lights and marry you just as the sun's setting." Her smile broadened. "I'd wanna keep it small," he continued. "Just us, the celebrant and our friends. And I don't want anyone to have to get dressed up. I certainly won't be. I don't want any tuxes." She smirked, but nodded once more. "I just want us to say our vows, become Mr and Mrs Woods, and then for all of us to have a great evening together." He paused. "Obviously, if you want something more formal, we can talk about it…"

"I don't," she whispered. "I want it just how you described it. It sounds absolutely perfect."

"It does?"

She nodded. "I can't think of anything I want more than to marry you, in the snow, in your forest."

"*Our* forest," he corrected. "Christmas Eve," he said suddenly.

"You wanna get married on Christmas Eve?"

He nodded. "Yeah. That gives you roughly ten weeks to find a dress." As the sun's rays glanced across her face, he noticed tears welling in her eyes. "Don't cry, baby," he whispered. "You've got nothing to cry about."

"I'm only crying because I'm happy. I'm so happy, Nick."

He held her closer. "Good," he said, "Whatever other vows I make to you on Christmas Eve, I promise you right now, I'm gonna spend the rest of my life making sure that you spend the rest of your life feeling safe, and happy, and loved." He kissed her gently. "I can't guarantee to do anything conventionally, Bex. I can't even guarantee to do anything very well. But I can absolutely guarantee that I will love you with all of my heart, until the very last breath leaves my body."

And as he spoke those words, he rolled her onto her back and kissed away her tears as the sun rose around them.

The End

Keep reading for an excerpt from Suzie Peters' forthcoming book
*Stay Here With Me*
Part One in the Recipe for Romance Series.

Available to purchase from July 20th 2018

# Stay Here With Me

Recipe for Romance: Book One

by

Suzie Peters

# Chapter One

*Ali*

My eyelids are starting to droop. But then, I've been working on the wording for this new mail shot for ages, and I'm getting nowhere with it. I check the time in the corner of my computer screen and decide, at just a few minutes before eleven-thirty pm, that I really should call it a night.

"Are you going to bed any time soon?"

My sister, Tess comes in from her bedroom, walks through the living room into the study area and leans over the back of my chair.

"Yes." I yawn, stretch, and look up at her. She's got shadows under her eyes. "I could ask the same question of you though."

"I've finally finished reading the last book I needed to get through. I've made my notes and, as a result, have discovered another two books I really ought to read, so that went well. I was just going to get a glass of water and then I'm giving up – at least for today," she says, going back out into the hallway and through to the kitchen. "How's it going?" she calls.

"It's not." I reach out to switch off my computer, just as my email pings, letting me know I've got a new message. "More junk," I murmur.

"Might not be," Tess says, coming back in and taking a sip from the tall glass of water she's brought with her. "Who knows, it could be Gordon Ramsay, asking you to come and re-design his restaurants for him."

I laugh. "And what would Gordon Ramsay need with a restaurant consultant? I doubt he needs help with his menu, or his decor, or staff management. You have seen those programmes he makes, haven't you?" Tess laughs with me. Still, I can't help it. I go to my mail app and check anyway. It won't be Gordon Ramsay though, I know that much.

"Good God," I whisper.

"It's not him, is it?"

"No, of course it isn't. But it is an enquiry from my website." The first one for months.

Tess comes and looks over my shoulder again.

"So it is. Well, that's great," she says, her voice – though still quiet, as always – full of enthusiasm.

"Before we get too excited, let's see what they want me to do."

I click on the message and wait for it to open, and together, we read:

*Hi,*

*My brothers and I own an Italian restaurant in Hartford. We feel it's in need of a complete makeover, in terms of the menu, the layout of the kitchens and the design of the restaurant itself. I wonder if you could contact me by email, or on the number below to discuss the project and your availability.*

*I look forward to hearing from you.*

*Kind regards,*

*Rob Moreno.*

I look up at Tess.

"A complete makeover," I whisper. I know what this means. It means weeks of work for one thing. But it also means income. Quite significant income. Don't get me wrong, we're not poor. We're very far from poor. We've got money in the bank – granny saw to that – but the idea of actually earning again, after the year I've had, feels good. It feels really good.

"It sounds like a big project," Tess says.

"It does. It's a shame he hasn't given me the name of the restaurant, or I could look up their reviews."

"You can ask him that when you get in touch. I take it you are going to get in touch?" she asks.

"Of course. Not now, obviously. It's far too late."

"I guess they've just closed for the evening and he thought he'd send the message before going home."

"Yes, probably. But I doubt he wants to hear back from me right now. Besides, I don't want a potential client thinking I'm still working at this time of day. He'll assume he can call me at midnight every night. No, I'll send him a message in the morning."

She leans over and gives me a hug. "I'm really pleased for you," she says.

"I haven't got it yet." I don't want to get ahead of myself.

"Even so, it shows you were right to get the website re-done."

Tess is right. It might have meant spending quite a bit of money to have the site re-designed, but it seems like it could just have been worth it.

"After what Liam did, I didn't have much choice, did I?"

"It wasn't Liam. It was Fiona."

"I know. But Fiona did what she did because of Liam." I don't cry about him anymore. I did that for the first few weeks after he broke up with me. Then, after the tears, came the anger. Anger that he'd chosen another woman over me, that he'd been seeing her for most of the time we were together and that he'd got her pregnant, and decided to propose to her. I think I was entitled to be angry… bloody angry, actually. And at least the anger helped me to stop crying. Then, after the anger, came the shock. His fiancée, Fiona, was one of those online bloggers. I'd never really seen the point of them, not until the night Tess pointed out the item Fiona had written about my company. What was really galling what that, when you searched online for my company, her blog posting came up ahead of my own website. And it was scathing. I can still remember the feeling of cold, abject horror I felt when I read her hurtful words. I contacted Liam by text and insisted he get her to remove the article, or I'd sue her for defamation. He was apologetic and promised he'd deal with it. Two weeks later, when it was still there, I got my father's solicitor to send a letter and she obeyed the demand to remove the posting. By then though, the damage was done. My business was all but dead.

That was when the self-pity started. I wallowed for a while, sitting in the flat, eating custard tarts and chocolate digestives by the packet, and watching episodes of Jeremy Kyle, just to remind myself that there were people out there with worse lives than mine.

Of course, one of the problems with programmes like that is that you get involved. You try and pretend you're not interested but, deep down, you desperately want to know whether the woman who claims she's always been faithful to her boyfriend and that he's just jealous and possessive, really has been cheating on him with his best friend. Normally, I flick through the channels when the adverts come on, but I found myself watching avidly, in case I missed the next instalment of each story. And that's when I realised I had a problem. Not only was I interacting with the people on the TV programme, often shouting, commiserating, or even crying with them, I'd also started to yell abuse at the adverts as well. There was one in particular, that got shown in pretty much every ad break and became really annoying. It was for a company that handled personal injury claims. They made a big deal about all of their lawyers being personal injury specialists and, after the third time of hearing their slogan that particular morning, I found myself screaming at the screen that they wouldn't be much use if they were private fucking wealth lawyers, would they? It was a sobering moment, especially as I don't usually swear very much. It was almost as sobering as the moment, later that day, when Tess arrived back home at the same time as our online grocery delivery and, as she signed for it and began unpacking, she informed me that I hadn't actually ordered any food – not real food anyway. I'd ordered custard tarts, chocolate digestives – in both milk and plain flavours, just in case I felt like a change – tea, coffee, bottled water, toilet rolls and bleach. And that was pretty much it.

By then, there was also the tiny matter that I was living in old leggings because I couldn't actually do up the zip on my jeans anymore. The way I saw it, I had a choice. I either consumed all the custard tarts I'd ordered, with a bleach chaser, or I snapped out of it.

I snapped out of it.

In fact, I decided to re-invent myself. I changed my website, updated my company logo, buried the TV remote down the back of the sofa, and threw out the custard tarts and digestives. I even ordered real food, and got it delivered the next day. We could eat properly again.

I started going to the gym. I lost the pounds I'd gained and – most important of all – I learned to smile again.

Tess nudges me. "Stop thinking about him," she says.

"I wasn't," I lie. "Okay, I was, but not in the way you think. I'm over him now."

"Good, because he was never good enough for you."

"I know." I really do. She's right. Liam was only ever interested in Liam and I want a man who's interested in me. There's got to be one out there somewhere, hasn't there?

"It's going to mean you being away quite a lot, isn't it?" Tess says, nodding to the computer screen.

"Well, Hertford's only about an hour away – depending on the traffic."

"I think you might have to help this guy with his spelling," she says, pointing to the screen.

"Why?" I follow the direction of her finger.

"Because he can't spell Hertford, and he lives there – or at least works there."

I look more closely and she's absolutely right. He's spelt it with an 'a', instead of an 'e'.

"Well, he doesn't need to be able to spell, I guess." I cast an eye over the rest of the message. "He seems to have got everything else right." And then my gaze settles on the telephone number. "That's odd."

"What?"

"The phone number," I say.

"What about it."

"It's got too many digits. And it starts… Oh, my God." Realisation dawns on me.

"What's wrong?" Tess asks.

"It's not Hertford in Hertfordshire. It's Hartford in Connecticut."

"In America?" Her voice has dropped to a whisper.

"Yes."

"I—I suppose that would explain why he was getting in touch at this unholy hour of the night. What's the time difference?" she asks.

"Five hours, I think. So it's six-thirty pm there."

"I suppose you could maybe call him now then."

I look up at her. "I probably should. If I wait until tomorrow, I won't be able to call until the afternoon." I let out a long sigh. "The thing is, Tess, this changes everything."

"Why?" she asks.

How can she not understand? "Because if I take this job, I'll have to leave you on your own. I'll be gone for two or three months."

"During which time I'll be busy writing my dissertation." She moves around and perches on my desk. "I'll be okay," she says, trying to sound stronger than she is. "You've got to at least try and get this job, Ali."

"I can't."

"You must. I won't forgive myself if you turn it down because of me." I can hear the emotion in her voice and I swallow down my own. "You need this," she says.

"And you need me." She does. Tess has never been strong. We've been glued together since our parents died. The thought of breaking that bond for two or three months is almost unthinkable.

"We can text, and call, and Skype," she says. "And I'm twenty-one now. I need to try and stand on my own two feet at some time." I wish I could believe she meant that. "At least make the call," she adds. "See what this guy has to say for himself, find out how much they really want to do and if it's worth your while, then we'll decide from there." She holds out the telephone to me.

I take it, looking up into her eyes, and she smiles down at me. "Okay," I say, checking my computer screen and dialling the number before I can change my mind.

"Rosa's. How can I help you?" The voice on the end of the line is deep, soft, and obviously American, but sounds a little harassed.

"May I speak with Rob Moreno, please," I say in my best 'office' voice.

"This is Rob. What can I do for you?" He's polite, I'll give him that.

"My name's Alison Bishop. You sent me a message about upgrading your restaurant."

"Oh yeah," he says, sounding surprised. "I didn't expect to hear back from you today."

"Well, I was working on something else when your message came in."

"I see. Um… Can you just give me a minute?" There's a pause.

"Yes, of course." I wait, listening to the noises in the background. He's covered the mouthpiece and all I can hear are muffled voices and the occasional clinking of a glass. Then, after a minute or so, the noise diminishes and then disappears altogether and I wonder if we've been cut off.

"Hi," he says. "I've just come back into the office. I can't hear myself think in the restaurant."

"Oh, I see."

"So, you got my message?"

"Yes. I just wanted to get a brief idea of what you were looking for. You… you do understand that I'm based in England, don't you?"

"Yeah. I chose your company intentionally. I wanted to get a European feel for this place."

"Your restaurant is Italian though. Why didn't you look at Italian designers?"

"Because I came across your website, I went to your personal profile, and I liked what I saw."

I can feel myself blushing. He's flirting with me. I can't even remember the last time a man flirted with me, but I can remember that it feels good. Even so, I need to stop smiling and focus.

"What exactly is it you're looking for, Mr Moreno?" I ask, trying to sound as businesslike as possible.

"Call me Rob, please." He's not going to let me. "It's kinda hard to explain over the phone," he says. "I was hoping you'd be able to come over and take a look at the place, and that we could sit down together – you, me and my brothers – and discuss what you can do for us."

"You want me to fly to America?"

"Yeah."

"At who's expense?" I ask. It's not that I can't afford it, but I want to know the kind of people I'm dealing with.

"Well," he says, "how about we agree a compromise on that?"

"Such as?"

"You buy your ticket. There's a hotel just a couple of doors away from the restaurant; you can stay there. If we end up employing you, the air fare and hotel costs can be part of your fee."

"And if not?"

"Then I'll reimburse you."

That seems fair. Either way, I'm not out of pocket. After all, it's his choice to ask me over there.

"Okay," I say, looking up at Tess. She's nodding her head. "When do you want me to come over?"

"Is the end of this week too soon?" he asks.

I think about all the things I've got to organise. "No. I should be able to manage that."

"Great." He sounds really enthusiastic. "We'll look forward to meeting you."

We end the call and I hang up, and put the phone down carefully on my desk, unable to believe what's just happened.

"So, you're going then?" Tess asks.

"For a preliminary meeting, yes."

"And if they give you the job?"

"Then depending on the start date, I imagine I could well have to stay out there. There won't be any point in coming back here. I'll have to source suppliers and contractors." I look up at her. "Are you okay with that?"

She nods and leans forward, hugging me. "Yes. Like I said, you need this, Ali."

She's right. I do.

## *Sam*

Jane's eyes fill with tears, but I'm not easily moved, and as much as I know this is for real, I just stand and look at her.

"I'm sorry, Sam," she whispers.

"I know you are."

"I don't know what else to say."

Neither do I, if I'm honest, so we stand and look at each other for an awkward moment before I realize that, as her boss – well, one of them – I should take the lead.

"I know it's not your fault, Jane." Well it is, but blaming her isn't gonna help. "But we had three customers send their steaks back tonight. Steaks you'd cooked."

"I know," she snivels. Why do women do that?

"You've been here for over two years now. I thought we were beyond the stage of me having to check your work, but I think the best thing is if we go back to that – at least for the time being." I pause. She's supposed to be in charge of her section, and this is a backward step for both of us – one which is going to take up a lot of my time, but needs must. "I want you to pass everything by me before you serve it. Okay?"

She nods and wipes her nose on the crumpled Kleenex in her hand.

"I'm really sorry, Sam."

"It's okay. Just try and get it right tomorrow."

She nods and sniffles again, then ducks past me and back into the kitchen.

"You could have been a bit kinder." I turn and come face-to-face with Rob, who's just come out of the office. He leans against the wall of the corridor that leads from the restaurant to the kitchens, the office and the entrance to my apartment.

"I *was* being kind, compared to how I might've been. And besides, I'm her boss, not her counsellor."

"Her boyfriend just left her for another woman," he says.

"And?" Ed had already given me this nugget of information earlier in the day, while suggesting I cut her some slack after I yelled at her for the second time in her shift.

Ed opens the door to the kitchen, letting it swing shut behind him, then leans on the wall beside it, opposite Rob. "I guess it went well with Jane," he says. "She just ran out the back door in tears."

"Why is this my fault?" I look from one of my brothers to the other. To be honest, it's kinda confusing, being as they're twins and – if it wasn't for the fact that Ed's got longer hair and is wearing chef's whites, while Rob's dressed all in black – they're pretty much identical.

"Because you've been on her case all evening," Rob says. "You, better than either of us, know how she must be feeling." That was a bit low. Okay, so we all know that my ex-wife cheated on me, but I don't need Rob, or anyone else reminding me.

"Thanks for that," I say, going to move past them toward the kitchen.

"Sorry," Rob murmurs. I ignore him and push through the double doors.

The whole room has been cleaned down now, the surfaces cleared and sparkling clean, and everyone's gone home for the night. Apart from Jane's mistakes, it was a good service – and by 'good', I mean 'busy'. I like it when it's busy, because then I don't have time to think. I don't like thinking these days, because all I tend to think about is Amber. I shake my head to banish the memories just as Rob and Ed come in behind me.

"I need to talk to you," Rob says and I turn to face him, glad of the intrusion for once.

While they may look the same – apart from the hair – my brothers couldn't be more different in their temperaments. Where Ed is shy, quiet and placid, Rob is playful, mischievous and downright annoying. Ed works with me in the kitchen, although we don't really do the same things. I'm in charge – and that makes Ed quite happy. He's a pastry chef – and that makes me completely delirious, because I'm really, really useless when it comes to pastry and desserts. And Ed is absolutely brilliant. He'd be even better, if he'd just have little more self-confidence, but then Rob says I've got enough for both of us. That's not true. I just tend to hide my professional insecurities better, especially in front of him. Rob works front of house, meeting and greeting the guests, showing them to their tables and making sure they're happy. And, if they should happen to be female, under thirty and vaguely attractive, it's highly unlikely that they'll leave without Rob picking up their phone number. He's the most outrageous flirt I've ever known – and I should know; I was married to the best. Fuck… that's Amber getting into my head again.

"What's up?" I ask, sitting up on one of the preparation surfaces.

Rob and Ed lean against the countertop opposite. "I've got something to tell you." Rob looks from me to Ed and back again. For once, I get the feeling even Ed doesn't know what's going on.

"What have you been up to?" I ask Rob.

He looks down at his own feet. "Earlier today, I—I contacted a restaurant consultant—"

"A what?" I interrupt him.

"A restaurant consultant. It's someone who comes into places like this and checks out what we could be doing better, then puts it right."

I can feel my anger starting to rise already.

"Okay," Ed says. "And?"

"And I asked her if she'd come visit us."

"Why?" I ask him.

"Because we need to update this place," he says, looking me in the eyes.

"We do?"

"Yeah. And you know it."

He's right. I do know, but that doesn't mean I'm gonna take this lying down. "And we need someone else to help with this, because…?"

"Because we're all too busy," he replies. "If we wait for the three of us to get around to it, we'll all be retired."

"What's she coming to look at?" Ed asks.

"Re-designing the outside of the restaurant, the restaurant itself…" He pauses. "Updating the kitchens and the menus."

"What?" I yell.

"Don't fly off the handle," he says.

"Why the fuck not?" I jump down from the countertop. I'm a couple of inches taller than both of them and I walk over, using my full height. "Where the hell do you get off making a decision like this without asking Ed and me?" I ask Rob.

"I haven't made a decision," he replies, holding his hands up in surrender to my foul temper. "I've just asked her to come over at the end of the week and take a look, then sit down with us and discuss what she can do to help."

"Come over?" I repeat. "Come over from where?"

"From England."

"England?" Even Ed's staring at him now. "Why England?"

Rob sighs. "Because I thought we could use a European angle."

I run my fingers through my short hair. "Our restaurant is Italian. We're Italian-American. So, if you really had to go down this route, then an Italian, or an American I could've understood. But someone from England?"

He smirks. "Funnily enough, she said that."

"Then maybe you should've damn well listened to her. She's making more sense than you are. How the fuck is some pompous English woman gonna have a clue about us and our market?"

"She's not pompous. She sounds really nice."

Light starts to dawn. "Oh Christ. Don't tell me, you saw her picture on her website and she's a beautiful brunette."

"No. She's a beautiful blonde, actually."

"Fucking hell, Rob." I raise my voice – again. "Did you have any other reason for choosing her, apart from her photograph giving you a hard-on?"

"Yeah," he says, sounding offended. "She has some really good testimonials on her website."

"All of which could be faked," I tell him, stating the obvious.

"I'm not an idiot." I'm tempted to question that. "I looked up the places who'd given her the reviews. And then I contacted them by e-mail and asked for their real opinion."

"And?"

"And they all told me she's absolutely brilliant at what she does." I don't really have a reply to that. He obviously did his homework. "And her fees are more reasonable than any of the other consultants I looked at."

Speaking of money… "Who's paying for her to come over here?"

"She is."

Is she crazy? "Really? She's gonna pay to come over here, not knowing if she's gonna get the job?"

He looks at the floor again. "Well, I said if we didn't give her the job, I'd reimburse her."

"*You* will?" I ask.

"Yeah. *Me*, not the restaurant. I get that it's my idea. I get that I went ahead and did this without consulting you guys, so I'll pay for her flight, if we don't end up using her. If we do give her the job, we've agreed that she can add it to the fee."

It seems fair – although I'm not going to admit it.

"When's she coming over, did you say?" Ed asks him.

"At the end of the week."

"You don't have a precise day, or time?" I say.

He shakes his head. "No. She's got things to arrange at her end."

"So all we know is that she's gonna be here sometime before the weekend."

"Yeah." Rob looks me in the eye, answering me, even though I hadn't meant it as a question.

I shrug. "Okay… well, on your head be it. I'll listen to what she has to say, but I just hope you're ready to pay the woman back, because she's gonna have to be real impressive for me to let her have anything to do with this place."

*… to be continued*